Chapter 1

Gina was sixty-two, and it h
last had sex, maybe more since the menopause, depending on
when you counted from. She had not been near a doctor,
clinic or other gynaecological medical intervention for at least
five years. And yet they'd said, not more than five minutes
ago, that she was pregnant.

The hospital walls were the colour of day-old
mustard. The designer would have called it something like
'field of ochre'; others would call it sludge, but to Gina it
looked like bile, which causes the sort of indigestion that had
brought her here in the first place. She lay still and silent. If
she didn't move, it might not be real. If she said something,
fear would make it sound harsh. A voice that could gut a fish
at forty paces.

The cup of sweet tea at her elbow suggested she was
in shock. Not denial, because denial, subconsciously at least,
is deliberate, a provisional shield for the brain. Shock is in-
your-face, unexpected. News of the reputed pregnancy
certainly hit that nail. But she couldn't drink sweet tea with
milk, no matter how deep the shock. Milk in tea turned it
into something it was never meant to be: a diluted,
cardboard-colour pastiche of its robust, fragrant, dark grey
self – a metaphor for colonial oppression, she remembered
vaguely from some presentation her eldest had done years
ago at school. Gina was hungry, although where she found
the energy to be hungry in her current situation was a
mystery. If she swivelled her eyes to the left, she could see a
digestive biscuit, so she needed to get the tea changed in

order to eat the biscuit. She wondered about the best way to achieve this without drawing attention to herself, a minor matter to momentarily obscure the planet-sized, urgent, impossible matter of pregnancy. She'd been doing senior yoga for a few months and her instructor had said 'Just breathe and it will all be OK.' Probably with less challenging situations in mind, to be fair. Exhaustion suddenly descended like a blanket, wrapping her in a cocoon, biscuits, tea and pregnancy momentarily left on the outside.

She had arrived at hospital early that morning, having crept out under cover of darkness, leaving a bland, truthful – or, at least, not untruthful – note to explain to Gordon the Lodger why she was gone. In the cab she'd agreed with herself that when she got the all-clear, she would stretch and swim more, eat a bit less, cut down on caffeine, alcohol and saturated fat, but not go to extremes; since she'd turned sixty she'd spent the odd moment now and then considering the trade-offs between life-shortening clogged arteries, alcohol-induced dying brain cells and, well, the pleasures of caffeine, cheese and wine. She had got the all-clear less than an hour ago: no malignant growths, no scary bad cells taking over her insides. She was, in general – pregnancy apparently notwithstanding – in good health. Normal blood pressure, normal liver and kidney function; worth shedding a few kilos but nothing to stress about. Pretty good overall. Would an unexplained foetus count as a malignant growth? She felt a drench of self-loathing at thinking that thought.

'Hello, matron,' said the nurse from the examination room who was sitting at the end of Gina's bed. Matron came in and sat on the chair next to the tea and biscuit. It would be polite to open her eyes and acknowledge the arrival, but Gina

32 to 33

Sula Murray

Published by hitthedecks.co.uk

This novel is a work of fiction. The characters and events portrayed in it, including references to Delayed Embryonic Settled Implantation, are the work of the author's imagination. Any resemblance to actual persons, living or dead, is entirely coincidental.

Cover design by Natasha Murphy

didn't want to give up her darkness to say hello to a stranger in a blue uniform. She could tell matron knew she wasn't sleeping and wondered if she'd call her bluff, but they sat there like that for a while until Gina's tummy rumbled, sending a wave that forced her eyes open, squeezing her upper body like a tube of toothpaste. She needed every technique from senior yoga just to get the strength to peep out.

The nurse looked pale and worried. Whether this was on Gina's account or something of her own, who knew? Her name badge said 'Allegra'; she had been the assigned lead for the oscopies and ultrasound that today's appointments were for – or had been for until half an hour ago. Allegra had done the booking-in at 7 a.m., taken a history shortly after, and checked up on Gina several times. The routine 'Welcome to Valley Health Care Facility' and how are yous. Why did 'health care facility' sound so sinister? It was a hospital. Call it that. Or at least a clinic. Irritation was another useful displacement activity.

'How is the backache now, Mrs Flowers?' asked matron.

'Much the same.'

'And the indigestion?'

'Ditto.'

'Any new symptoms?'

'Not really. I'm more tired than usual, but that might just be post-Christmas, which was really busy.' It was absurd, but the three women formed a coven of pretence to get through the moment, carry Gina forward with niceties and faux normalities. No one shouted 'Pregnant at sixty-two. Of course you're tired. What's with the chit-chat?' Today was the seventh of January. Monday. Sometime around mid November, Gina had started keeping a food diary, trying to keep track of intermittent indigestion and bloating. She wrote down what she ate, when she ate it and how she felt, looking for incidents of dairy or gluten or acid or alcohol – please God, not dairy or alcohol – making her feel grim. No pattern emerged. By mid December she was learning to live with the indigestion and didn't notice it nearly so much, when along came the backache. Google suggested that although she wasn't in the typical age group, best to rule out ovarian cancer. Any cancer in fact. Searching online for symptoms is a dangerous thing, but it seemed unlikely it had actually caused her to be with child. If she was. Which she wasn't. Not really, surely? Not possible.

A week before Christmas she had phoned her GP and for the first time pressed zero for 'urgent medical appointments only', feeling that this was simultaneously an overreaction and not drastic enough. Having had anything going in childhood, from scarlet fever to whooping cough, everything with a spot or a pustule or a rash – sometimes all three – Gina felt she got illness over and done with by the age of twelve. Since then, apart from one suspected broken ankle (which after a very long time in A&E being triaged down the list every hour or so turned out to be a bad bruise) and a cold every five years, she had been grateful for excellent health. Until this winter. Perhaps it was her turn to get something unspeakable.

Dr Manes had seen her that afternoon. Gina managed to stop herself opening with 'I've Googled it, and I think I've got ovarian cancer.' Had ice or heat helped the backache? No, and that suggested it might be something

4

skeletal. She was asked if she drank enough water, and the doctor noted the reply: 'About two litres a day as we're supposed to but usually as squash, pink grapefruit squash.' Which might, apparently, explain the digestive irritation.

And then, just to rule out anything suspicious, 'Here's a form for a blood test, and if you go today we'll have the results on Monday.'

'Will that rule out ovarian cancer?'

'It will test for it, yes.' Dr Manes tore off a prescription for strong painkillers for the backache – 'Just in case. Over the Christmas period' – and she made a follow-up appointment for Christmas Eve.

That's when Gina felt the thread of fear looping from her brain to her veins, forming a fence around her chest. Why did she need an appointment if the doctor expected it to come back clear? Why not 'You can just press option two for test results'? She didn't mention the fear to Dr Manes, who would not be able to make it go away whatever her response. She thanked the doctor, got in the car and drove to the walk-in blood test place. The queue had reached 23 and Gina's number was 61, so it was just on six when she got home, changed and went to the neighbours' drinks, pressing down the fear in her chest like pressing the plunger in a cafetière, holding the grounds of possible despair under a murky liquid laced with keep calm and carry on Christmas.

At night, she trawled through happy, carefree photos of family. Over that week, she looked at every mince pie and wondered if it would be the last time she ate mince pies, then decided she didn't want one anyway. She didn't tell anyone what the GP had said and no one asked, which was mildly surprising until she remembered, as she did every hour or so,

5

that she hadn't told them about the appointment. She waited for stabbing pains or nausea. None came. She waited for loss of appetite or blood somewhere blood shouldn't be. Nothing. She pulled herself on a mental vision of Santa's sleigh through seven days of child-minding, party-making, loading dishwashers and peeling vegetables. On Christmas Eve at 11 a.m., the GP said the blood test was clear, nothing sinister but she'd book Gina in for a routine ultrasound, colonoscopy and endoscopy to see if any of those could find something to explain the indigestion.

'How long is the wait?'

Dr Manes had not expected further conversation after this delivery of good news. She registered Gina's ongoing anxiety and took her time, given there was a collection of patients in the waiting room who had to be seen before Christmas. Her reindeer earrings looked incongruent with her neat black two-piece.

'Well, you're not urgent, so for a routine appointment perhaps eight to ten weeks. A bit more actually, because it backs up after Christmas, but hopefully before Easter.'

'I'm going to Australia. In January. To see my son.' In those far off, non-pregnant days of late December, all of three weeks ago, the most important thing had been to stop herself, all the time she was away, wondering if she was dying, to prevent a residual trail of doubt about the indigestion inching across her mind, ruining her Sydney summer. 'What about if I pay for it?' Given the four thousand pounds Australia was costing, peace of mind for another eight hundred had seemed sensible. And that's how Gina ended up in Valley Health Care Facility in the first week of January. First in gastrology and now... now in obstetrics.

She'd had a mild sedative for the (all clear, unnecessary) oscopies, and after they were done, a very nice sandwich and cup of tea – without milk. They knew to ask first in the adult suite of gastrology, whereas by the time you got to obstetrics they'd infantilised you, making assumptions on your behalf like assuming everyone took milk in their tea. She'd expected to be hungrier following the overnight fast, but at that point, with going home on the near horizon, the cheese and pickle seemed to be enough. A short rest, then off to a final check ultrasound, another ten minutes and she could get dressed, get a cab and go home to watch rolling news all afternoon, guilt-free because you're not supposed to do anything else. It was perfect that it was also cold and raining; she took a somewhat schadenfreudian pleasure in the contrast with the sunshine that waited for her in Sydney.

Gina had asked the ultrasound technician how many he usually did in a day. Around fifteen, he replied, and she wondered if she could have remained so pleased to see each new patient as he apparently was to see her. She noticed 'Graham Neville, Sonographer' on his name badge and wondered who his name reminded her of. An author, politician, footballer maybe. All of this frivolous speculation was only this morning, this hour, not some other lifetime or some other life. She had confirmed her name and date of birth for the third time that day.

'Hop up on the bench for me,' he'd said. Speaking to everyone as though they were five years old was clearly part of his bedside manner. 'See if you can just open the gown over your tummy for me. That's grand. Are you comfortable? The gel is a bit cold to start with, but it'll be over in a jiffy.' Slightly tired from the oscopy sedative and the early start, she closed her eyes and started just to drift when she caught an astronaut-like nuance in the atmosphere. Soundless. Weightless. The scanner stopped. She could feel the technician's hand shake, such a slight tremor. Gina dragged her eyes open, pulling them from the undergrowth of consciousness. His blanched face belied his steady voice, steadier anyway than his hand. He asked her to confirm her name and date of birth. Gina imagined this endless repetition of basic data was like being in prison or the army, although she had no experience of either of these things and found it strange they came to mind.

'They haven't changed since I hopped on the bench,' she said, going for levity with a tinge of sarcasm, even when clearly there was something perturbing. She had struck the wrong note, his voice now with a pleading edge.

'Please, Mrs Flowers, could you just confirm.'

'Fifth of July, 1956, and my name is Virginia Eleanor Flowers.'

She didn't ask what the matter was. She just knew he wouldn't tell her, like police never tell people on doorsteps why they are there until they get inside and get everyone sat down. 'I need to get a senior technician,' he said. 'Just to check something. I'm quite new.'

And he was gone, presumably before she could question him, had she been inclined. Maybe the newness explained his cheerful interest of three minutes ago. Even harping back to the desperate scenarios that had been running through her head all Christmas, Gina's thoughts were an insufficient match for the lingering sedative. She lay half-asleep on the hard ultrasound couch, wondering how long she'd got and if they'd let her have morphine or, better, heroin, which she'd always fancied trying and terminally ill seemed like the best time.

*

Three people edged in to the very small room where Gina lay beached on the couch. Was that a lot for a routine ultrasound on her liver? Technician One hadn't returned, for which she guessed they were both equally thankful.

'Mrs Flowers, I'm Mr Evert Grant, chief medical officer. This is Amal, our senior ultrasound technician, and Allegra you know already.'

Mr Grant was strikingly handsome; Gina shuffled through a hazy timeline of classically handsome fictional on-screen doctors from Kildare to McDreamy via Clooney – what was Clooney's character's name? Evert Grant outclassed them all. Plus, unlike them, he presumably knew a thing or two about actual medical stuff. Drawing her eyes away from Mr Grant to face up to whatever he had to tell her felt like hauling a lorry uphill.

He picked up her chart and asked her name and date of birth, next of kin, and then for Stan's date of birth. 'Fourteenth of September, 1983,' she said. 'But he's in Australia. So he is kin but not very next, not exactly handy. I'm going to see him tomorrow. He's an oil technician. In Sydney. I've got another son, Evan. Fourteenth of September, 1985. I know, same day two years apart. What are the chances. More than you'd think actually. I looked it up at the time.'

Her nervous babbling ebbed into the clinical air, the professionals standing like the music had stopped in a game of statues, waiting to start again.

'Do you mind if I have a look?'

Mr Grant and Amal took up the prime positions, one at each side of Gina's tummy, and the scanning started again.

'Mrs Flowers,' he said slowly, the voice for five year olds not confined to the technician. 'Your notes say that you have told us there is no possibility you are pregnant. On admission, before the sedative and before this ultrasound, we have clearly documented your response that you cannot be pregnant.'

'Yes. Or no. I'm sorry.' Gina tried to focus, to help, to answer this random question. 'Correct. There is no possibility I am pregnant.'

'Could you tell me why you seem to be so sure?'

Gina thought maybe the sedative had dropped her into a surreal side universe where she was terminally ill but they wanted to distract her from that with easy, irrelevant questions and maybe next up would be who was the current President of the United States. She nearly said 'Trump' just to show she knew the game.

The dregs of sedation were in the last stages of wearing off, but the effort of thinking, making sense of the question, was like being asked to figure out Pythagoras. Whoever he was. What made her think of an ancient Greek she didn't know anything about except his name? And triangles, she recalled.

'Sorry. The question.' She mentally firmed up what was required of her with images of the grim reaper, that scythe, at the end of her childlike kaleidoscope. 'I confirm I did tell you, not you personally, the clinic, everyone who has asked me, that I am not pregnant.'

'Could you tell me why you seem to be so sure?' he repeated. Mr Grant's gorgeous gaze held hers, not a rabbit in headlights, more akin to hostage syndrome.

'Well,' she said, 'I am sixty-two. I am ten years post-menopause and it would be many months since I last had sex. Certainly more than nine. In fact, nearer nine years.'

'Yes,' said Mr Grant. 'I see then why you'd say that.' It still hadn't got through to Gina that he was saying she was pregnant. It wasn't so much that she couldn't see the writing, she couldn't even see the wall. 'It looks as if you are around thirty-two to thirty-three weeks.'

'Left to live?'

'Pregnant. Your general health is good.'

Later, when she looked back on this unbelievably crass denouement, she thought maybe her body and her psyche were more in tune than she had recognised. Consciously, she had no idea that she was pregnant, had not arrived here to attempt to hide or reveal her condition. She had good reason to know for sure she was not pregnant and tell them that. Yet over time she came to think maybe her psyche was one step ahead, had begun processing the dilemma a while before. And that was what had prevented total meltdown, staved off impulses to shout they were stupid, hadn't they heard her, no one gets pregnant at sixty-two without having sex and with no eggs. The inner part of her mind had been working on protecting her and this new responsibility while she'd drifted on in ignorance for – apparently – thirty-two to thirty-three weeks.

But right then, she had just thought they were mistaken. Or that she was the victim of some sort of underground medical experiment. Mr Grant's extreme beauty supported this theory. Gina closed her eyes again and marshalled some words.

'I can't be pregnant. Do you think someone else's scan has got stuck in the buffer?' She was pleased with this thought; it seemed entirely logical. Things got stuck in buffers all the time, especially printer buffers and surely scanners were printers' first cousins. Printers were the evil robots of technology with autonomous malevolent agency. With a printer, you often had to clear the print queue and start again. Or turn it off and on again. She could see them looking at her, sympathetic, patient looks.

'No. That's not possible,' said Mr Grant when she managed to focus on him. Silence again. Eventually, in a softly querulous tone, she said, 'Maybe it's a phantom pregnancy, whatever that is. I've heard of them. I think my uncle's Labrador had one once.'

'No. That is not the case. A phantom pregnancy wouldn't show a foetus on a scan.' Mr Grant seemed very sure of himself.

'Doctor Grant.' Gina felt like she needed to speak slowly, to ground the conversation in a measured reality. 'In your medical experience, is it possible that I am pregnant, given my circumstances?'

He took his time to answer. Gina felt he was considering how best to accuse her of lying.

'We cannot rule out, Mrs Flowers, that some detail of your medical history is mistaken. This would be the most likely explanation.'

'Let me see the scan.'

Amal manoeuvred the machine. There did seem to be a baby floating in her body. The outlines were a bit sharper round the edges than they had been in the 1980s, when she'd last had any reason to be personally interested in the quality of pregnancy scans, but otherwise familiar. She asked Mr Grant what sort of doctor he was and he repeated that he was Valley's chief medical officer, a gastro surgeon by specialism, which made sense when they were checking her liver, less so now, but it did seem unlikely he would mistake a liver abnormality for a foetus. She asked if she could see a gynaecologist and he said he'd see who was available and that there would be another consultation fee. Then he left the room.

Amal tidied up Gina's clothing, wiping off the gel, and invited her to sit up. Amal asked – finally, someone asked – if she was OK. Gina nodded, the magnitude of the lie undiminished by being unspoken. Then, despite being tall and wearing the armour of a white coat and name badge, Amal left the room like a mouse hurrying behind the skirting board when a cat comes in.

Allegra, stalwart Allegra, the slightly unpopular friend you ignore until she's all you've got and you really need someone, was still there. Gina began to cry. Not, at this stage, because she didn't want to be pregnant but because she couldn't be pregnant. That would have been like crying because she didn't want a broken leg when she didn't have a broken leg and no one was going to break her leg. The foetus image thing notwithstanding. She was crying because it meant they hadn't found what was causing the bloating and the backache, and she might still have ovarian cancer the day before she went to Australia. Allegra held her hand. Was there anything worse than paying someone to hold your hand?

'Mr Howard is the obs man. He's outstanding and he is here today, so hang on for him. I'm going to take you to a single room now. Is there someone I can ring for you?' Gina shook her head, got up and started to take off the gown until Allegra put paid to that very minor improvement in her situation. 'Mr Howard will probably want to do his own scan. Maybe best keep that on.' They held each other's arms as they changed rooms, as if one of them might suddenly make a break for it. Gina lay down on the bed in the new room and stared at the ceiling. 'I'll get you some tea with a couple of sugars.' Gina, stunned, forgot to say no milk, no sugar.

So there they were, waiting for Mr Howard, Gina staring at the ceiling not drinking tea, longing for the digestive biscuit, Allegra holding her hand in nearly as much of a daze as her patient. Then matron arrived. When she had decided enough time had been spent in sympathetic silence, matron said, 'Do you want me to charge Mr Howard's consult to the same payment card?' Then, having completed the main purpose of her visit, matron went away. Maybe not Nurse Ratched but a suitable understudy.

Chapter 2

Mr Howard arrived a few minutes later, making Gina feel like she was a stop on a peculiar tour, visitors taking turns to view the curiosity. It's a big ask for a man to understand how the news of pregnancy affects women, and all women differently at that, but Gina reasoned Mr Howard as a consultant obstetrician must have a better idea than most.

'Mrs Flowers. I am Gerald Howard. I understand you've requested to see me because you find yourself unexpectedly pregnant.'

'Impossibly pregnant.'

The first technician knocked but did not wait for an answer before wheeling in a scan machine, setting it up beside her bed, his head slightly cocked, a slight overbite on show. He was wearing an incongruously fluffy hospital-issue grey fleece. It would only have needed his nose to twitch for the rabbit impression to be complete. Graham Neville then stood to one side, keen to put distance between himself and an old pregnant woman: minimise the potential for contagion.

'Could I start by taking a look?' asked Mr Howard. 'Allegra has organised a different scanner for you just to allay any concerns about the buffer.' Gina was touched by this small consideration.

Mr Howard didn't wait for her formal go-ahead. His movements were gentle and precise, lifting the handheld wand like a conductor raising a baton to quieten an orchestra. Gina still thought some variation on her buffer idea was the best explanation, despite the different scanner, so she asked him if there was some way the scan they'd seen earlier might not, in fact, be her. He said he wasn't a fan of that theory. Then it was on with the gel again. 'This might be a bit cold.' Because a slather of cold gel was the biggest of her worries that morning. Morning. It was still morning.

'Or a huge baby-shaped growth. A cancer that looks like a foetus,' Gina went on, not knowing which would be worse: an actual baby or an actual cancer. At least someone else looks after the cancer, and she would just be a passive participant in chemo and radio and… sometimes she really didn't like herself at all.

'I just need another minute, Mrs Flowers, then we'll be able to have a chat.'

A few moments later, the orchestral movements stopped and he ran his hands over her stomach with a soft flourish, like the 'hands that do dishes' advert, and took the seat next to her bed. Rabbit wiped the gel, and Allegra arranged Gina's gown to its least revealing folds.

'Mrs Flowers, we will, of course, do another blood test, but we have in the meantime tested the urine sample you provided as routine on arrival. In my opinion, there is no doubt at all that you are thirty-two to thirty-three weeks pregnant.' He paused then added gently, 'Just to be clear, it is not simply my opinion.' He stressed 'opinion' and went on. 'You are without doubt pregnant.'

Gina closed her eyes again and huddled under the comfort of the blanket fog. Everyone was quiet and still. The atmosphere was what coming out of a coma might feel like but with a side of nappy-filled nightmares.

'Pregnant? With a baby? Are you even a doctor, Mr Howard?' It could have sounded rude but the twin undercurrents of incredulity and desperation saved it from discourtesy. 'You know I'm sixty-two?'

'That is what we have on file for you. Yes, I am a doctor. Surgeons use mister instead of doctor.'

'Why? All that training then call yourself mister again. What do female surgeons do?'

She pulled herself back on track with a monumental effort. 'And I haven't had a period for at least ten years. Probably eleven or twelve. The last one I remember as a proper one, not just spots, was the year of my fiftieth.' Gina wondered if this was how a spy felt under interrogation, trying to remember your story with a few powerful people holding your life in the balance and deciding whether to believe you.

'It would be very unusual for a pregnancy to occur so long after the menopause.' Mr Howard was aware his words were a caricature of understatement.

'Especially when I have been celibate for nine years. And three months.' Gina was surprised she managed to come up with this, but somehow, counting in the fog, tracing back, she landed on the year: 2009. Any last possible chance of conception would have been before George was seriously ill, just a few months before he died, a few months after his fiftieth.

'I think, Mrs Flowers, if you don't mind, if I could just examine your tummy one more time, then you can get dressed and we can talk through the circumstances. Hospital gowns don't help anyone think.'

He ran his hands over her abdomen again, more firmly than before, pushing very slightly here and there until she felt a foot poking through the flattened expanse of her midriff. Gina could see this was no 'stuck-in-a-buffer' mistake. It was the reverse of not believing someone is dead and then seeing the body. She shut her eyes and went back to the virtual blanket. It was only ten-thirty in the morning.

During the following twenty minutes, Allegra got her up and helped her dress, as if she'd been run over and couldn't do anything for herself, certainly not put on shoes or do up buttons. Gina had come in wearing a box jacket, a loose white shirt (the bloating), dark blue trousers, flat ankle boots and a Liberty scarf with an understated necklace. The scarf had been a present a few years ago from Evan. His wife was expecting Gina's third grandchild. These thoughts made her weep silently, a few tears of self-pity, self-loathing and lingering disbelief. Self-pity because she was full of pity for herself and had not yet got round to balancing that with thinking about women who desperately want to be pregnant and aren't; self-loathing because, while she thought thirty-two to thirty-three weeks must be too late for an abortion, surely there was an exception for sixty-two-year-olds; and disbelief because... well. She would not be alone with that one.

Allegra led Gina, fully dressed ergo now able to think, down another set of corridors towards Mr Howard's room. He came out of a side laboratory and fell into step beside them.

'How are you feeling? Now that you're up.'

She had no idea how she was feeling. She could identify numb, other-worldly, in suspended animation, but these weren't really feeling, more like complete lack of it, like a cosmic out-of-body denial, so she just looked at him and didn't say anything.

'Well, please come in. Sit down,' he said as the small party turned into his room. The sound boomed in her ears on this most outlandish of mornings. 'Your blood test has confirmed the ultrasound, the urine test and my physical examination. It seems from what you've said that this pregnancy wasn't planned or expected.' He saw the bafflement on her face and changed tack. 'You seem well in yourself despite the unusual circumstances. Can I ask—'

Gina could wait no longer. She had to get a grip, stop being a passive recipient of this nonsense and get some information.

'Doctor, how is it possible that I am pregnant in my circumstances? It isn't possible, is it? What could have happened? What other explanation is there?'

There was another prolonged pause. Gina understood that Mr Howard was considering if she was mistaken, mendacious or crazy. So she thought she'd take the lead and was surprised to find her voice assertive and sensible, like talking to a customer about the need for proper VAT receipts and not just credit card slips.

'Whatever your doubts, I know my date of birth. I know my gynaecological history and I know my sexual history. So while I see that for now you think I am wrong – whether lying or just gravely mistaken – about one or more of these, perhaps you could work on the assumption that I'm not, and tell me how I could be pregnant. Or what else it could be.'

It wasn't a bad speech in the circumstances.

Mr Howard searched for a tactful approach. 'I do think it would be very helpful to firmly establish and independently confirm those key things,' he said, 'and I will explain how we can do that. However, as to how you can be pregnant in those circumstances, it is very unusual to say the least. I have never come across anything like this combination of circumstances which has resulted in a pregnancy. I do know there are some clinics that are exploring conception in older women. Do you have any history of contact with those?'

She wanted to say, 'Now you think I've been doing some fancy footwork on the IVF front in an illegal anonymous clinic with white walls and hushed silences, well-paid nurses and doctors banned from their own countries' professional registers experimenting, for thousands of dollars, on sixty-something women who want a baby. Or, if I haven't got thousands of dollars, a three-floors-up reverse version of a backstreet abortionist.' But deference to the medical profession, deeply embedded in many women of her generation, plus that she needed and thought she liked Mr Howard, tempered the reply.

'No.'

The denial was firm and convincing. Which was easy because it was true. She paused while she worked up to asking the terrifying, shameful question. They could all see there was something major squirming its way out of her throat into the world.

'Would I be able to have a termination?'

'It—' Mr Howard summoned up his professionalism. 'It wouldn't really be a termination. You're about thirty-two to thirty-three weeks pregnant. The foetus is viable. It would be a planned prenatal foetal demise. PPFD.' Mr Howard let that find a crevice in her brain. Planned Prenatal Foetal

Demise. She could see the capital letters. 'It is not, however, impossible. It is, more likely than not, possible.'

'What if it is not alright? The foetus. What if it is—.' Her mind slithered about looking for a word. 'Underdeveloped. Or overdeveloped. Or not really a baby.'

'From the tests we've run so far, there is no suggestion of any abnormality. But even if that is not the case – and there are further tests, intrusive tests, we can run – the foetus is viable. I don't perform PPFD operations because it is not an area in which I have any expertise. If you wish to end your pregnancy at this late stage, I would not perform that procedure. But I could put you in touch with… a suitable service. Qualified, excellent people who could assist you.' Another extended pause. 'Is that what you want?'

'Maybe. No. You mean I'd be murdering it?'

'Is there someone we can ring to be with you?' asked matron. Gina looked at this voyeuristic stranger, barely having realised she had come in to the room. Something to do with invoices, no doubt.

'No.' It was firm, not far off a shout but still just on the side of everyday. Maybe matron meant well, maybe she just wanted to tick the box: 'The detained person was offered one phone call'. But she was way off-beam. What did she think she was going to do on Gina's behalf? Phone a friend and say 'Can you come and be with Gina? She's pregnant and is a bit distressed about killing her baby?'

Mr Howard was still considering abortion niceties. 'It would not legally be murder if it was approved through the proper channels. But the foetus appears viable outside the womb as of today. It is maybe more a moral than a technical judgement. But it should be your judgement, of course.'

No one seemed sure what to do next. Gina decided she had to get them to see that she wasn't manipulating the truth. That would help a bit, at least. 'How would you like to verify my age, my gynaecological and sexual history?' she asked. It was only twenty past eleven in the morning but it felt like a different decade from when she'd come in.

'It's something for tomorrow,' Mr Howard replied. 'You need an urgent appointment to see your GP and discuss next steps. Matron will ring your GP and make sure they see you this afternoon. You are at most eight weeks from your due date and if the pregnancy proceeds, you need a care plan. Yours will be – is – a high-risk pregnancy because of your age and you will need care on the NHS. We only do routine procedures at Valley, but we can provide a private room for pre- and post-procedure if that helps. But the delivery must be on the NHS.' He paused, thinking. 'Yours is a very unusual case, Mrs Flowers. We will need to find a team experienced in the most similar types and we will be in contact with the best people. If you would like to come and see me again tomorrow, and decide to go ahead with the pregnancy, I will explain my background and see if you would like to be in my care.'

And for this ten minutes of non-advice, non-information sales pitch – as she, perhaps wrongly, saw it at the time – she later realised she had been charged £275.

*

Later that Monday morning on his 15 minute break from the scanner, Graham Neville put tomato sauce on his bacon roll and sugar in his tea, treats he usually only allowed himself on a Friday. Graham was less than six months post-qualified as a sonographer, but he knew it wasn't every day you did an ultrasound on a sixty-two-year-old pregnant woman. He said 'To go' to Viki in the staff restaurant, zipped up his fleece and went outside to eat, smoke and think.

Chapter 3

Stan didn't mind living in Sydney, although he was going to leave. Nothing personal, Australia. Moving countries was pretty much what he'd done for the last few years – ever since Carran – when he wanted to get out of a relationship. He didn't invest too much in anywhere, viewed each location as temporary, and gradually identified reasons to move on. Despite its perpetually bronzed image, he found that Australia grew dark early in winter, and cold. In summer it was often unbearably hot, and some people were uptight and not-so-gorgeous, just like anywhere else. If you had no interest in sport, it was hard to have a conversation. If you did like sport, you had an opinion on every ball that's ever been thrown, hit or kicked, and you shared it widely, especially with people whose bored expressions and desperate body language screamed not-interested-leave-me-alone.

This time he had a better reason to leave. Stan worked for Big Oil, analysing things the general public don't know exist, and he was shockingly well paid. Minor molecule incursion was growing in importance and there weren't many technical experts in the field, so broadly Big Oil would do a lot to keep him happy. It didn't matter where he worked, meaning whenever a personal relationship got tricky or dull, or he felt he could hear her biological clock, he would ask for a transfer and they'd say, 'Sure. Where to?' Stan had never told anyone how much he earned except his accountant. Last time he saw her, she asked him what on earth he did for all that money, because it never struck her that he worked especially hard. He didn't, and made no pretence otherwise. He worked from eight till four, five days a week. He went out at lunchtime, mostly to a coffee shop on the harbour front about twenty minutes' walk from his thirty-fourth-floor office in the central business district. He didn't think about work at all when he wasn't there. He didn't manage any staff or train new people, had no top- or bottom-line responsibility, didn't do anything dangerous or safety critical. His job title of MMI analyst meant that most of his colleagues assumed he was somewhere in the middle rankings of the organisation. He was well-liked, respected, but not someone who was seen as a powerhouse or a future leader. Sometimes he felt like he was in camouflage.

What he did was save Big Oil money. In a return-on-investment way, for shareholders at least, he was worth the big bucks. Stan was one of those shareholders, being a valuable employee, and it so happened that the next three months would be a good time to exercise his options and top up with a whole heap more cash, this time tax-free. Stan knew if some senior people demystified his work a bit, invested more in understanding what he did, they'd kick themselves at the lost opportunity to make even more money. He told them this on a regular basis; it was in all of his quarterly reports. His recommendations routinely included making his work stream more visible, but no one acted on them.

One benefit of the lack of external understanding of his job was that he had been building expertise in how to apply minor molecule incursion analysis to worthwhile, poorly funded projects, to bring innovation and efficiency to organisations on the front-line of climate justice. He didn't really need ever to earn again if he lived sensibly, and so he could start helping to save the world. His time has come. Or it would soon after his mum's visit. Gina arrived in a few days and Stan was slightly surprised how keen he was to see her.

They had a plan. Gina would arrive on Thursday. A few days in Sydney, up the coast, Northern Territory, fly to Tasmania, back to Sydney for a few more days. Soon after she arrived he planned to tell her he was handing in his notice at Easter and going to live in Scotland for a bit, on the coast, doing his own research. Stan didn't think she'd panic at him giving up his job; she, if anyone, discreetly suspected he was well-set financially. She told people he paid for her ticket but she didn't tell them it would be business class.

Before all that, Stan needed to tell Alison that his mother was coming and he would then be leaving. They'd been together around a year. Alison was his age, had divorced in her mid twenties after a stagnant two-year marriage both parties wished had never happened, and now she wanted to settle down – by which she meant a house in Manly, a four-wheel drive and children – and she wanted all this with Stan. Alison knew he earned a lot, although she was probably out by a factor of ten, but she had no idea he was planning major life changes. He thought Alison might, albeit reluctantly, move to the UK with him, but he didn't really want her to. It was going to be a brutal conversation. For the duration of any relationship, Stan was the ideal boyfriend, faithful, funny, generous and sociable, and this seeming perfection led to trauma above and beyond the normal fallout when he called time. He honestly didn't know if he had post-Carran commitment issues, or if he just hadn't met a life partner yet. Children? Maybe. He would be a good financial bet at the very least. But for now, he didn't want Alison and his mother to meet because he was moving, solo, back to the UK, so what would be the point?

Gina would arrive around midday on the Thursday, and they had decided over multiple calls and texts that going for lunch and a harbour trip would be the best way for her to keep awake until evening in the hope that would reduce jet lag. Stan had made up the spare bed, bought some mint tea and arranged dinner on Friday with some friends of his parents who had moved here decades ago and Gina hadn't seen since, though they were in touch a couple of times a year. On Sunday they would start travelling north.

Walking up seventeen flights to his office before getting the lift for the last seventeen, he wondered if it was pathetic to be so looking forward to going on holiday with his mother. At thirty-five it didn't really feel right. Alison would surely have liked to have come with them but a) he hadn't yet told her his mother was coming, b) it would only be to make him feel less like a sitcom caricature secretly in love with his mummy, and c) it would just make it even worse when he told her he was leaving Australia in a few months. Gina would, in Stan's view, like him to be bringing a girlfriend or fiancée or wife, although Evan had relieved any major pressure on the grandchild front. Two in fifteen months and another on the way. Mind you, careful reading of Evan's texts suggested this latest one – unplanned, recklessly conceived – had pretty much done for his brother and sister-in-law.

*

Gina was lying flat on her sofa, seeing for the first time in the eight months she'd lived there how pretty the ceiling rose was. Not original, but it added a bit of interest above the magnolia walls. A notch up, ceiling-wise, on the examination room. It was 12.45 p.m. and she had four hours to wait for her GP appointment.

Matron had reluctantly called a taxi for Gina. They had wanted to keep her in but she'd insisted on coming home, although now she wished she hadn't, the patient version of buyer's remorse. 'Alone with your thoughts' they say, and if she'd been in the Arctic Circle she couldn't have felt more alone with hers. The clinic didn't have grounds to advise against her discharge because she was well and, as far as they could tell, in sound mind. An unplanned pregnancy even at sixty-two isn't an illness or, on its own, enough to call into doubt rational decision-making. For now, matron had to agree to Gina's firm insistence on going home by herself, which came more from a place of wanting to feel normal than a desire to make her own cups of tea.

Gordon the Lodger was out and not likely to be back until his latest tour group finished their punishing schedule of stately homes, afternoon tea and other things English. Gordon lived in Fort William and stayed with Gina when his private tour-guiding took him down south, which was several months a year. Gina thought of him as a paying guest, a term from her childhood that she didn't think was current any more. The arrangement suited them both.

She explored techniques for how to think about her situation. She found if she held her head in her hands, very still, her brain would stop swerving from totally blank to multicoloured crazy, and then she could let her thoughts in one at a time. An orderly queue instead of a tidal rush. She could turn each of them over and consider them carefully. In the aftermath of her first widowhood, a friend of her mother's had told her that when things are overwhelming, when you don't know how to cope, don't look ahead. One day at a time, one morning at a time or one hour at a time, and then make a plan just for that. It was advice she had returned to often. So for the next hour she decided to sleep. She'd always been good at napping and hoped sleep would give her its best restorative shot. Riley, with a dog's unerring instinct for keeping silent company in times of distress, got up on the couch beside her, sensing her weakness, her reluctance to shove him off, and he immediately pretended to be asleep so she wouldn't have the heart anyway.

An hour or so later, calmer if not refreshed, she went back to the turnstile at the entrance to her mind, letting just a single thought in, keeping the others back until that one had been processed and found a home. One. Am I really pregnant? Yes. The baby foot nudging her midriff could be nothing else. Two. How? Can't answer that so it goes in the doctor box. Three. Who is the father? No idea. Had to be George but couldn't be George. Needs some input from the doctor, make a list of questions to ask – also in the doctor box. Four. Who to tell? No one. Unsustainable. Oh. Maybe Greg. Her brother was a proper grown-up and Gina had been the first of the family he'd told when he was to be a father at forty-five. Laura may have been something of a surprise to her dad but at least she'd been feasible. Within known parameters. News of her niece had merely been unexpected whereas Gina's news was… ludicrous. Five. When to tell them and in what order? Not today. Not at all, if she took the planned prenatal foetal demise option. Conference call? Mass email? Back to don't tell anyone. Six. Practicalities. Cot, breastfeeding – dear God, absolutely not – so bottles, then. Sterilisers. No, one of those neat machines Amelie had that made milk just the right temperature. The thought of this advance in bottle-making brought a disproportionate comfort. Space in the flat. Life-changing upheaval for twenty years. Oh my days, some holding pen for the mind this turned out to be.

Arranging these thoughts then allowed the unspeakable one through the turnstile. Question zero. Should she keep the baby? Suddenly the thought of adoption burst onto the scene like a car you'd only noticed as you were about to crash into it. Abortion, adoption or single parenthood had confronted mothers for centuries. But at sixty-two?

Heaving herself up as though she were suddenly morbidly obese, she wondered if she should change her clothes for something looser. She had a couple of shapeless frocks and baggy jumpers somewhere. She went to the bedroom and stared at her outline in the mirror. Medium height, medium length on-its-way-to-grey hair, had considered herself a size 12 – until now at least – middling sort of face made less ordinary by careful make-up. She'd good reason to be grateful to the assistant in Selfridges who'd shown her how to apply foundation and eye liner. She smiled often and the lines showed. There was no obvious bump. She did have excess flesh but it was flat and flabby, like having one of those doughnut peaches or a swimming ring strapped around her middle, not the rounded, protruding, front-facing orange she'd contentedly had with the boys.

Running her hands over her distorted midriff, she supposed her abdominal muscles had been stronger then, whereas now there was room for a full foetal stretch across her middle: no need for curling up into a football-shaped bump. This baby could do a starfish, no bother. And then there was that foot again, suddenly poking at her wrinkled folds, reminding her of fresh butter on mouldy bread. It was grotesque; she was instantly nauseous, weeks of morning sickness in one swoop. She rushed to the bathroom and vomited into the toilet, retching and reeling until she could stand up only by holding tight to the bath edge, with her other hand on the shower screen.

She didn't change her clothes. It wasn't like anyone would care what she was wearing. Having thought changing might make her feel better, the effort of doing so was just too much. Yesterday, last week, most of her life really, she'd been the efficient person with lots of stamina, the go-to woman when you needed something done. Now she couldn't even change her shirt. She wondered if she was depressed, but it seemed hard to believe that depression was not there at eight o'clock in the morning and full blown by mid-afternoon. She'd always thought of depression as a systemic, developing thing: a process, a gradual dampening down of who you are and how you view your world. Not something that you could get in an instant over coffee, like cutting your finger or having a heart attack. But then, Gina asked herself, what did she know about depression? More or less than she knew about late middle-age pregnancy? She picked up her passport, driving licence and birth certificate, rooted around and found her NHS card and a letter from the pensions people telling her she'd be sixty-six before she received her pension. Fleetingly pleased at her ability to locate them at short notice, unlike keys and glasses, both of which eluded her regularly, she set off for the surgery wearing the same trousers, shirt and jacket that she'd put on at six that morning.

*

It was a twenty-five-minute walk. Every step felt artificial, as though she were an imposter in her own body. She was tense, ready to hide in a doorway or turn in the other direction if she saw anyone she knew who might say something incendiary like: 'Gina! Hello! How are you? When are you off to see Stan?' Gina fantasised Dr Manes saying, 'So sorry, Mrs Flowers. That must have given you a bit of a scare! As if you could be pregnant!' Pause for an embarrassed smile. 'It's called a false positive gynaemotonomo. Go home, have a glass of wine and a good laugh about it.'

Then the foot had another go, half jerk, half kick, all 'I'm here. I'm real.' Gina sat down on a low wall and put her hand gently round the outline of the foot, reminding herself of the mother-to-be of thirty-five years ago. It was so obviously a foot, a baby foot, but she allowed herself to consider what she might have swallowed that could be that shape. Andre, her oldest grandson, who had beautiful manners and ate everything from moules marinière to curly kale, had been with her a couple of weeks ago. He had a small toy ship that was sort of oval and square at the prow. True, it was hard to see how she could have swallowed it without noticing, but was it any more fanciful than falling pregnant at sixty-two, at least ten years post-menopause and highly celibate?

She checked in at the console in the surgery and wondered idly how long it would be until no human would be involved in diagnosis and routine care. She had a neighbour, Maya, who had worked at Heathrow but was now replaced by boarding pass apps and online check-in. Maya had been LHR woman and girl – a storybook of passengers trying to check in fridges as hand luggage and claiming implausible relationships with senior executives in the hope of an upgrade. Years ago Maya had said that staff joked about passengers writing their own tickets and going through turnstiles to get on planes. Prescient if slightly chilling. And that was just aeroplanes, not medicine. Gina took these displacement thoughts to the waiting room.

She was ten minutes early but some klaxon had alerted Dr Manes to her arrival. Rather than 'Virginia Flowers to Room 3' flashing up in lights, the doctor came in and asked Gina to come with her. Dread of what she'd hear spread through Gina. She felt like someone in the dock waiting for the jury foreperson to pronounce guilty or not guilty. A whole life hanging on that one word which they knew and you didn't. Yet. She thought of the time she'd been arrested at immigration in Dallas: 'It'll be OK. It has to be' mixed in equal parts with 'People get locked up for life without parole by mistake.' In Dallas it had been OK. How many Virginia Eleanor Flowers were there? At least two, but she'd managed to convince them she wasn't the one on the wanted list. The wanted one was nineteen, thank goodness, and she had been fifty-five.

She sat, heavily, thumping down into a well-worn chair where numerous patients had waited for boil treatment, a terminal diagnosis or the sunshine of an all-clear. Dr Manes asked how she was. Gina stared again. She literally had no idea what to say. Fine, because she wasn't ill? Depressed, but was she? Terrified, but what could a GP do about that? Numb, but not completely numb – she'd felt the foot. So she stared.

'Mrs Flowers,' Dr Manes said, very gently. 'You are thirty-two, maybe thirty-three weeks pregnant and we need to discuss your care.'

'What are my options?' She managed a whisper. 'You know. Options.'

'Well, I think first it would be very helpful to establish your history and how you are feeling so that we can plan appropriately. Make sure everything is progressing… normally. For a pregnancy. Satisfactorily might be a better word.'

'Do you believe me? What did they tell you?'

Dr Manes paused for quite a long time. Gina imagined her credibility on trial in the doctor's mind. If someone you love with all your heart, trust completely and know to be one of life's good guys gets accused of a horrible crime, there must be a period, a nanosecond maybe but more likely an ongoing, raw and rough nagging ache, when you wonder if they did it. Gina recognised the melodrama of her thoughts. She was just the GP's patient.

Dr Manes said, 'Mrs Flowers, there is no "they". I am your doctor. It is my job and – though this sounds a bit soppy – my privilege to care for my patients. Mr Howard and everyone at the clinic is working for you and with you. Your circumstances are so unusual that it is really a question of… of establishing everything exactly. I think it would help to find evidence that there is no mistake. It would help us as doctors and it would help you. You need to trust us. We really do have your interests and those of your baby at the centre of our care.'

Despite feeling a rush of gratitude and gladness almost pushing her to tears, Gina found her truculence was made of stern stuff. 'How will it help me, this evidence? I know the truth. I don't need to provide evidence.'

Another long pause. Gina wished she could find the grace to put into words her appreciation of Dr Manes' thoughtfulness.

'Getting the best care will be easier if everyone has access to all the facts, and evidence is the best way to do that. And if… when… if you tell people, it will be easier – less difficult – if we are all clear. About the evidence.'

Gina considered this, surprised to be still rational enough to know both that Dr Manes was right, and that it didn't mean the doctor didn't believe her exactly, though it could very well mean that. But first things first.

'What are my options?'

'Do you mean about continuing with the pregnancy?'

'Yes.' Then, for what would be the final time: 'Is there any doubt? That I'm pregnant?'

'No.'

Gina put her hands on her cheeks and now felt the tears sliding into her fingers.

'If you mean, can you have a termination.'

There was another silence.

'I do, yes. I need to know the options. I'm sixty-two. What will I do with a baby younger than my grandchildren?' It wasn't a question Gina expected the doctor to answer; she just needed to give voice to her fear.

'It is too late for a routine termination. Any ending of the pregnancy would be an assisted foetal death.'

'You mean murdering a live baby. What Mr Howard called planned prenatal foetal demise?'

'Well, not murder as such, no. But it is very likely the foetus would be viable at this stage, so it would be more complicated than… than if you were, say, just a few weeks pregnant. Mr Howard will be more up to date than me with current terminology in this field. But yes, essentially we are talking about the same procedure.'

'How would it work?'

'You would need to see a specialist. Tomorrow. It isn't straightforward, but your circumstances are not straightforward. I can't really say more than that. It is a matter for Mr Howard.'

'He doesn't do planned prenatal foetal demises. He told me that. He did say he might know a service.'

They sat in silence for a while.

'Do you think that is what you want?' asked Dr Manes finally. 'If so, I do need to make a referral today so that you can have appropriate pre-op counselling and information. Tomorrow. And speak to Mr Howard so we can find someone to refer you to.'

'I'd give birth and then they'd kill it?' Gina's head suddenly jerked up as if to make sure she was alert enough to prevent defaulting to baby-killing because she was over-tired or not paying attention. 'How do they do it? Do they just let it die, starve it to death, or do they do something? An injection?'

'Mrs Flowers, I don't think I'm the right person to help you with this. If you do want to see this as an option, I need to make a referral, urgently.'

'What do you know? How does it happen?' Gina could see Dr Manes thinking, not knowing what to say. She thought she'd help the doctor out because she liked her. She'd probably have helped her out even if she didn't like her because trying to please was deeply ingrained. 'Please could you make the referral. I don't think it is what I want but I make better decisions if I know all the options.'

Dr Manes picked up the phone and asked someone on the other end to make an urgent appointment for tomorrow morning for Gina with a late termination counsellor. 'Tell them it's a P-twenty-seven-W.' So that was her. P-twenty-seven-W. 'And set up a call for me with Mr Howard as soon as possible.'

Gina put thoughts of termination to one side and shifted back to Dr Manes' original concern. 'What evidence do I need to provide?' Dr Manes looked at her computer, and Gina appraised her, which was an indulgence. It wasn't like she didn't have other things on her mind. Mid thirties. Shoulder-length hair, mascara and lipstick, no jewellery, clothes that weren't M&S but weren't exactly edgy either. A white shirt covering – Gina realised as her GP changed the angle of her chair to focus on getting Gina to focus – a bump. Less than thirty-two weeks but a bump. Dr Manes saw her realise. Neither of them acknowledged it verbally, but a tiny frisson of something that could have been sisterhood crossed the room like a sparkler-strength shot of lightning.

'Whatever your… options… there are three things we need to firmly establish: your date of birth; when you reached menopause; when you last had sex.' She thought again for a moment. 'And to confirm that you have not made any clinic-led or home-based attempts at IVF or other form of fertilisation.'

Gina needed to consider again if this might all be a dream, which did seem unlikely – but then what about today had not been unlikely? – and, if so, how she might wake herself up. What were the signs you were awake and not dreaming? There was a saying that if you are mad, you never think you are. Perhaps if you are dreaming, you don't consider the possibility that you are dreaming. On that unscientific basis, she was awake: this was her reality. Dr Manes was waiting patiently. It was only just after five o'clock. This time yesterday, Gina had been packing. One swimsuit or two? Hair straighteners? If she had a foetal demise tomorrow, it might still be relevant. Finally, Gina replied.

'So I can answer those questions, but you're saying they, you, won't necessarily believe me?'

'I am saying in something as unusual as this, it is best to have independent verification. Evidence. Proof.'

Gina understood, intellectually. Of course she did. She understood it was so preposterous that without proof, documents or test results that no one could argue with, she'd always be in the margin of doubt. She was boiling with confusion and rage and indecision, so she gathered those enemies of logic together, shaped them into a neat square and put them into a mind-box. A bow around the box for good measure. Then she put it in a recess of her brain. She could picture the brain's furrows and hills, and she chose a location right at the back to hide the box. She would come back for it.

'Well, I've brought my birth certificate, passport, driving licence, NHS card and a letter from the pensions people. I'm hoping that along with my surgery records that will sort out my date of birth.' Gina was trying to keep her tone neutral but could hear the undertow of resentment. She hoped Dr Manes didn't detect it – or forgave it. There was a pause.

'Of course, Mrs Flowers, these documents aren't for me. Honestly, I'm not sure who they are for, but I do think it is very wise to have them. I think Mr Howard will want them.' She stopped and Gina knew she was working out how to get something unpalatable across. Just as she started to say it, Gina realised. These documents proved a Virginia Flowers was born on the fifth of July 1956. They didn't prove Gina was *that* Virginia Flowers. And that is what Dr Manes said, tactfully.

Staring blankly at people remained Gina's default mode of the day. Dr Manes was still talking.

'It will be very important for your care to firmly establish your identity and your age. But we must move on with planning that care while that process is underway. If there is a process. I don't really know.'

Gina decided to be sensible, treat the enquiries like airport security. No matter how daft some of the things seemed, airport security needed passengers to do things their way and you were not getting on a plane without complying.

She needed people on her side, so she'd help them to know who she was.

'Is there a test I can do to prove I am me and I am sixty-two?' In her mode of compliance, she tried hard to keep the swing between petulance and sarcasm under the tonal radar.

'I really don't know if that will be necessary, Mrs Flowers. I am certainly not saying that. I think for now we should proceed with the documents you've got and the information you've given us and wait to see what Mr Howard has to say.' Dr Manes hesitated and then went on. 'We will be able to get a good approximation of when you went through the menopause by examining your ovaries in ultrasound again.' She paused. 'I'm not sure what tests can be done to establish the length of time you've been celibate. One step at a time. My main concern is the health of the baby and your health. So tell me, please tell me this time, how are you? How do you feel?'

Gina shook, shuddered and abruptly wailed. Dr Manes tried to comfort her, like trying to marshal a stampeding crowd with a single megaphone. The doctor was – presumably – a happily pregnant woman of thirty-something years, and Gina was an inconsolable sixty-two-year-old pregnant mother without a husband – ashamed, embarrassed, frightened, tired, angry, foolish, still a little in denial: all these emotions fighting it out for first place. There was also a maggot of hope it was all a mistake. A maggot because it shouldn't be there. Exhausted, she slumped and stared, nodding her acceptance to go on.

Dr Manes talked a lot about a care plan. The information drifted past Gina like a glider coming in to land before veering off the runway.

Eventually Gina asked for a taxi and promised she'd see Mr Howard first thing. On leaving, suddenly she was standing up and walking as if she was pregnant. What a difference half a day made. Ignorance is bliss. Knowledge is power. She felt neither blissful nor powerful.

She craved alcohol. To relax, to take the edge off. It's what she did most days but only since she'd turned fifty and the boys were fully grown. She wondered if she had created, unknowingly, an alcohol-dependent baby. Dr Manes escorted her to the car park, repeating 'Please get someone to come over and be with you' as Gina got in to the taxi.

*

Just before 9 p.m. in England, 8 a.m. in Sydney. Gina knew she had to ring Stan. She was almost packed for the flight on Tuesday – tomorrow – night, just chargers and washbag to go in. Sandra was going to leave work early to take her to the airport, so she'd have to phone her as well. Gina could easily have taken a taxi, but Sandra was Stan's godmother and wanted her friend to take a Departures hug across the world to him. Gina was not often given to procrastination, preferring to deal with emails on receipt and get unwelcome tasks off her to-do list first, but this evening was different. She booked a taxi to the clinic for the morning. Taxi switchboards don't ask awkward questions like 'Why? You went there yesterday. Is something wrong? Is there someone who should come with you? How can you contemplate murdering a viable baby?' None of that. Just postcode, time and destination.

Next, she heaved herself off the sofa again, made a cup of tea and cheese on toast. When George Douglas, her first husband and her sons' father, had died, the boys were still small and there were days she had no idea what to do, how to make the hours pass, keep them occupied. She used to look at the clock at nine in the morning and think if she could get through two hours, it would be eleven and she could have a sit-down coffee. She'd had a stand-up, walk-around coffee every half hour, the act of making it as much the comfort as the result. But a sit-down coffee was a minor triumph: it meant she had passed two hours of those very long days; two more and it would be lunchtime. And so the months had gone by until the diminished, reconstituted family achieved a fuzzy resemblance of their normal. Evan stopped asking if Daddy could see them from heaven, and Gina – hallelujah – could respectably go back to work.

She had worked as a bookkeeper then, before training as an accountant simply for the money. She had always much preferred bookkeeping, and a few years ago, when she could afford to, had gone back to it. Accountancy had been a heavy responsibility for her, although over time as she witnessed the auditing and financial mismanagement that littered regulated industries with little political or individual accountability, she'd felt on the wrong side of that fence. George Douglas had dropped dead at the railway station – a brain haemorrhage at the age of thirty-six. Gina had been really sad for him and the boys that he'd died so young. She had never felt much good as a wife; being a widow, she realised to her shame, wasn't that awful for her. There were times when remorse – at how she could feel like that when the boys were bereft – still fell into her mind unbidden but not entirely unwelcome; it meant, she hoped, she cared deeply on some level. She wouldn't have wished George's death on any of them, of course, but she was quite good on her own. The life insurance had paid off the mortgage, and once she'd qualified they could have a couple of holidays a year with clubs and activities so she didn't have to entertain the boys or worry about what they were doing. It suited them all. She thought from time to time that it was highly probable – especially when people new to her status as a young widow were voicing sentiments of sorrow or recognising her loss – that she and George would have divorced if he hadn't died. She used to wonder if she should tell the boys. She probably wouldn't. Maybe they would find it useful, to contextualise their childhood, but more likely it would be an inappropriate disclosure: a weight shifted from her shoulders to theirs.

She'd seen a grief counsellor a year or so after George's death. She wasn't clear how it had helped her directly – perhaps she wasn't grief-stricken enough – but she'd noticed the boys were calmer for a while when she got back each Tuesday, a little less clingy as the weeks went on, and so she supposed there was a link. It helped her feel more in control, if not less conflicted. There were times when she felt like someone had thrown a sack over her head, and even though her hands and the sack hadn't been tied she couldn't get out, yet she found she could focus on the boys, blot out everything except what they wanted for their tea. This Monday evening, more than thirty years later and lonely to her soul, she managed to stop herself thinking all the crammed-in thoughts: doctor, identity, celibacy, menopause,

43

tests, fathers, Australia, pregnant, pregnant, pregnant – hideous. She focused on getting another cup of mint tea and opening the tin of shortbread she'd bought to take to her friends in Sydney.

An unexpectedly helpful thing the counsellor had said was, broadly, don't lie. To herself or her children, especially. Which sounded obvious as a guide for life but was both harder and more liberating than she'd expected. Sometimes, Gina came to realise, the truth takes us prisoner before setting us free, but she found it was the way out of the majority of her muddles, personal and professional. She didn't have to be a rank over-sharer; not lying doesn't mean telling everyone everything. Equally, said the counsellor, don't hide behind lies of omission. Apply the concept of appropriate disclosure. If you are going to lie, have a very good reason and admit to yourself what that reason is. These things were said often and firmly. They had got Gina through the boys' teenage years with less jeopardy than would otherwise have been the case, and she often referred herself back to that advice.

And yet here she was, plotting lies plural to tell Stan. She knew a lie to be very rarely standalone. It brings other supporting lies in its wake, webbing together into that well-recognised tangle, a concert of deceit. 'Stan, oh no, I'm so sorry. I was so looking forward to it, but I can't come because…' She considered basing her lie on the deaths of people close to her but unknown, or only vaguely known, to Stan; something medical but not life-threatening preventing her flying; Riley suffering some dreadful but curable canine disease so her mother couldn't look after him and he couldn't go in the kennels; sudden and crippling fear of flying. She came up with two ostensibly viable alternatives. One: she'd lost her passport so she'd be a couple of days late. Two: she was pregnant and the doctor says she can't fly there and back in time to give birth, always assuming she didn't legally murder the baby before the flight took off. Thirty-six weeks is the limit for flying. Maybe she could get there and back and they couldn't actually stop her, but at her age they'd strongly advised against it. And Australia had a heatwave, the mere thought of which now made her feel nauseous. And what if it arrived early and she had to explain all over again she was sixty-two, celibate, post-menopausal and pregnant? Gina imagined herself saying all and none of those things to Stan on WhatsApp, and wondered what this melange of nonsense having a punch-up with the truth was doing to her psyche.

She Googled the lost passport option: best to get her lie as truthful as she could. There were emergency appointments available, at a price, for tomorrow. So if she were to ring Stan now, he'd Google like she'd just done, book her an appointment and then a cab to take her, wait and bring her home.

She didn't ring him or Sandra that Monday night. She couldn't get the words 'I'm pregnant' into her throat yet, let alone out of her mouth. She wasn't due to leave for the airport until 5 p.m. tomorrow for a 9 p.m. flight. About twenty hours before she absolutely had to tell somebody something.

*

With take-home pay only a baby step above two grand a month, it would be a long time before Graham was in touching distance of buying a house in west London. Just thinking about it made him feel foolish, embarrassed by the ridiculousness of his ambition. How could he ever save the deposit on the four hundred grand needed for a one-bed? Sonography might be a secure profession but it was never going to get him on that ladder. And it was boring. Vitally important, but God it was dull. Or had been dull – until today.

Chapter 4

Gerald Howard usually started work around eight-thirty in the hospital over the way and came across to Valley on Mondays and Fridays for the private clinics. He hardly dared hope Gina Flowers was for real. She was real, of course; her pregnancy was real, no doubt. Looking at her, she could be sixty-two; she could also be fifty-two, so on the outer bounds for a natural conception even post-menopause, or seventy-two. She was – he hunted about for a neutral description – well presented.

Mr Pelham was coming at nine and Mrs Flowers was due at eight, so here he was at half past seven, prepping for what could be the most interesting patient he'd ever had. Obs and gynae, like much medicine, involves a fair number of people who just need reassurance: some with easy fixes; many with chronic ailments that would go on and on, mitigated a bit by pills, ointments or incisions. And then there were a few with life-threatening conditions in need of the best, most skilled care. For those, Gerald Howard was the man. Within this, once or twice a year, something unusual came his way: quads or more, conjoined twins, upside-down and back-to-front babies – or very young mothers, victims of statutory rape, who could still make his seen-it-all heart sink a little lower. Mothers over forty-five were increasing, although biology had not yet reshaped its parameters to accommodate career paths, so many had assisted conception of one form or another. In any of these circumstances, Gerald Howard was who you'd want. The oldest woman he had ever delivered of a child was fifty-three.

Gerald still frequently brought to mind her mud-coloured face and torn body after the birth. She had had a religious objection (almost certainly what got her in to the pregnancy mess in the first place, he thought) to just about anything medical, so pain relief, a Caesarean, even forceps were off-limits. By the time her twenty-three-hour labour was over and her baby safely yelling, most of them in the delivery suite could not bear to look. And if they could hardly stand it, how on earth the poor mother did, only her God knew. He had learned a lot from that delivery and would need it all if Mrs Flowers was for real.

Gerald had contacted Bill Pelham, a master of P27Ws, and asked him to talk to Mrs Flowers about a PPFD. They had worked together for a number of years post-grad, although Bill now mostly practised in private hospitals and well-equipped palaces in major cities, managing pregnancy options for popstars and princesses. He was, however, based in London and could be relied on to fit something in if Gerald asked, as Gerald would do for him. Hopping on a private plane to do a thirty-minute how-are-you-today appointment that any half-competent midwife could have done for one of Bill's more attention-seeking patients had never sat comfortably with Gerald. Today was one of the few times he felt the quid pro quo had been worth it. If there was to be a P27W, Bill would be the man to do it. Plus he would let Gerald assist and get a first-hand look at the phenomenon that was Virginia Flowers's uterus. A tiny compensation if she decided not to proceed to term.

Gerald hoped to persuade Mrs Flowers to let him scan her ovaries and take a really good look at her womb and its surroundings before her consult with Bill. The size and shape of her reproductive organs would tell him approximately how post-menopausal she was: say, within a year if it was in the last five, or within two or three if the last ten. Beyond that, he wouldn't be able to say how many years, but it wouldn't matter.

Valley Health Care Facility had nicer surroundings than the NHS maternity suite. Birthing mothers could pay for a single room just because they wanted one, rather than it being allocated on grounds of need. Prenatal consultations benefited from appointments at the time booked, complementary coffee and biscuits, and consulting rooms with inoffensive paintings and a view over gardens – or a tasteful shutter arrangement if it was the car park aspect. Gerald had asked Mrs Flowers to come here so she could wait in a private side room between procedures.

He felt tense at the thought of losing her as his patient – if she was what she said she was. And he believed she was. His first delayed embryonic settled implantation patient. Only three women had been reliably documented as potential DESIs. None of them was over sixty and although they were some years post-menopause, they weren't celibate, so there was always room for doubt as to when fertilisation had occurred, hence 'potential' against their diagnosis. And to the best of his knowledge and research, none had given birth. Of all the clinics in all the world, Gina Flowers had walked into his.

Evert Grant came in, halting Gerald's mental preparation for his career-defining patient.

'You're in early, Evert.' Gerald suppressed his irritation at the disturbance by letting each exhaled breath add a thin layer to the invisible barrier between him and the chief medical officer. The two doctors rubbed along in mutual professional respect, if no more than that. Gerald acknowledged Evert was an excellent, even outstanding clinician, and as CMO of Valley he would not allow clinical standards to be compromised; he also made sure patients paid for everything from coffee, plasters and garden views to an expert opinion. Gerald would have liked to be an NHS man through and through, but Mondays and Fridays at Valley were helpful verging on necessary to pay for his father's care home and save enough to afford the same for himself and Rosalie one day. He used to be surprised how many of his NHS patients respected and trusted him more because he also had a name for himself privately. It should have been a hundred times the other way round.

'You're here on a Tuesday,' Evert replied.

'Virginia Flowers,' said Gerald, as if either of them needed the explanation. 'I am reasonably sure it's a DESI. Delayed embryonic settled implantation,' he clarified, mindful that guts, not gynae, were Evert's speciality. 'I intend to verify today. I can do her post-menopause assessment. Bill Pelham is coming to talk her through her P27W options. Her GP has checked her date of birth and she is sixty-two. If she is Gina Flowers.'

'What about her length of abstinence?'

'I spoke to Arak Mudonak in Cairo yesterday evening. He'd like to be on the delivery team. We talked through the internal visual checks. He has a few untried ideas we can add in, but I'll need Mrs Flowers' consent for a scope and she might not be keen. And we don't want to take any risks at all – none at all. Maybe not even a scope. So I think on abstinence we'll have to go with what she says, and we will only know for sure after the child is born. Arak thinks the visual checks will be valid even after a birth, but of course he hasn't anything empirical.'

Evert stood there waiting for him to go on. Gerald needed both a sounding board and to practise what he'd say to Gina, so despite a small stab of resentment at Evert's presence, he went on.

'After the birth, we can also do some internal swabs to help establish or eliminate recent sexual activity. It will be a delicate matter to raise with the patient, because ideally we'll do the checks immediately after delivery, perhaps even before the placenta. I need to consider that further. If the swabs don't find anything, which we wouldn't really expect but let's try and cover all fronts, and Arak's visuals don't come up with anything, then essentially we're trying to prove a negative – but on strong grounds that the negative exists. The clincher will be a DNA test on the baby and the father. Assuming we're allowed to do a DNA test and we can find a putative father to test against. Or fathers.'

'Do we know who the father is? Might be? Possibilities? I'm not familiar with the parameters. I believe I've only read about DESI in an American medical journal and that would be a while ago.'

'No. Not yet. If Mrs Flowers is levelling with us and it is DESI, it could be any sexual partner since puberty.'

Both doctors thought about that for a while and wondered to themselves where Virginia Flowers lay on the spectrum between a one-lover woman and what their mothers might have called a good time girl. Her GP records showed she had had two children in her twenties – sons now in their thirties – nothing in the records to suggest different fathers, and that she had sought help for how to cope after the boys' father had died of a brain haemorrhage when they were very small. Couple of lovers before, a couple after? A free-love compendium of men and women in the 1970s followed by grief-riddled sexual encounters with anyone who'd have her? Or one man all her life, no one matching the dead-husband-on-a-pedestal?

They agreed Mrs Flowers would have to give birth over the way in case of complications. They would need the very best O&G team available, which only the NHS could put together. Both men also knew that in the event of a delivery, they'd be on the medical conference and PR circuits and potentially in the coroner's court. From where Evert was standing, if something went wrong, well, better the birth was on the NHS. Valley's insurance was not designed with sixty-two-year-old, post-menopause celibate birthing mothers in scope. Neither of them knew Mrs Flowers's financial circumstances to make a guess about private pre- and postnatal care. Evert said he'd see what he could do on costs if it was helpful. Valley going for credit but being very much at arm's length about anything tragic or involving insurers felt suitably but unsurprisingly grubby to Gerald. But if Gina was going to give birth at sixty-two, a quiet, comfortable room was the least she needed, and while the NHS would almost certainly offer her a solo in the circumstances, it would be with the sounds of other labouring mothers as a backdrop, most of them less than half her age and some young enough to be her granddaughter. And the real possibility of being bounced back to a multiple-bed ward in the event of a mother in even greater need.

In any case, Bill Pelham might put paid to it all. Neither Gerald nor Evert were squeamish about terminating pregnancy. Indeed, both often thought it was the right call. But this was a baby, not an embryo, and there was a slick of disquiet about such late termination that sat very uncomfortably with their still-remembered oaths to do no harm, despite a firm belief in the mother's right to choose. Both also had a knot of pending disappointment if Mrs Flowers and her baby did not come through for them.

*

Mrs Flowers arrived soon after, listening to Evert's offer to see what he could do about room pricing in her exceptional case, much as someone might listen to an undertaker discussing cut-price coffins. Used to a more receptive audience, Evert was uncharacteristically starting to flounder during the list of extras he might include.

'Mr Grant,' said Mrs Flowers, 'you do know I'm sixty-two and unexpectedly having a baby in seven weeks, don't you? I'm seeing a man in a few minutes about murdering it. And there's adoption. Meal packages haven't yet made it to the top of my to-do list this morning.'

Gerald was sitting in what he hoped was a supportive pose at his desk. He couldn't leave in case a tiny reassurance that only he could give was needed. He could see in her face that she knew she was being rude and that she knew she would want – crave – the private facilities. Standard polite discourse had deserted her as if lasered out by the horror of her situation. He was mildly enjoying Evert's discomfort at her approach.

'Can I fly?' she asked with barely a break.

Neither doctor was sure who she was speaking to. A few moments of silence went by until Gerald picked up the gauntlet.

'Fly?' he said. 'Do you mean in a plane?'

'Unless the old-mother-late-pregnancy combo gives you wings, I would need to take a plane, yes.' Her tone was pitiless, sarcastic. Gerald recognised it as a defence mechanism of some sort, and wasn't completely surprised when she acknowledged this, as if offering a one-off compensation payment. Speaking to both of them she said, 'I'm sorry about my tone. Being rude to you doesn't make things any better, but I can't seem to help it.' A small current of relaxation shimmied round the room.

'You want to fly somewhere? When? Where? How long?'

'Australia. Tonight. Three weeks.'

'No. No. No.' Despite his three-fold denial, his absolute certainty in his professional opinion, Gerald was flustered, a feeling as rare as it was unwelcome to him. He was appreciated by colleagues not only for his skill and experience, but his complete focus on the task in hand. Fluttering now like a dandelion in a strong wind, he could see that if Pelham didn't get his patient, some smooth suntanned Dr Bondi-Sydney-type would. Pregnant women can usually fly until thirty-six weeks. Unless it's twins – and it wasn't. Or there is a risk of complication. He had her on that.

'Why? Why do you want to take a plane?'

'My son lives in Sydney and I am due to go and visit him for three weeks. My flight is at nine o'clock tonight. Can you stop me?'

'Probably not. Although your airline might ask for a certificate and I wouldn't give you one. You would be travelling against medical advice. Any insurance would not be valid. Giving birth on a 747 with a couple of cabin crew – maybe an off-duty orthopaedic specialist three business class gins ahead if they put out a call - and some drop-down oxygen for company over the Indian Ocean, should that arise, would not be ideal. Medical care in Sydney is extremely expensive. They will not have an expert team prepared. I would strongly suggest you reconsider.' Gerald sounded like someone going against the clock on a quiz show.

He was ahead, but Gina gave her dream a last flag-wave.

'The airline isn't going to know. I just look fat. My passport shows I'm sixty-two so pregnancy is hardly going to occur to them. I will check-in my own bag. They won't even see me until after take-off.'

Gerald's years of helping pregnant women through bereavement, shock or while facing dreadful decisions to be taken in a hurry came to his rescue. Clasping his own hands as if he were holding hers, his voice became calm and soothing. 'I can't stop you, and if you choose not to tell your airline, you could – just possibly – get away with it. But please do not travel. I cannot tell you how strongly I advise against it.'

They were sitting in a half-circle. Gina, in the middle, started to cry. Loudly, raising the pitch with each new breath, moving towards hysteria. Gerald handed her a box of tissues and tactfully backed away from the exchange, bringing Evert in on his side. Which was also, of course, his patient's side. Evert's bedside manner had been a strong point since he first changed a catheter as a fourth-year medical student. It was why so many patients recommended Valley. He was astounding at remembering names and conditions, making people feel special. It was time NHS doctors only had for their most gravely ill patients, not for varicose veins and routine oscopies.

Several minutes passed as Gina sobbed, Evert no longer discomfited, instead simply waiting: being present, Gerald thought. He'd often heard of it but not seen Evert in action before. Gina was wearing the same jacket as yesterday, bought on that trip to Dallas with George Flowers' sister, Amanda. The shape and material reminded Gerald of one Marlon Brando might have worn playing a hard-hewn motorbike mechanic in the late fifties in a small town with a diner and a gun store, before he made it big and broke hearts.

Gerald was a fan of Brando and many things American. He'd met his wife, Rosalie, in a diner a few miles outside Nashville when he'd been to see Springsteen and stopped to eat at the first quiet place outside the city. Rosalie was arranging her father's funeral. Old man McGrath had wanted a jukebox, milkshakes, hot dogs and waffles for his send-off, and Rosalie had left her sky-high office in New York to organise this with her old school friend Collette, Flat Jack Cafe's owner. The diner had looked like something straight out of Grease and that was just how Collette worked very hard to keep it. Familiarity had bred success for her as easily as it supposedly bred contempt for others. Arrangement-making over, Collette had gone to make some calls, leaving Rosalie drinking iced tea at the only Formica table with a space when Gerald asked if he could share it. Polite and friendly, as people in those parts generally were to strangers, she asked if he was enjoying his holiday. Three weeks later, having flown home in the meantime, he went back to New York to see her.

Gerald's patients didn't really see him as a man, just an expert in their wombs or ovaries or birth canals. They rarely looked at him properly, perhaps because he had literally seen too much of them, heard too much about their troubles and tragedies, intimacies that most of them would rather have kept entirely to themselves. A few revelled in the attention but most cringed. He wasn't remarkable to look at: average height and build, mousey hair neatly cut, average complexion, hazel eyes and a smile that was generally at half-mast. Rosalie was a few years older than he was but not enough to open a gulf of age-related reference points or incompatible fitness levels. Theirs had been a meeting of smart but very differently agenda'd minds: he the field-leading specialist in an underfunded area of public medicine; she the sharpest PR woman in the world's sharpest, most glamorous city. They had married, both for the first time, when Gerald was thirty-nine. He was constantly astonished to find himself saying 'my wife'. It was a joy he hadn't thought would come his way. As a teenager and young man, he had been no magnet for women, and as he got older found his work and music sufficiently satisfying. He did not want children; he wanted a dog, though lacked the time to look into the practicalities. His mother had lost four children before dying giving birth to him, which was a tragic, unfathomable story that Gerald never quite got to the bottom of. His father had been utterly unable to talk about it and other relatives were thin on the ground. Both his parents had been only children and themselves orphaned by the time

Gerald came along. On the day Gerald qualified, his father had a catastrophic but not fatal stroke.

Gina's tears slowed to a gentle weeping and she crumpled the tissues into a tight ball. She didn't apologise; that wasn't necessary, but it was usual. Nor did she attempt a joke about waterproof mascara. Patients routinely apologised for being emotional. On delivering devastating news, Gerald found almost all women repeatedly said they were sorry for weeping, even as they stared down the barrel of stage four cancer in their third trimester.

Evert had been characteristically still, poised almost, assessing the best moment to pick up the medical thread. 'Mrs Flowers, Mr Pelham will be here in half an hour. We have a room next door where you can talk to him. After that, perhaps Mr Howard, you and I can meet again, because whatever your decision, we have to make some arrangements and we have to start that today. I am going to order some tea, poached eggs and toast for you now and you need to eat that before seeing Mr Pelham. Allegra will bring it for you. Then we will take the next steps one at a time. You are in our care. We will be looking after you.'

Gina nodded. The offer of breakfast was a first for Evert as far as Gerald was aware, and he wondered if Mrs Flowers would get a bill for it at some point. Gerald closed his eyes for a moment and imagined his disappointment if she chose a termination. He felt it as sharply as a surgical knife making an incision.

*

Jeremy Hazell had had annual check-ups at the Valley, paid for by a long-standing private healthcare plan. When he died he left a legacy that paid for this mean little office, previously drenched in beige gloom, to be refurbished – as long as they named it the Hazell Room. Mr Hazell hadn't come Bill Pelham's way medically, but he thought of him every time he had a difficult conversation in here. There was speculation that the legacy had actually been intended for the 'Breatheasy' unit over the way, which had so often helped alleviate Mr Hazell's respiratory distress, but the wording in his will was ambiguous and the NHS cagey about room-naming, so it had come to Valley.

Evert Grant had given Bill Pelham a brief on Virginia Flowers – reportedly sixty-two, five-years-plus celibate, ten years post-menopause, pregnant. Only the pregnant bit was certain; even so, the first thing Bill intended to do was to rescan and check that, although it was unlikely that three doctors, matron, two scan technicians, two urine tests and a blood test would all be wrong. Still, he needed to see the scan himself.

Maybe Mrs Flowers wasn't sixty-two or celibate or post-menopausal. Or none of those things: even one would make pregnancy… unlikely. Delayed embryonic settled implantation was a textbook possibility only – possible in the way that the Queen winning Wimbledon was presumably possible.

Evert knocked and opened the door, holding it for Mrs Flowers, who looked plump around her middle, strained around her eyes but otherwise unremarkable. 'Mrs Flowers, this is Mr Pelham. He can talk to you about your options.' At that, Mrs Flowers's expression registered a tiny spasm of shock before settling back to blank. It was as if some kind of PTSD was isolated to her face. She crumpled into the green corduroy-covered chair, her legs shaking, her hands catching the arms of the chair to stop her falling to the floor. Evert nodded, hovered for a moment and left, saying Allegra was waiting just next door and to give her a call whenever they were finished so they could move things on.

Mr Pelham wasn't sure how to get started. Like Gerald Howard, professional self-doubt and lack of confidence only rarely put in an appearance, but this patient's restrained distress was more painful than most. Pitiful. Very few women presented for a termination after twenty weeks, and almost all of those had foetal issues he could calmly and clearly discuss with them, along with the very small risk to their own health. He was no Dr Death and did not take his responsibilities lightly, but he believed in a mother's right to exercise her choice, sometimes a much less agonising choice than received wisdom would have you believe, in a safe and responsible environment. Sometimes it was to end a desperately wanted pregnancy in tragic circumstances. Gina Flowers, however, was unique.

Outside the hospital he didn't talk about his work. He would deflect conversation away from things medical and had grown comfortable lying to casual acquaintances about his profession, which had become everything from a lawyer to an IT consultant. He had a postgraduate diploma in medical law and was something of a software geek, so neither of these presented any difficulty. Although he went for IT in legal circles and law with IT types.

Mrs Flowers suddenly grabbed the consultation reins. 'I guess your interest is my age, how pregnant I am and whether I can stand an op. I suppose it doesn't make any difference to you how I got pregnant or if I am lying about anything other than my age.'

She seemed aggressive. Sometimes the teenagers and younger that Bill saw were similarly raw, though they'd say something like, 'Suppose you think I'm a slag,' or 'Just take it out. Take the fucking thing out.' More often, they'd say nothing, clinging to the adult with them, whether the nurse, social worker, mother or sister, needing it all to be over. He mostly considered the under-twenties to be victims of circumstance and had no problem with them lashing out at a random doctor if it helped in any way for them to come to terms with the decision. Quite often, he sat with them longer than they expected, asked again if they'd like to talk and did his best to find everyone some peace. And – more frequently of late – he wondered about the foetuses and how he could square his conscience with aborting a foetus but not – of course not – with terminating a newborn. This baby would not be a newborn, not exactly. He couldn't rationalise it, it just was. He used to be asked to provide comment when abortion was in the news, but reporters weren't interested when he responded that he understood completely why people felt conflicted. The media wanted a firm, preferably strident view, and he didn't give good soundbites. Frank ambivalence, seeing both sides and respecting difficult individual choices, wasn't media-friendly.

'I'll start again,' she said. 'I'm sorry. I'm on edge. Please could you talk me through my termination options. Non-birthing options. I am definitely sixty-two. They say I am thirty-two to thirty-three weeks. They say you do P-twenty-seven-Ws and that is what I'd need. They say you're

61

the best at it, but I don't know if I want to murder my baby or even whether the law says I can. I am sorry. I started badly. We haven't got much time.' And she started to cry quietly.

Sensing she was already weary of confronting her barely believable story and the medical intrusion into her life, he handed her a box of tissues and waited a few moments. She nodded, signalling she was ready to hear him. Mr Pelham decided facts were the best place to start.

'The law allows a termination if two independent doctors agree there is a significant risk to the health of the mother. P-twenty-seven-W is our shorthand for post-twenty-seven weeks, and in general only highly experienced obstetricians consider such cases. Given your age and how little we know about birth in women over fifty-five, I believe two such obstetricians could be found to certify such a risk. I certainly would.'

He paused, aware that he may have planted the idea that if she didn't have the abortion, she was going to die.

'Mrs Flowers, for us to certify the mother is at significant risk, the bar for that is not what you might consider significant. It takes account of psychological and physical health. I have reviewed your medical history, checked your indicators, and apart from your age there are no obvious risks to your physical health. That said, your age is itself a significant factor that we need to consider. Along with your mental health.' She nodded, so he went on. 'Legally, you would most likely receive the necessary permissions. If you do decide this is what you want, we would need to obtain the certifications and operate as soon as possible, tomorrow ideally. It does not give you much time for reflection but we would not want to delay. I know that your GP has arranged pre-termination counselling for you this afternoon should you decide on that.'

'How would you do it?'

Bill looked at the woman before him and struggled to see a pregnant mother. She looked chubby round the middle, apple-shaped but no bump as such. Mostly she looked… too old. Not ancient. If you saw her at the school gate fetching an eleven-year-old, you might at a stretch think late mother but more likely, early granny. But here in the Hazell Room he could not credit her condition. And he did not want to answer her question. He did not want to tell her the safest way to terminate would be for her to give birth to her by then lifeless baby.

'I think the best thing is for me to have a look. I'll just ask Allegra to sit in with us on the ultrasound.'

'I haven't felt it. Haven't felt any movement today. Do you think I could have poisoned it with unkind thoughts and angry fluids? Killed my baby in utero instead of killing it outside?'

'I don't think so,' he replied. 'But we do urgently need to check.' And they both knew a significant part of Gina would be relieved if the decision had made itself.

*

Mr Pelham may have said she couldn't kill a foetus by drowning it in poisonous fluids produced in reaction to its presence. He may have said not only did that not happen, but also if she produced that sort of acid in that sort of quantity, she would at the very least have desperate indigestion and, most likely, excruciating stomach pain. Yet Gina wasn't convinced. She felt a raging river of guilt was flowing round where her blood used to be, and it was poisonous – lethal – like having hydrochloric acid instead of blood cells and plasma.

Then just as she got up to lever herself on to the ultrasound bed again, helped by the junior ultrasound technician, the rabbit/footballer one, from yesterday, the foot stuck out. She pointed it out to the two men as if they hadn't noticed it already. She was put in mind of a shark in a children's swimming pool. 'Look, look at that foot.' There was disgust, fear and a soft scrape of anguish in her voice.

'Good, good,' Mr Pelham said. Then he felt foolish. No one knew what good looked like in this situation.

'This is my third ultrasound in twenty-four hours. Is it like X-rays? Can it damage the foetus?'

'No. It's completely safe. Risk-free – unless you fall off the scanning couch. And I don't say that about many things medical. Do you need some help to get ready?'

She shook her head, incredulous that just over twenty-four hours ago she'd had no idea she was pregnant. She had been worried about cysts and ulcers, a sneaky bit of cancer hidden from previous tests, but had no concerns about planned prenatal foetal demise. Now she was embarrassed, ashamed about her condition. Having no logical reason to be either was no help – it wasn't as if she'd planned this or failed to take some elementary contraceptive precaution. She gathered her words slowly for her next, almost unsayable question. What was she hoping to find out? Something to make it easier to decide to kill her baby?

'Mr Pelham, can you tell if the baby is alright?'

There was quite a long pause. Gina felt she was becoming a connoisseur of pauses.

'We can tell some things with a good degree of certainty. Sex. Relative size and shape of the head. Number of limbs. Heartbeat. Length and weight. These are all good indicators of general foetal health, and scans to date have not revealed anything untoward in those indicators.'

Another pause. Gina waited. He'd have to go on, and she appreciated it must be hard to frame the words sympathetically but accurately.

'There are other conditions we can test for with further procedures. This ultrasound will not help us with those. You will wish to discuss them with Mr Howard if you decide to carry the baby to term. This ultrasound is primarily for my information. It can't help you decide if it is best for you to continue to carry the baby to term or if we should consider – you should consider – on our, on Mr Howard's advice, if an earlier birth would be helpful. With the excellent nursing and medical care you would have— a baby has a good chance of viability at thirty-two weeks. So if an early delivery is recommended, that in itself would not be a major cause for concern.'

As soon as he'd said it, the double-edged sword was visible. Gina could see it hanging from the single light bulb inside a tasteful wooden shade above the ultrasound table. Dead baby, problem over, mother-as-murderer on one edge; unwanted baby, life-altering problem, bus-pass mother on the other.

By now, Allegra had dressed her in the gown, the scanner was swabbed and prepped, and Graham from yesterday was spreading the gel. Gina needed to see the monitor again and asked him to turn it to her. Mr Pelham, who would normally have insisted his line of sight was more important, had to use his left hand and stand at an awkward angle to see over her shoulder. The throb-throb of a steady infant heartbeat felt as loud as a drum in a wardrobe. It was a boy. Another one. Couldn't this one at least have been a girl? Done her that little courtesy? Or would that have made the decision harder? Murdering a daughter when you don't have any, who could do that? Murdering a son when you've got two – and two grandsons, a third on the way – well, who'd miss him?

Mr Pelham took his time, rolling the scanner steadily and carefully over her middle, which looked fat but flat. 'Do you want to know the sex?'

'I think that cat is out of the bag,' she replied. He nodded. Eventually he turned off the ultrasound, Graham wiped off the gel and left. Helped by Allegra, Gina got back to the seat in the Hazell Room where Mr Howard and Mr Pelham waited.

'I am going to have it,' she said. 'It's too real. If I went into labour now, it – he – would almost certainly survive.' She thought as she sat down that she'd made the decision, but she couldn't seem to stop scraping at the infinitesimal possibility of a pain-free, guilt-free, baby-free future. 'If I have an abortion… would the baby feel… anything?'

'We do everything we know how to keep the foetus comfortable.'

She imagined hearing those words if for some reason she had no choice; perhaps it was her life or the baby's, a baby in a multiple pregnancy singled out, a severely damaged foetus that would not survive its birth. In those circumstances, she'd have to face that choice – but she didn't have to. If she ever wanted to sleep peacefully again, Gina had to have the baby.

'Finally, Mrs Flowers, I need to make it clear that if I were to perform a P-twenty-seven-W op for you, it would have to be decided today. If you change your mind and come back next week, I will not do it. You may find another doctor who would. But I need to impress on you that any decision is much, much better taken today.'

She nodded. 'Yes. I understand, Mr Pelham. Thank you very much for seeing me at such short notice.' He shook her hand, wished her well and left. Allegra held her other hand. Mr Howard asked if she'd want a few minutes to compose herself, and then they could talk.

*

There was so much ground to cover, but they got through most of it in the following hour. They were Gina and Gerald by the end, and Gina remained relatively composed, tears thankfully absent for a while. She wanted to know, like many of Gerald's expectant parents, about the chances of various conditions, but broadly it was too late for testing – and if she was not going to abort, what was the point in testing anyway? So they agreed to set those aside. Foetal alcohol syndrome – about which Google was especially alarming and commentators especially vilifying of mothers who had so much as eyed a glass of fizz since thinking about getting pregnant – sat like a heavy doormat of worry in Gina's thoughts. Christmas had come and gone, she'd been to several social events over the summer in what would have been the very early stages of her pregnancy, and in general she probably consumed the maximum recommended fourteen or so units of alcohol a week. But FAS doesn't show in the womb, so she'd have to wait. It was unlikely, as were other conditions. Some, Gerald suspected, were more likely at her age – although pregnancies at her age were so rare even that wasn't certain – but still not likely.

Bill Pelham's good long look on the scan earlier that morning had confirmed shrunken ovaries entirely consistent with being ten years post-menopause. A post-delivery womb scrape and further scan, internal this time, would finally confirm this, but the medically fascinating conundrum was how hormones necessary both to detect a pregnancy and then carry it to term were compatible with being post-menopause. They weren't, in any textbook Bill Pelham had read, or written for that matter.

Matron, meanwhile, had double-checked Gina's GP records and seemed very clear both that Gina Flowers was sixty-two and that this woman was Gina Flowers: blood group, eye colour, height, proofs of address – all matched. And there was the testimony of the long-serving practice receptionist. So that left just the manner of conception in doubt. Not much was known about delayed embryonic settled implantation. A few years ago, it had been the subject of a workshop at the World Congress of Gynaecology and Obstetrics. Somewhat ironically, recalled Gerald, it had attempted to explore the three identified cases (all three disputed) as models for how fertilised eggs could be stored in the womb rather than outside it and released only if a woman wished to have a child after nature had decreed her child-bearing years were over. Gerald had lost track of the cases, although he had now put out urgent calls to various experts to see what he could trace. The faint shimmer of a possible new post-fertility treatment would likely be of wide interest in the specialism.

Of most interest to Gerald was who the father was. If DESI could happen at all – and there was no other explanation, if everything Gina Flowers said was true – then there were no norms for the most likely father. The most recent sexual partner, maybe, but the mother's eggs would be older and fewer. The first? Freshest eggs but longest storage time, perhaps diminishing the likelihood. The sperm of her most frequent partner would perhaps have the most opportunity but this could be offset by the quicker swimmers of another candidate. Or time of day or month, location, position, internal and external temperatures, father's genes, or any number of other variables. Gerald could not ever remember having felt this mix of emotional giddiness and intense professional responsibility. He imagined it might be how an astronaut felt prior to lift-off, albeit without the risk to his personal safety. He was aware that the investigation needed was not likely to be welcome, except in as much as Gina surely would also want to know.

Gerald broached the issue of paternity.

'Gina, with this being DESI,' – no more 'if' he'd decided – 'have you wondered at all about the conception father?'

'Yes. Fleetingly,' she replied. 'I've got to deal with Australia. And how to tell people. And how to look after a baby. A baby I am unprepared for. I will be eighty-one before he leaves school.' She paused. 'Or he will be an orphan. But, yes, a bit. I've thought about it a bit.' She added slowly, 'What should I be considering?'

'Well, our priority is your care. From now until delivery and then until after recovery, you are my responsibility as the obstetric lead. After that, you will have options. Perhaps social services might be able to help if you want to talk about adoption.'

Gina looked at the floor. 'I couldn't kill him, but I might be able give him away.'

Gerald was surprised to find how in tune he was with Gina, unusually empathetic. Perhaps it was because Rosalie was not so far from her in age and he could imagine Rosalie's horror – and his own – if she found herself pregnant. He embraced Gina's acerbic responses, hoping he was a safe repository for her distress, warming to this less technical role. In general, he believed clinical competence was as far as his obligation to patients went, and in that he overflowed. He cared deeply about his other patients, medically, but he didn't want to look after their emotions. Gina was different.

'I'm sorry,' she went on. 'It's just that I'm meant to be going to see my son in Australia tonight. I've got a flight booked. I've packed. I've been looking forward to it for eight months. I don't know who to tell or how to tell them. My mother is eighty-five. My eldest grandson is four.'

'Gina, my opinion has not changed. You need to postpone your travel plans. You absolutely cannot travel to Australia tonight. You must face up to that.'

'Thirty-six weeks. I thought thirty-six weeks was the limit. I'm thirty-two to thirty-three. I could get there and back.' Her voice betrayed her lack of conviction. This was one last grasp at normality, one last turn of the roundabout.

'No. Definitely not. You cannot travel. You must stay here and make arrangements for the birth. You must get some antenatal care and rest. You must prepare. I cannot physically stop you trying to travel, but I am telling you, again, in the plainest way possible that you should not do so.'

They sat in silence for a few minutes. It was 9.50 a.m. in the clinic, mid evening in Sydney. 'I need to call Stan. My son.'

'Are you going to tell him why you are not going?'

Something had settled in Gina's psyche and it made its way to the top of her mind at just the right time. She would need someone with her for a short while. Stan had time booked off work. He could come over for two weeks and help sort out practicalities. He was a very practical boy. Man. He was thirty-five, a man by any measure. He was good at arrangements, calm, and he would be the easiest person to have around.

'I think I am going to tell him that I need to have an urgent gynae procedure that is not life-threatening but does need to be treated immediately. And I will need to recuperate. So please could he come here as soon as possible.' She paused. 'He'll want a lot more detail, like what is it, but he'll come.' She looked at Gerald to see what he thought.

He took it slowly. 'That is, in principle, a very good plan. I do wonder, though, if you should consider telling him the truth and just ask him to keep it confidential until he arrives. It would give him time to get used to the idea while he travels.' It was Gerald's turn to pause. 'Let's start with this question: why will it be better to tell him when he gets here than before he leaves?'

Gina held up her hand to count off reasons on her fingers, noticing that they were fatter than normal. She didn't wear rings but she did really like her fingers, felt they were one of her best features, helped by a weekly manicure. Even in the bizarre count of reasons not to tell her thirty-five-year-old son she was pregnant, she admired last week's pre-holiday choice of polish.

'He'll worry. He'll think I've got it wrong. He might tell someone. He'll ask loads of questions, like who is the father.' Her little finger was still cradled inwards on her upturned palm. Then: 'I'd have to say it out loud.'

Gerald was so confident in his rebuttal, Gina wondered fleetingly if he'd ever been to a don't-lie counsellor. 'Yes, he will worry. But no more than with your cover story. And he will probably think you might have got it wrong, anyone would, but he will need to get over that hurdle at some point and he might as well get started. Ask him strictly not to tell anyone and trust him to do that. Tell him you can't answer his questions until he gets here, because you have to see doctors, but you only found out today.' It was a useful point to draw breath. Gerald was keen to take advantage of the paternity opening but decided to counteract reason five first. 'From now on, you will have to say it out loud, so perhaps he is a good first outing for the words. I'll give you the room to have a think and then perhaps we can pick up on the question of paternity. Just ask Allegra to fetch me when you've made the call. And if you decide not to tell Stan, we'll work with that.'

Gerald opened the door, sidestepping Evert Grant with his hand raised to tap for entrance. 'Mrs Flowers, would it be convenient now to have a word about room arrangements? And do you have a card handy for the consultation fee for Mr Pelham?'

Gina wanted to think about phoning Stan but politeness reasserted itself, displacing her urgent personal need in favour of someone else's less pressing enquiry. Plus, Mr Grant was a senior hospital doctor, a medical professional who had done all that specialist training, had all these brains and was undoubtedly busy – his time worth more than hers. He offered her an en suite room at what she understood was a very reasonable rate. She managed to talk about including some nursing care and meals, the accountant in her doing the negotiation almost without her input. But no check-ups or tests or procedures, nothing medical or clinical. Just a room next door to the NHS facility where she would… be admitted. She tested the phrase 'give birth' in her head, but wouldn't let those silent, terrifying words out.

She thanked Mr Grant and said she'd think about it. This wasn't the response he expected, but he refrained from mentioning the limited time and availability. This was still a health care facility, not a sofa showroom. Gina wondered what was in it for him: some sort of publicity or medical kudos? Would she have to be interviewed by magazines, describing her joy and fulfilment? Maybe get some tasteful soft furnishings or an imaginary swimming pool, with the Valley Health Care Facility logo winking in the background? Might she actually be able to sell her story to pay for all this? Oldest mum in England: My push-and-tell nightmare.

*

Graham Neville carefully took a picture of four screens of Virginia Flowers's notes. He had to use his login to view her records again, outside an appointment, which he thought, if he had to, he could explain as training follow-up. He'd brought an old smartphone with him – no SIM – and had also managed to get a photo of her, unobserved as far as he could tell, as she got out of a taxi first thing.

He had no idea what to do next.

Chapter 5

Gina phoned Stan.

He was stunned. 'Proper floored,' Gina's father would have said. Stan didn't believe it, although she didn't think he thought she was lying, just that she was… what? Deluded. Deranged. Playing some sort of outlandish prank. Simply wrong, toying with a late mid-life wish-fulfilment scenario. She didn't know what he thought but he didn't think she was pregnant. He asked some questions she didn't want to answer – couldn't answer – except to say she was thirty-two to thirty-three weeks and couldn't travel.

'So, you're not coming?' Stan asked, still a question and not a statement of understanding.

'No. The obstetrician says I can't. I know the cut-off is normally thirty-six weeks, but given my age and the distance, he has strongly advised against it. Said it would be against medical advice. I'd have no insurance and if something were to happen mid-flight, it would be… messy. The airline wouldn't be happy.'

'Who's the obs man? What's his name?' From ten and a half thousand miles away she could sense Stan typing 'Gerald Howard obstetrician England' into a device. She was faintly surprised she hadn't done that herself, so she said, 'Hang on a minute' and looked up Gerald on her phone. He was good.

'This is the man who says you're pregnant? How do you know it's him, not some imposter? Is he really registered with the GMC? Have you checked? Are you in England?'

She couldn't be bothered with those questions, the only ones she could have answered properly. 'Stan, please will you come over here instead of me coming to you?'

He agreed and said he'd cancel the flights he'd booked for her and text her his flight details. She went over the don't tell anyone, not anyone, not his brother or his grandmother, and heard the faint intake of breath as the implications of his mother telling her mother her only daughter was pregnant at sixty-two began to come alive. He said of course not. She suspected not believing her made that easier. It was 7 p.m. on Tuesday, Sydney time, so he should arrive in the UK on Thursday.

*

The armchair in the Hazell Room had a table attached that could swing over to hold a meal or a drink. Like in a fancy cinema. Or a nursing home. Gina swung it round, found her diary, which had those blank notes pages she'd never used before, and started three lists.

List 1: people to tell and when to tell them

List 2: things to do

List 3: possible fathers

She made the first and second; the third was a heading only. It seemed sensible to talk to Gerald before making list three, but at least she had written the words, put empty bullet points underneath and made it official.
She pressed a bell. Allegra tapped and opened the door a moment later, and Gina told her that whenever Mr Howard was available she was ready.

They agreed that Gerald would accept her history as she told it. Postnatal tests would confirm it. Gerald was glad to believe her. DESI meant that anyone who in normal circumstances could have been the father could, in fact, have been the father. Gerald used gentle language, avoiding the euphemistic but not as direct as he might have normally been. Gina was going to have to dredge up four decades of sexual history for dissection, and he thought phrases like 'could have been the father' easier to hear than 'anyone you had sexual intercourse with'.

Gerald saw that Gina had three sheets of paper on the horrible integral table put there so patients could sip tepid water through a straw without needing assistance from staff. Two were written on, looked like lists; the other was blank except for a title and some empty bullets.

'Anyone? No matter how long ago, no matter how often or not, no matter anything except that?' she asked.

'One of your fertilised eggs has been in your womb for some time. Essentially, it's been hiding. You may have a tiny cavity where it implanted and now it has been dislodged. Or it may have been cocooned in the lining. So, if it has been there ten years, it could have been there forty years.'

'I've read that older eggs are less likely to...' She hesitated, tried again. 'There are less of them and they degrade. The foetus is more likely to be damaged or not carry to term.'

Gerald was skilled at imparting information, detached, calm, balanced: don't patronise; don't overload; explain, don't advise. Confirm understanding. Repeat. When training students he had often felt this was the most important part. 'Let's separate a few things. Some conditions do not present until after birth, and that is true for all babies. But as far as we can know at this stage, your baby is fine. You are now thirty-two to thirty-three weeks. As you discussed with Mr Pelham, if you were to deliver now there is an excellent chance of viability. And we are going to do what we can to ensure you don't deliver yet. I do think, however, that a planned Caesarean would be the best course. Your muscles will not be as strong as they were when you had your sons.

'We don't know about the… let's say… storage conditions in utero. But this embryo has implanted and has grown to a normal size for thirty-two to thirty-three weeks. So let's work with that. Do you want to talk through the paternal scenarios?'

'Paternal scenarios,' said Gina flatly, closing and rubbing her eyes, looking at the ceiling not at Gerald when she opened them. 'I never thought I'd have to share my whole sexual history with anyone. I mean never, no one. There are some things that are just mine and I wanted to keep it that way. Lots of bits of my life, actually. I don't know yet how I'm going to avoid telling my friends and family. They'll want to know, of course they will. So if I can't give them one surefire father, they're going to ask about possibilities. Or worse, speculate among themselves.' Gina shivered, or maybe it was a shudder. 'I don't want to tell anyone except you unless I absolutely have to. But I don't find it easy to say it's not your business – or to lie.'

'I understand that. I'm fifty-three, Gina. I would be uncomfortable if I had to revisit such matters.' Gerald's discomfort would be admitting he had only ever had one lover; it was clear from the direction of the conversation that this was not the case for Gina. 'If you prefer, we can simply go with "father unknown". And your friends and family would have to accept that, because if we don't make efforts to identify him, the father will remain unknown. Would you like a bit more time to think about that?' Even as he said it, Gerald crossed symbolical fingers in his head, his breathing made slightly shallow by controlled anticipation. He was satisfied he had kept his tone neutral, believed he'd hidden his eagerness to start investigating.

'No. At some point I'll need to tell—' Such a long pause, he wondered if she'd completely lost her thread. 'My son. This son. About this whole thing. Or I might have to write him a letter because I'm so old.' She paused and Gerald didn't interrupt with platitudes. Undeniably she was old to be a new mother.

'He'll ask.' Gina continued slowly, picking her way along a path littered with tiny emotional bombs and crushing, massive practicalities. 'And I'll need to be able either to tell him, or say I tried and it wasn't possible.' Another pause. 'What I'm not clear of is what you'll need from the… prospects.'

'DNA matching would be ideal. Other things would be excellent indicators. Are you still in touch with any or all of them?'

'No.' Gina drew the slide table towards her and started on the third list. 'There are definitely five. Possibly six, if we start from the beginning and go right through. Have you got time?'

Gerald most certainly did have time.

*

Stan was sitting in the waiting room of the minor injuries unit of the midsize hospital in his suburb of Sydney. He wasn't injured but he had really wanted to talk to someone…he picked through words like choosing from a box of chocolates….dispassionate. He'd booked a flight to London, cried off work citing a family emergency, got his dog walker to look after Wilson, and then made his way to the hospital where he knew Rob was on duty. Rob was the only doctor he knew, had only ever been known to get passionate about body-surfing, and he was coming to meet Stan for a coffee.

The best part of an hour later, Rob came through, out of uniform, shift over. 'Sorry to keep you, mate, but I'm free now for an hour.' Rob had always been the type to set boundaries, decide the rules of any engagement and stick to them. It was reassuring, but irritating too; even his close friends, like Stan, could resent being scheduled in to a timetable for a drink, kick-about or family emergency. Stan had sometimes wondered if this lack of creativity had confined Rob to minor injuries rather than medical glory. 'What's the problem, mate?'

'Medical confidentiality. Does it apply to me?' Stan asked.

'Well, I wouldn't treat you, not normally, so you're not a patient but if you want to run something by me, then yes, of course I'll keep stum. Unless, you know, danger to self or others. Do you think you're sick?'

'No. No one's sick. It's more confidentiality by proxy. Someone else.'

'Don't tell me who it is then. And if they're not sick, what? Alison's pregnant?'

'No. My mother. My mother says she is pregnant.'

'What?'

'My mother. Says she is thirty-two to thirty-three weeks pregnant.'

Rob had never let emotion, even a low-grade emotion like surprise, get in the way of practicalities. 'She's coming out next week, isn't she? Should she be flying?'

That lack of imagination again: check the rules on flying before you wail 'What? Your sixty-two-year-old mother is pregnant? The mother you thought was finished with men, and finished with… younger woman things, your mother who is a grandmother – that one?' It was, of course, Stan who wanted to wail, but still.

'Seems unlikely, mate. And not my area but I guess if she had help, it might be a goer. What is she? Late fifties?'

'Sixty-two.'

Rob looked at Stan. 'That would be quite a story. I mean, maybe not a medical miracle exactly but very much in that ballpark. Bit of a corker, I'd say.'

*

Evan was fretting about why his mother wasn't answering her phone. It rang out before going to voicemail so it wasn't switched off, wasn't out of battery. Maybe it was on silent, but that wouldn't be like her. Maybe she didn't hear it, but ditto: his mother was as wedded to her phone as any teenage digital junkie. Her assortment of WhatsApp groups, family pictures and Instagrams of rescued badgers were a marvel – and frequently a bore – to behold. She should be at home packing. He tried the landline. No reply. He rang Amelie. It was as good an excuse as any to phone his wife.

'Mi, my mother's not answering her phone.'

'Try again in an hour. She'd call if there was something wrong. She'll phone before she leaves. Are you really worried?'

Evan knew he couldn't admit to being really worried, especially on such flimsy grounds. Amelie would hate it. And he wasn't worried, exactly. He knew he was his mother's ICE contact, with Stan being in Oz, so if something had happened… he drew breath and rationalised. 'Yep, I'll call back in an hour. Of course. See you tonight.'

'I'm going to the People's Kitchen tonight.' Amelie cooked twice a month at a night shelter. She cooked French-style, which some guests adored but many disguised with tomato ketchup. He'd not exactly forgotten, but what with that and her cultural programme, the late meetings and pregnancy yoga, it felt like looking after her children or spending time with him weren't so much last on her agenda as not even items. At best, he would be under any other business. He wondered how Amelie would feel about doing nothing. He didn't think she'd ever tried it. Let alone doing nothing with him. He had tried so hard, and succeeded so well, in being a present father, an exemplary parent, that he'd ended up sixth fiddle to Amelie's work, interests, friends, time for herself and good deeds. Suddenly he was resentful. He very rarely phoned her during working hours with a worry, so he must have been really worried. But she just wanted to get on with her things, he thought, trying not to sound petulant even to himself.

Evan decided to go and see his mother and he was on the road within ten minutes. A tiny act of defiance. He might send Amelie a text when he arrived. He needed to know if it was a foolish overreaction or a perfect instinct; and he needed Amelie to know she'd been on the wrong side of the equation. It would take him forty minutes to get to his mother's house. He'd never done that before, arrived unannounced. What if he found her on the floor, having hit her head? He'd be a hero. As long as she recovered and he wasn't too late.

Or maybe she'd accidentally left her phone on silent.

*

Mr Howard asked Gina to work chronologically. He asked if she minded if he took notes, his fingers already over his keyboard. Gina had sensed his anxiety that she might not go through with the paternity search. And while it wasn't her priority now, after the birth she would want to know – and the baby, child, boy, man that he would become would want to know – and it seemed sensible to get a few details out now. Would the father, if he was alive and could be found, want to know? Would she tell him?

It was still only Tuesday morning. Only twenty-six hours since she'd known, no longer than a flight to Sydney. It felt like she'd time-travelled since yesterday, every hour a week of confusion, decisions and headache. Stan's text came through. He was arriving at 5.30 a.m. on Thursday morning. She texted back to say can't meet you, get a taxi, safe travel, lots of love, thank you, and when she pressed send the phone was slippery.

She had shed enough tears in the last twenty-four hours to fill a baby bath. They had felt more like an overflowing gutter than tears of sadness, grief, despair, joy or laughter. Right now, these salty numbers were relief. Stan was on his way. She sniffed, blew her nose and told Gerald that Stan was on his way.

'Good, good,' he said. 'Glad to hear you will have someone with you. Will he perhaps be your birth partner?'

Gina thought this might be the clumsiest thing anyone had ever said to her, right up there with her first father-in-law's enquiry as to the state of her virginity. David Douglas's intention had been to let her know it didn't matter – 'Really, it doesn't matter at all. No one expects to marry a… I mean, if George's mother… but that was a different time' – and was just trying to get to know her or – worse – make conversation. But by the time he'd scraped the sides of embarrassment for both of them, it was too late to retract his assertion that practice made perfect. They rarely spoke after that, each of them politely waltzing away when a potential for conversation arose, finding glasses to wash or children to mind, and certainly not unless within the protective cover of at least a medium-size group. But the idea of having Stan as her birthing partner was grotesque. Sandra. She would ask Sandra.

'Paternity,' Gina said, marshalling her mind back from random memories of the early years of her first marriage. 'The father.' The ridiculous birth partner suggestion meant talking about the baby's paternity was now a relief. 'Chronologically.' She paused to think, looked at the list she had drafted. The facing page had 'Present for Anton's birthday' – ten days away. Anton was Evan's eldest, about to be four. This child would be Anton's uncle or half-uncle. Gina looked after Anton and his brother every other Friday. That would stop. Spanner in their childcare works. Maybe

84

she could manage this Friday with Stan's help and that would give Evan two weeks to make a plan. Although they must have a plan for this week because she should be in Australia.

Gerald was looking at her patiently. She dragged her mind away from comforting minutiae, her thought process like a snowplough turning in a blizzard.

'Roland was the first. Ibiza. Really hot. The weather. I don't think we used hot or fit like now, back then. Maybe hot but not fit. He was a trainee journalist, just accepted on to a BBC course of some sort. It was just a couple of months before my eighteenth. Twice or three times, maybe, more fumbling than action. I'd started taking the pill for the holiday, but I wasn't that careful about checking if it had kicked in. I worried about it for two months after we got back.'

'Do you remember the name of the pill?'

'Microgynon.' She surprised herself with this bit of recollection. 'Blue packet. Is that enough detail for now?'

'Whatever you can easily remember and feel comfortable with. We can come back to details as we need to at a later stage.'

Gina felt the need to retaliate, reverting to formality as she did so. 'Mr Howard, I am not comfortable with any of this. Right now, my overriding emotion is self-pity. Some shame, but more self-pity. And I don't like myself for that.' She sighed. 'I'm sorry. I'm tired.' She put her elbows on her side of his desk and her head in her hands in a classic pose of dejection or despair. Gerald didn't know if it was a protective gesture or to help her remember.

'The next was Eddie. He had just qualified as a mental health nurse and we split up when he was accepted to train as a doctor so he could be a psychiatrist. It was unusual then, maybe still is, to make the transition from nurse to doctor. Anyway, he moved to Glasgow for med school and we lost touch. More accurately, he dumped me but I don't suppose that affects his paternity chances. Between his shifts, his study, me working in Paris one week a month, him living in Exeter and me in Cambridge, frequency wasn't really… well, frequent. We were together, though more apart than actually together, for a couple of years and he came to my twenty-first, left for Glasgow the next day. Never saw him again.'

'Still on the pill?' Gerald asked, registering how Gina buried her distress through those last few sentences.

'Yes, though sometimes I ran out if I overstayed in Paris or was giving my mum a break from looking after my dad. I didn't bother going to a different clinic, just sort of managed. Caught up as and when.' She paused. She needed to finish but was hot with embarrassment. He might be a leading obstetrician but Gerald didn't routinely need a list of lovers to deliver a baby.

'Three. My third sexual partner. I married George Douglas in 1980. January 1980. He was mangled by a hit-and-run three months later. On Easter Day. Months in hospital. He recovered fairly well physically, eventually. That's what they said anyway. So we went along with it. He's the father of my sons. Once he was discharged from hospital, he went back to work. He was a civil engineer. But he couldn't do his pre-accident role on bridges because he was terrified of traffic and bangs. We didn't talk about PTSD then, but I think that was what he had. The only desk job they had was in Birmingham and we lived in London, so we moved because the desk job was less money and Birmingham was cheaper. I got pregnant three times. Two to term. I had come off the pill as soon as we were married. We both wanted children.'

'But the marriage didn't last?'

'George had a brain haemorrhage in 1988. At the station. They said it was nothing to do with the accident. Stan was four, Evan just two.'

It all seemed such a long time ago. Gina may have occasionally suspected the marriage would not have survived if George hadn't died, but she wasn't so omnipotent as to think she'd killed him with her thoughts of leaving. Unlike killing her baby with bile, which had seemed so clearly a possibility a short while ago. She was glad she hadn't shared her perfidy with anyone else at the time. Grieving widow she had been, much more in sadness for her sons and for George – who was a good man who died far too soon – than for the loss of her husband. She was genuinely sorry he was dead, that he wouldn't know the boys or they him. That could, and in those days frequently did, make her weep, which was useful because society and certainly George's family had expectations of grieving widows. George had been an only child and Gina recognised the heartsore daily existence of his parents who had adored him and, to be fair, her – to as great an extent as they could anyone who wasn't George. They took comfort from the boys, and she moved back to London to be near them and the free childcare they provided. At least until Alexandra Douglas was admitted to a high-dependency early-onset Alzheimer's unit almost at the same time David left her for a third cousin. But by then the boys were teenagers and childminding was less of an issue for Gina.

The day of the accident had felt worse than the day he died. She had been expecting him to die for the seven years since the accident, so it wasn't a shock when two policewomen arrived at her door. But immediately after the crash when they were so newly married they hardly knew each other, when he was in intensive care, and when people said 'Mrs Douglas' and she didn't realise they meant her? At first they thought he wouldn't recover, then they said he would but not fully – though they never said what that meant – then they said he was young, fit and lucky and he'd be fine. He looked the same; the cuts, breaks and bashes healed. He could think and calculate. They had two children. But Gina wasn't surprised when his brain exploded inside his head and she always thought George wouldn't have been surprised either.

She couldn't bring to mind the feel of him, his touch or his laugh. Neither of the boys laughed like him, although how she knew that when she didn't know how he laughed was a mystery. She could not remember any films they'd seen together, any songs they'd sung along with or his favourite food. He was like a husband-avatar and she his ghost widow.

Thinking these thoughts, imagining saying them out loud to Gerald or anyone else, she was a bit surprised not to dislike herself. Would she really have left her post-crash, not-quite-himself husband? She sounded horrible. But she couldn't see how relevant any of that was to paternity. This murkiness could stay in her head. She'd become quite friendly with Mairhaid, the third cousin and her stepmother-in-law apparent, who made her laugh a lot more than George's mother ever had. The boys were not best pleased at that, although they got on with her fine, taking the view that they had to accept their grandfather's choice. Anyway, their grandmother wasn't any the wiser by this time. But they didn't see why their mother had to push the boat out and be personal friends with Mairhaid. It was easier to make people laugh when you hadn't lost your only son.

Gerald sat still, sympathetic and patient. 'Are there many more, Gina?' he said. 'I mean, not that it matters how many. We have all morning.'

'I won't need all morning.'

He reddened. 'I meant take your time.'

'Three more. Who is your preferred candidate so far?' It was her turn to wait while Gerald gathered his thoughts. She guessed he was looking for the most tactful presentation.

'I think the best way to approach it is to DNA-test the baby to see if there is a match with your sons, if they are agreeable. We will need their consent. If there is a full match, then George will be the father and we need look no further. Gina, is there any chance at all that George is not the father of one or both of your sons?'

It was as if she'd crawled to a place of safety and a battering ram had been right behind, crashing through the door. She hadn't been unfaithful to George. Ever. In her imagination, perhaps, yes, some days. But not physically. But if a fertilized egg could have hidden in her womb to come out decades later like a tiny Rip Van Winkle, then presumably – if the father was Roland or Eddie – it could have done so to become Stan or Evan. She felt sick and then she was sick, lurching over to the handbasin in the corner of the consulting room and bringing up far more vomit than she'd expected from two poached eggs. Mr Grant's treat breakfast, no longer free-range on sourdough. She ran the tap as Gerald pressed a bell. Allegra came in to hold her up and Gina half-collapsed into her embrace.

Until he'd said it, Gerald hadn't realised how his question could sound. A double barrel: had she been unfaithful to George so another man could have been the father at the time, as it were; and could a fertilised egg already have been there when she got married? But it dawned on him as Gina supported herself on the sink, dragging Allegra down to a stooped position of rescue.

'Oh, Mrs Flowers. Oh no.' So Gerald reverted to a formal mode of address in times of stress as well. 'I don't think so. I don't think you'd have two, three sets of dormant embryos. No, no. Just that if there is any doubt about the paternity of your sons, it would show up if they agreed to a DNA test, and it would be best to be prepared.'

Gina's tone was raspy, as though she'd been too long underwater and came up gasping for breath. Which was how she felt. 'Well, if you mean did I ever sleep with someone else while married to George, the answer is no. But am I reassured that this implantation, secret embryo-hiding thing couldn't happen twice? Also no. If it can happen once, why not twice? Or three times?'

It was Allegra who suggested they could maybe pull George's medical records and there might be something there to help, when Gina remembered. 'George was AB negative. I'm AB positive. The boys are both AB negative. They look like George. And they look alike. Sort of.' In the light of this information, the chances of them not being his was, Gerald assured her, very small.

'More or less than me being pregnant right now?' she countered. He didn't answer. Gina wasn't expecting him to. Things were tricky enough.

'Do you need to take a break, Mrs Flowers?' Gina understood Allegra's concern: she was holding up a pregnant, haggard, green-tinged old woman. Yesterday Gina had been early sixties, late fifties in a friendly light; right now, in the acid bath of one hundred watts angling back from the over-sink mirror, she'd added a couple of hard-life decades to her appearance. It was shocking.

'I'll get us all a coffee,' said Gerald. He left the room as Gina made it back to the chair, put her head between her knees and tried to steady her thoughts. She'd been in the airline brace position once before during a frightening landing on a plane with two burst tyres. It had been a long ten minutes. She doubted she had been the only one making improbable pacts with the future if she survived. The future she could imagine now seemed only to extend in very short timeframes: this interview, then what? Maybe Stan arriving.

She became aware of Allegra gently tapping her arm. 'You're OK,' she said. 'Just not looking your best right now. Nothing that a shower and a bit of make-up won't fix.' Gina felt a surge of irritation at her kindness, swallowed it down and nodded. Never mind a shower and some mascara; it would be like painting the front door of a burnt-out building.

Gerald knocked, then seemed to think better of it and came striding in without waiting for an answer, bearing three paper cups of decent-enough coffee, even though Gina's had milk in. No sugar was offered. From Allegra's half-hearted sips it looked like she missed it.

'Shall we do another one?' asked Gerald, as though asking a child if they wanted another bedtime story. It seemed like Gina morphing into a wizened hag had spooked him.

She looked at her list. 'Four. Jerome. Une affaire sans lendemain.' God, she had loved that phrase: an affair with no tomorrow. The others looked at her, politely, humouring her, which, unreasonably, irritated her again. 'French. For one-night stand. It was actually two or three nights, four or five perhaps, over a couple of weeks. Paris. Mid-nineties. Four or five years after George. George the first, I mean.'

Silence still from both members of her audience. She sighed deeply. She hated this coincidence.

'My second husband was also called George: George Flowers. He died ten years ago. Sepsis. He was the last. Number six. Five if you don't count Ibiza Roland.' She nearly hadn't started seeing George Two at all because he was called George. It felt wrong and that hadn't changed, even though they'd been married eight years when he died. When Gina had left the hospital carrying a rucksack with his coat and watch, she stood and looked at people getting on buses, buying parking tickets, carrying on as if the world had not fallen in on itself. They would go home and watch soaps, cartoons and the news as usual. She'd realised how much she had loved G2. At first she thought they'd been content, compatible, not delirious but comfortable and easy. Good enough for both of them. G1 had brought loss, mostly deflected loss at that, missing the father of her children rather than the man himself. G2's death had brought grief so dense it felt like living in a thicket of thorns. The price we pay for love, as they say. She pulled herself back to those days in Paris.

'Jerome was divorced, and although I think he may have been seeing someone else at the time, he lived alone. I didn't really care. This was just a fling. Contraception never came up apart from one awkward moment in the first stages. He said something about being very French, which I took to mean he would let practicalities take a back seat to romance. I didn't check. I was too far down the road for that and I was reckless. Stupid. Lucky.' Gina wanted to move the conversation on. 'Alan was next.'

Gerald pulled back. 'Could we just go back to Jerome for a moment? Do you recall any arrangements? Any contraceptive arrangements?'

The clarification was unnecessary. She didn't think he'd been talking about travel plans. She felt defensive. She'd had a scare with Jerome. A tiny bit of her had fancied a cute semi-French bébé, all chic outfits and well-designed baby accessories, like the colour-coded bottle sterilisers she'd seen while shopping in 1990s Paris. Not a Mothercare staple at that time. But it had just been a scare: no more than four days late and no one knew. She hadn't expected to sleep with anyone on that brief trip, hadn't been sleeping with anyone for a long while, so she was unprepared. As was Jerome although she'd felt him not being contraceptively prepared might have been a decision not an oversight. Anyway, she'd chanced it and got away with it. He'd been brought up Catholic and she had a friend whose time at a convent school left their circle with a detailed if only semi-accurate understanding of when 'it' was safe, together with a working knowledge of First Communion and the unattainably perfect example set by the Virgin Mary for all womanly matters. After the first time, she and Jerome had made calculations about her fertile dates, reckoned it was safe. Her rhythm was in the right place. But hey: Paris, French lover. Honestly it would have made no difference at that point. They told themselves it was low-risk and carried on.

Feeling a twin drag of shame and resentment, which in time would become familiar, Gina gave Gerald a slightly censored version of Jerome, reluctant to lay out every detail of her past for scientific examination. Jerome had helped her back from cold storage. With him she'd found the sort of sexual normality that had stopped not just post-G1 but for a while before that. Sometime after his accident. 'Does that make him more likely?'

'If he was right about your cycle, and given the transient nature of the relationship, maybe not.'

'Short,' said Gina. 'Short relationship. Not transient. It was important to me, and to him, I think. It just didn't last. Wasn't meant to last.'

'One more?'

'Yes,' she said. 'Number five. Alan. One night. One condom. I think. The best sex of my life. No, more than that. The best twelve hours of my life.'

'That might be relevant,' said Gerald as again Gina started to cry as if seven months of pent-up hormonal pregnancy crying was coming in one torrent. She thought back to the day George Flowers and Alan collided.

*

'Yes please, no, maybe. Yes, I think so. Thank you. Just the dark blue case.'

It would be one less thing to be responsible for, at least until she got to baggage reclaim. By checking in her hand luggage, all she would have to keep hold of was her handbag, her boarding card and herself. Eliminating the risk of forgetting her dark blue case, prompting one of those announcements about personal items and controlled explosions, felt like a good move in her state of unreliable concertation brought on by exhaustion and elation scrambled together. Feeling faint with hunger and happiness, she went through security and in search of a lunch heavy on carbs, low on nutrition, no taint of anything green or healthy, which she was sure Edinburgh airport would provide.

A couple of hours earlier from her hotel room outside Kirkaldy, sitting on a bed she hadn't slept in, Gina Douglas had phoned George Flowers.

'I need to cancel tonight,' she said. 'Not cancel, postpone. Can we rearrange please?'

'You could just have stood me up,' he said. 'If that's what you want to do really, just say.'

'George, I have just had to track down your company number without the benefit of a phone book and not knowing exactly how to spell it, explain to the receptionist I wasn't family but my call was personal and important although not life or death urgent, explain to you who I was and generally go to quite a lot of trouble and personal embarrassment to ask for this postponement. If I had been inclined to stand you up, that would have been much easier. Although,' she clarified, 'I've never stood anyone up. It feels unkind. And I haven't had the opportunity much.'

'You didn't need to explain who you are to me. I recognised your voice. And you could just have asked Sandra for my number. Are you alright?"

'Yes, thank you. Tired but fine. Difficult day yesterday. So difficult I resigned and I need some time to tell the boys and so on. Stop my mother worrying. Do the admin for my new job. And clear up loose ends at CRCL.

'I didn't want to ask Sandra, and anyway she'll be at work.'

George was leaving the next day for his six weeks on rota in Dubai so they agreed to have dinner the night he got back. In the event, she decided to go to the airport to meet him, taking him so much by surprise he hadn't quite got over it by the time they married a year or so later. He'd had one of those car services booked to go straight to the office which brought a slightly awkward angle to the reunion, the driver keen to get away and on to his next fare not hover at an uncomfortable distance in arrivals while his passenger sorted out his love life. Gina had nevertheless floated back to the short-term carpark.

'Here's it. Fish and chips. No peas. Do you want tomato sauce? Brown sauce?' Her plate of carbs, grease and calories had arrived.

'Mayonnaise, please, and a cup of tea,' replied Gina.

'You had a good trip? Work or what?' Doreen the waitress continued, fishing a grubby sachet of mayonnaise out of her apron. 'I want to go somewhere on a plane for work, someone else paying. But you don't get much of that waitressing.'

'I don't get many tips,' Gina smiled.

'Right enough,' agreed Doreen. 'Tips here are best I've ever had. People just leave whatever they've got in our money.'

'Work *and* what,' answered Gina as Doreen went off to get the tea

An hour later, eyes closed against take-off, Gina felt the previous night become part of her, melting slowly through her skin. It would be a while before it was fully absorbed, not instant but no more than six weeks.

*

Patients lie. Not always, but frequently. They leave out information they see as embarrassing, either in fact or just to talk about. So it's 'a few beers a week, Doc' instead of borderline drunk and incapable most nights; 'social smoker' without mentioning that includes ten cigarette breaks a day with similarly addicted colleagues; 'I've no idea how I could have got herpes', as if the tumble with a random guest in the cloakroom at a wedding last month wasn't relevant; or, most prevalent of all, 'Yes, I've been doing the exercises, sticking to the diet just like you said'.

Gerald didn't think Gina was lying, although a lot more about her sexual history was going to be needed if the father couldn't be identified from the DNA. He did not relish having to ask those questions. What Gerald wanted was to pinpoint the biological markers immediately, eliminate the candidates until there was just one, and then delve in to the very deep details of that – only that – relationship and the medical histories of the parents to try to understand how an embryo had somehow survived years *in utero* before implanting. An embryo would be expected to degrade over time and, therefore, wouldn't the foetus show signs of that degradation? But as far as could be told from the scan, this was not the case. Remarkable.

He listed the six candidates out loud in chronological order.

'Roland. Late teens. Microgynon. Two or three times over a few days. Possible not actually consummated.

'Eddie. Early twenties. Microgynon. About two years, on and off.

'George Douglas (G1). Twenties to thirties. Father of adult children. Eight years. No contraception.

'Jerome. Late thirties. No contraception. Dates method. Four or five times over a week.

'Alan. Forties. Multiple times over one night. Condom at least once.

'George Flowers (G2). Forties to fifties. Vasectomy. Ten years.'

Gina hadn't really wanted to talk about Alan but when she had, it was an unadorned story of the best sex Gerald had ever heard about, read about or had been described during his medical school years by pumped-up trainee doctors using all their powers of exaggeration and embellishment. He certainly couldn't do it justice in his notes so he didn't try. Facts only. Alan and Gina had worked together for just a few weeks and had both attended a work meeting with an overnight stay. Gina had just met George Two, although they weren't yet an item, but she knew George, at least, wanted to be. Going up in the lift in the hotel, 'We've Got Tonight' came on the muzak and the rest just followed. She'd been quite hazy about the precise number of condoms available or used, certain only that there had been at least one.

It wasn't yet midday. Gina had been led away, not exactly a prisoner leaving the dock, by Matron and Allegra so they could persuade her to admit herself to hospital that day. Gerald would have liked to remain at his desk to think out his plan for the birth and for the path to identifying the father. But he was late for his clinic over the way, so had to leave his thoughts until later. Concentrating on a clinic list of routine complications would be tricky with Gina's case to occupy him, like trying to give directions to a stranger when you'd just been given the all-clear from cancer. He had arranged to see Gina the next morning to move things forward. In the meantime, he put on his slim-fitting black rain jacket and crossed the dividing line to the NHS hospital across the gardens.

Chapter 6

Gina was reminded of the feeling she got when she had the first glass of champagne on Christmas Day around 11 a.m. Total buzz, total detachment, *carpe diem*. She never thought it would be possible to get that on your own in a suburban taxi during daylight hours on a Tuesday. And it wasn't possible, not for her anyway. What she felt was a reverse of that benign bonhomie: flat, self-observing detachment and no desire at all to seize this particular opportunity. It was only early afternoon.

She had always been good at logic; it was why she was in finance. Maths made sense. Spreadsheets could be controlled. As long as you input the right numbers, the correct – although often unwelcome – results would come out. Deficit. Surplus. Logic. She ran her hands through her hair, wondering if she'd keep her colour – well, not exactly *her* colour, that was grey, had been since her early thirties – with a baby. Baby. The word reverberated inside her head with a mocking, banging beat, a warped football chant of derision: ba-by, ba-by, ba-by, too-old, too-old, too-old.

Back to logic. She was pregnant. Gerald needed to figure out who the father was. Gina didn't begrudge him his professional OMG moment, although she wished it hadn't been her who had provided it. But she had to work out what to do. She rejigged her earlier list. One: a birth plan. Two: tell people. Three: stuff. Four: Who is the father? Five: What to do with the baby.

It was hardest to frame her thoughts about five.

When things are really difficult, she remembered, take them a day at a time. Or if that's too much, half a day; and if that's too much, an hour. She was maybe at no more than five minutes at a time. She could do One: Gerald knew what he was doing and she'd agree to whatever he said was best for a birth plan. Two: Hail, Mary, full of grace, pray for me now and at the hour of needing to tell my mother I'm pregnant. And friends. Friends wouldn't be so bad; it was acquaintances she dreaded. She could face friends, not in person but on a video call. With a stiff single malt, ice and soda. Which she can't have for months, except she already had, so what would a few more matter? Three: make a list, go online, getting stuff would be easy enough, if an expense she hadn't exactly planned for. Her spending budget for Australia would cover a cot and nappies but not twenty plus years of shoes and X-boxes. Four: now she had made the decision to identify the father, Gina was relieved to have no choice but to leave the technicalities to Gerald. She hoped she wouldn't need to describe much about highs, lows, positions, timings, feelings or fluids to get a fix on the baby's paternity. But Five. Five was heartache. She closed her eyes and breathed in. And out. And in. And out. Breathing to cope, to settle herself, regain control, become calm. It wasn't enough not to murder her child, to give birth to him. He would need a life plan. A carer. And in. And out.

It was around twenty minutes in the taxi from the hospital to her home. She arrived not long after midday and paid the driver, mildly astonished that he needed to be paid, that the world was, in fact, turning as normal, just like it had when G2 died. She was pregnant, but taxi drivers were still doing airport runs, playing the wrong station on the radio, taking fares.

Gina noticed a car that looked a bit like Evan's on her street. Looked exactly like Evan's, in fact. Was he having a crisis just when she needed all family crises to hold fire for a few weeks while her situation took centre stage? Her phone was on silent, had been all morning. There weren't any calls she wanted to take and she hadn't wanted to be tempted to look before discarding someone. She took it out now and saw three missed calls from Evan. She phoned him the very same moment as someone looking just like him got out of the car that looked just like his.

'Have you left Amelie?'

'No. Not yet anyway. She's more likely to leave me. I'm too lazy to cause such upheaval on purpose. And don't forget she's pregnant.'

'Me too. I'm pregnant.'

They stood on the pavement, as shocked as each other, Gina unsteady on her feet at the enormity of saying it out loud. Evan put his arms around her, took her keys and they went indoors. Her luggage for Australia was still in the hall. Evan said nothing, wondering if Gina was having a breakdown or making— what, a joke? He certainly didn't say congratulations or ask when it was due. They sat down, both on the sofa.

'You first,' she said. He didn't argue; he wanted a bit of time to assess her state of mind. Obviously, for Evan, Gina couldn't be pregnant. But it is an odd thing for your sixty-two-year-old mother to say. He didn't even look at her shape to try and confirm or disregard the assertion. It was too preposterous to warrant a visual check.

'It's just that you didn't answer your phone and it was ringing, so it wasn't turned off, and you never do silent so I got worried. I rang Carmen to ask her to pop round but she's in Spain. So I came to see you're OK.'

'Carmen's daughter is getting married and the reception is in Spain. I was invited. I would have gone if I hadn't been going to Australia.'

'Tonight?'

'No. I'm pregnant. I can't fly. Thirty-two to thirty-three weeks pregnant.'

Evan was usually a thinker, didn't try to avoid every gap in a conversation, no inane comment just to fill a space, but this was a significant silence even by his standards. It was the sort of pause when someone says something stridently political you disagree with and you don't want to collude by glossing over it, but neither do you want an argument because you don't know them and hopefully will never meet them again. Eventually he settled for: 'I didn't know you were seeing anyone.'

'I'm not. I haven't been. No one since G2.'

Evan was having trouble processing the information that his sixty-plus mother had said she was pregnant with no obvious channel of conception. Was she mad or misinformed or what? Now he looked at her waist. 'You've thickened out a bit. Is it one of those phantom pregnancies that will go away?'

'No. I'm pregnant. thirty-two to thirty-three weeks.'

'Is that possible? I mean, can it be a mistake? How can you be pregnant?'

He asked her what day of the week it was, how many cousins she had, the middle names of his children and then she said, 'Stop, Evan. Just stop. I have not got early onset. I am not deluded. I am – completely unexpectedly – pregnant.'

'Did you plan it? Go to a clinic in Hungary or Brazil or somewhere, because it isn't legal here, is it? Do you want another baby?' Gina couldn't place his tone. Somewhere between incredulous and, harder to detect, sympathetic. If she'd been doing a wine tasting she'd have added 'with a note of hostility'.

Gina closed her eyes and leaned back against the sofa. The weight of exhaustion was tangible, like holding a huge, heavy, unwanted present she couldn't just hand off to someone else or put in a bag to take to the charity shop next week. There was a coffee shop at the bottom of the road and she asked Evan to get her a double espresso and whatever he wanted. Just so that she could practise opening her eyes and getting words out. As he got up, her phone rang. Stan.

'Mum, it's me. I'm at the airport on my way to Singapore, change on to the Dubai flight, then on to London. Couldn't get anything direct. Everyone going home after Christmas. Are you OK? Are things still the same?'

'Yes. Evan's here. He just arrived because I had my phone off and he was worried.'

'Have you told him?'

The boys used to be so close, but since Stan had been living overseas, and especially since he'd moved to Australia, they'd only seen each other every couple of years. Evan hadn't visited, too expensive for four of them, and he hadn't accepted Stan's repeated offers to pay. Now Gina wondered if Stan was a bit protective of her… news. She should have told him she was going to tell Evan. Or told them together.

'Yes. Just now.' She paused. 'But fair to say it hasn't really sunk in.'

'Good,' said Stan, and she was satisfied that he meant it.

The weight lifted a little, the unwanted present shedding a couple of kilos. But she had doubts that either son believed her, not that it mattered much, and she certainly didn't blame them for that. She thought of things that were hard to believe, like the moon landing or men pulling a jumbo jet uphill in a competition; either of those seemed perfectly plausible compared to her situation. In seven to eight weeks, probably earlier as Gerald thought a planned Caesarean would be best, there would be no room for doubt. At this point, her son *in utero* kicked and Evan jolted back as he saw it. Gina felt like she had a bit part in *Omen III* meets *Rosemary's Baby*.

'See you on Thursday, Stan. Safe travels.'

'Wait, mum. What's happening? What have you found out?'

'Nothing, really. I see the obs man, Gerald – Mr Howard, Dr Howard. He is a proper doctor but he's a surgeon so now they call him mister. Why would you do that when you've worked all those years? I see him again tomorrow to work out a birth plan. I can't believe I just said that. Had to say that. I need to lie down now. Lots of love.'

She cut him off, swiping the red phone icon up as if the firm press of her thumb would transmit to him not to ring back. No texting from business class – first class, maybe – lounges.

Evan was still staring at her midriff, with the baby banging out a kick every few moments. Just when you

105

thought it had gone back to sleep, there was another one. Gina really did need to lie down.

'Do you know the father?' asked Evan.

'I did,' she replied. 'But not any more.'

'Who is he?'

'I don't know.'

'You just said you did.'

'Well, it depends how you meant the question. Do I know the identity of the biological father? No, not exactly. But whoever it is, I did know him. I need to lie down.'

'What, now?'

'A pregnant mother with six weeks to go needing a nap is hardly unusual. I'm exhausted.' Evan was pushed from confusion to concern, both registering on his face, jockeying for pole position. 'And I haven't been pregnant at sixty-two before,' Gina went on. 'Don't let me sleep for longer than an hour. Then I'll have the coffee. I've got too much to do.'

She lay down on the sofa, pulled a throw over her and fell asleep in the same way a puppy suddenly collapses when tiredness just takes over.

*

Evan sat in the cafe rather than go back to his mother's with its taint of absurdity. He felt able to think watching the double-macchiato brigade, of which he was often one, get a late lunch. A cafe was normal. Something was far from normal at his mother's. He rang Stan, hoping to catch him before he left.

'It's me. Can you talk? Mum's not here. I'm in a cafe down from hers.'

106

'Yes, boarding shortly. Not ideal, best I could get. Does she look pregnant?'

'Not exactly. If you saw her on the tube and she looked twenty-five years younger, you wouldn't know whether to stand up or not. Could be pregnant, could be chubby around the middle, hard to tell. Except the baby kicked. I saw its foot.'

'I didn't know she was seeing anyone,' said Stan, 'and surely you'd think she was past it. She's sixty-two, for fuck's sake. And if she isn't over the hill, why the hell did she let it happen?'

'She said she isn't seeing anyone. Hasn't since George. She didn't deny going to a clinic but she didn't say she had. Said she did know the father but not any more. Suppose that rules out a clinic then. Unless she harvested some sperm.'

'What, without the dude knowing?' The two men were silent for a few seconds, both conjuring and then discarding images of how exactly that might happen, all the more disturbing with their mother as the protagonist in this mental drama. 'If she's pregnant – it's still a big if, right? – do you think she'll keep it?'

Evan let out a breath. 'Thirty-two to thirty-three weeks. That's quite far gone. So I don't know if she could, you know, not keep it. I don't think it is such a big if. You didn't see the foot.'

'Will you be there when I arrive? Are you staying with her? What about the Triple As?'

'I'm just trying to work it out. Mi is going away this week, a design show in Nice or some such. I'm going to ring her mum and dad, see if they could stay at ours for a couple of days. Tell them mum's not well. I can't bring the kids here, not now. Too much.'

'See you on Thursday. Ev, if there's anything that just needs money, I've got it. Seriously.'

Evan was about to talk about splitting it, and anyway their mother wasn't on the bread line, probably 'comfortable' would be the right description, but he caught 'Please now turn off your electronic devices' and Stan had gone. And suddenly, like Gina earlier that morning, he wasn't sure being financially comfortable at sixty-two allowed for eighteen additional years of child-rearing.

Just as he was getting another coffee and something to eat, Amelie rang to see if he had got hold of Gina.

'I'm here with her now. Well, she's sleeping for a bit and I'm in that Italian cafe getting something to eat.' He kept his voice low, barely a match for the hubbub and road noise.

'Is everything OK?'

'She's pregnant. Well, she says she's pregnant and I think she is.'

'Who's pregnant, Evan. Someone you know?' The slightly querulous note made Evan realise what Amelie had latched on to was the notion that he'd got someone pregnant, not that his mother was pregnant. It was understandable, he supposed, but dear God, was this how far gone their relationship was? Amelie thought he was sleeping with someone else? But Mi was pregnant herself. How could she think he would do that? He really valued a life as uneventful as it could be with two (soon to be three) under-fives; extra-marital complications were not his style, not at all. Unless the baby wasn't his… Dear God, he thought for a second time. The thinking all took some seconds and a lot of compressed effort.

'Evan, you have to tell me.'

'My mother.'

'What about your mother?'

'She's pregnant.'

'Your mother?'

'Yes.'

They both felt her tension ooze out of the conversation. They might have to acknowledge what had passed between them in these few minutes, but not now.

'I want to stay with her tonight. Stan's coming. He'll be here on Thursday morning. But in case she isn't pregnant – what if it's a breakdown? – I don't want to leave her.'

'I have to go before six tomorrow and I can't get home until the weekend. So what are you going to do about the kids?'

The rush of togetherness he'd felt when revealing his non-affair vanished in that instant, drowned by self-pity and resentment. Was there nothing, nothing that he needed, that would tempt Amelie to stay home and keep house for a couple of days? If her sixty-two-year-old pregnant mother-in-law didn't rate higher than selling curtain fabric at two hundred euros a metre for houses on the Riviera, then he couldn't see how his aching heart would ever get a look in. He hung up and quashed her ringback as firmly as Gina had quashed Stan an hour ago.

An hour ago. He paid and went back.

*

His mother had woken up and was in her bedroom making lists. Cot, steriliser, buggy, car seat. 'I remember they wouldn't let you take Anton home without a car seat,' she said as Evan tapped on the door and inched in. 'When your dad picked us up, I just sat in the back seat and put the seat belt round you.'

'You're still pregnant, then.' Evan tried to frame it as both a joke and a question but neither seemed to hit the spot. Gina sat down heavily on the bed.

'I know. I don't believe it either and I've seen the scans, felt the kicking foot and listened to the medics. I feel like I've been given a terminal diagnosis and I don't want to believe it and then I hate myself because I'm not ill, I'm pregnant, and I don't wish this baby dead, or at least I didn't take the chance I had to kill him. Arrange his planned prenatal foetal demise.' She paused for a few moments. 'That's what they call it after twenty-seven weeks. But I have to work out what to do. First, I think I have to tell your granny.'

The enormousness, the sheer unthinkability of telling Liv Redcar that her daughter was pregnant made mother and son draw breath. Evan sat down on the bed next to Gina.

'I suppose you have to?'

'I see her twice a week, love. Are you suggesting I can hide a baby from her?'

'Yes. Yes, I think you could. For a bit anyway. I mean, she thinks you're in Australia for three weeks. She's got Riley, then when you get back she's going to Minorca for a month. Why worry her? You can hide for a good few weeks.'

Despite the farce of a sixty-two-year-old woman hiding her pregnancy and then the baby from her reasonably fit eighty-five-year-old mother, it was a very, very attractive course of action and Gina warmed to it rapidly. 'Mum, I have to go home soon. The kids,' said Evan.

'That's fine. Can you come on Thursday when Stan's here and I've been back to the doctor? I'm sure he'll recommend a Caesarean so I will have some dates.'

'I can bring some stuff. We won't need the cot for a few months.'

'God, no,' said Gina. 'Thank you, but I'm going to order it online with one of those services that puts it up for you, like I did for Anton, and then if you do need it, it won't be a problem.' Evan suspected 'it won't be a problem' was code for 'That way, Amelie can't complain', so he left it.

'Come home with me tonight. Mi is going to France tomorrow.'

'I think they will insist I get admitted soon, so I am going to work through my finances and other lists in the next few days. I need to be at home. Passwords, papers, that sort of thing. I need to make a will. Gordon the Lodger will be in later, so I won't be alone overnight. Stan should be here really early on Thursday. His flight is due in at half-five so I need to be here for that. Could you take my luggage out of the hall before you go?'

Evan went to the shops for bread, milk and a ready meal for Gina. Which he swapped for spinach, fruit and a steak. Then he put the ready meal back in the basket. Who knew what she'd want to eat, and if it was full of preservatives it would be OK for one night. Gina lived on a quiet residential road, terraces of late Victorian houses, lots of them now flats – including hers, which was on the ground floor so had a garden. That would be a blessing with— He paused before using the word even in a silent conversation with himself. A baby.

At the bottom of her hill, turn the corner and there was a busy through road with late-opening shops, cafes and takeaways. He was walking quickly back with the shopping, aware he needed to leave in the next ten minutes or would miss the nursery and after-school club deadlines. Turning in to his mother's entrance he saw Sandra about to ring the bell. 'Sandra!' he called too loudly. 'Sandra, it's Evan.'

'I know,' she replied. 'It hasn't been that long. Three weeks, I think. Is everything alright? Is Amelie OK? The kids?'

'They're fine, thanks. Are you looking for mum?' The slight quickening of his words betrayed his anxiety.

'I'm taking her to the airport,' said Sandra. 'I'm a little early, but I didn't want to risk being late so thought I'd make sure I was here in good time.'

'It's only a couple of miles from your house.' Evan realised it sounded like an accusation. Sandra was giving up her evening to take his mother to Heathrow and had considerately arrived in plenty of time, and his statement made it feel as if she was trying to hide something. 'She's pregnant,' he said.

'How's it going?' said Sandra, a little baffled by the turn of conversation. 'Gina said she was well, a bit tired but still working and doing fine. With your help, of course.'

'Not Amelie. Well, Amelie, yes, she's pregnant. Fine, thank you. So is my mum.'

'Your mum's fine?' Sandra had picked up the tremor in Evan's voice. 'Or not?'

'Fine. But also pregnant. I shouldn't have said anything. I don't know who she is going to tell. Didn't she cancel her lift? She's not going to Oz.' Evan fumbled Gina's keys out of his pocket, almost dropping the shopping, his anxiety about being late for the pick-ups outdoing that for his mother now that Sandra was here. He opened the door, shouted 'Bye! See you tomorrow. Got to go. Sandra's arrived.' And left. He was nearly at Andre's nursery before he noticed he'd been singing along to the Frozen soundtrack all the way. Let It Go didn't feel like a viable option in these circumstances.

Gina heard Evan shout something from the front door which sounded like goodbye in long form. She had to ring Sandra, who was due in an hour to take her to the airport. She was going to ask her what she thought about her not telling her mother. Sandra was a senior manager of a social work department, calm, funny, good at decisions. They had started training together as accountants, but Sandra had soon realised that was a waste of her talents and pushed her way on to a social work course at the last minute. She didn't talk much about her work, not to Gina anyway. Her daughters were each a year or so younger than Stan and Evan. For a while, Gina thought there might be something permanent between Stan and Yasmin but had been glad it had run out of steam when Yasmin left for a recording gig in Berlin. Her friendship with Sandra was one of the few unblemished, easy relationships she had ever had, and she didn't want it trampled on either by Stan in hobnailed romantic boots or some new fancy of Yasmin's.

Gina was ringing Sandra from the sofa at the same time as she heard a phone and Sandra's head came round the door.

'Gina, what's going on? Why are you beached on the sofa? Evan seemed in a daze. Has something happened?' She looked at her phone, saw the call was from Gina and asked why she was ringing. Gina stalled by asking her why she was early and Sandra chuntered off into a story about missing gloves and fear of Terminal 5, all the while watching like a sparrow-hawk might watch a mouse, looking for any clue of movement or direction.

Suddenly, Sandra changed tack with an ambush worthy of a military strategist. 'You can't be pregnant?' Gina stared at her. 'Something Evan said, but... what was Evan doing here? Are you ill? Are you going? Where's your luggage? It was in the hall last week.' The bird of prey hovered. The mouse quivered then nodded.

Gina filled her in, tea going cold in its I Love Grandma mug, a no-doubt last-minute purchase by Amelie at Christmas for one of the little boys to give her. Looking at it, Gina realised maybe she could just about manage a baby, but a small child? No. Eight hours with Anton and Andre and she needed to lie down in a darkened room watching quiz show reruns for the rest of the evening. She couldn't do it seven days a week, she just couldn't.

'Are you sure?' Sandra pressed on.

It was the first time Gina remembered ever being irritated with her friend. 'I've seen four doctors, had two blood and two urine tests, three scans, it's got a foot and I can feel it move,' she replied, dully but with an edge. 'And no, I'm not going to Australia. Stan is coming. He's on his way. That was me ringing to tell you I don't need a lift.'

Sandra sat down. 'Gina Flowers, you are the most reliable friend I've ever had. The Best. What on earth— fuck, this is a humdinger.' Sandra rarely – very rarely – swore. The last time was when Yasmin won a Rap Writer of the Year award, but the shock of Gina's pregnancy knocked a talented musician winning a songwriting prize into next week. Suddenly, Yasmin was Doris Day and Gina was the Sex Pistols.

Gina asked Sandra to be her birthing partner, if she could get time off work. She wouldn't miss it for the world, Sandra said, as if it were an invite to Beyoncé's farewell tour, not a labour ward. And for a moment it felt good to Gina to have some enthusiasm – joy, even. To Sandra, babies were a gift, a perspective all the more valuable because it must have been tested at times in her work. She stayed until Gina went to bed at eight, knowing Gordon would be in later. Gordon the Lodger needed to move out. Another problem, losing his ad hoc rent. But she slept deeply and for that felt better in the morning.

*

Graham decided to wait. He'd build up a portfolio – a portfolio indeed! – of pictures of Mrs Flowers and wait until he could use them. No more logging on to her records. No risky moves. He might hang around in the car park, take pictures of her visitors. He rationalised this strategy as sensible – certainly not stalking and anyway, he hadn't decided anything yet – but the nuggets of disappointment

115

and contempt that he felt for himself were as present and uncomfortable as a stone in his shoe.

Chapter 7

The plane was going to be at least an hour late, so Stan thought it likely his mother would have left for her 10 a.m. before he got to the house. Finishing the last gorgeous red but tasteless strawberry of his airline breakfast, he considered whether to go and meet her there or go to the house. He'd been a dedicated finisher of airline meals since the family's first package holiday to Agadir when he was a teenager, a week which still ranked as one of the best in his life. It had been one of those all-inclusive resorts, so drinking Coke at 9 a.m. and spending the day on a banana boat did not bring down any of the usual censures about cost or suitability. His mother had been relaxed, properly so, for the first time in ages; in truth, for the first time Stan could remember. They'd nearly missed the flight because Gina had been delayed getting back from Paris, and his grandmother hadn't helped by keeping to fifty on the motorway: 'I'm not going to risk my licence because your mother is behind schedule'. She seemed to have pulled out of the ten-year slough since his father died, and started to look forward. He remembered her playing table tennis with him and Evan, insisting she could take them both on at once, that she'd been really good at it at school. They had unwisely bet their birthday money on that game. It wasn't that she had been outwardly or operationally miserable for ten years. But on the tourist-packed sands of Agadir beach, they saw a woman they had dimly thought must be in there but had so far only caught the occasional glimpse of.

Stan idly considered for the first time if she had maybe had a holiday romance or a new lover at home, but he couldn't recall any such figure or subterfuge. While there was no reason for a widow of ten years not to have a lover, Stan was fairly sure his mother would not have broadcast a relationship until it had a permanent label firmly attached, as she finally did with G2.

He decided to go straight to the house, drop his luggage and then work out what to do. By 'what to do' he knew he meant how to get into the hospital and make sure it was all true. He sent Alison a text in reply to several from her to say he was in England, and found the best words he could to end the relationship, only slightly startled at how irrelevant she now seemed. Last week they had attended her nephew's baby-naming, and he'd been part of her family's in-jokes; yesterday he hadn't made the time to tell her he was going to England. Hell, he was shallow when you looked at the evidence. He was really important to Alison, central to her life, probably the most important person in it, yet he'd jumped on a flight and left her behind with no contact, less thought indeed than he'd given his rented apartment.

He changed his shorts for jeans, tugged a fleece out of his hand luggage, put his seat in the upright position and prepared for landing.

*

Three days in and Gina was finding it hard to remember her previous life. It seemed utterly incredible that right now she should have been in a transit lounge in Hong Kong. Eleven

118

months in the planning and her flight had taken off without her.

Gerald came in wearing a dark navy suit, a shirt but no tie: a contrast from his work wear of the last two days. It looked as if he'd been taking style advice overnight. Why would that be? Press, students, lectures to colleagues, decent suit happened to be in the cleaners; but that wouldn't explain why he wasn't wearing a tie.

'Apologies for keeping you waiting. I had to do a couple of procedures over the road.' He reached in to a drawer, took out a tie and smiled a further apology as he deftly made a perfect knot. 'Where shall we start?' Gina wasn't sure if this was a rhetorical question or directed to her, but given she had no clear view on where to start she left it to him to answer. 'Perhaps you could just finish your outline of paternity by telling me about your second husband.' Gina went straight in, finding a rhythm in setting out the story.

'George Flowers' first wife had had two children before she married him and didn't want any more. And as I understand it what she wanted, or didn't want, she got. So he had a vasectomy a short while before the marriage. He didn't like to talk about Renée, but I formed the impression it was a condition of the marriage. I'd seen a few pictures of her and she came to G2's funeral. She reminded me of Princess Margaret or Margaret Thatcher, someone like that, with a certain carriage, confidence and bearing. Like a dressage horse.'

'How long before you and George started a sexual relationship would the vasectomy have been?'

119

Would this dissection never be over? She did the calculation as best she could. 'I can't be sure exactly but at least ten years and maybe up to twelve.'

'And he and Renée didn't have any children?'

'No.' Gina looked at Gerald and wondered if he was thinking that maybe G2 had only told her he had had a vasectomy because he did really want children and knew she didn't. It had crossed her mind at the time, even though she was in her forties by then. But nothing says 'I don't trust you' like asking your future husband for proof of a vasectomy. And as the marriage progressed, she came to know G2 was not that sort of man and she had been ashamed of herself.

'And you had an active relationship throughout your marriage?'

'George was a commercial planner, shopping centres and things, and worked in the Middle East, so he was only at home for one week in every six, plus holidays. But, yes, we made the most of that. Two years before he died, he got skin cancer and initially went downhill very quickly, then stabilised. But he couldn't fight off sepsis when he got an abrasion and it got infected.' She really could not say any more. Enough.

Gerald could almost hear Gina's tears forming, building into an unshed dam.

'You have had your share of tragedy, Gina.' He left quite a pause as she recouped some of her composure; she moved to very slightly safer ground.

'George's sister, eldest sister, Amanda, didn't come to the funeral. She sent me an email, something like: "All the others are coming so as George would have said, you'll have a big bunch of Flowers. But I am going to come in a couple of weeks when you might need some company."

'I was puzzled that a funeral service in a church with a God I don't believe in taking centre stage – outranking even the deceased – could bring me so much comfort. Perhaps it was because George and his God had been pretty close and I was glad he had that. Or the singing or the number of people saying it was a beautiful service, he was such a nice man, "Is that his wife?" pointing at someone else, not me. Amanda was right about the bunch of Flowers coming, including a dumpy cousin I'd never heard of let alone met, as well as siblings, nieces and nephews. Renée looked elegant and told me that she had spent days looking for an outfit so as not to look frumpy for George. I had spent too long looking for an outfit George would never see, but wanted to look good for him, and that was my place, not hers. I could see that she'd not want to look frumpy for the guests, for herself even, so I could see it – but not for George. That wasn't fair.

'When Amanda came over, her timing was just right. The boys had to get back to their own lives, and leaving their grieving mother with a kind and capable step-aunt for a while was a relief to everyone. We took George's ashes to Cornwall and scattered them in the Atlantic so they could float their way to Florida. Amanda helped me sort George's stuff. We were drained and got drunk – not drunk, just took the edge off – because we couldn't do it without semi-anaesthesia. He had a US dollar savings account and Amanda eventually managed to get control of that and help some of his family.

'Every couple of years since, we meet up in a different city, me and Amanda, climb its tallest building and eat in its best restaurant in memory of George. We email or phone on birthdays or when something newsworthy happens – a new grandchild, a house move. I told Amanda at Christmas that I was going to Australia.'

Gerald waited until he was sure she had said everything she wanted to say, relevant to paternity or not. He needed to have her attention again before going on. She looked at him and nodded. 'Sorry, bit of a tangent.'

'In terms of the father, we can't take any definitive steps until the baby is born and we have, with your permission, DNA for comparison. If your sons agree, we will first test one of them for a full-match sibling. If they are not willing, we can discuss if there is another way to do that.'

Another pause. Gina realised he was trying to transmit how much it would help if one of the boys agreed. She was able to provide that reassurance at least.

'I can see that DNA from the boys would be helpful and much easier than any other route. I don't think they will object, but if they do – and I would be really surprised – I'll explain why it matters so much to me. I would be astonished if they then withheld permission. I'll ask them soon.'

Gerald was quite still, weighing the timing of his next suggestion like a leopard judges when to pounce. Or a blackmailer chooses when to reveal his hand. 'If your first husband is not the father, we will need to consider one of the other candidates. Apart from the knowledge it will give you for your new son, your existing sons and yourself, it will be an extraordinary insight for medical and especially fertility research.' Gina felt she knew that already. That this was now some sort of scene-setter for a new hurdle. Otherwise, why restate the obvious? She waited.

'I would… would you… allow a private detective to start tracing the other candidates? Entirely discreetly, not contacting them, not getting in touch at all. Just trying to establish in the first instance if they are, for example, still alive and where they might live.' Gerald did his best to maintain eye contact during this delivery, not wanting to look in the least… shifty. Shifty and Gerald had never yet shared the same airspace and almost certainly never would again.

Gina didn't know where she found the capacity to be shocked. But she was, profoundly, as though she'd fallen down the rabbit hole and was eating cake with the Mad Hatter. It was a perfectly legitimate suggestion – logical and sensible, even. It underlined that Gerald was very keen to identify the father. Over the years, she had become accomplished at keeping her own counsel. Wrapping her distaste for some matters in polite layers of well-chosen words. She'd had plenty of practice with some of her accounting clients.

'I don't know what that would cost exactly,' she said, 'but I am sure someone good would be expensive and I don't know if I can afford it.'

'If money was not an issue,' Gerald persisted, 'would you agree?'

Gina surmised he'd got the financial angle sorted but wanted to hear him say so. 'Why wouldn't money be an issue?' she asked.

'I have not yet made specific enquiries, but I do know of funding to support this kind of research. I would anticipate we could access sufficient funds to cover the cost of a detective and researcher.'

'Researcher?'

Gerald paused again. This was turning into a very stilted conversation, the sort you might have if you bumped into a sacked colleague outside M&S. 'The identification, and therefore the medical research, would very much benefit both from tracking down paternity possibilities and understanding more about your history with each one.'

She could see that. Didn't mean she wanted it to happen but she could see the sense in it. 'Why now, though? Surely we can test Stan and Evan and if that means George Douglas is not the father, only then do we need to do the other stuff. And it will be obvious if George Flowers was the father.' The awkwardness was mounting.

Stan would have arrived at the house by now and Gina wanted to see him more strongly than she had ever wanted to see anyone in her life. She hadn't yet told her mother she hadn't gone to Australia, although she had sent her a text yesterday saying she'd be in touch once she'd met up with Stan. A truthful lie. So she didn't really have time for Gerald's constant lulls and him picking his words like a good choice would change the meaning.

'Why it will be obvious if Mr Flowers was the father?' asked Gerald.

'The baby would be mixed-race. He is the only man I slept with who would make that possible.' She repeated: 'Why so quickly?'

'Because once you have had the baby, you will be, like all new mothers but to an intense level, exhausted and preoccupied. But now, you have maybe four to six weeks to rest physically – absolutely rest – and you can brief the detective and the researcher. If we wait until after the birth, it might be some months before you have any energy to devote to matters other than the baby. This way, we have a head start on the groundwork.'

And so Gina agreed, like suspects finally agree to confess to crimes they didn't do: to make it stop. Make him go away. She didn't think she liked him very much any more. And then, somehow, in the next hour she had seen Mr Grant, agreed the rate for however long she needed a private room in Valley starting tomorrow, signed two forms approving the hire of a detective and a researcher (funds to be sourced by Mr Howard), and agreed to set up an appointment with a lawyer, which the fund would also pay for. A taxi arrived to take her home and the driver said, 'Same time to bring you in tomorrow, Mrs Flowers?' Her life was truly not her own.

*

'Gina told me you were coming and I thought you might not have a key. Gordon the Lodger has left for a five-day Stratford and the Cotswolds special.' Sandra had opened the door to Stan's ring. He dropped his bags and hugged her hard.

'It's so good to see you.'

'You too.' Sandra took a couple of steps back from the front door into the hallway. Gina had spent the last few months getting the flat more or less how she wanted it. There were three bedrooms, Gina's en-suite, another bathroom, a really big kitchen, a small office space, a separate living room and a reasonable garden, big enough for Riley to bark at squirrels on the occasional day she couldn't be bothered or wasn't able to take him out. It was well fitted out and recently painted, not much clutter. For anyone planning to have a baby at short notice in their sixties, it was the right sort of flat: no steps, no lifts to be out of order, easy to clean, straightforward to toddler-proof. Stan dragged his bags into the hall and they went in to the kitchen.

'I never imagined a baby living here. Visiting, yes, of course. But not a baby living here. I've seen it on video but I didn't picture a cot in the corner.'

'Neither, I guess, did your mother,' replied Sandra. They both looked round the kitchen as if it was an estate agent's 360-degree online special, imagining a buggy in the corner by the French doors, feeding bottles and paraphernalia on the window sill. Surely Gina wouldn't breastfeed, even if she could, thought Stan. His instinctive 'Yuck, no!' reaction was a ghost of adolescent revulsion at anything to do with parents and sex. The image of his mother breastfeeding was not one he welcomed. The implications of a new (half?) sibling were starting to take root as realities. Stan looked at Sandra with a 'What now?' expression.

They filled each other in on the last couple of days and how they thought Gina was. Sandra added: 'I did see Gordon this morning as he was leaving, and told him you were coming and Gina wasn't going to Australia. He is now obviously worried about her, probably imagining she must be ill. I said I'd text him tonight. I'll see what Gina thinks about that. He also said you were welcome to use his room, and he can make other arrangements for accommodation if we let him know. You can use the other room this week. We can make up the bed. I've got an hour before I need to leave so I can help. Or is there something else I can do?'

126

'I can do the sheets.' Stan sat down. 'Sandra, what on earth is my mother going to do?'

His godmother made coffee as she spoke. 'At first, I thought she might have made a mistake. It's not that I thought she was deluded. It was just so hard to see how it could be true. I know her. I know she—' Sandra changed tack. Discussing her friend's personal story with her friend's son: no. 'But now I really think she must be pregnant. She told me about this DESI thing.' Then seeing Stan's expression, she explained what she understood about delayed embryonic settled implantation. 'She told me she had decided against an abortion, even though she would probably get permission, because the baby is likely to be viable at this stage and she didn't want to murder it. Her words, not mine.'

'So is G2 the father?' Stan asked.

'I don't know. Gina doesn't know. The doctors don't know. She might find out a bit more today.'

'But what is she going to do? With a baby? She's sixty-two. She lives on her own, mostly. She would be nearly eighty by the time it—'

'He,' interrupted Sandra. 'It's a boy. No. Shouldn't have told you. Please forget that.'

'Forgotten. By the time he, it, leaves school. It's crazy.'

They talked a bit about what they obliquely referred to as 'arrangements', covering everything and achieving nothing. What if it is early? What if it has extra needs? What if she doesn't recover well from the birth? What about feeding? Night feeds, a cot, money? When Sandra left it was a relief finally to stop identifying seemingly endless problems with no apparent answers – no obviously good or

127

straightforward answers, certainly. Stan put the heating back on, partly because he was tired and feeling the difference in climate, partly to make sure the house was warm when his mother got back. But mostly to try to take away the chill of despair, or displacement at least. He phoned Evan, who didn't answer but did send a text saying he'd come over after school although he'd have to bring the kids. He'd read that before he looked at several missed calls and three texts from Alison, the last one asking him to ring her urgently. He supposed he owed her that.

'Stan, where are you? What's going on?'

'I'm at my mother's. In England. It was sudden. She's seeing a doctor at the moment.' Given Stan's dereliction of duty to his partner of fourteen months by imparting the information at long distance with no warning that he had flown to the other side of the world, she took it very calmly. No histrionics, not even a 'How could you leave and not tell me?' Alison was so in love with Stan she could rationalise even such a shocking negligence.

'I'm sorry. Is it serious? Is there anything I can do? Should I come over?'

'I don't know if it is serious. And thank you, but there's nothing you can do. Wilson is at Fairview. Bree will keep an eye on the flat.' If Alison was seething or shredded with hurt that he had found time to organise kennels and talk to his cleaner but not to her, she kept it to herself. He needed to work out the least bad way to underline that the relationship was over. He understood she was shocked that he was suddenly on the other side of the world, and that she would have expected to have a role in what happened next, but he had sent her the text. Alison was still speaking. She could come on Sunday.

'Alison, I need to concentrate on my mum right now. My brother has got stuff of his own and he needs me to help. I'm sorry it's such a shock for you. But we're over, you and me.'

Alison drew a breath, controlled her emotions. The effort she made reached Stan's dulled conscience even over thousands of miles and a phone on speaker. He stilled himself, stopped trying to read other texts and emails to concentrate on this conversation to get it finished, get the message understood.

'Please, Stan. Let's talk about it when you get back. It doesn't matter when or what happens. If you need to move to be with your mum, I can do that. Stan, please.'

Stan had been here before, although in less dramatic circumstances. This was a rerun of his time-to-move-on speech delivered out of the blue to a blameless lover. He wasn't going to backtrack. No false hope.

'I don't even know when – if – I'm coming back. Probably to sort stuff out, maybe. But it doesn't make a difference to us whether I am or not. It's over, Ali. We have had a good time. But you need to find someone else.'

'Have you? Are you even in England?'

'I am, yes. My mother is at the doctor's and I don't know what the news will be when she gets back. I am not seeing anyone else and haven't since I met you. I'm just not where you are. I'm not looking for commitment. I haven't got it to give. But there is no one else.' He heard Alison start to cry, and she hung up. That was pretty much that, then.

He dozed off for a bit and was woken by the sound of Gina's taxi. Remembering and regretting the efficient brutality of his conversation with Alison, he got up and went to open the door. He was nervous about how his mother would be and how he'd be with her, images of how it should have been, meeting at Sydney airport, filling his head as he stood in the hall.

Chapter 8

Admission procedures done, Gina sat in the chair in her bedroom at Valley. The soft furnishings were a dark rose colour, reminding her of her grandmother's front room in the early sixties, when it was considered modish, a bit unnecessary, even close to effrontery to have 'those sorts of colours'. Her grandfather asked what was wrong with bracken green or dung brown more often than Gran wanted to hear. Her far from home-from-home at Valley had a double bed, for which she was grateful, expecting a narrow single. A double stopped her feeling like this was a cell. She wondered if all the rooms had doubles. Later, Allegra told her they only had two double rooms and Gina thought she probably had Mr Grant to thank, which she also thought she ought to have remembered to do at some point.

The previous night, Gina and her sons had talked. One pressing problem was when to tell her mother. The conversation began and ended with: 'She's eighty-five.' There was no longer a 'What to tell her?' Someone would have to say either: 'Gina's pregnant. The baby is due in four weeks'; or 'You've got a new grandson and it isn't Evan's. Or Stan's. Or Laura's.' Mention of Gina's niece had given them all the same idea at the same time.

Greg worked on railway signals doing something very specialised that only about five people in the country knew about, all of them coming up to retirement, so goodness knows – and certainly not the railway operator – how the East Coast Main Line would cope in a few years' time. With his free first-class rail travel, Gina hadn't felt bad about ringing her brother and saying she had something urgent to discuss, and please could he come down in the next few days. He knew she should have been in Australia and it couldn't be good news, so he was currently on the 0640 from Doncaster and expected to arrive at Valley shortly. The signals could obviously get by without him for a day at short notice.

There were only fourteen months between Gina and Greg. From childhood to late teens they had fought over just about everything: attention, toys, records, friends, bedrooms, food, comics. When she was sixteen and he'd just turned eighteen they fairly abruptly worked out they were good friends, and it had remained that way ever since. Both the Georges had been very fond of Greg, partly because he was such a good brother and partly because he was easy company. What he had been less good at was relationships, never making his mind up about a woman until she'd got fed up and moved on. Stan's approach to romance, since Carran at least, reminded Gina forcibly of Greg's, but backwards: it was Stan who moved on. Finally, much to Greg's delight, a fleeting relationship with a work colleague had resulted in Laura. Most of the family assumed an alcohol-filled one-night stand on his part, and a desire for a child before it was too late on hers. Laura's parents had drawn up schedules for childcare and finance, and basically rattled through her childhood years on a spreadsheet and love for their daughter. Neither had settled into a permanent relationship, and while friends on both sides speculated that one or other held a torch for their co-parent, it really was not the case. They were both lonely sometimes but content enough.

The fifteen-odd years age gap between Laura and the Douglas brothers meant they hadn't had a lot to do with each

132

other growing up. Travelling in a gap year, however, a cousin in Australia with a spare room was a useful asset and Laura had stayed several weeks with Stan last year, getting to know Alison a bit. Probably a bit better than Stan.

Greg had been alarmed when Gina had asked him to come straight to the hospital, but he'd lived forty years in Yorkshire and was their father's son, so concern was not something he would easily give voice to and definitely not over the phone. He was a man of minimal words. They rang each other most weeks, but once Greg had asked how she was and received 'Fine' in response, he would have been quite happy to leave it there. Laura was becoming a similarly thoughtful speaker, not given to the chatter and endless opinions of many of her contemporaries; about halfway between her garrulous mother and taciturn father.

Greg arrived just after one o'clock, bringing lunch. Valley's unchanging 'delightful light lunch' of a sandwich, an apple and a cup of tea was aimed at its core market of day patients. There was a chain coffee shop with baristas at the NHS hospital 'over the way' (as Valley staff always referred to it) and Gina had decided to go there for coffee or tea twice a day. She had to remind herself there was nothing wrong with her; she was not in confinement and was free to waddle off any time.

They ate the cheese baguettes, crisps and melon in silence, more or less. Silence wasn't awkward with Greg, being his default. Gina noticed him looking at her for a clue as to why she was in hospital, asking himself if she looked pale or had lost weight and so far coming up blank. She was dressed in loose clothing – though not strictly maternity wear

– so he probably wouldn't have noticed her middle. Anyway, it had been several months since she'd seen him.

'You didn't go to Australia, then? Is it serious, Gin?'

She told him. It wasn't worth being pregnant at sixty-two just to see the look of complete bewilderment on her brother's face, but it was a minor side benefit.

'And I need to talk to you about what to tell Mum. That's the main reason I needed to see you. Thank you for coming. And for lunch. God, I was hungry. I love a cheese baguette.'

Greg sat on the bed and held her hands, the closest he ever came to a physical gesture of comfort, and something he hadn't done since G2's funeral.

'I thought you were dying. I can take a pregnancy. So can Mum.'

Over the next hour or so, they worked out that what Gina really needed from Greg was for him to lay the ground with their mother. And to make sure Liv went to Spain next month as planned. Liv went to a lunch club on Fridays and always straight home afterwards, so Greg called a taxi and went to see her. He booked in to the hotel opposite the clinic and said he'd be back early evening.

*

Rosalie McGrath was well connected. Her contacts included researchers and private detectives – and a considerable choice among them. When Gerald had told his wife that he needed one of each – the very best one of each – she knew who to ask, how much they'd charge, and how to persuade Brad to take the case. Gerald had thought it likely that at some point Gina would need help to handle the media. He wasn't sure how to encourage her to ask him about that and was acutely aware of professional boundaries. And yet there would be no one better placed to help Gina than Rosalie. He had asked for Gina's permission to tell Rosalie the background necessary for the investigation team, but so far that was the extent of it.

Over the years, Rosalie had sent him patients who were painfully wading through the frequently unsuccessful treacle of being treated for infertility. He had always made it clear he was her husband, which universally reassured rather than repelled. He had often found her clients' desire to have a baby was intricately linked with their ambition to have family photos appear in glossy magazines, but it was his place to treat the presenting problem, not to question motive.

The private detective was Brad Saunders, and Sophia Olobo was the researcher. Gerald had wanted to meet them before introducing them to Gina. They were expected just after lunch, and were booked in to the hotel across the road for a week. Gerald was now hurriedly drafting the retrospective funding proposal to cover the investigators' per diem rates, plus legal advice and miscellaneous expenses. Although he'd had no difficulty convincing a contact from a US fertility and child-life research charity to front up the money, Gerald was somewhat twitchy about the source of funds, backed as it was by a prominent American pro-lifer. But the chair of trustees was a decent, straightforward woman who had supported several of Gerald's requests over the last decade. In any case, he didn't know many – any, in fact – foundations that could complete a transfer of such a considerable grant within twenty-four hours. Seventy-five thousand dollars was within the chair's personal discretion, no need for a committee; Gerald was familiar with the huge amount of private money spent on research in the States and from time to time simply had to make his uneasy peace, professional and personal, with the implications.

The first stage of research would not take that long overall, but gently piecing together Gina's history could not be done for eight hours a day: she would be exhausted. As quickly and sensitively as she could, Sophia would take the factual histories of Gina's relationships with all six potential fathers, handing over to Brad as much identifying detail of the four not known to be dead. Then Brad could start work on confirming the current whereabouts and personal situation of the four.

Gerald went to make sure Gina was settled and give her an update on the investigation team. She agreed Sophia could start on Saturday, and Brad as soon as he got information to go on. There was no enthusiasm in her manner. She had accepted this as, if not inevitable, then the least worst course of action. Gerald then trudged over the way. He was usually glad to leave Valley, but today was as anxious as a lover waving a sailor off to war.

*

Greg got out of the taxi, glad to leave the driver to entertain someone else with football scores, moans about potholes and the state of the government. He could see his mother through the slats of the blind on her front window, making him feel a little uncomfortable, almost voyeuristic. The news wasn't going to get any lighter no matter how long he spied on her. It was an Edwardian terrace house with stained glass in the door, bins on a neat two-foot strip of paving behind a raised bed, which looked remarkably vibrant for the time of year. He needed to ask her what she was feeding her plants. He thought the front door had maybe been painted since he was last here, and found himself falling into this as an opening topic.

'Hallo, Mum. Have you had the door painted since I was here? It used to be light grey, didn't it?' On stooping to hug Liv, he saw her face lose its colour and her eyes fill with tears.

'Yes,' she replied. 'In November. Raj did it for me. Said he was doing some painting anyway, but I'm not sure he was.' At which point Raj came out of his front door, just a metre away from where Greg was standing awkwardly.

'Greg! It's you. Just checking it wasn't someone untoward, you know. Liv didn't say you were coming. How are you?'

'Fine, Raj, fine, thank you. Very well. Spur of the moment visit. Mum didn't know. I was in the area, visiting Gina. Came on the train this morning, stopping overnight. Not with Mum. And how are you?' It was a bizarre conversational wriggle, courtesy momentarily trumping the need to allay Liv's fears. If, in fact, that was what he was going to be able to do. Greg gathered himself. 'Haven't got long, so I need Mum to get the kettle on. Nice to see you again, Raj, and thanks for checking me out. Good to know there's a friendly eye on things.'

Liv stepped back into the hallway and moved into the kitchen. 'I got such a shock when I saw you. Thought there must be something wrong, you must be ill or worse, but you told Raj you're well. Is that true?'

'It is, Mum,' replied Greg. 'I'm fine.'

'Why didn't you ring then? I'll make the bed up. It's lovely to see you, but I haven't got anything in. I might have a Marks macaroni cheese in the freezer. I don't know if it's cook-from-frozen, but it's only three so it might be OK if I defrost it now.'

'I'm not stopping overnight. I'm staying with Gina. Near Gina. In a hotel near Gina.'

For Liv, it wasn't so much a penny dropping that there was something up with Gina, not Greg but Gina, it was more like a heavy weight had descended on to each of her shoulders. She sagged on to what she now called the day sofa in the kitchen, which Greg remembered as the new sofa when he was a child: one they couldn't actually sit on for the first five years after it arrived to dominate their then very small front room, in case they dented the cushions.

'It's Gina, then. Is it cancer?'

'No, nothing like that. She's not ill.'

There was a long silence while Greg worked out what to say and Liv went through myriad causes of Greg coming to see her about Gina, like she was looking for a bargain at a car boot sale.

'Not one of the boys?'

'No. Mum, it's difficult to say this so that it makes any sense, but Gina asked me to come and tell you she's pregnant.'

Sometimes it was hard for her children to credit that Liv was eighty-five. She had been blessed with good health – physical and mental – smooth skin and an interested hairdresser. Years of caring for her husband with a progressive disease had made her value every moment of lightness. But right now she was clutching her white blouse at the neck, clawing silently at the arm of the sofa, her mouth slackly open and, with the look she gave Greg a mix of confusion and distress, wouldn't have looked out of place in a drawing of Bedlam. Greg went to sit beside her. 'She's fine, Mum, fine as can be. It was a shock, but they're taking good care of her in the hospital. Stan's here. She's OK.'

There was a silence of the sort when news of an unexpected death is delivered. The same stunned look, chill in the previously warm air, a stillness and a reckoning: a reckoning that finds many wanting in meeting the needs of others. Greg held his mother's hands and said, 'No one's dead, Mum. We're all OK.' His attempt at reassurance brought her no visible comfort. Greg admitted to himself he had expected his mother to react better. No, not better. Be less shocked? How naive was that. Her sixty-two-year-old daughter was pregnant. He took three deep breaths, something they'd trained signal operators to do to compose themselves in times of crisis. It seemed trite, a waste of precious time until you saw how effective it was. And it brought clarity on what he needed to say.

'Mum, shall I tell you what I know? So you don't have to ask questions?' There was no nod but seeing a few tears and blinks, he realised he was on the right track. 'Gina is thirty-two to thirty-three weeks pregnant. She is going to have the baby. They might've let her abort, but it would be viable so she doesn't want to.' A tiny nod of instruction to keep going. 'She is about ten years post-menopause. She hasn't slept with anyone since George. Something very rare has happened to her. So rare, no one knows about it. No one has seen a case. It is called delayed embryonic settled implantation. They call it DESI. A fertilised egg suddenly

139

released after years hiding away in her womb and planted itself and is now a baby. A foetus anyway. A big, baby-like foetus.'

Another tiny nod. Greg's ability to retain and then explain detail, essential for his safety-critical work, had never before been so useful in his private life. 'She's in a private hospital next to the NHS one, where a really good team will deliver the baby. Instead of her going to Australia, she phoned Stan and asked him to come here. I came down this morning and she told me. She asked me to come and tell you.'

'So whose baby is it? Who is the father? I thought George, second George, had... you know, the snip.'

'I didn't know that,' replied Greg. Why would I? Why did his mother? he thought to himself. 'But as far as we understand it, anyone could be the father. Anyone Gina has ever slept with.'

And at that, Liv gave in to the tears and wept quietly in her son's arms. After all, he realised, it was a hell of a thing to hear at eighty-five.

*

With the physique of a man who had never even looked at a full English, here was Brad, chowing down on an All Day Breakfast of organic sausages, free-range eggs, baked beans, mushrooms, black pudding and bacon as if it were calorie-free – and maybe even good for you.

Years of making his appearance non-descript, blending into any background, meant not only would most people walk by without registering his presence, but also those outside his tight personal circle who came into contact with him when he couldn't avoid it – delivery drivers, neighbours, a very few others – found his physical characteristics hard to recall. His own family thought he lived in the US. Every year he rented the same house in Florida for two months, filled it with the minimum needed to look like he lived there and they came for a holiday. To them he was something to do with cybersecurity, so they expected him to be away frequently so not needing much in his house, and they did not expect him to talk about his work. He actually lived in west London, eschewed personal relationships and pretty much lived to work. It was a state of affairs he had decided would be worth it for another few years; when he reached thirty-nine he was going to find a wife and write a book. He knew he was lonely and had often considered living what the papers would call a double life: one identity for family, the other for work. But deceit – personal deceit, at least – wasn't his style; the house and holidays in Florida he defined as professional. He knew more than most how lies soon wrap around deceivers like a boa constrictor, even though they would protest – and he often believed them – that they never meant for this or that shabby outcome to happen. In the meantime, it was just him and his contacts.

Rosalie was his favourite and most lucrative client, although he had nearly refused this assignment. His fee was high and frequently double the going rate. She handled some serious names. On this one, she was forgoing her commission, at least in the first stage, because her client (Virginia Eleanor Flowers, previously Douglas and née Redcar) was a patient of Rosalie's husband rather than wealthy and needy. Flowers was apparently pregnant at sixty-two and not by any of the usual natural or artificial channels. Brad knew all about Gerald Howard. After his first investigation for Rosalie, he had checked them out, right down to visiting the diner where she'd said they'd met and making sure there really had been a Springsteen concert in Nashville that weekend. If Gerald was ever going to have an affair, Brad would know about it – probably before Gerald. Whether he'd tell Rosalie, he hadn't quite decided.

While she waited for Brad to finish his meal, Sophia had a cheese omelette and two espressos. At their short first meeting the previous evening, neither of them had said very much beyond personal introductions and investigative objectives. It was she who had suggested they meet for brunch before seeing Gerald. Having spent yesterday afternoon sketching out a provisional approach based on the very terse written brief from the charity, she wanted to talk to Brad about how much information he would need so that she could ensure Mrs Flowers was comfortable with what Sophia would need to disclose.

'Nothing at all about sexual positions, frequency of intercourse, intensity of feelings,' said Brad, referring to the most intimate of the recollections Sophia would, over time, be trying to elicit from Gina. 'But absolutely anything that might help identify and locate the four living suspects.' He corrected himself: 'Four non-husband paternal candidates. Who may or may not be alive. I've got what I need to know about George Douglas and George Flowers. If Mr Howard is right and the Douglas sons will agree to a DNA match, I don't need to do anything about George Douglas. I will find out about George Flowers' life, his first marriage and vasectomy in particular, but I don't need anything from you

142

to get that moving. I'm going to start there this morning.' He handed Sophia a mobile. 'Please use this – and only this – to contact me.'

Sophia was silent for a moment, trying to work out the answer to the question that had arisen in her mind. Brad anticipated it. 'It's not about you. Not about trust in you. You know phone hacking? When this story gets out, journalists from all over will want a piece of it. By then, this phone and its records will be crumbs in a landfill. The network provider's records will be irretrievable. Use your own phone as normal. Keep this one for me and Rosalie, and Mrs Flowers if you need to give her a number or ring her. Talk to Rosalie about how to keep notes.'

'Rosalie from the charity?'

'Mr Howard's wife. She hired you.'

'She works for the charity? The charity that hired me? It's a medical research foundation. I'm meeting them next.'

Brad left it there. Not his patch. 'I'll be in touch.' By the time he had left, Sophia could barely remember what he looked like; certainly, she couldn't have picked him out from an identity parade.

*

Sophia was in the final stretch of her thesis on the medical history of offenders, completing a PhD in criminology. Her well-connected and respected supervisor had helped her gain security clearance to interview men – and a few women – for her study. It was that supervisor who had recommended her services to Rosalie, and told Sophia to charge three times what she had first thought of. Rosalie had known Professor

143

Solo since their university days and while his recommendation meant Sophia's ability was a given, Rosalie needed to check that Sophia was someone who Gina would not only trust but like.

Sophia was softly spoken and easy to listen to; her interviewees never struggled to hear what she was saying although her voice was low, mellow even. It was a technique she developed for her work in prison – loud voices were a red flag for staff and prisoners alike but she didn't have time to repeat herself so she had worked on voice and volume exercises to find her optimal pitch. Quietly dramatic to look at, Sophia was just on the verge of being a head turner. For prison visits she wore a semi-camouflage of too much make-up and a headscarf. Today her makeup was limited to lip gloss.

Sophia was very likeable. She smiled a lot, listened properly and made Rosalie feel comfortable, which was a rare feeling for Rosalie in the company of someone she was not only hiring but who was much younger than she was. This was partly because Rosalie resisted feeling comfortable, equating it with complacency. PR success was not built on complacency. It was built on rigour, obsessive checking, lightning reactions, confidence in your judgement, good decisions – and contacts. Feeling comfortable was as alien to Rosalie as leaving the house without her phone, or spending a second longer than necessary on anything. Except if Gerald was involved. What if she hadn't been in that diner that day? Although no more sentimental than she was complacent, Rosalie thought of Gerald as her father's parting gift to her.

Sophia had turned up bang on time. They were using Gerald's office at Valley. 'Good to meet you, Sophia. I'm

Rosalie McGrath. We spoke on the phone. Professor Solo speaks very highly of you, and I hope you will find this project interesting. It's certainly unusual.' During this short speech, Rosalie had shaken Sophia's hand, taken her coat, pulled out a chair for her and gone back to Gerald's side of the desk where she sat down. 'I thought it would be good to meet before I introduce you to Mrs Flowers.'

'Could you tell me a bit about yourself and your charity, please? It was all very rushed yesterday and I feel I don't have a clear picture.'

Rosalie already knew the outstanding balance on Sophia's student loan and what her PhD grant, a small amount of teaching and a cataloguing job in the library, amounted to each year. She knew there was no family money for Sophia to count on; her parents were both working, still paying a mortgage with enough savings to replace the washing machine if it broke but very little else. They took a holiday in Europe most years and an extended trip to see family in Harare every three or four. Sophia was the first to go to university, followed by two younger siblings, one yet to graduate. Proud though the Olobo parents were, they did wonder if their finances would stack up in the face of all this education.

'The medical research charity is funding the research stage of this project, Sophia. I work in public relations. Mr Howard is my husband. A patient of my husband's needs a research and investigation team to undertake work on her sexual and marital history. Confidentiality is essential at this stage. Mrs Flowers is thirty-two to thirty-three weeks pregnant and, understandably at sixty-two, somewhat taken aback by this unexpected development in her life. My

145

husband is the senior obstetrician, and he asked me to source and recommend a researcher – which is you, Sophia – and an investigator, Brad, whom you met earlier. I am not engaged by Mrs Flowers. I have not yet met her. But I undertook to source you and Brad because I have significant experience in this area and my husband has none.' Both women sat still for a few minutes while Sophia processed the various threads.

Rosalie texted Gerald to let him know Sophia was ready for the full brief. He would arrive in about fifteen minutes. Rosalie decided that this time could best be spent by reassuring Sophia of the importance and validity of the project, addressing head-on some of the fears that Rosalie assumed she would have, so that by the time Gerald arrived she would indeed be ready.

'I work for some very well-known people, some very wealthy people, some very important people, and some who fall into all or none of those categories. My agency takes care of situations, mostly of our clients' own making, that they would rather not be in, or that they wish to exploit for financial gain. We are mostly called in on a reactive basis to fix a problem. No, we are not Scandal or Call My Agent, but that gives you some idea of how the industry works at its most extreme. Sometimes, like this case, we work proactively. I don't mean scheduling interviews with celebrity gossip magazines; that's not our bread and butter. Briefing well-paid sources with information that clients want to manage into the public domain is our business, for example. As is keeping information out of it.

'I hope that explains my connections in research and investigation fields and why my husband suggested to Mrs Flowers that he locate her investigation team and then, with her permission, referred it to me. The medical research charity is funding the research because it could have implications for areas of fertility study they support. That is as far as my involvement goes at this stage. When Gerald arrives he'll be able to tell you exactly what he hopes you will be able to establish with Mrs Flowers.'

'Are you hoping Mrs Flowers will become a client of yours?' asked Sophia. 'Presumably it will be a big story. And Brad suggested I ask you about how to take and keep notes. I mean, I know how to take notes. What's different here?'

'About Mrs Flowers, yes, I probably am,' admitted Rosalie. 'There are very few new stories, very few clients with situations I haven't seen a hundred times. And I need to address that with her. Gerald wanted to get Mrs Flowers the best possible research team, and it needed to be done overnight. He happened to be married to someone – the best possible someone – to be able to do this. I want to help him. And I believe it will be very helpful for Mrs Flowers. Anything else is for her and her alone.'

Rosalie took a slim laptop from her bag and handed it to Sophia. 'No handwritten notes. Not at any time, no matter what. No jotting things down at home that you remember late at night. Everything goes in here. You can type or you can speak and it will transcribe your words. Files are saved automatically to a dedicated secure server. If needed, we will be able to retrieve any previous version, so don't worry if you delete something you later find you need. It connects to a VPN with end-to-end encryption. There is a charger pack. Only charge the laptop from the charger pack; charge the charger pack separately. Mouse, keyboard, laptop stand. If there is anything else you need, please ask. A taxi account has been set up for you; feel free to use it entirely as you wish for a month, including personal use. I am going to ask you now to sign another non-disclosure agreement. The NDA you e-signed yesterday covered these preliminary discussions. The new one covers the next stages. After you have had your chat with Gerald, a lawyer will explain to you what is involved and the consequences.'

Rosalie looked directly at Sophia. Whatever her peers in the industry might say, there was no such thing as a good judge of character, even among PR professionals. Especially among PR professionals. And certainly no substitute for a watertight NDA and sanctions for breaching it. There was only the assessment of the risk of assuming someone was on the level. It wasn't about the personality. It was about the risk of being wrong, weighed against what could be lost if the risk wasn't taken.

Gerald arrived and Rosalie left. Even for the brief time they were in the room together, Sophia was aware of a warmth in the room that wasn't there before or after. Neither Gerald nor Rosalie seemed like cold fish; but their sum was greater than their parts.

*

'Ms Olobo, I am very pleased to meet you. Thank you for taking this on at such short notice. I am Gerald Howard, the lead obstetrician for Mrs Flowers. Please call me Gerald.' He paused.

'Sophia,' she filled in, as she assumed was expected. 'And I appreciate your wife finding me for this project. I don't know a lot yet but it is very interesting. Really interesting.'

Sophia was comfortably on first-name terms with many of the people she encountered in the course of her studies, be they professors or lawyers, or the inmates usually known by their surname or a nickname. But there was something about the medical profession that meant she felt presumptuous using the first name of a doctor. The psychiatrists she had interviewed had all offered their given names, but she had been unable to shift from Dr Akbar or Stevenson or De Luis. Mr Howard may have started with 'Please call me Gerald' but she wouldn't do that; not yet, anyway. Sophia settled for one of those slightly uneasy interactions when she needed to be sure she had Gerald's – Mr Howard's – attention prior to speaking to him to avoid using any name at all. She'd trawled online for easily available information about Gerald Howard, and it was clear he was very highly regarded not just at his own hospital but internationally.

Over the next hour, Gerald outlined what he needed from Sophia, suggesting how she structure her 'enquiries', as they coyly referred to the intrusive and mostly unwelcome questions she would be asking Mrs Flowers. While Gerald wanted to know everything about Gina's history, he had decided it was best to take it in two stages. First, get information that could help Brad locate the candidate fathers, and capturing anything else that came out as part of prodding those recollections. 'Collateral facts and feelings' was how Sophia relayed back to him her understanding. Gerald hoped there would be quite a lot of collateral. The more invasive questions could wait for stage two, whenever that might be;

Gerald did not want to risk overloading or alienating Gina at this early juncture.

Sophia asked for a few minutes to think and quietly ran through her current and previous research cases. The collateral disclosures on those occasions had, in every case, been deep and illuminating, but those participants had nothing else to do. Talking to Sophia, or anyone they weren't locked up with, was a break. Some had a streak of narcissism and many – although this was rarely acknowledged – wanted to impress her. Gina Flowers was a woman with a deep dilemma, not a criminal in need of attention or redemption. Nevertheless, Sophia would hope to draw out more than the basics. She looked at Gerald.

'I've had some thoughts on how best to work with Mrs Flowers that I'd like to run by you now, if that's OK. I'll tell her a bit about my background. I want to reassure her that the focus of my research to date hasn't been a subject's criminality but their medical and familial history. I am concerned that my research interests might unnerve her somewhat, and I want to make sure it isn't an issue.'

Gerald knew the answer but asked the question anyway, maybe needing to reassure himself that Sophia would have the same view of full disclosure. 'I had that same concern when Rosalie suggested you and told me about your areas of expertise. Is it necessary to be explicit about it?'

Sophia was taken aback by Gerald's question.

'It is, yes. Definitely. I can't imagine you would expect me not to share this information with Mrs Flowers. It wouldn't take much for her to find it out anyway. She is much more likely to trust me if I mention it, relevant or not, than if one of her sons Googles me. If your question is a test,

I hope I've passed.' Gerald cast his eyes awkwardly to the corner of the room. Sophia moved on. 'A bit about my background and how I understand my work fits in to Brad's work. Essentially I will provide him with facts. And only facts that might help him locate the four non-husband candidate fathers. I intend to get an outline so Brad has something to work on at once, and then I'll move to the deeper dive for your research or if Brad runs into a dead end. Rosalie has given me instructions on note-keeping, and I will tell Mrs Flowers about those arrangements. If she asks why it's necessary, I will refer her to Rosalie – is that OK?'

This was something of a dilemma for Gerald. Was he pimping his wife to a patient? Or worse, a patient to his wife? Rosalie did not need his help to find clients; in fact, he often wished she would take fewer. But he'd known she would like to represent Gina and there would be nobody better to do it. But there was a clear conflict of interest – involving Sophia would not make that go away.

'My preference,' said Sophia, 'would be for Rosalie to meet Mrs Flowers with me and explain exactly how we got to where we are now, what she does, and why she believes these lengths are necessary for confidentiality. I would also like to tell her about the demands, requests – no, instructions – Brad made for communication between us. Unless you object, I am going to ring Rosalie and ask her to do this and, after I've met the lawyer about the NDA, you can introduce us to Mrs Flowers.'

Her research had layered in to Sophia a substantial level of professional confidence, although this had not meaningfully been put to use outside a subject interview until this moment. Over the previous year, she'd interviewed 'the

Suitcase', whose wealthy family said they believed in his innocence. No one else did – probably not his lawyer and certainly not Sophia. The Suitcase trafficked unbelievable amounts of cocaine boldly packed in Samsonite luggage, relying on bribes and his family's high profile to see him through airports. The family had invested heavily in dealing with steely prosecution lawyers, defence barristers looking to make a reputation, overconfident hangers-on and assorted public-relations ructions, including a leak from Suitcase's cellmate about Sophia's work ('Suitcase unpacks his baggage to pretty young student'). Sophia had watched and learned from the weary grinding of a criminal justice system, which oddly mostly managed to retain employees who were relatively incorruptible. Suitcase was her watershed interviewee; she knew after him that she was good at her job.

Gerald had a clinic over the way but would be back at three-thirty and asked Allegra to find out in the meantime if Gina was agreeable and if she would like her son to be there. He left Sophia to the lawyer and to contact Rosalie, then headed off to the more humdrum business of floating vaginas and overlong labours that waited for him in the NHS. The multi-headed hydra that was Gina Flower's pregnancy was reaching full throttle.

*

The late afternoon meeting had gone reasonably well for Sophia. Gina Flowers had looked exhausted and was clearly only just coping with the demands on her time and her body. Sophia had tried not to look too long or too often at Gina's figure and had come to the conclusion only that she looked a bit plump, sagging somewhat when she stood up and walked round the room. It wouldn't cross anyone's mind she was pregnant, but Sophia couldn't be sure if that was merely inbuilt resistance, the automatic disregarding of such a ludicrous notion in someone who looked over fifty. Over sixty, even. Or by the end of the afternoon, in touching distance of seventy.

She had reviewed the second, enhanced NDA, taking advice from the lawyer, who assured her he was acting only for Sophia despite being paid by someone else. They'd made a few changes, got it signed, witnessed, done. And Rosalie had met Gina.

Sophia had listened to the conversation by default rather than invitation. Gina had wanted to finish their introductory session, but Rosalie arrived before the end and neither asked Sophia to leave. The lawyer had also waited and, despite the lawyer being in another room, it did all feel a bit too cosy for Rosalie and her contacts. Which Gina had tactfully verbalised: 'I do very much appreciate your time and coming to meet me at such short notice. And having an investigator, a researcher and a lawyer on tap. With your husband being my consultant, it feels very much an in-house affair.'

'Yes, it does,' agreed Rosalie. 'It is, although we do all have professional boundaries and obligations. You have a lot to think about. The only person you should absolutely definitely not change is Gerald. You'll need someone to make sure the press don't get a whiff of the birth, or are silenced if they do. Or if you decide you want them to, to handle the media activity. Manage opportunities. But that does not have to be me or anyone from my company. So let me make a pitch now, and then I will leave, and if you want to you can call me to follow up.'

'What about the lawyer and the investigation team?'

'Those were simply contacts I provided. They are not PR people and I have made no charge for their services, though they are of course being paid by Gerald's funders, because the investigators are essential to get the medical side of the project underway, and the lawyer is essential to set things off on a proper foundation. The lawyer will explain that you can stop using the services at any time with no financial repercussions. All – let's call it intellectual property for now – remains yours.'

'I'm sorry. I'm tetchy. I do want to hear, first, your view on why I need someone, please.' Gina, sitting alone on the bed, wished she hadn't told everyone she'd be fine this afternoon. Stan was still intermittently sleeping off his jet lag, she'd shushed Evan when he'd offered to find someone to pick up the kids so he could be with her, and Greg was with their mother.

If Rosalie had been handing Gina the nuclear code, she could not have made it appear more weighty yet, simultaneously, simple. It took just a few sentences to explain that keeping the story out of the media would be next to impossible for the family. Someone not bound by medical ethics or family loyalty, or susceptible to a bribe, would almost certainly try to sell it. A media management agent would spot potential leak sources, limit them and either explain why it would be a very bad idea to break confidence or find their price for silence, nearly always without threatening – say it softly – bankrupt-inducing legal action. The story could be managed rather than exploded in the tabloids, where truth and privacy pulled as much weight as a shallow wave in a tsunami. But the really interesting part, at least as far as Gina and Rosalie were concerned, was the opportunity to exploit what Rosalie called 'Gina's story'. Sophia thought it likely that Rosalie was aware of the effect on Gina of naming it such.

Rosalie had been leaning on the radiator. Her look, like most things in her life, was carefully put together: bespoke jeans, cashmere cardigan with a silk scarf picking out complementary shades, Chanel No. 5, a designer-messy haircut with perfect highlights. Yet not intimidating, not trying to impress or put anyone else down. 'Here is my number, which is secure and calls are encrypted, should you want to follow up. If you would like any general advice, or want to check anyone out, I am happy to do that without charge.'

'What's the name of your firm? Your website address?' asked Gina.

'Rosalie McGrath Corporation. No website. You won't find much about me online: the odd medical conference dinner with Gerald but nothing professional. We do a lot of social media but it's project-specific and doesn't lead to the agency.' Rosalie could see how hard this was for Gina. Most of her clients already knew a bit about media management before they came to her, even for the first time. And they came to her. She did not go looking, not any more. She told Gina and Sophia the story of how she'd got started in PR, offered to get a birthday present for Gina to give Anton if that would help, wished her well and left. Her next meeting was with an Oscar winner who had just found out she was not the birth child of her Oscar-winning parents –

155

and was wondering how to turn that into several million dollars.

Quite a Friday afternoon. Baby-shock day plus four.

*

Jed Waller III was as harmless as he was spineless, as healthy as he was handsome, and came blessed with rich parents who were not only going to give him the family business but surround him with hand-picked clever people to run it. None of these were the reason Rosalie McGrath agreed to marry him; indeed, he didn't get the business until many years after their engagement was called off. But he was due to open offices in Hong Kong, Singapore and Australia – that at least was the reason his father gave for the travels – and Jed wanted her to go with him. So they needed to get married, everyone said at the time. Jed wanted to marry Rosalie very much, and that was flattering because every other girl in Anstack, Tennessee wanted to marry Jed. Back then, when Rosalie was nineteen and Jed twenty-three, it was still that kind of place.

Rosalie wanted to be a journalist and was spending what she and Collette called 'the picture money' for a long-distance course at a New York institute. The McGrath farm did alright, much better than some, but Rosalie preferred to pay her own way rather than explain why she wanted a heap of money. She was halfway through the course, getting good marks, and it seemed like the other side of the world would be good for material; plus, married to Jed, no one would expect her to earn, freeing up her days for writing and researching. It wasn't the most romantic way to approach a proposal, but Jed didn't notice and Rosalie didn't care. Either it would work out or it wouldn't, and Jed was nice enough. And she wanted a break from the farm. Years of Clem McGrath telling his daughter she was pretty as a milkmaid didn't mean she wanted to be one.

Three weeks before the wedding, a low-slung, heavy-looking Ford pickup the colour of old blood stains eased slowly up the McGrath drive. On the porch, Collette was wearing the purple bridesmaid's dress she'd come over to try on, looking, as Rosalie said, like a cross between an angry grape and a hibiscus in full bloom.

'Well, I swear, if that isn't Aidan Jones driving that truck,' said Collette. 'What the glory-me does he want?' Jones got out of the pickup. Less than ten minutes later he left, taking the pictures with him.

'I need to tell Arlene. And I need to talk to Jed.' Rosalie watched the pickup's tyres kick up dust. Shivering with rage and guilt, she wasn't yet thinking straight.

'Well, honey, Jed won't want to know. He is ignorant and blissful made flesh, that man. You know Jed won't want to know, and your whole marriage will be right there on the line, clear as any line can be. This may be 1981, but his family ain't exactly fans of women's lib and I'm not even sure this counts as that.' Once Collette was on a roll, Rosalie couldn't help but listen. 'Arlene will not want you raking all this up now, not four years later she won't, when she thought it was all buried. So whoever you talk to, whoever you see, you tread careful, girl. More careful than if you were walking through your daddy's cow fields in your white wedding shoes.'

The pictures had been taken by a lanky middle-aged Texan two or three years back in a studio off Broadway – the main drag in Nashville. Rosalie had seen an advert for glamour models ('No more than 18 years old. Good money paid') in the back of the Anstack Argus, listed in the want ads like regular jobs, waiting tables or fixing cars, although you didn't have to be under eighteen to do either of those. She'd taken the bus one hot Saturday to find out what 'good money' meant. It meant she had to take her top off, pout and thrust, hold some uncomfortable positions and vile objects for minutes on end; generally, as she recognised at the time, demean herself and her sex. But she'd negotiated four times what the Texan first offered and, once he saw how well she could follow instructions and maintain a pose, doubled that again on subsequent trips. She'd told Collette about the pictures, though not about how much money she'd made, and given no thought as to where they would end up. They had ended up with Aiden Jones when the Texan went home to Dallas and hired Aiden's man-and-van to do a clear out.

Figuring that Jed Waller III's fiancée would be keen to keep her back street glamour past from the groom-to-be, Jones came over to extract a favour, the type of favour his slurried imagination assumed back street glamour girls would do, for keeping his former classmate's secret. With a grounded menace that was seriously out of kilter with her hotpants, halter-neck and leisurely drawl, Rosalie said that Aidan going with Arlene before she was sixteen was a crime and set out what would happen if the pictures were not destroyed. Jones backed himself into the driver's seat still yelling threats, though now deflated. It was the grubbiest of tit-for-tat spats leaving neither side with so much as an egg cup of dignity.

Rosalie and Collette both knew that Arlene, the kind of studious hard-working girl who still wore pigtails in ninth grade, had had a crush on Aiden like a steamroller on a beetle. She had wept for a month when he turned out to be a callous seducer, and it wasn't until she'd got a place in vet school that she seemed to forgive herself that first, terrible foray into relationships.

'I need to tell Jed, Collette,' said Rosalie, 'or I'll be wondering all my life if he'll find out. If Aidan Jones gets soused, forgets about Arlene and tells him. But I think you're right, I don't think Jed'll like it. Or more like he'll think his daddy won't like it, and hell, he'll be telling his daddy because he tells his daddy everything. Come to think of it, that's the best thing about us moving away. It'll be a lot more trouble for Jed to go running to his pop about what colour shirt he should wear.'

Collette was right. Jed Waller III ignored Rosalie's request – put it no higher than that, it was a request not a plea – and asked Jed Waller II what he should do. Waller II told Rosalie to give back the ring and paid her ten thousand dollars to leave town without a word. A week later, Rosalie was on another bus – five days and thirteen states to New York – to finish her course in person. She took Collette's advice and didn't tell Arlene they'd used her story to blackmail Aidan.

When people asked Rosalie over the years how she got into media management, she said she started at the seedy, shady end of the business and worked her way out. If they asked for her advice, she'd say be first on the scene, identify the levers and keep your own counsel.

*

159

'Graham? From ultrasound?'

Graham jumped, started sweating and felt dizzy all at the same time. They were on to him. Gina Flowers's people. He'd lose his registration. They couldn't send him to prison, surely not, he hadn't actually done anything, but he'd never work again so maybe he'd end up in prison anyway because he'd have to steal. He turned to look at his accuser.

'I thought it was you. I'm glad I saw you again. I just wanted to say thank you for my scan last week. It was so dreadful but you made it easier for me. Well, not easy but... you know. Thank you.' Graham's vision was blurred, stopping sweet tears of relief, holding them on the precipice of his eyelids with strength and control that came from fear. He had no idea who this woman was.

'Glad it's all OK. Happy to help,' he said, as if he was working in a burger bar and they were talking about a bag of fries.

'No. I'm Lena Frost. It's not all OK.' She spoke slowly, realising that her tragedy was just another case to the sonographer. He'd scanned, dispensed pre-packaged kindness, reported and forgotten. She couldn't feel any worse but the foolishness of thinking he'd care – about her, Lena Frost and her lost baby, a whole week later – turned her crimson. 'I'm sorry to have bothered you.'

Chapter 9

On Saturday, Gina's first question for Sophia was, 'What did you think of Rosalie when you met her?' Sophia told her, and said that Brad had been a contact of Rosalie's for a very long time and he said she was the best in the business. Sophia had brought coffee and lunch as agreed and set up a workstation near the window in Gina's room. A sunless, mild January day looking in on them did nothing to lighten the institutional feel. They agreed to work chronologically so they started in 1975 with Roland.

*

Gina didn't really drink at all in those days, even on holiday. She tended to be up before breakfast service had finished, not hungover in bed until four in the afternoon, when the partying could start again. They were a group of eight, all halfway through A levels; the other seven were still in bed when she walked down at 11 a.m. for a milky coffee at the small bar they'd gone to the night before. They'd left around midnight. The others had gone on to the Ding-Dong Disco, and Gina returned to their shared room to read, her torch batteries fading – the hotel lights went out at ten. She'd chosen that bar because the barman ignored her. Elsewhere, the waiters ranged from feeling they ought to be friendly to tourists, through desperate to practise English, to outright harassment. But in the Bar Es Cana, the waiter brought a coffee, took her pesetas and that was it. He was tidying, clearing and setting up for the greater reward of the evening;

at least she hoped for his sake it was greater, because it was long hours and hard work. So he polished glasses, wiped surfaces and took no notice at all of Gina with her book, unless she caught his eye for 'Un cafe mas, por favor'.

Today, an English guy she'd seen around with a group of his mates came in with a book in his hand and ordered a coffee at the farthest clean table from her – all of four feet away. Bar Es Cana could have been subtitled 'Smallest bar in Ibiza'. He kind of nodded; Gina kind of nodded. Then she saw he was reading *Looking for Mr Goodbar* just at the same time he noticed she was reading *Looking for Mr Goodbar*. She half-laughed. He blushed and she said, 'What do you think?' and later that week Gina thought they might have had sex. It was hard to tell exactly. He clearly didn't believe she was on the pill, which was a relief because she wasn't sure how effective it is when you've only done five days. He insisted on double condoms, something of a trick in which she had no magic touch, and he didn't seem to have any more of a clue. Roland also did a lot of counting backwards from ten but to what purpose Gina wasn't sure. By the time all the necessary technical manoeuvres were complete, Gina couldn't have said if she had actually lost her virginity and not noticed the point of impact, or if it had just been high-octane messing around.

Their levels of discomfort with the relationship – was there another word for what it was, she wondered – were equally matched, along with their desire to have an acceptable excuse for peeling off from their mates, which hooking up most definitely was. The respect it garnered for both of them, much-wanted but not really earned, kept them going, more or less, until the end of the week, when they didn't so much as exchange their home towns, never mind an address or phone number. Gina liked Roland, liked his company, liked very much the substance he brought to her hitherto lamentable love life. If he hadn't been so obviously out of sorts with something he wasn't talking about, she felt they might have made more effort. She pinpointed him as her first love, and although this clearly would not come across in her retelling decades later, she had somewhat romanticised the few days they spent not actually avoiding each other: dark-blue starlit Mediterranean nights, shared picnics on the beach, a regretful farewell due to circumstances beyond their control. The farewell had actually been half each of a baguette with some cheese, put together and sneaked out of the buffet breakfast in Gina's beach bag, eaten on the stone sea-break near the hotel, and an acknowledgement that it hadn't been too bad. They got on their respective buses for a four-hour wait at the airport, where they had several stilted farewell-again encounters on the way from one queue to another, before their separate early-hours flights home. Mediterranean nights were dark blue and starlit at that time of year, so that part at least was true.

*

Sophia had gently pulled facts as Gina told her Ibiza story, careful to catch the hard bits of information within the narrative. It was delicate work and incongruously put Sophia in mind of combing nits from her sister's fine hair. By mid afternoon, she had a page to upload to the secure server and share with Brad.

Roland Leonard Stevens. Age 66 (born 14.02.54). 21st birthday Valentine's Day 1975. Left university in 1975. Keele Uni (80–90% sure it was Keele). Studied English. Came from a naval family. Father in the marines or something to do with ships. Went to work for the BBC in central London on a training scheme for journalists in September 1975. GF and RLS met in Ibiza, summer of 1975. Spent time together but not a full-blown romance. GF stayed at the Hotel Es Cana in the village of Es Cana and RLF was in a hostel round the corner next to a Catholic church. He was there with 3 friends, one called Bob and ?the other 2 both called Dave (sure about Bob and at least one Dave, 50% 2 Daves). They didn't see each other again after their flights home on the August bank holiday that year. He was flying to Gatwick. Height probably 5' 10" to 5' 11" (based on him being a 'good few inches' taller than GF but probably not over 6ft). Eye colour unknown. Accent and physical appearance unremarkable.

Sophia had been surprised Gina could remember Roland's middle name. Turned out he didn't like Roland so used his middle name, although he'd introduced himself to her as Roland. His mates had called him Lenny (though Gina thought maybe he'd said his family called him Roland) and Gina had asked why, and then remembered Leonard because it was her father's first name. It was Stan's middle name but – Gina had said, making them both laugh – after her dad and not unrequited love for Roland. Drawing out the details took longer than Sophia had expected. She was used to interviewing prisoners who wanted to talk and had often spent hours in lock-up planning what to say: they knew they had very limited time to get their point across. Much of what some prisoners told her was only loosely, if at all, connected to the truth: life stories embroidered much as unflattering data might be by politicians. Gina was the opposite, recalling things she had never expected to need again, let alone tell someone else, and taking pains not to mislead or set up any red herrings.

They took a break around 3 p.m. with a cup of tea Sophia again brought from the cafe in the NHS hospital, which they all now referred to as 'over the way'. The two women chatted about normal things for a while: box sets, family, dogs. Cafe conversation, a short interlude of the everyday, as welcome as it was artificial. Then they moved on. Gina's relationship with Eddie Grainger had lasted much longer, just short of two years, although she came to realise she hadn't known him well at all.

*

It wasn't pulling yourself together that was hard, Gina thought: it was keeping yourself together. She'd gathered up her bravest face and widest smile the day after she realised that Eddie had left, and toughed it out for what remained of her twenty-first birthday weekend, answering questions about his whereabouts with vague allusions to work, trains, friends he hadn't seen for ages and anything except what she knew but couldn't believe to be true. He'd left. Without a word. Keeping herself together over the next few months was a different story. She had told people fairly soon that they'd split up, amid genuinely puzzled enquiries as to why. That, she didn't know. She could live with a relationship that had just run its course, been strung out too long in the face of distance and competing priorities, but not the humiliation of not knowing if this was, in fact, the case.

She couldn't tell anyone how she felt. Not about not being together any more, that was common enough, but that she had not been worth a conversation. She knew he was alive, never thought he was dead in a ditch somewhere, because if he had been someone would have told her. But she'd meant so little, been worth so little, he'd cared so little that he didn't say, 'Gina, it's over'. It had taken fifteen years, one rebound marriage and intermittent self-imposed moratoriums on men before she'd begun to feel less worthless. That was the damage Eddie Grainger had done for the want of a goodbye.

> Philip Edward Grainger (spelling of
> Philip not certain, could be double-
> L). Always known as Eddie in time
> GF knew him – father also Phil. Age

now probably 68, 69 or 70. GF
remembers his birthday was at the
end of April, best guess 26th. A few
years older than GF but ?how many.
Born in Dundee or somewhere like
that, brought up in or around
Arbroath. Father died when he was
10: accident at work as a fireman.
Mother's name something like Morag
or Moira. School in Brechin, took the
minimum number of exams he
needed for nurse training, then left
for Glasgow. GF thinks PEG told
her it was in the local paper at the
time, it was so unusual for a male.
Qualified and then did psychiatric
nursing. He mostly worked in Exeter
while they were together but can't
remember anything about where or
address. When he came to see her, he
hitched and (for Paris) took the bus
and ferry from London. He was with
GF in Cambridge for her 21st party
on 11 July 1977, but left the next day
and she never saw or heard from him
again. GF and PEG met through the
sister of a friend of GF's. Asked the
friend a while back what he was
doing now. The friend didn't really
keep up, though she thought PEG
had qualified as a doctor. He'd lost

touch with her sister so this was just
the grapevine. 5' 11". Blue eyes.
Strong Scots accent, east coast.

To give Gina a respite, they agreed to take the next
day off and start again on Monday. Sophia left and passed
Stan arriving. She didn't know for sure it was Stan, but he
was headed towards Gina's room and had the look of his
mother. Beauty may often be in the eye of the beholder, but
some things and some people are objectively beautiful. Stan
Douglas was objectively beautiful: lightly tanned, just over six
foot, dirty-blonde hair and well-arranged features. He said
good evening as he passed and again to someone else further
down the corridor where he stopped for a chat, a trickle of
charisma flowing down the bland hospital corridor. A small
part of Sophia wished he'd stopped to chat with her just so
she could enjoy his face a little longer. She knew a number of
very nice men, kind, considerate, funny, but she couldn't
bring to mind any beautiful ones.

*

Stan popped his head round his mother's door, finding her
lying on the floor with her feet on a cushion, playing a word
game. He said he just had a couple of calls to make, would
get them something to eat and left. He had considered
discussing his plan with his family but, acknowledging that
his mind was made up, he was just going to inform them and
not ask what they thought. He was going back to Australia in
the next couple of days, finish up there and then come home.
Permanently. He could do it in a week while his mother was

safe in hospital, and he would, fingers crossed, be back by the time she had the baby. The longer he left it, the nearer the due date. And if he didn't go until afterwards, well. Piece of string and all that.

Not long after six he was back with Gina, bringing fish and chips sealed inside two Tupperware boxes. He helped her off the floor, which she didn't like but judged was better than the ungainly struggle to lever herself up while the baby-containing tyre around her middle lurched and slithered from side to side. As they ate, Stan told Gina about ending his relationship with Alison, the smell of grease and vinegar lending a sheen of normality. They were both worried about being told off for having takeaway chips in the hospital, so Stan turned on the extractor fan in the bathroom and opened a top window to let in just enough cleansing night air without lowering the room's temperature too much. His mother was tearful, partly about the whole baby thing but also, she said, because she felt like she couldn't even make a cup of tea when she wanted one, as though she were in a nursing home. Prison, thankfully, seemed to have dropped down the metaphor list. She didn't talk about going home, however badly she wanted to; it was now 'baby first' and that meant hospital.

Stan rinsed the Tupperwares and then took the fish wrappers outside. It was cold, wet and dark, and it would be colder, wetter and darker at this time of year in the west of Scotland. In Sydney it would be high summer. He thought about that for a few minutes, leaning on one of the pillars where the smokers stood, aware of a lingering haze of tobacco smoke. He found he was sure he wanted the move. Ideally, he would want his share options paid out; and technically there were another eight weeks or so to work before he could resign. There were some compassionate leave clauses in his contract and he reckoned that caring for his pregnant sixty-two-year-old single mother could be compassionate grounds. He would need Gina's permission to tell them and make them believe him. Plus a flight, a text to his department head, and an employment lawyer. Cleaning his hands on the tiny wipe, tang of lemon disinfectant mixing with the stale oil, he went back inside to find a woman sitting on his mother's bed.

'Hello,' he said. 'I'm Stan, Gina's son. Would you like me to come back in a bit?'

'Oh, I'm not hospital staff,' replied Rosalie, at which Stan frowned. 'I'm Rosalie McGrath. Nice to meet you, Stan.' Stan looked at his mother. He thought he knew most of her friends and certainly thought he'd have known any who'd be visiting her in hospital in… her condition. The phrase made him wince: it sounded so old-fashioned – and it applied to his mother.

A few minutes after Rosalie had left Gina the previous evening, Gina had phoned her, agreed terms and felt the first stirrings of control since The Shock. Rosalie was back to see if she needed anything immediately and to outline how they might handle things.

'Rosalie is a media manager,' said Gina. 'We're talking about PR. Protecting me from the press and then selling my story.' Stan was surprised Rosalie didn't bat back this bald and unflattering description of her profession, but she smiled a genuine smile, and they all chuckled. Not enough hilarity to be a real laugh and still with an undertone of embarrassment, but it felt like a marker of progress. As the moment petered out, Gina looked at Stan to see if he disapproved even if he didn't say so, ready to defend her decision to work with Rosalie.

'I'm impressed my mother has managed to get a PR person in the room so fast. How did you get in contact? Mum, did you just Google 'best PR person for older pregnant woman' or what?' Stan's wariness was deftly put, neutral and on-guard at the same time.

'I'm Gerald Howard's wife. Which has nothing to do with my ability and experience for this job but has everything to do with how your mother and I have come into contact. And a potential conflict of interest.' Rosalie answered for Gina.

'Well, yes,' replied Stan, 'and…' He discarded 'a coincidence' as too critical, 'convenient' as too sarcastic and settled on 'lucky' with a question mark in his intonation.

'Could you run through things again, please, while Stan's here?' Gina asked. 'Then he can tell Evan and Greg and my mother. I think they'll take it better if Stan is happy. They might think I've been duped or drugged.'

Rosalie's suggestion – and she carefully called it no more than that – was that prior to the birth, the bare fact of the pregnancy be limited to hospital staff, family, Sandra and professional advisors. Some information for potential fathers was obviously required and would need to be managed with NDAs. Rosalie would gather Gina's thoughts on coverage, the story, appropriate media and come up with a plan for approval. That would happen over the next few days. She would talk to the family and Sandra, explaining Gina's wishes and how they planned to monetise the story. After the birth, a press release would be sent out but with media management already settled.

Stan said he needed to sleep on it. In fact, he still just needed to sleep having been on the go since arriving, never mind residual jet lag. He decided to raise his own plan with his mother to boomerang to Sydney while Rosalie was still there. 'Rosalie, I need to run something past my mother, and if we go ahead with your services it would be helpful to have your view on it. Can I confirm if you have signed an NDA please? Sorry if that sounds a bit rude.'

'Not at all. And not yet. But it is a good question and a good point. We generally sign the NDA on engagement, but I have one here and an e-signature app, so let me do that.'

Chapter 10

Stan and Evan had agreed they needed to talk to Dr Howard. His wife being their mother's media manager seemed all a bit… cosy, maybe? Undeniably convenient for Gina, for them too, and they did recognise that media management would be needed, but Rosalie McGrath couldn't be the only PR person on the patch. They'd had a somewhat fractious exchange of texts with their mother and eventually got her permission to talk to Gerald. Gina had been clear she was very happy with Rosalie, grateful the matter was sorted and the boys were not to change the arrangements or imply she, Gina, had instigated the chat with Gerald.

Dr Howard agreed to see Stan after his Monday NHS clinic and before his private clinic at Valley. The advantage of Gina having Rosalie on speed dial to set that up with Gerald at twelve hours' notice on a Sunday was not lost on Stan, although Dr Howard made no reference to it. Evan couldn't sort out the logistics of childcare and work to get there when Dr Howard was free and before Stan left for the airport, and anyway they felt it didn't need two of them. They weren't ganging up on Dr Howard, just looking for reassurance. *Mr* Howard, Stan reminded himself.

'Does it feel odd, being the medical lead and the husband of the PR lead?' opened Stan. 'Any conflict of interest?'

'Yes, it does feel odd. And no, I don't think there is an actual conflict of interest, although there could certainly be a perception that that is the case. I'd like to explain if I may. If you have time.' Another of Gerald's pauses ticked by as he carefully lined up the words he wanted to use, sifting and checking for the best combination. He'd honed this art over years of delivering unwelcome news to prospective parents. How to prepare them but not frighten them, to offer comfort but not false hope, ease the transition into years and decades of caring for a disabled child or tell them their dream of parenthood was not going to be realised in this, or perhaps any, pregnancy. Sometimes there was just the mother, with Gerald the only person to witness her anguish.

'During pregnancy and until the birth, the priority is the mother. Always. It's a dilemma I came to terms with years ago. If it is either mother or baby, it's mother.' He watched Stan, seeing a glimpse of shock. 'Your mother is safe. She's sixty-two and giving birth is exhausting. Euphoria often takes the edge off the physical toll but even for young mothers – well, 'labour' is no misnomer. But your mother will have me and the some of the world's top obstetricians to look after her physical welfare. And she has you all.

'I have declared the potential conflict of interest in confidential registers at this hospital and Valley, and informed my professional colleagues. Drs Mudonak and Maynard each offered to become clinical lead, and I know Rosalie offered to provide the names of other media management agencies. Your mother refused both offers. I asked Gina if she would submit an affidavit stating her position, which she is going to arrange with her lawyer. I am comfortable, ethically speaking, with the way we are proceeding. I swore a Hippocratic oath more than thirty years ago. In the work I do, I am reminded of it every day. But. If anyone at any time thinks there is something to worry about, please let me or someone else know.'

174

It was obvious that Mr Howard had not quite finished. Stan surmised he was not as familiar with addressing the media issues.

'Rosalie has put together a project,' Gerald continued. 'The crux of your concern is, I believe, that your mother's consultant and her closest, non-medical, professional advisor during this period are married. And that I, as her consultant, introduced your mother to my wife. I understand how it looks and the implausibility of the coincidence. I cannot change those things, although should your mother choose at any time to change or withdraw from any of the arrangements, we would facilitate that without question. I can tell you that nothing will get in the way of my care for Gina and her baby.'

Stan nodded. He had had to ask and Mr Howard had treated him courteously and seriously. Why then did he feel foolish? He thanked Mr Howard and walked over to say goodbye to his mother.

'Safe travel, love,' she said. 'Thank you for coming and for coming back.'

'Wait for me, mum – and you too, little one. Don't meet the world before I get back.' They hugged awkwardly, not because they were wary of physical affection but because there was a flattened bump in the way.

*

Brad's cousin John rarely travelled farther than his local supermarket. He wouldn't so much as take a day trip to central London to see the sights. The idea that he might ever go abroad was as reckless to him as walking a tightrope across the Grand Canyon. Brad's mother and John's mother were twins. Brad and John may have been cousins, not brothers, but their physical resemblance was marked. John's gregarious nature contrasted with his limited horizons. He worked in a builders' merchant at the end of his road. He was a cheerful man, enjoyed his job helping plasterers and plumbers find what they needed, chatting about thread sizes and trowel types. He had a girlfriend who wanted the same things as he did, including a regular Friday night takeaway and being able to pay the mortgage. His life now suited him.

A number of years ago he had fallen into debt after a short-lived but high-octane gambling spree. Online gambling had become irresponsibly easy and before he was blocked by the virtual casino, he'd placed several thousand pounds' worth of bets he couldn't pay for. He'd asked Brad to lend him a few hundred pounds to keep the payday loan company at bay and Brad had asked how much he really needed. Brad gave him enough to pay the debt and cover a deposit on John's flat, which to both of them seemed like a fair price for Brad to get a passport in John's name, the discreet use of John's identity and occasional ratification of details. The loose arrangement between them was that when the ten years on the passport ran out, another thousand or so per year would cover the next decade. Beyond this, Brad was John's comfort blanket. His earnings covered his day-to-day needs, but if his mum ever needed anything or his roof fell in, Brad wouldn't let him down. John stopped looking for the golden nugget and, despite dreaming occasionally about a big win, never so much as bought a lottery ticket.

Brad didn't need to work undercover for the majority of his assignments, but he preferred it. He booked travel as

John Freeman and moved comfortably between personas, as easily as changing shirts. John had come to realise slowly that if things came to light he would not be viewed as wholly innocent. He had absolute trust in Brad, despite not knowing basics like where Brad lived, and took seriously the instructions to keep the arrangement to himself. There were letters from a credit card company or a bank occasionally, less than half a dozen a year, and if his girlfriend Belinda was ever curious enough to open one, the worst she might wonder was if he was having an affair.

Brad had started work on Gina's case with the General Register Office, moved on to other open sources, finishing with data and records which were, you might say, off-grid. By the very early hours of Monday, a week after the confirmation of Gina's pregnancy, he was mostly certain of the biographical details, family history, physical descriptions and current whereabouts of Roland (Lenny) Stevens and (Philip – one L) Eddie Grainger. He couldn't be completely sure until the visual check, and an in-person confirmation of a salient fact. Hackney for Roland or the Highlands for Eddie first? There was an 0940 flight to Inverness on Monday morning – today – with seats, and who didn't want to go to the frozen north in early January? He booked a ticket and a cab for 7 a.m. – both in John Freeman's name – and looked forward to a full English at Heathrow.

*

Sophia arrived at Valley not long after eight, just as Brad was checking in at Terminal 5. Hospital mealtimes during the week, even in a private facility, were early: breakfast at seven,

177

lunch at noon (or eleven-thirty if you were unlucky) and dinner at five. She already felt that questioning Gina was like teasing out a splinter with a rusty penknife, and they had not yet touched on the most sensitive matters. That was for later. For now, it was the identification details that mattered and they started the day in Paris, 1992.

*

Gina hadn't much liked Paris. She loved France, just not Paris. No one was ever good enough to be in Paris unless they were Parisian or impossibly famous. She had been working there one week a month for several years, staying in the spare room of her friend's grand-mère. There was the deepest bath imaginable, which was never filled to more than a tenth because the boiling water ran out after a few minutes and the cold not long after that. Gina developed a system of running the boiling water, then the cold, having a pastis on the tiny balcony and then it would be about the right temperature, although it only came up to just over her ankles.

Jerome she met through work, at an awards do for '1992 Franchise of the Year' or some such. Her company, a supplier to Jerome's franchisor, had to buy a table for the celebration dinner at the Plaza Athénée. No one wanted to go except Gina, who was after all in Paris, far from home with no childcare issues thanks to George's parents who moved in to her house Monday to Friday for a week a month, her father's illness preventing her own parents from physically helping out. So she went. She met Jerome at the bar and she made him laugh, describing her tussles to look less English, more continental. 'Black,' he'd said. 'Wear black and a scarf, an interesting necklace, and get yourself a good bag.' He had eight sisters, he said, so he should know. It had been sound advice she used often.

He'd told her he was still technically married but lived apart from his wife and the divorce was on its way. It was probably true, and anyway it suited her to believe him. This was her last month in Paris: the account had grown under her supervision and she had recruited a French partner, so from now on she would only come maybe twice a year.

It had been nearly four years since George Douglas had died. Gina knew she had married him to feel safe and wifely after the devastation of rejection by Eddie. But after George's death, with two small children and needing to keep his parents onside, she had not contemplated another relationship and had not had the confidence to have even a discreet fling. Until Jerome made it sound so easy, so French, so normal.

She had been a bit taken aback by his approach to contraception – what had been called the rhythm method in her sex education classes, which only the girls had received because – clearly – it was a girl's responsibility not to get pregnant. George's accident had slowed that part of their life long before he'd died, and Gina hadn't given much thought to contraception since soon after Evan was born. On that post-award, free champagne, how-much-I've-missed-this night at the Plaza Athénée, she didn't have anything of her own to suggest. Once they'd agreed by way of slight shoulder shrugs and raised eyebrows that they'd spend the night together, Jerome booked a room.

For the remaining time Gina was in Paris, they alternated between his apartment – modern, next to a deafening bypass but with loads of hot water – and her room, which had the tiny balcony, a grand view, beautiful ceilings and not much else. They made no attempt to keep in touch. But they had taken each other a little farther on the road to healing.

*

Sophia asked Gina if she wanted a nap or at least a decent break, but Gina said she was better in the mornings and anyway they came round after lunch to take samples, measure things, hook her up to charts and generally get in the way. They left Paris and moved to Kirkcaldy.

David Harper knew his worth in the world, saw himself very much as one of the important people. Gina didn't like him from the beginning. That said, she didn't have much to do with him directly. She sent him weekly management accounts; he stuck a list of questions on her desk and she typed up a list of replies. Other than that, she dealt mainly with his PA, who also didn't like him much, but as she lived eight minutes' walk from the office and needed to go home at lunchtime to let out her ageing dog and check on her ageing mother, she felt the trade-off was worth it. While Gina had sometimes thought David was a bit curt, she'd vaguely supposed he was just busy and a bit of a genius. She knew his subject was physics, and he was totally across all the technicals of CPRL's work, which frightened and impressed the phone engineers.

She visited the Kirkcaldy site every quarter and liked the site manager there. On that day, after they'd run through the site's figures, he had taken her out to lunch and talked about some ideas he'd had for developing the business. He asked her if she could run some financial models for him to present to David next quarter. They worked on these for an hour or so until the management meeting.

She had been surprised to see Alan at the meeting. She knew him to say hello to but otherwise not much. Travel requests generally came her way and she didn't recall seeing one for him. Even so, she was shocked when she heard David pull him apart in public. Everyone knew Alan had done a really good job in sales, brought in a lot of business and helped reassure a few valuable but nervy engineers who weren't yet certain mobile phones would be a lasting thing. A mobile was known either as a Mars or KitKat depending on its shape, weighed about three kilos and was mostly used in cars. Alan's riposte to David became legend. For months after she'd left CPRL, any meet-up with former colleagues always included 'You were there when that sales guy told David Harper what's what'. After Alan left the room – quietly, taking his time to gather his things, not storming out, thanking the Kirkcaldy site manager for his time – David cut him to shreds to the four employees remaining around the meeting table. It was dreadful. Unprofessional. David looked like a small bitter man who'd been bested by a subordinate, his misuse of power exposed. Then Gina found the word: he was a bully. So she stood up, said that Alan might have skipped a couple of procedures but she couldn't listen to any more, at which David said, 'Caught the heart of the middle-aged widow, has he?'

181

The week before, she'd been approached about a job to start in three months. At the end of the week she tidied up and left, with David threatening to sue for breach of contract because she didn't work her notice. She did the Kirkcaldy figures for the site manager before leaving.

But on that afternoon she went back to the hotel and saw Alan in the bar. She'd planned on watching a bit of telly, phoning home, writing her resignation letter and making lists of things to do before she left CPRL on Friday, plus activities to do with the boys before she started the new job. She waved at Alan with uncharacteristic familiarity and rang the agent about the new job from a phone in the foyer. CPRL didn't give its staff mobile phones.

When she joined him at the bar, they chatted for a bit, debriefed and dissected the meeting, and Alan offered her a lift to the airport in the morning. Someone from the site usually collected her and took her there so she rarely hired a car.

In the event, she got a taxi.

As they entered the lift, there had been no plan. They had not exchanged charged glances of lust. There had been no flirtatious smiling or light brushing of skin. Not a whisper. They'd simply talked in the bar, 4 p.m. somehow providing the intimacy that often only comes pre-dawn. He had told her he was at something of a crisis point: work, children, marriage – all seemed to be askew at once. She remembered thinking he was having proper, potentially life-altering doubts and not just a wobble. She had listened, a bit flattered maybe by the veiled confidences. Not *Strangers on a Train*; no one was going to murder anyone, but there were echoes of the safety of confiding in someone you had no connection to, would never meet again. Getting into the lift, she said resigning today was the most reckless thing she'd ever done, although a new job in the pipeline had made it easier, and that made them both laugh. They were laughing as the door opened at the third floor, the lift emptied and they could hear 'We've Got Tonight' muzak its way into their ears. Before they reached their floor, the fifth, a bomb exploded.

Since then, Gina had thought that a bomb would be the best way to die – though she knew it was both naïve and crass to think that way. Exploding into tiny airborne pieces, carried on stardust and surrounded by light.

Alan was a little over six foot with strawberry blonde hair cut neatly, if a bit longer than you'd expect for a corporate salesman. He wasn't conventionally good-looking, more rugged than handsome. There was a film, *Risky Business* with Tom Cruise, that reminded her still of that night, although Alan was Tom Cruise's physical opposite. Gina and Alan were far from teenagers on high jinks, but there was both depth and spontaneity to the performances in the film that took her from Kirkcaldy to Chicago. She watched it every few years in the way others watched *Some Like It Hot* or *It's a Wonderful Life*.

They both knew it was not going to be an affair. It was never going to be repeated. There was no need to discuss it. She was the one who was single, so in the morning she said to him, 'I won't tell anyone. Not a hint. No one. Because once you tell one person, drop one hint, you've lost control of the story. I promise.'

'It'll never be this good again, Gina,' he said. 'Not for either of us, will it? I don't know where it came from. I'll think of it every time I get in a lift.'

183

Gina didn't know if that was a joke or not. She wondered if he meant he'd think of her every time he got in a lift or just, you know, the night. She didn't ask, nodded and went to pack, order a taxi, change her flight to the one after his. She couldn't risk being in the confines of a car or on a flight with him, not even a coffee in the departure lounge, hiding lust in plain sight. Later that week, she helped him with the admin of leaving CPRL: payroll, holidays, personal items. Through David's PA.

What's the meaning of life? That was. Is. Camus, Gina thought, but maybe a philosopher, someone she'd read at school, said if you're incarcerated with just your own thoughts for company, you can spend years remembering the events of one day, the details of one room, and the time passes. Every butterfly's wingbeat, each drop of rain will come back if you wait and practise. Recollecting this one night had seen Gina through darkness, loneliness and self-doubt. She waited and she practised and every time she needed it, it was there for her. She couldn't know for sure it was the same for him but she thought it might well be.

*

By mid-afternoon, Sophia had another two pages to send to Brad.

> Jerome. French. ?Surname.
> Something like 'Matisse' but
> definitely not Matisse. Begins with a
> B or P. Born in Lyon. Now aged
> about 70 but wide margin on that, at

least 5 years either way. Birthday was either 4 or 14 July. Gina couldn't remember if it was Independence Day or Bastille Day. Lived in Paris in 1992 and had moved there about 10 years before that. Catholic family, at least 7 siblings, maybe 9, possibly all sisters. He was the middle sibling, all alive in 1992. Separated before 1992 from Nicole (80–90% certain on name of Nicole). No children. In 1992 owned or operated or was in charge of a number of car dealerships in Paris. Height about 5' 9", not tall. Wore glasses since childhood for short sight. Was vegan. Very knowledgeable on wine but not a show-off. Possible, but unlikely, that Jerome was not real name.

Apartment in Paris brutalist, modern, but was no more than 10 minutes on foot from Notre Dame, 4th floor near a bypass or motorway. Gina might recognise the street name or a picture and can look at Google Street View over the next few days if that would be useful.

Less than half an hour after sending the report, Brad messaged Sophia: 'Don't ask Gina to check streets for Jerome yet. Unlikely to help. If get stuck, might change that but other info more useful'. The next text said: 'Loads to go on, really good stuff, thx'. Sophia had expected him to be on the brusque side of business-like; his supportive comment was unexpected.

And then there was Alan. Sticking to the facts for this part of her reporting, Sophia kept all nuances to herself. This fleeting encounter had apparently defined Gina's identity from her early forties, grounding a self-confidence she had never really felt before and which nothing since had shaken.

> Alan. Surname forgotten (may come back to Gina). Best guess at age now 65–70; wide margin of possible error. Worked for Car Phone Repairs Ltd (known as CPRL) for a few months 1998-99 as did Gina. Company HQ was in Southall, repair warehouse in Kirkcaldy. CPRL taken over by a subsidiary of Samsung in about 2000. Lived in west London, Ealing or Acton, maybe Hammersmith – north of the river. Married but marriage possibly in trouble so might be divorced. Wife's name was Sarah. He had flown from Edinburgh to Heathrow in mid-June 1999 around lunchtime. Sister stood for Scottish parliament in 1999 Holyrood election. 6ft. Brown eyes. Salesman.

While Sophia and Gina still had a lot of work to do to uncover the more subtle, difficult to talk about details that Gerald needed, they did feel they'd made a good start on the practicalities.

*

Brad parked the hire car outside the trendiest-looking hotel on the banks of the River Ness. He had booked for the Sunday night, which was already over, so he could take immediate occupation even though it was only 11 a.m. on Monday. He was tired and needed a few hours' sleep before settling into observation outside Eddie Grainger's house. By the time he would get there it would be almost dark, which meant he would be harder to spot, as would his subject. Absent some hideous coincidence like a marital infidelity it was unlikely that Eddie expected a private investigator to be trying to find him and therefore equally unlikely that he would be on his guard. So although Brad would rather have had the benefit of daylight, he rarely did anything professional when he was tired. He went to bed and slept until the alarm at 4.30 p.m.

The fourteenth of January was his father's birthday, so he rang him when he got up, mindful of the time difference with Florida, where his dad would expect him to be ringing from. And was able to answer accurately if not truthfully when his dad asked, 'Have you just got up, son?' He bought tickets for his parents to visit him every year in lieu of birthday presents and with each trip his relief that the time to stop hiding his life was approaching increased.

According to research undertaken by specialists in data for people who need to know these kinds of things, the car least likely to be noticed or remembered by casual passers-by was a grey Toyota Yaris. If a bright blue Rolls-Royce was one hundred on a scale of memorability, the car Brad was sitting in opposite the house he believed to be Eddie's was a two. Not long after 6 p.m. the man Brad presumed to be Eddie left his house with two dogs and walked along the well-lit avenue to the Guinness-black river with its bank of shadowy trees and assorted bridges. Eddie didn't stay out long. It was minus four. Satisfied that the man who had come out of the house was the right height and within the right age range, Brad went back to his hotel to continue enquiries on Jerome and Alan, which so far had proved as tricky as Eddie and Roland had been straightforward.

On Tuesday morning, from the Yaris Brad watched Eddie leave the house again with the dogs not long after eight, only returning close to eleven o'clock. In the meantime, he had seen a woman leave the house in a mid-range SUV with a much older man – an old man, Brad thought: maybe her father or father-in-law. She'd come back less than half an hour later on her own, and Brad's hope was that either Eddie or his wife would go out to fetch the older relative later in the day. And so it was: not long after 3 p.m. he was following at a short distance. While he was satisfied to be on the move, he wasn't frustrated by the uneventful hours in the car. He had practised concentration and stillness since taking up martial arts as a teenager, finding self-knowledge and gratification in the control he developed. He far more often found himself surprised at how quickly a stake-out had passed than he did wishing the time away.

'We do day care as well as residential care, and also respite care if you need a short break from looking after an elderly relative. I'd be very happy to make an appointment for the manager to show you around our facilities. Would you be available tomorrow? Then she's off, but Friday perhaps as an alternative?' The receptionist at Saint Anne's Nursing Home and Day Care Centre looked at Brad with her pen poised, daring him to decline with a direct gaze and the threat of ink in the diary. He made an appointment for the following day, at ten-thirty.

As he was leaving, he fell into conversation with Eddie and the old man, also on their way out. The cold and wet that waited for them outside the lobby made Brad's get-up unremarkable: beanie, scarf, and collar pulled well up, covering the stubble he'd been leaving unchecked since the start of the investigation. A pair of plain lens glasses, one of maybe twenty he used from time to time, and some stage make-up added ten years to his appearance. The men exchanged names and pleasantries and got to talking about care. Eddie's east coast accent remained intact, unsullied by years in Edinburgh. Brad was not able to place it, so had to ask. Eddie Grainger told this pleasant stranger that he was originally from Montrose, not far from Dundee, and that he was a retired psychiatrist who had been able to source recommendations from colleagues in the Highlands for his dad's care. Saint Anne's was top of all of their lists. Brad shared a few details about his work in IT and how he was thinking of relocating to the Highlands from London to be nearer his mother. He thanked Eddie, returned the Yaris and got the late afternoon flight to Heathrow. Piccadilly line to Holborn, four stops to Liverpool Street on the Central, and then overground to Hackney. Roland tomorrow. He phoned the home to cancel his appointment for the next morning, booked into another trendy hotel for Tuesday night, had a shower and went to bed.

*

Rosalie didn't much do excitement. Whether royalty or celebrity, big names were her everyday. Professionalism. Detachment. Decisions. These were what her clients valued. She cared very much about their lives while they were under her contractual services, but she did not get excited. Everyone else did enough of that without her joining in.

Her excitement about Gina Flowers was an exception: partly because it involved Gerald; partly because it was really human, not manufactured; and partly because Gina so needed her, though Gina did not fully appreciate that yet. She hoped Stan's impending conversation with Gerald would move that forward.

Rosalie had got up early that Monday, 3 a.m. early, to be available for at least part of the working day in Australia, spending time sorting out matters for Stan's short trip back: a first-class flight, a driver and assistant for the duration of his stay, a lawyer and a media manager. Stan had sent several texts over the weekend, insisting he didn't need the flight and assistant, and Rosalie now knew that he didn't need her to pay for them, but she'd gone ahead anyway and he'd given up protesting. The lawyer he did need. And the media manager. Rosalie intended to manage the post-birth media in

Australia herself, but until then she'd be busy here and someone had to work with the lawyer to help Stan's company understand that if they didn't let him exercise his share options on compassionate grounds, they would regret it in a few months. Stan would be on his way to Sydney later, twenty-four hours travelling, and that gave plenty of time to sort out syndication and exclusives, and make sure everything was properly handled.

Rosalie understood this kind of control could look like exploitation; to some extent it was. Families in unexpectedly newsworthy situations generally did not have experience of media attention, of their news value, of how to create and market themselves, although they frequently had what Rosalie called TOI: their own ideas. Managing TOIs was one of the harder aspects of her job. Having to cope suddenly with media was a bit like arranging a funeral. Who negotiated seriously with a funeral service? With a time-sensitive need, the bereaved often lacked their usual critical faculties in the face of trauma. Professionals were available and knew what to do. They made money, their clients felt better. Win–win. One person's exploitation was another's situational benefit maximisation. Take the PR agent out of New York, but they'd bring their workspeak right along with them.

'Hit the Decks' was on board. It had a solid, growing online following, needed a big story to break the US, high editorial standards and a modest print circulation. Its coverage was serious but not nerdy, took offbeat areas the public hadn't realised it was interested in like 'Why People Claiming Benefits Buy Designer Handbags' and found the story behind them. Readers were wide-ranging in age, class and political leaning. 'Decks' was ready for Gina and she was perfect for them. A few months ago they'd published a dedicated Australia edition for the first time and meeting the Sydney-based editor was now on Stan's itinerary. Stan didn't yet know about 'Decks' or, indeed, any other detail of his Rosalie-produced to-do list but once he did, the need for an assistant would become very clear.

Rosalie had considered media from mainstream tabloids to high-fashion glossies for the exclusives. 'Hit The Decks' was neither of those, but it would afford Gina some distance from the mob when she needed it, and a quirky angle. So that was press, print and online. Now they needed broadcast. It was so clearly laid out in her mind how this should go. She needed at least three of the living paternal candidates. She needed the family. She needed a healthy baby boy, ideally delivered by her husband. She needed complete control. She needed Gina to see what a good idea all of this was. A TV series, eight parts: the intro, one episode featuring each candidate, and a wash-up. That would be new territory for Rosalie and her desire was startling even to herself. 'Executive producer: Rosalie Howard.' She thought she would keep McGrath for the agency. It was too early to loop in Gina but not too early to lay the groundwork.

Rosalie was going back to New York, catching the 6 p.m. from Heathrow, timed so she could meet Stan for a drink in departures, allay any final fears, and probe for details he didn't know she needed to know and so hadn't told her. She'd then spend the rest of the week closing down with her two live clients on the east coast, which might mean she would lose them for a few months until they got fed up with whichever agency or pop-up PR person they found to replace her and came back. She could live with that if she had to. It wasn't that Rosalie had no one else in the US office who could do client-facing work; she did and they could do a very good job. But these two clients had been with Rosalie since she had signed them as teenagers; they had helped make her reputation with intros and seamless discreet recommendations. Neither would take well to being sidelined for a UK-based nonentity. Rosalie would say she needed to spend a few weeks in London: they knew her husband lived there. But if asked directly why, she would not try to dress it up as anything other than it was: a more important client. And she anticipated not only that they would ask, but they were no more than 50% likely to see it as a fair trade even had Gerald been in need, if she'd had a genuine compassionate reason for leaving Baseball God and Sound Machine Angel. The celebrity stratospheres of Baseball and Sound Machines required a titanium sense of self and that not uncommonly brought with it blindspots to the needs of others.

If things had not gone well with Gina, Rosalie would have stayed in New York for the foreseeable. She would have helped Gerald if he asked, but Gina was either Rosalie's client or she wasn't. And now she so nearly was.

She went in to work with Gerald. He was due to see Gina at lunchtime, after his National Health clinic for diabetic mothers with other complicating risk factors, and before his private clinic for multiple births. Rosalie texted Gina, who said 'can you give me half an hour', so she and Gerald went over to the hospital coffee shop, a rare treat for them: to do something small and everyday together. They made a big effort for things like his father's eightieth, her friends' second weddings and landmark birthdays, and his various professional social events, but just getting breakfast out together on a weekday – she wasn't sure they'd ever done that before except on holiday.

When she entered her room, Rosalie found Gina up, dressed and suddenly obviously pregnant, as if the baby had realised his time was coming and had turned from being a flabby pancake to a grotesquely oversized rugby ball. It was utterly incongruous. Gina Flowers was just too old to be pregnant. It very unfairly put Rosalie in mind of seeing an old man with a teenage wife, the contrast between wrinkles and peachy skin always sending a shiver of misery through her mind. Gina Flowers definitely needed PR.

'Hello again. Thank you for coming back. I had a shower and I look pregnant now, don't I? Is it just because we know? I keep thinking of Dorian Gray or Benjamin Button. Something all wrong in age terms.' Gina had the over-bright delivery of the ultra-nervous.

'It might be because we know,' said Rosalie. 'But, yes, I do think you look pregnant today. Which you are. How are you?'

'Well, at the weekend I thought I might never manage to have a shower again, let alone wash my hair. You know about Stan going to Sydney tonight and then coming back next week? Stan talked to Gerald earlier. To make sure about the ethics. I am going to talk to Gerald about the earliest safe date after Stan gets back that I can have a Caesarean. There's a service in London that comes to your house, decorates a room, buys what you need and leaves everything ready, so they are coming this afternoon. My friend Sandra is going to go through my clothes and bring me a few things I can wear. I am going to rest and think about the baby. And who the father is. Was. Might be.' Gina drew breath, trailing off, aware of the babbling.

A private nursery service coming to visit the house of a sixty-two year old woman who lived on her own would have been a red flag even to strangers to media management. The nursery service staff would have radar to put an air traffic control tower to shame and a list of media contacts willing to risk a few hundred pounds in cash for a possible story. These sort of services would have clients who asked for discretion, clients who already had PR agents and NDAs controlling contracts for pictures of the nursery and guidelines on the look, but there would always be one who didn't realise their own value. An upmarket nursery service would be on the lookout, like an antiques dealer at a house clearance, except their prize would be the naive Premier League wife or the unwary politician's squeeze. Rosalie needed to get this tied up in advance, tighter than a wet knot.

'Gina, we need to talk.'

Gina's eyes filled with tears. 'God, I'm so sick of crying all the time. I'm sorry. I can't seem to turn off my tear ducts. I have cried more in the last few days than at every funeral I've ever been to put together. I'm sorry. I just didn't want you to leave.'

'That's not what we need to talk about. Well, only indirectly.' Rosalie recognised the moment a client was in, and this was that moment. Gina was now definitely in. 'I've come to confirm that you want me to work for you. And if you do, I need to go to the US tonight but I'll be back overnight on Friday. I'll handle everything, including the baby service. You can't let them come to your house today.

You'll have to do it by video link so they can only see your top half but you can see their samples. And you'll need make-up and the right lighting. So if you do want me to work for you, we need to talk money, control and ground-rules. You are the client but I'll be in charge with nothing but your and the baby's interests at heart. Just so we are clear, that includes financial maximisation for you. Money. You have to trust me and you can.'

Gina was still clearly trying not to cry again. Rosalie broke the rule of her professional career to sit with an arm around her. Not a hug exactly, just a gesture.

The baby service was put off until the next day so Rosalie could get hair and make-up organised. A good make-up artist, one from Rosalie's tried and trusted portfolio, would need an hour to make Gina camera-ready, looking no more than forty-five. 'Decks' got the green light for London, Sydney already signed, syndication rights to follow. The two instructions Gina gave Rosalie were to provide enough, ideally much more, but at least enough money for the infant's upbringing and future, and to keep the shock-horror circus in check. Gina understood on an everyday level that there would be media interest, but Rosalie knew she had no idea how traumatically that could manifest itself. Newspapers trample first, print soon after and look for the truth last, if at all – in this sort of case, they published and never minded who was damned. That could be resolved in court if anyone had the wherewithal to take them on, which they usually didn't, but if they did, the proceedings just helped sell more papers.

'Normally at this point we might look for a ghostwriter to get started on a book,' said Rosalie. 'But I think a podcast series would work better, covering the human and scientific angles, and then it could be written into a book, serialised in a magazine or paper later. Or on screen.' Gina was silent.

'And for that,' Rosalie went on, 'it would add a lot to have the candidates.' Still Gina said nothing: no outbursts or objections, whether fake or real, no endorsement, no reaction at all. 'My proposal is that we put together a project team. A psychology researcher – no reason why that shouldn't be Sophia – a journalist and a lawyer to undertake different parts of the project. Pick up from where Brad leaves off.'

Gina looked puzzled.

'Brad's the investigator,' Rosalie reminded her. 'To find the fathers. Potential fathers. Paid for by the foundation. He'll be finished once they are located, verified and, if you agree, invited to contact us. Contact our lawyer, Nick Hewen.'

'Of course,' replied Gina. 'Sorry. Hard to keep track sometimes. He's using the information I give Sophia.' Rosalie nodded and went on. 'The project team – Sophia, Nick so far - and I have a journalist in mind who will collate the interviews. With the candidates, the medical team and the family. That way we have the best opportunity to maximise payments for everyone – you, of course, Sandra, the boys and the fathers. And, naturally, the baby.'

The room was very still, as if bad news was being delivered. A few minutes passed in uncomfortable silence. Yesterday's empathy seemed long ago and far away.

'Gina, do you have any questions?'

'No. No questions. But I want an agreement that every participant can withdraw at any time and can withhold consent to using their material. And I can veto all or any of it at any stage. And nothing apart from the background confidential research happens until after Barney is born. It just feels like such a lot, unmanageable.' She sighed.

This was not what Rosalie had hoped for. It left far too much scope for individuals to dent the value of the whole. And for Gina to scupper it entirely. She said so, and they talked about how they might flexibly frame the agreements to reflect her wishes but keep some control. And however unmanageable it felt to Gina, it was Rosalie's day job. Finally, Rosalie said, 'Deal?' and Gina nodded. 'I'll get working on the legal agreements now, put the further research in place, and you can put everything aside until after baby Barney makes his appearance.' A pause. 'Barney?'

'I didn't want anyone else's thoughts on his first name so I had to decide it now. I'm open to middle names if I need to be. And last names. If one of the Georges isn't the father, and no one else cares, I think I'll go for Redcar for his last name. Redcar was my maiden name. If it's allowed. I don't even know if you can choose a surname or you have to have a parent's.'

Rosalie nodded, seeing the sense in all of that and glad that Gina was thinking and planning to some extent. At least she wanted the soonest possible safe birth, so maybe there would be just another few weeks to wait for the main event. 'You can. Give him any surname you choose. I checked. Barney could definitely be a Redcar.'

*

Evan had struggled to concentrate on the final stages of the quarterly output for a long-standing client, which he badly needed to finish – so badly his mortgage depended on it. The work was dull beyond belief. Having Evan work on that newsletter was like getting a combine harvester to rake an allotment. A few times a year Evan suggested a rebrand, new layouts, a slight change of emphasis or style, or even just a new font to try and keep things fresh. But Financial Advisory and Investment Bureau knew its clients and that they did not like change: even moving from Times New Roman to Arial might be newfangled enough to make some of them take their very lucrative business elsewhere. For years Evan had turned out copy with broadly four plots: it has been a very challenging year; despite some volatility the markets have performed well overall; the economic outlook going forward is uncertain; a steady hand is needed on the investment tiller. The subliminal message was 'You've got a lot of money, stick with us and we'll make you even more. Or at least not lose too much of it'. Amelie's work life had a glamorous aspect, no denying it: photo shoots in exotic locations and interesting buildings. It was also hard work, long hours and badly paid, so while most of their friends would assume that Amelie was the breadwinner, her salary just about covered her clothes and the kids' clothes, whereas Evan's more mundane occupation bought the sourdough. And paid the mortgage.

He didn't think Amelie would leave him while she was pregnant, although he wouldn't have bet the house on it. They had both been utterly dismayed at another pregnancy, barely discussing it for the first few weeks, but neither had mentioned 'taking care of it' and so they'd stumbled on to

199

this point. Four months to go. At least this one of his mother's grandchildren would be younger than her own child, if only by a matter of weeks. It crossed Evan's mind every couple of days to wonder if Amelie's baby was his, could really be the result of careless-just-this-once, fingers-crossed sex. On balance, he thought it probably was, but still.

He arrived at his grandmother's after lunch, at Greg's request, just to make sure she hadn't collapsed with delayed shock, and to press her to go to Spain at the end of January as she'd planned. Evan and Liv had become close after her husband died and it had matured into friendship as Evan got older and his own boys arrived. Growing up, it was his paternal grandparents who had largely taken centre stage, desperate in their bereavement and consoled by caring for their grandsons. And for the last few years of her husband's illness, Liv struggled to find energy to devote to anything except his care. They'd talked about those times in recent months, Liv finding from conversations with her contemporaries' children and grandchildren, mostly at funerals, that many of them wished they'd asked more questions while they had the chance.

Today, Liv came to the door in her dressing gown, something Evan hadn't seen since he turned up at her house after a music festival, wet through and only faintly aware it was after midnight. She hugged him so long he had to gently detach her arms and steer her into the kitchen. 'It's OK, Gran. It's OK. We'll be OK.'

He listened to his grandmother explain her fears. Which were, almost exclusively, about Gina. She'd be having an anaesthetic, major surgery – that was bad enough, although middle-aged people did those things all the time.

But give birth? Bring up a child starting at sixty-two with no help? 'We'll all help,' said Evan.

'Of course we will, but Stan lives in Australia, you have two small children, another due very soon, and a wife who is sometimes present, sometimes not. I am eighty-five. Greg can fit a car seat at least, but other than that, he lives six hours away. Which honestly is probably not the worst thing, because he may be a world expert on signal failure, but I wouldn't trust him to change a nappy without going through half a packet, and they're not cheap, and still failing to catch everything. Seriously, Evan, your mother is facing a dreadful ordeal. Women are not meant to give birth at sixty-two, even by Caesarean. Am I the only one that understands the measure of the trauma?'

'Well, Stan, Greg and I are men. So you understand it best. Mum doesn't seem traumatised. She seems to be coping.'

'Coping is what your mother does, Evan. Particularly when there is no alternative except collapse.' Liv was right. When they'd been burgled on Christmas Eve; when her husbands died; when the boss at her accountancy firm had been convicted for embezzlement and for two years the investigators tried to prove she was in on it too. When Stan came home high with a stash in his pocket. When Sandra had a breakdown and her family had moved in. So, yes, coping was Gina's thing.

'That's something good, Gran. Mostly. I think.' They tacitly acknowledged the truth of this while recognising the drawbacks of being designated a coper. 'Stan is going back to Sydney tonight for maybe a week or two, to sort out work and his flat,' Evan went on, hoping to ease some of Liv's anxiety. 'Then he'll come back, probably permanently but if not, for long enough to stay with Mum and help out.'

Liv started to cry again. It was one of the few physical characteristics she and Gina had in common, this easy way with tears of distress or laughter. It used to embarrass the boys but they'd got used to it. These, however, were tears of relief, and she asked no further questions about money or what Stan would do about a job, usually major preoccupations for her.

'Gran, Mum wants you to go to Spain as planned. She thinks you'll be rested then for after the baby comes, and there isn't anything any of us can do beforehand. The doctors have got her all settled and you can FaceTime.'

'Sweetheart, I want to do whatever your mother wants. And if that would make her feel easier, then that's what I'll do. I've been thinking about it and I was expecting it. That it would be easier to have me out of the way so you don't have to worry about me too.' Evan recognised this as a double-edged sword of possible but not certain acquiescence but left it unchallenged. 'So when Stan gets back, he can look after Riley. And when I get back, I can make cups of tea in the middle of the night for your mum. If she needs me, promise you'll phone me and I'll charter a private jet,' she finished. He said he would and he meant it, knowing his grandmother didn't take a taxi without a full cost–benefit analysis and careful scrutiny for suitable train and bus alternatives.

*

'We need to go over the list again, Gina,' said Rosalie. 'See if anyone else has come to mind. Like when you put a crossword down and then come back to it, that elusive clue is suddenly obvious. Every single person since Monday 7 January until right now that you have had any contact with whatsoever. Then I need to check again if there are any weak links. You need to make a subject access request to Mr Grant and your GP to see if anyone we wouldn't expect has accessed your records. Our surveillance is solid but we've still got a few weeks to go.'

Rosalie's southern accent had prevailed over years in Manhattan, and Gina distracted herself from the fantastical notion of surveillance by setting Rosalie's words to a country and western tune in her head. 'Our surveillance is solid but we've still got a few weeks to go' fitted nicely into 'You picked a fine time to leave me, Lucille.'

'And if you think of anyone else after I've left today, text me immediately. Without delay. Gina?'

'Sorry. Yes. Subject access requests. I'll do it today.'

Chapter 11

There was a board bearing Stan's name as he came through Sydney arrivals; Rosalie had organised for him to go straight to the lawyers. 'Hello,' he said to the driver. 'I'm Stan Douglas.'

'G'day, Stan. I'm Ted. Ted Taylor. Taylor's Cars.' Ted looked past Stan.

'Only hand luggage. We can go straight on. They're expecting me. I know it's early.'

'There's a lady who said you'd give her a lift. I asked her to wait in the coffee shop,' said Ted. But Alison hadn't.

On the way into the city in the car, she told Stan she'd been to see Wilson, and the kennels said he was coming back this week to make arrangements. They shouldn't have told her, but anyway they had and here she was. They didn't know what day or flight, but she knew he'd be on BA so she had met every BA flight for the last three days. It was stalking, and that wasn't like Alison so he pre-empted what was coming.

'You're pregnant.' She nodded. 'It couldn't be an accident, Alison. We both know that.'

'I want a baby. I'm thirty-four. I love you, even though you don't love me. So I set out to get pregnant and I didn't tell you because you'd have finished it. And you finished it anyway, but I am at least pregnant.'

Ted came through on the intercom. 'We're here.'

'What do you want me to do?'

Stan looked at Alison. 'I've got a whole day of meetings I don't want to cancel but I could meet you about seven.' She nodded. 'Ted, please could you take Alison wherever she wants in between times. I expect to be finished here in a couple of hours, but I think you've got the itinerary.'

By the end of the day Stan had met the lawyers, met the media managers, met his line manager, fetched Wilson from the kennels for a few days, put his apartment on the market, and checked into his dog-friendly hotel. He showered and changed and went out to meet Alison, swerving with double jet lag between grumpy and euphoric.

By the end of the week, his company had agreed to him exercising his share options in return for a six-month consultancy agreement to hand over to a new person not yet identified, though Stan was fairly sure they wouldn't manage to recruit before his consultancy was up. That was a problem for another day. The lawyers were taking care of the paperwork, and he had sorted out the beginnings of a back story with 'Hit The Decks' Australia. He had paid his dog walker to look after Wilson for six months. And he had suggested to Alison that they go back to the UK via Los Angeles with a forty-eight-hour detour to Las Vegas to get married. They might as well.

*

It wasn't the wedding she would have chosen and it definitely wasn't the wedding – albeit a second – that her family would have chosen for her. But it was a wedding. They both accepted it might not work. If either of them had had more time to think, they might have done things very differently or not at all.

Alison had lived in Sydney all her life. Holidays were on the Gold Coast, apart from a trip to Bali for her first honeymoon and a cruise round New Zealand for her parents' ruby wedding anniversary. Stan didn't know what would happen about his plans for Scotland, but he thought they were delayed at worst. Despite the importance of their decisions that week, they talked about things very little. Talking wouldn't change reality. They were just going to give it a go. There was no sudden rush of fatherly joy for Stan, no blinding light that this was what he'd always wanted, sort of. He had a lot on his mind, and he wanted to support the mother of his child, and it seemed that giving it a go was the least imperfect solution. It saved a lot of confrontation and actual decisions – getting married aside – and that suited his mood.

The remainder of his time in Sydney, Stan had spent seeing his friends without Alison, explaining that she was pregnant, that they were going to get married in Las Vegas and give it a go, that he needed to move back to the UK for family reasons and his company had been very supportive. He promised to come back after the baby was born and wet its head. Despite it seeming an unromantic, even dispassionate, arrangement, it was at least grounded in authenticity. There was no pretence. Alison was pregnant. He was going to be a father. They were going to give it a go.

He had to tell his family as well, but figuring there was little left that could surprise them now, he just phoned Evan and said they'd be back on the twenty-fourth, the following Thursday morning, London time. His girlfriend's name was Alison, she was pregnant and they were going to stop in Las Vegas to get married. Evan was given the job of telling Liv.

Stan rang Gina. It was at this point that it all felt too much. Stan had always thought of the joy it would bring his mother if he ever did announce a baby was on the way; this wasn't how he'd imagined it.

'I didn't know, Mum. Alison wanted a baby and she's thirty-four. She didn't know I was planning to finish with her. She didn't even know that you were coming to visit me. God, that feels so far away now, can't believe it was only last week. So, not knowing any of this, she got pregnant and she didn't ask me for anything. I suggested we get married. I just think we need to see how it goes. She is nice. I think you'll like her. She's going to change her name so there will be another – well, not another but a new Mrs Douglas. She wants the baby to have my name. I'm not really bothered.'

'Congratulations. And to Alison. Sometimes the topsy-turvy things work out for the best.' His mother said more reassuring practical things and made a joke about not being able to find a wedding outfit anyway. Rather than seeing the best in things, she'd always been good at not seeing the worst. She didn't catastrophise – a word she didn't even recognise until a year or two ago. She'd had plenty of 'steady as she goes' practice when Stan and Evan were very young and had honed her skills in subsequent years. But Stan had a very definite impression that, in this, both he and his mother were in some hazy form of uncharacteristic laissez-faire, unable due to circumstance to sort things out as they might usually have done. So they chatted for ten minutes or so, mostly exchanging anecdotes about Wilson and Riley, and it didn't feel a bit like they both had major life events hurtling down their personal trajectories at an unstoppable, unthinkably fast pace.

Stan and Alison married in Las Vegas, with the photographer as one witness and the hotel manager the other. The reservations and photographer had been arranged by Rosalie. The couple did not discuss this milestone. Blank-eyed punters in the early-hours casinos spent more time talking about putting a two-dollar bet on red than Stan and Alison spent talking about their wedding. They were subdued, uneasy in each other's company. Alison was sixteen weeks pregnant, nauseous and tired from the travelling. She'd spent a good bit of the journey looking at Stan's uninterrupted flow of business-class champagne, simultaneously ashamed of and trying to contain her resentment. No wonder she was exhausted. For now, they ignored that they were newly-weds, ignored the magnitude of the circumstances and decisions of the last couple of weeks, overlooked Alison's dream of perfect nuptials second time around – another dress, off-white this time, friends, family, first dance but built to last – and slept.

Alison assured Stan she had enough savings to manage for a year if she didn't have to pay for rent and he told her not to worry about it. She had wanted to travel economy so Stan said his mother's PR company was organising the flights. At the very least, Alison would be entitled to a share of some of the money the extra frisson his own paternity would add to the 'Hit the Decks' exclusive. He'd have to ask Rosalie to explain it to her. But in the huge bed of their huge suite in the huge hotel on the Strip, they each slept on their own side. Stan dreamt, as he did from time to time, of Carran. He had been so sure she'd say yes when he gave her the engagement ring that he'd organised a surprise party for the following day. But she'd said no – not then, not ever, they just weren't right together – and she'd moved out. Moved, he found out a few weeks later, to South America to teach English and perfect her Spanish. Her mother wouldn't tell him where and although now, more than five years later, he no longer expected to hear from her, it didn't stop the dreams and the wondering.

*

For Brad, Wednesday was Roland (Lenny) Stevens. On a street in Hackney – red lines, bus lanes, relentless traffic and stopping confined to twenty minutes in the loading zones – sitting in an observation car would have been as subtle as a cactus in a tulip field. So Brad waited at the 41 bus stop, his bike tethered to a lamp post behind him. Ten or eleven buses had gone by before a woman came out of Roland's house, talking on the phone as she turned left towards the Overground. Ann, presumably: Roland's wife. Ninety minutes or so later, Brad watched Roland set the house alarm, double-lock the door and head to a coffee shop. Turning his navy waterproof inside-out, he put on a different pair of glasses, followed Roland in and ordered an almond milk flat white. The closest he could get to a full English was a ham and cheese croissant, so he had one of those. The coffee shop was between the morning and lunch rushes, the table next to Roland free. Brad took out his laptop. He needed to confirm something about this man that matched what Gina knew about Roland: either that his birthday was Valentine's Day, that he had been offered work as a trainee journalist for the BBC at some point, or had been to Es Cana in Ibiza in 1975. He almost didn't bother when the barista called out: 'Lenny, your toast's ready,' and Roland got up to fetch it, but he wanted to minimise any possibility of coincidence. And finish his breakfast.

This wasn't the Highlands. While Brad had never found it to be true that Londoners or, more accurately, people who lived in London, were unfriendly, they were less likely to strike up a conversation with a stranger unless they needed directions or to share an Uber when there was an incident on the Tube. He would only get one chance to get his confirmation without leaving an impression. Botched attempts would result either in a shutdown or Roland repeating the conversation to his friends and family: 'There was this odd bloke in Coffee Canteen today. Kept asking me when my birthday was and if I'd ever been to Ibiza.' The reason for tracing Roland had nothing to do with illegal or underhand activity – no drugs, no affair (or if there were, these were of no interest to Brad, at least not at this stage) – but keeping the investigation confidential and the candidate unaware were as important to Brad as if Roland was a Mr Big. He finished his coffee and stood up to leave, taking out his headphones, putting on his outdoor wear and shuffling his chair around Roland's table to make more room and very lightly bumping Roland's cup.

'Sorry, mate. Did it spill? Wasn't paying attention.' Brad removed one of his earbuds.

'No, it's fine,' replied Roland. 'It was nearly empty. What are you listening to?'

'Podcast. BBC. On technology and disease. Funny, a few years ago and we'd not heard the word podcast.'

'Certainly not when I started with them. Still had the test card.'

'You were there a while ago then?'

'Forty-five years ago. Stayed in journalism but went on to fishing magazines. Love the BBC, mostly. But it wasn't for me.'

Brad picked up his bike and cycled home. Easy enough to check out fishing magazines.

*

Although he had contacts he could pay, call in a favour from or chalk up a favour to, Brad liked to use those contacts only when essential – for speed or because there was no way he could find the information by other means. That generally meant investigations for financial services companies or high-profile clients of Rosalie's. He hadn't ruled out using them for Alan or Jerome, but was some way off that yet. He went back to his notes on Alan first.

It was straightforward to identify women who stood in the Holyrood elections in 1999, a much longer trawl to then check for any who had brothers called Alan or any variation of Alan. It took Brad the rest of Wednesday via registers, long-neglected sites, broken links and dead ends to find there were just two. Of these, an Alan Mackintosh had married a Sara McLeod on 29 May 1987. One of the witnesses was Joanna Mackintosh, who had stood for the elections – Alan's sister? Brad needed to confirm that; another hour or so of diligent research and it was done. That meant the other Alan – Dunbar – was less likely; he had apparently married a Theresa Cole in 1993 with no subsequent divorce and no record of Theresa's death, but

211

worth eliminating to be sure. It was past 8 p.m. so Brad found something to eat, filed his report to Rosalie and spent some time reviewing a request for his services from a major bank.

*

The hospital was quiet in the evenings, routine cases having been discharged, with only bed-rest maternity patients and those needing a professional eye kept on them remaining. Anything really worrying had been transferred over the way before 7 p.m. and the start of the night shift. Gina was alone, thinking about her latest scan which had confirmed thirty-three weeks with the baby looking fine. Concern was expressed about the quality of her uterus and birth canal and her ability to deliver. A Caesarean was confirmed, not that this was a surprise to anyone. Gerald did not want Barney's birth to be an emergency. The baby was over two kilogrammes, nearly fully grown and all his internal organs were developed sufficiently that he would be able to manage on his own. Gerald wanted to deliver at thirty-six and a half weeks, considering that the optimum. He needed a few more days to get his medical team in place.

Patient confidentiality meant Rosalie was less worried about breaches in the hospital setting than elsewhere, but that was a bit like being less worried about jumping without a parachute at five thousand feet rather than thirty thousand. Gina didn't worry about what Rosalie was doing. Trust and her other preoccupations freed her up from that completely.

Rosalie had organised on-call cars for Evan, Liv, Sandra, and Greg, and for Stan and Alison when they arrived back. She found some help with childcare for Evan and a private midwife for Alison. Reasonable expenses were being covered by 'Hit The Decks' and the foundation; in the world of world exclusives, 'reasonable expenses' included private midwives and twenty-four-hour chauffeur services.

*

'Have a nice evening.'

The security guards had never spoken to Graham before, a nod maybe but not a spoken exchange of greetings or farewells.

'Are you new?' Graham asked, succeeding, he thought, in keeping a tone of polite, professional interest.

'I am, started this week. Better hours than where I was before. And not so many fights! Have a nice evening, Mr Neville.'

Graham got into his car on the passenger side and put the seat back down. He lay, semi-recumbent, not sure if he was hiding or recovering. Why did the guard use his name? How did he know it? Was it coincidence or were they on to him? On to what? He hadn't done anything. But extra security – that had never happened before. They did get some celebs here giving birth and they often brought their own people with earpieces and walkie-talkies, but this new guard felt different. Security had never spoken to Graham before. Was he warning him to have a nice evening because it might be his last night of freedom?

Chapter 12

'Gray, have you got a sec?' No-one had ever called him Gray before he came to work at Valley but all his hospital colleagues did. Graham was surprised how much a part of the team it made him feel. Only friends would call you 'Gray'.

One time, a few years back, he'd brought some cannabis in from Amsterdam for his then girlfriend for her twenty-first. He spotted a sniffer dog just before he went through customs, flushed the cannabis and crept through the green channel with liquid legs, a volcano in his stomach and fear all over his face. Those dogs were smart – would they be able to smell the traces? Was it too much for 'personal use'? He could say it had been planted. Once through, attracting no interest canine or otherwise, he'd bought two cans of vodka tonic from Marks and drunk them in the taxi home while phoning the girlfriend to break things off. If she needed cannabis smuggled, the relationship was going nowhere.

'Have you got a minute? Now?'

Amal wasn't Heathrow customs but Gray felt the same disabling dread. He inched into her office as if every step incriminated him.

'Just wanted to check why you accessed the records for Virginia Flowers the day after her scan,' said Amal, clearly with other things on her mind and expecting a straightforward explanation.

'Virginia Flowers? Did I? Can I check?'

'No need, you did,' she replied. 'Why?' His supervisor looked at him directly.

'I mean, can I check which patient she is?' said Gray.

'You don't remember?' If he said he didn't remember that would, literally, be unbelievable in the sense that no one, least of all Amal, would believe him – not unbelievable like Gina Flower's pregnancy was unbelievable. But if he said he did remember, why had he asked the question?

'No, well, yes, of course. I just wasn't sure of her name. I thought her, the patient I'm thinking of, had a shorter first name. Jane?'

'She's known as Gina,' said Amal. 'Why did you access her notes after the scan?'

'It was so unusual. Sort of training, really.' Gray was very glad of his prepared excuse. 'I wondered if I'd been wrong, caused a hoo-ha about nothing. I knew straight away I hadn't because Mr Grant came in, but later I wanted to see if it looked different to anything else. Any other pregnancy scan. Anything for the future. To learn about.' He pictured himself standing by a burning building with a can of petrol and a box of matches and the police saying 'How did that start?'

'You should have got me to sign if off,' said Amal. 'I'll do it now. Next time, check first. Amazing case, though. Poor woman. Her womb'll end up on a few training courses, I expect.'

Hunched over the toaster in the staff kitchen a few minutes later, Gray seriously considered if his career as a mole was over. Maybe he just wasn't espionage material. And he'd never make friends in prison, not these sort of friends anyway. He searched 'sell your story'. You could contact a journalist anonymously; just fill in an online form, few details and they'd let you know if they were interested. Protect their sources, they said. So they'd protect him. Although he knew you shouldn't believe everything you read in the papers and maybe that meant this too. Still. Anonymously. He set up a new email account, filled out the form and chewed slowly on his toast while he talked himself through it.

*

Brad's Spanish wasn't fluent but it wasn't far off, what with his Florida connection and deep love of rural Spain. His French, however, had been left at school, so he was grateful the librarian in the Bibliothèque municipale de Lyon, Yvette, wanted to practise her English and was well-disposed to help Brad find his great uncle Jerome, if he was still alive. Brad explained about his terminally ill grandmother searching for her youngest brother, lost years ago when she moved to England on marriage. French municipal records, while legendary in their detail, were held on a town or regional level, not on a searchable national database, so Brad had to start in Jerome's place of birth. But from an approximate year of birth and two possible dates, a known marriage and the name of his spouse followed by a divorce, Yvette established that a Jerome Pertus, born 4 July 1951, married to and divorced from Nicole Maradis was on the electoral register for the Vieux Lyon district, St-Georges section of Lyon's fifth arrondissement. The section comprised a manageable, for Brad, number of streets, well under half of which were residential. Pertus: Matisse? Brad considered asking Sophia to run Pertus by Gina to see if it dislodged a nugget from her memory, but with the birthday matching, he decided instead to first try to find another piece of evidence.

Residential addresses were not published with the electoral register. Brad was mapping out in his head how long it would take him to check out every home in every one of those streets when Yvette said she could check the records for management committees of apartment blocks, which typically listed all the residents, to see if his great-uncle was mentioned. A Jerome Pertus was the chair of the residents' committee of an apartment building not far from the centre of town: quite close, in fact, to the municipal library. A ten-minute walk, a check on the doorbell names and Brad had an apartment number. Sometimes you just got lucky.

He went back to his hotel for some more desk-based research and to think. Two hours of searching online got him only a little further: one photo in *Le Progrès* of a Jerome Pertus presenting an award at the Chambre de commerce et d'industrie Lyon Métropole, and one mention among alumni of a mid-level wine master course. Both straws blowing the right way, but no more than straws.

He decided to break in to Jerome's apartment and look for something concrete. Breaking and entering was something he did no more than once or twice a year and only when his pre-conditions were met: no criminal edge to the investigation; no reason for the suspect to be more wary of burglary than the general populace; ability to prepare; and low to theoretical chance of being caught.

Brad stayed in Lyon two more days: Friday surveying Jerome's building and environs; and Saturday mostly waiting for Jerome to go out. He would only need fifteen minutes in the apartment. Once in, he photographed a Renault pension plan and then waited outside until Jerome came back from lunch to take a full-face picture in the hope that Gina would be able to identify him from that. He was confident in his work, but he would need Rosalie's team to be able to answer 'How did you know it was me?' without relying on the pension plan. Brad was back in west London by 10 a.m. on Sunday. He filed his report to Rosalie and spent the rest of the day playing online poker.

*

Sophia could suspend judgement on her usual interviewees and look instead to understand. In her experience, and contrary to much received wisdom, understanding did not lead automatically to forgiveness, although it did often reinforce her anger and despondency about systemic pathways to violence, crime, and society's reluctance to tackle root causes. That was in her other life, which she had temporarily suspended for Rosalie's generous day rate and a taxi account. She found, however, she could approach her work for, essentially, a PR agency, with similar dispassion. Rosalie had talked her through the media plan that Gina had agreed. Any unease Sophia might have had about exploiting the birth of a baby had been dispelled. It was hard to see how else Gina would provide for a child for twenty or so years; selling her story was her best bet and, from what Sophia had picked up so far, it looked like a decent bet.

The second stage of Sophia's research with Gina was much less inviting than the first. Establishing the details Gina could remember about her lovers that might help Brad had been straightforward: dates, legal relationships, names, facts. Not feelings, sexual preferences, locations and frequency. Under Professor Solo's supervision, Sophia had interviewed some deeply unpleasant people, and in the last year she had been asked to focus her research on murderers. Examining childhood circumstances was a well-worn research path; the perspective of their physical medical history less so. She was able to talk with her supervisor about the horrors, the high too many of them got from violence. That high sustained some throughout their sentences, reliving the terror they'd inflicted in the wee small hours over twenty years' incarceration. There were two things these remorseless souls had in common, she thought: vanity, and a good memory, both of which enabled everyday deceptions on the path to fulfilment. 'We had no idea,' said the mother, the colleague, the neighbour to the press, and more often than not they didn't confront it at the time, thought Sophia. But afterwards, after the incontrovertible proof – usually a confession, because that way lay the only glory left open to the killer – the mother, the colleague, the neighbour, they understood they had known. They rarely recovered from that retrospective knowledge. But at the time, no. The soft doubts they'd had, when they saw grainy pictures or read about bus routes the suspect used, were explained away until they knew they'd known. How useful her research would prove in the end wouldn't be clear for some years yet. And then there were the ones who were sorry. What did they have in common, medically?

Sophia wrote her thoughts in a notebook she kept for the purpose of resetting her mind. She used it for every post-visit write-up, and when she'd been reflecting too much on the mayhem of psyche that came with her research. It helped her to rationalise. The world was not all bad, although she had slowly come to the view that many of her interviewees normalised horror to the point they might be evil. That was not the conclusion she had expected to reach when she started her PhD, but it was where she'd ended up. She hoped her funding would be extended but she hadn't yet worked out what for. Sophia shook her head to clear away the bad guys, knowing that she spent too much time mulling over them, and got back to thinking about Gina.

Rosalie had explained the longer term media plan: in-depth interviews with Gina for 'Hit the Decks', and an interview with each of the living candidates before and after the father was identified – if he was. Then there would be interviews with the sons, Gina's mother, brother and friend. These participants would all be paid a six-figure sum, with more if Rosalie could secure a TV drama. Rosalie's lawyers, using the details that Brad had confirmed, were going to write to all the candidates and ask for their cooperation. If they agreed to an initial exploratory meeting, Rosalie would pay for them to consult a lawyer independently and, if all went well, a journalist, perhaps more accurately a content producer, would take their stories.

The trickiest legal bit, Rosalie had said, was how to deal with identification or, indeed, anonymity. The lawyers were working on that. If the key players could be identified by people who knew them from the information that would be part of the 'Hit the Decks' story, then the cat would not just be out of the bag to the mainstream press, it would be running amok, scratching and clawing at Gina and those closest to her.

Sophia arrived at Valley to see Mr Howard ('Gerald. Call me Gerald') who wanted to brief her again, this time on the medical and what they euphemistically called 'social' details.

'Sophia, I need to know the answers to some questions that will be difficult to ask and Gina is likely to find difficult or upsetting to answer, if only because of the length of time since the events. One important point is that you do not record 'Not sure' as a definite answer, but it does need to be recorded. So, if the question was, to use an off-piste example, 'Did the woman's coat have buttons?' and the answer is 'Yes, I think so', what you need to record as the answer is 'Don't know' and then in the free textbox, put down how sure Gina is about the buttons and anything else she can remember. Using scales of one to ten can be helpful. Asking what type of buttons, how many, were they the same colour as the coat – all of these follow-ups can help us work out the probability of the recollection being correct.

'We are hoping to ask the candidates themselves about their physicality, so for Georges Flowers and Douglas only you need to cover the following with Gina: circumcision, erectile problems, and general physical and mental health. I have a guideline questionnaire.' Sophia thought 'guideline questionnaire' was the most helpful and welcome phrase she had ever heard.

*

Stan and Alison – Mr and Mrs Douglas – arrived to see Gina when she wasn't expecting them. She'd wanted to be on better form to meet Alison for the first time, and she was irritated with Stan for not checking with her first, not that it was taking much to irritate her in these final days of pregnancy. It was 2 p.m. and she'd just finished a perfectly nice lunch of salmon and salad that Sandra had brought in. Gerald had called in that morning as well, gently pressing her belly, taking blood and her temperature, which she was reasonably sure he hadn't done himself for quite a while until the last couple of weeks. He'd wanted her to have another scan the next day and she had to temper her fear that too many scans weren't good for the baby against his absolute assurances that they had no adverse effect whatsoever.

Sandra had asked her if she wanted to talk about it.

'Do you mean to you, or do I want a therapist?'

'Either,' Sandra replied. 'You can start with me if you like, or I can give you a list of recommended therapists. Or your PR lady will. I'm sure a shrink-type would be considered a reasonable expense.'

'What do you think about adoption?'

'I think,' said Sandra slowly, 'that if you decide on adoption, the baby will be absolutely fine. Right as rain. You might take a while to adjust. So might your family. And you need to consider if you will keep in contact.' She stopped but Gina knew she hadn't finished.

'I'm not really qualified to talk to you about adoption but—'

'You can find me someone who is.' Gina's interruption was brusque and tetchy, both uncalled for. Hormonal mood swings were doing a lot of heavy lifting in explaining Gina's scratchiness.

'Yes. And if it is a live consideration for you, perhaps do it soon.' Sandra stopped again and Gina didn't interrupt this time. 'In normal circumstances, I can't see how it would get easier to place the babe for adoption as time goes on, but in your situation, it might be different.'

Gina saw what her friend was trying to convey. Coping with a six-week-old baby screaming four times a night with help and family was one thing, but when he was a fractious, all-day-long toddler and the novelty had worn off, it might be easier then to give him away. Except she'd know him and – if the baby books were right – he'd know she was his mother. But what if Sandra was right? With the project money she could afford help but the responsibility, the lifelong responsibility, would be hers. Maybe the father would help. If he wasn't dead. Would she want that? And if she didn't, would she be able to refuse? And when she talked to herself about lifelong, did she mean her life – maybe twenty years if she was lucky – or Barney's?

'I need to think about it.'

Sandra kissed her, held her tight, said something kind and left. Gina continued thinking about adoption, which led, as so much seemed to these days, to her starting to cry. She texted Sandra to apologise for the scratchiness and got a blowing-a-kiss emoji back. Then reception phoned to say her son was here. They hadn't added 'with his wife' and Stan didn't have the good sense to come in by himself first and prepare Gina to meet her.

Alison came in first. 'Hallo, Mrs Flowers. It's lovely to meet you. I'm Alison, Alison Smith. Now Alison Douglas. How are you?'

'Alison, hello. Fine, Alison, thank you. Stan didn't say he was coming. You were coming. I hope you had a good trip. England in January is a bit of a contrast from Sydney, I expect.'

'It is. But I've been to the shops and I'm all kitted out for it. Fleece and waterproof, boots, sweaters, that sort of thing. And you need a flannie in Sydney in the winter so I dug out a few things to bring with me. Not as cold as Melbourne. Melbourne gets really cold, as cold as England they say.' Because there was nothing more pressing than the weather.

Stan wasn't given to constant chit-chat and Gina wondered how on earth he would manage married to Alison, who seemed to talk like the world would implode if she left a few moments silence. How did they get together? How had she not driven him away on their first date?

'I'm sorry,' she said, as if Gina's thoughts had appeared in a bubble over her head. 'I'm nervous. Would you like to see my wedding ring? It's beautiful. I chose it, but Stan bought it. In Las Vegas. We got married in Las Vegas. We're both pregnant. I mean you and me, not me and Stan. Stan's not pregnant. Obviously.' Alison looked out of the window in an effort to stop talking.

Gina nodded. This was not what she'd had in mind when she'd asked Stan to come back. Neither had he, but that didn't make Gina any less irritated. Two weeks ago, she'd been almost on her way to Australia to visit her son and the only worry she had was her dog's arthritis. Now she felt like a has-been in a mediocre sitcom. If Gina had been tired, scratchy and a bit overwhelmed before they arrived, she was exhausted, grumpy and flattened after these three minutes.

They stayed for half an hour. Stan had arranged to view two flats within five minutes' walk of Gina's house, after which he and Evan were meeting with Rosalie. Gina wanted to know if Alison was going too but didn't like to ask, so asked instead if Amelie was going.

'No.' said Stan. 'Rosalie did say to bring her, but she's not back from the Riviera or wherever her current maison fabulosa is. I'm not sure she thinks Evan has got the whole thing wrong or if she thinks he's having some sort of breakdown.'

'You'd like to think that would be enough to bring her back,' Gina said, then remembered about Alison and sighed at herself. She didn't want to share her mixed feelings about a daughter-in-law in front of a stranger, never mind that the stranger was also now her daughter-in-law. And seemed to have a head full of clotted cream.

*

Brad's long haul of searching online for Alans (and Allans, Aluns and the rest) that met most of the profile – eliminating and prioritising, concentrating on those in the UK, checking them all as far as possible for siblings, approximate age and location – had brought him to the two men left on his spreadsheet. There was no alternative but fieldwork. A morning's work scrubbed out Alan Henry Dunbar, head teacher of a Brighton primary school who was, Brad noted from a social media page, a shade over six foot four. It seemed overwhelmingly likely Gina would have remembered and mentioned a height in the top percentile so Brad's earlier working assumption that the other Alan – Mackintosh – was indeed his man seemed ever more sound. Joanna Mackintosh, Alan's sister, had narrowly missed being elected to Holyrood in 1999 for the Labour Party but was of no further assistance in tracking down Alan twenty years later. Brad drove halfway from Brighton to Leeds, staying overnight at a service station motel and arriving at the end of the M1 mid-morning.

He had very little with which to confirm Alan's identity except the names of his sister and his wife, no death or divorce having been recorded. Plus that he'd worked with Gina in Southall in the late 1990s in some sort of fledgling tech sales role.

He had found what he believed must be the right Alan's address, a whole floor of a converted Victorian building in a mid-size, tourist hotspot village about ten miles north of Leeds city centre. There was an open-all-day even in January pub opposite and Brad spent the afternoon there, ordering coffee and sparkling mineral water with lemon at half-hour intervals, and food around 5 p.m. The street outside was surprisingly busy and fortunately well-lit from dusk, sparing Brad a wait in his car. Anyone coming in and out of the building he noted. All were too young to be Alan or his wife, until just after six, when a top spec small Mercedes pulled into the shared drive. Brad was across the road in less time than it took the driver to gather her bag and phone and slot her key in the lock. From behind the hedge and with the help of automatic security beams and the light of the porch, he could see the woman would be about the right age for Alan's wife. She carried a branded well-constructed paper bag with rope-type handles: Mackintosh Munro; clothes, shoes, accessories. But whatever the bag contained it wasn't clothes, shoes and accessories. More like crisps, wine and a takeaway.

Mackintosh Munro was in York with one of those window displays that made passers-by feel that just by entering they'd become elegant and slim. It opened at 10 a.m. on weekdays. Brad guessed the clients were mostly locals, with tourists adding a layer of additional income to the regular purchases of women and their husbands looking for conservative chic. By a quarter past ten he had changed into one of those husbands, and not much after eleven he emerged with a plain navy handbag for his wife's birthday, several hundred pounds lighter and knowing that the owner, Sara Mackintosh née Munro, was indeed married to Alan, whose sister Joanna had stood unsuccessfully for the first intake of MSPs. Lynne had worked at Mackintosh Munro since it opened, speaking fondly of her boss's sister-in-law. Joanna was very supportive of the business and came down from Edinburgh a couple of times a year to refresh her work wardrobe, and for the odd special occasion purchase. Lynne knew Joanna much better than she knew Alan, who worked away a lot, although he was getting ready to retire. Sara was planning a cruise for them, meaning Lynne would need to sort out a carer for her mother for a few weeks to cover the extra hours.

Brad admired the beauty of the bag, its plainness really a showcase for the designer's skill with design detail. A few days after he got back home he dropped in to see John and gave the bag to Belinda. She knew an original when she saw one and wondered uncomfortably if it had fallen off the back of a designer handbag lorry. She'd never thought Brad was the type. Sensing her hesitancy, he showed her the receipt and said he'd bought it for a girlfriend who'd dumped him the night he was going to give it to her and couldn't now take it back to Leeds and anyway, the shop didn't do refunds. He swerved Bel's enquiries about the girlfriend with an ease born of practice and she didn't quite have the nerve to press him.

*

Months later, Gina acknowledged how close she had come to backing out of the project. If it hadn't been for the rapport with Sophia, who knows? Maybe the money alone would have been enough. But then again. It felt to Gina like Sophia appreciated how hard it was to spread out your life for other people to pick over. One million pounds was a lot, of course it was, and the baby would need it. But still. Sometimes it was only the thought of the alternative – going back to bookkeeping while caring for a child – that sustained her on the project, kept her selling her life. And persuading others to sell theirs made hers more valuable. The grubby sheen of a well-stocked bank account was seductive. Gina had often thought that while she would do a lot of unpalatable things if her family were in danger, money alone would not tempt her to go against her conscience or what she saw as the proper order of things. It seemed now she might have been wrong.

The interconnectedness of the contract terms scared her: if one father backed out, the consequences were such-and-such; if Gina herself backed out, ten times such-and-such. So she thought the best thing was to not just keep going but give it everything she could, taking comfort from the old saying about fish and chip wrappers being yesterday's news and not thinking too much about the depthless, infinite storage of online media which would be available to a curious, anxious or angry Barney to trawl from teenage years on.

'Let's take the candidates in chronological order again,' Sophia suggested.

As she talked, Gina wondered who she wanted to be the father. At least her memories provided no reason to be fearful of any of them. It would be easiest if the baby turned out to be a straightforward full brother to Stan and Evan. There wouldn't be a new set of relatives, curious, loving, horrified or indifferent. Given how inherently tricky the paternal situation was anyway, she came to realise that she really hoped George Douglas was the father. Anything that made the boys' lives easier, all three of them, and that would be the single biggest thing, although it would mean Barney never knowing his father. But he would have two full big brothers.

Her friend Maisie had introduced Gina to George Douglas, maybe with matchmaking in mind, maybe not. Maisie and her husband were moving to Hong Kong or somewhere and this was the leaving dinner. It was on the boring side of sedate, a bit like Maisie's husband, Gina had thought, and then she got stuck next to a man talking about bridges. He was serious and handsome so she gave him her number because she had to do something. She couldn't mourn Eddie for ever. There must be some reliable, nice men out there. George was a reliable nice man and when he'd phoned to ask her out, she said yes.

She hoped the father wouldn't be Eddie. Eddie had not broken her heart beyond repair but he had certainly badly damaged it, put it on emotional bypass for a long while. She had never really squared with herself how he could leave her without a word, not at the time or in the weeks afterwards. They had been girlfriend and boyfriend for nearly two years. She had been exclusive and had thought he was too. When, ages later, the news began to filter back that he'd got into medical school at the last minute and had gone up to Glasgow to prepare, there was no mention from mutual connections about another girl. It was years before she heard that he'd qualified, and several more before she found out he'd married. She had been in love with him and she had known that at the time. They didn't live together because she was spending time in Paris for a French company she was doing the UK bookkeeping for, though she lived in Cambridge where she was studying part-time. Eddie worked in Exeter on a constantly changing shift pattern. Neither of them had much money. They spent two or three days together every two or three weeks. They talked from pay phones every few days. He made her laugh, said lots of nice things, but she never really got to meet his family or many of his friends.

And then he left without a backward glance and not even for some love of his life. She sometimes suspected – and she had thought about it too much, far more than it warranted – that might have been easier. Easier, that is, than her just not being worth the bother of a conversation. It haunted her for years, all the years with George Douglas, all the years until Jerome, like a deep shadow on her psyche when it came to giving of herself. It carved out from her soul the ability to trust, to take people – not only men, but people – as they seemed in their dealings with her. The question of when would they leave and what wouldn't they say was always there. Whatever she did about anything, except at work, wasn't going to be enough. She wasn't worth it. So she hoped Barney's father wouldn't be Eddie.

In second place, after George One, she hoped the father would be George Flowers. He was a lovely man and she'd loved him. It would be complicated. He had four sisters back in Miami who would want to welcome their beloved late brother's son, a brand new nephew, into their lives and into their church, even in such inconvenient, biblically speaking, circumstances. G2 had not been evangelical, but he had been a true believer and a regular churchgoer. Gina would go with him occasionally because she liked the choir. His funeral had been at the Metropolitan Tabernacle, a huge church on the roundabout at Elephant and Castle, where he'd attended when he first arrived in England. He was an American very much at home in London. She decided if the baby was his she would have him baptised at the Tabernacle and explain to their son later that he could make up his own mind. And she'd ask Amanda, George Two's eldest sister and still one of her closest friends to be godmother.

She was getting ahead of herself, but it felt sensible to prepare. These administrative tasks, still very abstract, prevented her thinking about motherhood itself. She did not want the grind, the inability to just go out, the expense, the worry, the nappies, the lack of sleep, the responsibility. She didn't want any of it. It was easier for her, a non-believer, to think about who would be godmother.

231

Gina had hardly known Roland, never found out much about him in those few sunny days in Ibiza, so he could take whatever place was left. Jerome, not much more but she recalled him as being self-centred and a bit patronising, or at least as much as you could tell in knowing someone for less than two weeks. He was also very French in the best ways: attractive, attentive – a hard trick to pull off if you're also self-centred – charming but not oily, well read, a great cook, arty, and something of a puzzle, moving from mechanic to salesman to entrepreneur, as she vaguely recalled. She'd thought he was a fantastic lover, and he probably was, but then along came Alan.

Alan instantly replaced Eddie as last on the list. She did not want to look at her child and be reminded of that night every time. It would just feel inappropriate. She would have to discolour her memories, make them less intense, sanitise her too vivid recollections. So not Alan. But she was curious to find out if he remembered, and if he did, did he remember like she did or was that his normal?

*

Over the next few days, Sophia and Gina continued to pick over the carcasses of Gina's romantic past. It was a surprisingly varied narrative but nothing nasty, nothing forced, nothing rough. Which from a 'find-the-father' view was a good thing because Sophia could not see why anyone on the wrong side of that question would want to participate in airing it, or at least airing it truthfully, decades later.

Gina had been in love with Eddie and George Flowers; she had married George Douglas while subconsciously on the hunt for a safe haven after Eddie and was very fond of him. She and Roland/Lenny had used each other in Ibiza to prove the point of that sort of rite of passage holiday, which was to have sex in the sunshine. Gina was doubtful it actually happened, though it did come close, maybe close enough to inseminate her. The word 'inseminate' always made her think of pigs but she couldn't remember why. She had liked him well enough and would probably have seen him after they got back if he'd asked, but he didn't and she had been fine with that, if slightly surprised at the time. 'We were both inept and I remember thinking he had something else on his mind,' she had told Sophia.

Then she fell in love with Eddie, married George Douglas on a long rebound, regained something of herself a few years after George's death with a full-on week with Jerome in Paris, and came to love George Flowers very much. After having thought she'd settled for companionship and financial security, it turned out he was good fun as well and most things she wanted in a husband. She had been sad after his death in a different way from George Douglas: sad for herself rather than for the loss of her sons' father. That might be a tricky one to navigate with Stan and Evan if they ever came to know it. But the defining moment of Gina's personal life – probably her inner life as a whole, in fact – was the very short time she spent with Alan. Sophia hoped she herself might be so lucky one night.

Sophia noted and classified the physical and technical details of these relationships, gently and painstakingly working through Gerald's questionnaire, coming back to bits that seemed too much at first pass. She took care of Gina's memories as you would precious fragile objects: her grief and brief recollections of humour or joy, her squeamishness in talking about preferences and difficulties. She wrote her report over two long days, revisiting her laptop notes and recordings, and checking in with her senses. Gerald seemed to think it was good enough.

So, in order of preference: George Douglas, George Flowers, Jerome, Roland/Lenny, Eddie, Alan.

*

Gray now thought he had enough pictures and enough what he thought of as 'human interest' details to contact the journalist from the magazine: 'Goss and Celebs Behind The Scenes!' Not by phone, he'd no idea where there might be a phone box never mind a working one. Not from any device he owned. He considered buying a burner but didn't trust himself to chuck it away. And somehow he thought if he just bought a SIM and put it in his phone, they might be able to trace him. Whether 'they' was the hospital, the police, the magazine or Gina's security he hadn't articulated to himself. So a pc in an internet café – he'd been quite surprised they were still a thing – and a webchat. He got the bus to Oxford figuring less CCTV than a train station and Oxford would be a good place for anonymity, although he didn't take off his beanie or scarf the whole trip.

It took 8 minutes to agree a price; if everything he'd said was true and he had the material he said he had, they'd pay him £100k. He had three days to meet Simone - she'd come wherever he wanted - and provide some proof to be going on with. And a name.

Chapter 13

Nick Hewen waited for Rosalie in his members' club in Soho. There was a garden and he could safely leave his belongings to go to the bar or the bathroom without gratingly asking a stranger if they minded, just for a few minutes, keeping an eye on them. He'd trusted someone in a café before now and both his laptop and the stranger were gone when he got back. He also liked the club because it was a social enterprise, so the hefty membership fee and price of a coffee felt less like a rip-off and more like a donation. He didn't donate, by and large, and wasn't a figure on the legal circuit of fundraisers but he did support, over the long term, charities he thought were doing good work. It helped him square his comfortable lifestyle with the less fortunate circumstances of those he passed every day on his way around London. He knew he could do more without even noticing the financial impact, but he wanted to ensure money he channelled into good causes was effectively used, and he was going to address this when he retired. At least that's what he told himself and his friends who sometimes had a dig about his apparent lack of largesse. The notion that he would get round to altruism someday was another layer in his privilege comfort blanket.

Nick hadn't made it the hard way to success in his profession. His route had been smoothed and steered by his mother (a QC), father (a Circuit Judge), an exemplary education and an endowment to see him through studies here and overseas, and various services to iron his shirts and collect his suits from the cleaners. He'd seen solicitor work as more lucrative, though less prestigious, than the bar or judiciary, and he'd been right. He came from monied stock, and had consolidated and expanded that legacy far enough to be sounded out by private agents as to whether he had thought of relocating to Monaco. He hadn't and he wouldn't. He believed paying tax was a public good and would, in time, be looking at doing a high-profile bit of pro bono. Eco warriors taking on a global giant maybe. Not yet. Soon, but not yet.

Rosalie, his most interesting client – and among his most lucrative – came through to the small private lounge he'd booked, divesting her winter outerwear elegantly and without missing a step. She wasn't conventionally pretty, not striking or stop-in-the-street attractive. She had a warm and welcoming face, which Nick thought must be a big help in PR. She was elegant and homely at the same time. She exuded trustworthiness. And was nice, as far as he could tell based on all his dealings with her. He stood and shook her hand. Kissing clients, even his longstanding and favourite ones, was not in Nick's repertoire.

A few days ago she had called and provided the headlines, much as if delivering a lunchtime news bulletin. Today's meeting was to work out the legal position for what happened next. As part of the agreement they would sign, all the candidates would have their own legal advisor, paid for by the project, and Nick would tell them what sort of expertise to look for in a lawyer. (In the event, all of them came back to him asking for a recommendation, and he had given them all the same list of ten, with the caveat that each advisor would only take one client). Four coffees, a large bottle of water and some small plates later, he and Rosalie had final drafts of the various contracts needed to move things forward. They slid gently into talking about Gina.

'She's reasonably resilient, Nick, but she's not made of steel. God help her, she's pregnant at sixty-two.'

'I'm a few years younger than her. I would be horrified to be having a child. And I'm a man.' He paused. Saying he knew how someone felt was something he never did because no one did, ever. Shared similar experience might give someone insight to emotional pain or how to cope or strategies for middle of the night desperation, but it couldn't be how someone else felt. He considered if there was a potentially sexist angle to what he'd just said. He wasn't sure exactly what it might be, but it was always best to be on the lookout before it became an unwelcome diversion.

'I might not understand much but I am really sympathetic to her dilemma.' He considered that again once he'd said it out loud and it passed muster. He had no idea where Rosalie lay on the political or social issues spectrums, and while he wouldn't pander to anything he found completely unpalatable, he wouldn't lightly or gratuitously offend a client either. But saying nothing about everything wasn't an option; lawyers needed to have opinions, give advice, take a side (a welcome plus if it turned out genuinely to be the client's), and all that came with its own risks.

'She does need the money,' Rosalie said, 'and while she might sell her soul for it if that was the only way to provide for Barney – the baby – we won't ask her to. All we need are honest accounts from everyone and access to their stories. And, ideally, my genius husband to identify the father and for the father to be the man the public likes best.' They'd worked before on client image but it was often in the context of damage limitation. The soft-sell stories featuring beautifully staged pictures of beautiful people in beautiful houses were the territory of glossy magazines. Rosalie's work was much more subtle: so subtle that the media, and especially the public, didn't realise it was going on at all and her clients usually had no idea of the extent of background work. Gina certainly didn't. But she and Nick had managed the participants of a few high-stakes reality TV shows together and knew the territory. 'But, if push comes to shove, it's Gina and the baby first.'

'Understood.' One of the things Nick liked best about working for Rosalie was that she didn't need to talk – or need him to talk – all the time. She understood the place of a reflective silence.

'The candidates, on the face of it, seem decent enough. Our challenge in the research for the programme is going to be to mingle the science and the emotion, find the red herrings, the meaty backstory. If they each know who the father is before we've captured their reaction to maybe being the father, then it will be different. Lesser. So they won't because we won't find out until Gina has had a chance to adjust.' Nick nodded. 'Unless the father is one of the husbands, in which case it's different.' Rosalie continued. Quite different scenarios. So good to have you on board.' she finished.

*

Alison wasn't driving Stan away exactly, but she was irritating him. She had not been able to stop the nervous talking she'd developed seemingly while coming through immigration. It

238

either hadn't existed in Sydney or he hadn't been around her enough to notice.

She had not told her own family about Gina. The effort felt just too much to handle on WhatsApp. Her mother rang her daily and if the time difference had been less of a headache it would probably have been even more frequent. She wanted Alison to come back to Australia to have the baby and if that meant leaving her so-called husband, so be it. Alison's mother could not see how what she called a shotgun wedding would work, and somewhat illogically reminded Alison nearly every call that she'd always said Stan wasn't the type to commit. 'We're married, Mum.' Alison said. 'He's committed that much. And getting married was his idea.' Alison's mother lived in a small church-going community around four hundred miles from Sydney. While she wouldn't admit to being grateful that her daughter had at least got married before giving birth, she grudgingly admitted Stan was likely to shoulder his financial responsibilities, assuming he came back to Sydney and went back to that good job of his. Not messed about in England trying some experiment of working for himself with a baby on the way. Her mother's contempt for Stan was gradually fraying the long-distance bond with Alison.

Alison had given Stan a tidied up version of this and asked what he thought. He said her relationship with her family was entirely up to her and, given the crazy events of the previous two weeks, he understood her mother's concerns. If she did go home for the birth, he'd come over a month or so before the due date and stay until Alison was settled, but that wasn't his first choice. He was going to come back to the UK in the short term, but would consider New

239

Zealand after he'd finished in Scotland. If he finished in Scotland. He had told her about Scotland on the long flight from Vegas, and how he planned to get his new business started. He thought he could be pretty much be ready to move in the autumn. He said if she wanted to stay in Australia, they'd figure out the travel arrangements and visiting. He couldn't be more reasonable given that, as Alison admitted to herself – and what everyone else would be thinking – she'd got pregnant despite knowing not only that it wasn't what Stan wanted, but also she'd told him it wouldn't happen.

Stan didn't mind Sydney, although he didn't actively like it, preferred but didn't worship London and was indifferent to most Scottish cities. But he loved the coasts of Scotland, west and east. His and Evan's father came from Nairn near Inverness, and he and Evan had gone there most summers on holiday with their paternal grandparents who, having moved south for work decades before, never stopped missing the seductive Highland combination of water and mountains. Gina had liked their father's three sisters, who lived in the Highlands. Stan was a fairly solitary, somewhat lonely boy, Evan being much more sociable and friendly, less dogged by a constant fear of loss. Stan liked being able to cycle from one house to the next in the summer where the women of his father's side of the family always made him very welcome in a scones-and-hot-chocolate – but don't mention the tragedy – sort of way.

Alison, incongruously made fragile by Stan's utter reasonableness, decided she was going to have the baby with him here, but she would go home for a visit now, offering to be in Australia when Gina's baby was due to give the family some space and Stan time to help. Then she'd come back in a few weeks and they'd see. It seemed a decent enough plan in the circumstances, and Stan was touched by her consideration. They agreed to rent a flat for six months, decided the one they'd seen the day before would do, and get on with things. Which raised the tricky question of finances.

'I have enough savings to be OK this year if you can put down the deposit on the flat and we don't overdo the baby equipment. After that…' Alison began one of her nervy monologues about working and childcare and she'd rent out her flat in Sydney but, having given up her job without notice to come to England, she wouldn't get maternity leave and all sorts of other things. Stan tried to listen to everything she wanted to say and made it until she ran out of steam.

'I have enough money, Alison. I'll pay the deposit, the rent and give you enough each month so that you can stay here this year. We'll split food and household if you like, or I can sort those. Whatever. I want the baby born here because I won't be ready to leave, so I'm really, really comfortable helping with your finances to make that happen. And obviously with supporting the baby. Please don't worry about it.'

He went out for a run. Alison, tired as she neared the end of her first trimester, lay down on Gina's couch and wondered if he had forgotten they were married or just decided not to mention it.

When Stan got back, he came right out with it. 'Ali, you never used to talk so much. I get you're nervous but can you go back to normal?'

'If you can introduce me to the estate agent and anyone else official as your wife. And promise to meet me at

241

the airport on Easter Saturday which is when I'll be back.'
Stan nodded. Alison rang the wholly disinterested agent who
had showed them the two rental possibilities. 'Hello, Jason.
My name is Alison Douglas. You showed my husband and
me around Five Montmartre Mansions earlier. If they'll
accept an offer on the rent and get a deep clean, we'll take it
and need to move in within three days.' The agent, who
hadn't even troubled to find out the council tax or average
monthly bills, was somewhat taken aback by her approach.
He wouldn't have lasted five minutes in real estate in
Australia, Alison thought but kept to herself. She had
resolutely avoided using the words 'in Australia' since her
arrival. She had to phone back twice to find out if the offer
had been put to the landlord.

After the deal was agreed, Stan said, 'He wouldn't last
a week in real estate in Sydney.'

*

Later, Evan came over and Alison went to bed, partly from
ongoing jet lag, partly tact. Stan opened a couple of beers and
continued the day of straight-talking. 'Ev, what if the baby is
or isn't Dad's? What do you think? Either way.'

'I honestly don't give a fuck either way. He'll be our
brother. A bit odd, we'll feel more like his uncle, but I don't
care if he's a half or a full. Seriously. Not a bit. Just need
Mum to be OK. That's it. You?'

'What if she gives it up for adoption?'

'What? Seriously, no. She won't. I mean, no.' Evan
looked at Stan as if he'd suggested their mother might boil

242

the baby alive. 'But are you OK with the half thing? If it's not Dad's. Not our full sibling.'

'Yep. Like you, I feel it doesn't matter much. Weird, though, with Amelie and Alison. I mean, weird. It feels, I don't know, not real.'

'What if she can't cope.'

'Money. Ninety per cent of how you cope is money,' replied Stan. 'Not gazillions, but more than enough so you don't have to think too hard. That's why the project is the thing, why we have to do it. Apart from needing press minders anyway. I like that Rosalie.'

'You know her better than me. Met her more than once, anyway,' said Evan. 'But going on what you've told me and what she said on the phone, yep, we need her.' He drifted into silence. Then: 'Stan, I think Amelie might leave me. After the baby. Not Mum's baby, our baby. We never intended it. On bad days, I'm not sure it's mine. I'm going to get a DNA test. But I won't tell anyone. Except I've told you, obviously.

'It's really good to have you back. I'd got used to it but I miss you.'

'Thanks, mate. Me too. What if you do the test and it isn't yours? Isn't it better to just leave it?'

'Fuck, no. If it's not mine, I'll have to work that out, but not knowing for sure is not an option. And honestly, I think it is mine so it's less of a risk than you'd think.'

'Have you asked Amelie if she is sure it's yours?'

'Mm. She just looked at me. I don't know what it meant. But it made me see that we're lonely. I can't talk to her, and she doesn't want to talk to me. I'm not going to do anything about it now. Get the baby thing done and we'll see.

But I don't think I'll feel like I do about Anton and Andre if it isn't mine. I won't hate it. But I don't know if I'll want it. Not full-time.'

There was a knock on the living room door. They looked at each other. 'Must be Alison, forgotten something,' said Stan. 'You don't need to knock,' he said as he opened the door. 'It's not a teacher's office.'

*

When the car salesman had asked her about the car, clearly weighing up the wisdom of selling a relatively powerful SUV hybrid to a woman who had informed him she hadn't driven for more than ten years, she'd said it was a birthday present for someone in the family. Liv was mildly annoyed by his palpable relief, and torn between her recognition of his just about justifiable concern and her desire not to be classified as too doddery to buy a car. He offered to have it delivered to save her the trouble of fetching it and she'd been happy to accept. She knew what she'd done was a bit high-handed, but occasionally instinct was right and she was sure Gina would be glad when she'd got over her probable resistance. Now Liv needed someone to talk to. Not the boys, not Laura – she wasn't even sure if Greg had told his daughter. She hoped not because it would be a big secret for her to keep. Not that Laura would deliberately mean to break the confidence, but Liv could see her thinking she'd just tell so and so, they won't tell anyone, and before you knew it the Daily Mail had a headline the size of Big Ben. So that left Greg. She phoned him.

'Mum, are you OK?'

'Yes. I have noted for the last few years every time I ring someone they check I'm still alive first. I am. Though the shock might have hastened things on a bit.' It wasn't a good joke and she hadn't delivered it well. 'Sorry. Nerves. I just need to someone to talk to, Greg. I'm going to burst.' Gina liked to talk things through. Greg didn't and never had. Liv and her husband had been married happily enough, but now Liv struggled to remember any meaningful conversations they'd had; everything had been dulled by his last few years of ill health but he'd never been a big talker. Greg took after his father. Neither of them was uncomfortable with emotion. It wasn't a stiff-upper-lip thing. They just didn't feel the need to process feelings by talking about things. Liv did.

'Will I do?' Greg asked. She realised it was a sacrifice for her son and she loved him for it. 'Or Rosalie is going to sign Sandra up to the project tomorrow so after that you could talk to Sandra. Although as she knows already, and it's Sandra, you could probably talk to her now. But I can come down tomorrow if you like. Stay a few days.'

Liv hadn't thought of Sandra. 'I'm not sure I can go to Spain now. I know I said I would, but I don't know. I don't want to. I could look after Riley.'

'How is he?' Riley was a dog that even cat lovers warmed to and a safe, comforting topic of conversation. He wasn't pushy, not always trying to lick you or guilt trip you about a biscuit. He only barked if it was important and was a good listener. Liv went away a lot on holidays for older people, which often seemed to work out cheaper than staying at home by the time you took bills into account, otherwise she'd have had a dog herself. Having Riley was the next best thing. She told Greg there was a squirrel driving him mad in the garden and they discussed whether squirrels should be hibernating, deciding it was probably something to do with climate change. Things felt normal for a short while.

'It's another couple of weeks. So you don't have to decide now.'

'If I cancel today, I get half the money back. After today I lose it all.'

'Don't think about that. Let's see how things go. Mum, I can see a call coming through from Sandra so can I take it and ring you back?'

'Don't ring back tonight, love. Ring me tomorrow.'

Sandra came over to Liv's house around 10 a.m. the next day. 'Did Greg ask you to come?'

'No,' said Sandra. 'Though I can see why he might have. I rang him last night to ask if he thought it would be all right if I came to see you. I need someone to talk to and he said he thought it would be fine.'

Liv wasn't sure if Sandra was dressing this up to make her feel better but did it really matter? 'Me too. Come in.'

Chapter 14

Roland Stevens had been editor of *International Angling* for thirty-two years, retiring a few months before print publication ceased. The online version didn't do badly on subscriptions and adverts, but it was a different skill set and Roland couldn't be bothered to make the full transition. He'd done well to keep print circulation at a reasonable level for as long as he did, and many of his readers stayed loyal as the magazine switched to digital. He was not tech averse, definitely not, but fishing, he felt, was one of the few pursuits not enhanced by an app or pictures on Instagram. You went to the water, caught – or not – your fish, then either killed, cleaned and ate it or put it in the freezer all the same day, or threw it back quick as you like. Fishing was still and peaceful. Apps and social media were neither.

Angling didn't attract many women, and not much effort had been made trying to get a female presence in the sport. It was with an undercurrent of duplicity, perhaps, that Roland told his successor that getting women – or better, girls – into fishing was the unexploited reserve for growth. He'd thought about it and discarded it. Can't have women cluttering up the river banks in high heels, needing toilets, his owner had said whenever Roland tried to get female-led marketing into a budget. It was never going to work, he'd told himself, and so his readers generally thought. He'd had very few job applications from women over the years, maybe no more than two or three; not even during *International Angling*'s heyday when circulation was a quarter of a million a month and he'd needed a secretary and secretaries had been pretty much universally female. He'd got Jonno instead, and Jonno went by the title of editor's assistant, and that fooled everybody because Jonno was a man and therefore could not be a secretary. Never mind that he typed letters, made reservations, managed diaries and fielded calls. Sometimes, Roland mused to himself, he'd become completely immersed in angling because of the lack of women. He didn't know how to talk to them. He understood, of course, that he could have a conversation as he would with anyone else (although taking more care not to offend, especially recently), but he struggled to put this intellectual rationale into practice. It's not that he didn't like women, or thought them a lesser species or lacked respect. What he lacked was confidence, so it was easiest to simply avoid the possibility of exposing his deficiency.

He was sensible, logical, fit and lean. If you were to pick a team captain, be it chess or baseball or a jury foreperson, you'd pick Roland. When finishing up his traineeship as a journalist at the BBC, he had realised he wouldn't ever make the top tiers. He didn't want to end up reporting on local traffic, so thought he'd better specialise somewhere he felt comfortable. Print was the platform for niche pursuits in the early 80s and he'd done a lot of fishing while moving around as a teenager. His father had worked for an aluminium company and they relocated every couple of years to open a new factory – the US, Africa, Australia, the Far East. He rarely fitted in and didn't want to invest in friendships (though at the time he didn't think of it in those terms) because a few months later he'd have to leave. So he spent his weekends fishing: sometimes with a car and driver for company, if it was the sort of location providing those 'ex-pat benefits' for security reasons; and sometimes by himself on the bus, or occasionally a fishing club tour. Attending all-boys schools, his female relationships in his teenage years were confined to his, mainly older, relatives and the occasional rarity of a girl over 10 attending a family event.

He was eighteen before he knew it, applied for English at Keele and then the BBC just because they were there and he didn't put in the time to think about alternatives.

At college he came in to his own: bright enough but not super clever, an appealing face and he was nice. Kind, reliable, dependable. At least until the day of their final exams when he got Mary Batten pregnant. They'd shared the same dissertation supervisor. Three months later he refused to marry her.

He accepted he either had to support Mary's baby financially or pay for an abortion. He left the choice to her. But he would not marry her. She had told him she was on the pill when she wasn't. Had she been truthful, he would not have dipped in to sex for the first time under a table at the back of the stage in the student bar with only a torn tablecloth and a few posters about dreary bands and half-price beers hiding them from view. Mary told him the news at the end of August, the day before he was due to go to Ibiza with three of his friends, the BBC traineeship starting when he got back. She'd turned up to see him at his last day at Our Price in the high street; he couldn't have been more taken aback if it had been the reformed Beatles. The last time he saw Mary she was weeping at the bus station as he got on the coach to Gatwick. When he thought back on that time of his life, while he wasn't especially proud of himself, he thought he'd made the right decision. Just could and should have carried it out better. Asked how she was getting home from the bus station at least.

The day he returned from Ibiza, he detoured to Mary's house. Barely covering that odd English mix of tan on top of angry red, peeling skin, his 'Get It On in Ibiza' T-shirt and dirty shorts were never likely to repair his image with Mary or endear him to her family. He would have changed if he'd thought about it, but he didn't. What he wore had never been and never became much of a consideration for him. Mary wouldn't see him. Her mother asked him for money for the abortion, which he paid over three months using all his savings and half his first few monthly salaries, meaning he slept on various floors for the beginning of his traineeship. By some, now forgotten, roundabout route of old university acquaintances, Roland heard about Mary's wedding a couple of years later and vaguely hoped she'd be happy. He wondered if she'd tell her husband about the abortion. It had never crossed his mind to tell his parents about the not-to-be grandchild.

He'd met a girl in Ibiza because he'd had to – that's why they'd gone. He didn't have the inverted confidence to say 'Leave me out this time, guys' or 'I got Mary Batten pregnant and I can't face another woman, you can't trust them, none of them, ever'. They'd only have said 'Mary who? Didn't know you were seeing anyone' (which he wasn't) and ordered another round.

This girl was nice enough, conventionally pretty, mildly flirty and didn't expect him to talk too much, but he was not going to risk a repeat run when she told him she'd just started taking the pill. He'd tried to look as if he wanted to, and they'd given it a go a few times, but the precautions he insisted on were at odds with the natural order of things and he wasn't sure if anything really happened between them. By the time he got everything in place to his satisfaction, it had felt like opening a mediocre Christmas present wrapped in barbed wire. Apart from his guilt about Mary and general anxiety, he was not a confident or engaged lover, but the girl was very keen to lose her virginity and it was better than dealing with the constant hum of coercion from his mates. He was sure, however, that if there was an unwanted pregnancy, this time he was not the daddy.

Some years later, with *International Angling* on a sound footing, Roland married Ann, and some more years later, with the help of science, they'd had Eva. That made him question if Mary's baby had been his after all, which had not occurred to him at the time. But he never delved in too much to whose fault it was – his or Ann's – that they had needed the assistance of the expensive, discreet place on Cromwell Road. As a family, the Stevenses rubbed along very well although he was always aware of being on the outside of an inner circle of two. Given that his wife and daughter were women, he communicated with them tolerably well, certainly better than with any others, although that was a low bar.

Ann worked for Sainsbury's doing something with brand analysis. Eva tracked dolphins around the world, generally on a boat and sometimes in a bothy or a tent on a windswept coast. But never with a decent salary attached, which was OK; Roland couldn't be bothered to save dolphins, but he was happy to contribute financially to Eva's efforts, and he did conscientiously cut down on single-use plastics at her frequent and strident behest. At his retirement do, which nearly everyone enjoyed far more than Roland, his replacement had made a toast to new beginnings and this next exciting chapter in his life. Roland wasn't sure either of these would be welcome, even supposing they materialised.

*

Once his retirement was underway, his two busy women left Roland at a bit of a loose end for a lot of the time. He went most weekday mornings to the coffee shop on his road, buying a paper on his way and ordering the same thing: Americano, sourdough toast and then another Americano. A coffee cost the same as he'd earned in half a day when he'd first started work, but it occupied an hour and made him feel still part of a world where people had proper things to do, colleagues to meet and laptops to hunch over. He frequently exchanged a few words with the baristas and other customers, keeping alive a tiny rivet of connection with things external. This particular Friday in early February, he'd just started to notice the mornings getting a little lighter and the evenings lasting a little longer. It was raining and he remained at his table longer than usual, partly waiting for the relentless sheets of water to ease off but mostly to process the contents of the letter he'd just opened. As the fug came up, he felt interesting, like a character in a Hopper painting, all sad hinterland and moody vibes.

The letter had been delivered by hand as he left his house, jacket pulled around his neck like a waterproof tourniquet, by a young man on a bike. 'Roland Leonard Stevens?'

'Yes,' he'd replied. Almost everyone who isn't wanted by the police or other criminals says yes before they have time to think.

'I have a personal letter for you.'

The cyclist hadn't said 'You've been served' – this was a street in London not a US film set – but it would have felt right if he had. The letter was from Hewen Jones Solicitors and marked 'Addressee Only: Strictly Personal and Confidential'.

> Dear Mr Stevens,
>
> There is a matter our client wishes to discuss with you. It is of a highly personal nature and we would strongly recommend you consider carefully before discussing this letter with anyone else. While we will not be able to discuss the matter in advance of a meeting, we can assure you there is no question of criminality or concern for the health or wellbeing of you or your family.
>
> As a preliminary, we would suggest that Nicholas Hewen, our senior partner, meets with you to outline the matter in question and furnish you with information to enable you to make a decision as to whether to proceed to engage with our client. For this preliminary meeting, which

we anticipate will last about an hour,
we will reimburse any travel expenses
and pay a fee of £1,000 for your time
and inconvenience.

Should you wish not to proceed, the
discussions will remain confidential.

We would be very grateful if you
would telephone our office to make
an appointment. It is a matter of
some urgency so your response in
the next few days would be much
appreciated.

Yours sincerely
Hewen Jones

Roland looked them up. The Law Society website
informed him Nicholas Anthony Hewen had been a solicitor
since 1981, with only two specialisms identified, family law
and media law. The rain was easing off into a misty drizzle,
the risk of getting soaked coming from traffic spray and not
the skies, so he walked the three miles to Clerkenwell,
checked their office building and the nameplate and then
took the bus home. He wondered if it was some sort of a
sting. Or a scam. He decided not to tell Ann, who would
probably say it was bound to be a set up and he should
ignore it. He made the appointment for a couple of days'
time. Long-lost relative died and left him a fortune? That
didn't feel right. A child he didn't know about wanting to get

in touch seemed simultaneously the most likely and a very long shot, given his romantic track record, or lack thereof. The fee and the cloak and dagger were at odds with that theory too. His friend James had had a daughter trace him a few years back, after he'd lost touch with the mother who had not said she was pregnant; but that had been through an official agency, and he seemed to remember money was not allowed. Roll on Mr Hewen. It was the most intriguing thing that had come his way in years.

*

Nick Hewen was a few years away from retirement, though he looked as if he was a few years past it. He should have been able to stop working full-time a while ago, as many of his contemporaries had, but school fees and two difficult divorces had decimated his ability to save and provide a decent pension, although his definition of retirement savings and a decent pension were, by more usual standards, outlandish. His mother had been scathing about his divorce settlements, saying he'd never have allowed one of his own clients to give away so much and leave themselves so little. Similarly, his mother's idea of little was luxury to many others, but everything is relative. Nick did battle for his clients and was paid a lot of money to fight for their settlement, but he couldn't be bothered with his own. Plus, his mother was never a woman to hold back on 'I told you so' when a kind word or gentle gesture would have done much more for her son. He had, at least, learned from this and had close and comforting relationships with his own daughters, neither of whom had shown any interest in the law. Shauna was a primary school teacher in what Nick regarded as beyond the back of beyond, which meant it was more than ten miles from a cinema complex and choice of Michelin-starred restaurants. Tanya did something with computer programming that was possibly more profitable than legal practice. So he made do: if not in luxury's lap, then certainly sitting at its feet.

He only worked on very high value or interesting accounts these days, plus the odd retained client who had been with him since the early difficult years and would no more be palmed off to someone else than Nick would wish to palm them off. He understood professional loyalty as deeply as he mismanaged spousal loyalty. Rosalie McGrath was one of those high-value clients. Her latest instructions had seemed barely credible, and for the first time, Nick had been unable to proceed without checking. If Rosalie had been put out by his request to speak to Gerald, she kept it to herself, and allowed him to ring Gerald at the hospital for confirmation.

Nick was keen to meet the four candidates, get things underway, and he hoped they would all agree to participate in the project. Roland Stevens was due just now.

*

Hewen's office suite was unremarkable in decor and furnishings, although you might describe it as understated if you were being polite. Nick's desk was clear. Winter sun threaded through the Venetian blinds, laying a streaky bacon pattern on the floor.

'Mr Stevens, please come on in.'

Roland had slept without being troubled by the meeting, which had surprised him. He was curious but sanguine. He had not, certainly not knowingly, had any criminal dealings. He didn't buy lottery tickets so there weren't millions waiting for him. It didn't have the hallmarks of a negligence claim or something similar (not much risk with fish, he'd reasoned – unless you were the fish). On balance, it had to be either long-lost family, or he had – also unknowingly – some inside detail on a celebrity or a politician and the story was about to break.

*

By lunchtime, Roland was pretty much in the picture.

'Can I just repeat it back to you? I have understood it all, but it seems so far-fetched and I'd feel better if I could say it myself. It's probably the journalist in me.' Nick nodded his agreement; it was the sort of approach he would have taken himself.

'A woman I met in 1975 while on holiday in Ibiza,' said Roland matter-of-factly, 'is pregnant. She is sixty-two. As far as can be established, and it is widely accepted by the medics that this is in fact the case, she has not had sex since she was widowed over ten years ago, and she is many years post-menopause. The explanation is delayed embryonic settled implantation, known by its acronym DESI, and any man she has had sex with could have left the fertilised egg hiding in her womb for however long. Something dislodged it and despite her age and her physical condition, the embryo implanted and the baby is due in the next few weeks. She has had sex with six men and I am one of them.' Roland paused.

257

'I'll come back to that, if I may.' Nick nodded agreement for a second time.

'And now she wants to sell her story. You want me to agree to sell mine and to provide permission for the material to be used in a drama. For which I'll be paid, and I'll get more if I do an afterpiece. We're talking in the region of one hundred thousand for stage one, even more if I turn out to be the father or provide other as yet unforeseen cooperation.'

'Yes,' said Nick. 'That's pretty much it. If you're not pressed for time,' he went on to Roland, 'I'd suggest you get yourself some lunch next door – my tab is set up, they're expecting you – and we meet again at 2 p.m. It will give you a chance to think of any questions I might be able to answer immediately. And we can map out what happens next depending on your preliminary conclusions.' Roland nodded and somehow indicated by shifting his position slightly in the chair that he was not pressed for time, or if he had been would clear his afternoon to engage with this development.

'I need to remind you, as set out in the confidentiality agreement you signed on arrival, that you can only discuss the matter with one nominated individual. The consideration is now in your bank. Which means it is binding.' There was no hint of menace or threat in Nick's tone, but Roland knew that a breach of the agreement would not only be found out – after all, they'd found him in less than forty-eight hours – but the penalty clauses would be invoked.

Roland had nominated Ann as his one contact, but he did not contact her. He knew that once you told one person something, you lost control. And he didn't really want her advice or to try and please her or explain. In fact, he didn't like to communicate much at all, somewhat ironic for a journalist, as he had often thought to himself over the years. He was content enough as her husband, certainly wasn't going to upset any apple carts, and did enjoy her company from time to time. But she could be relentless. She would want endless details that he didn't yet have and would not understand his forensic approach to this. And if she didn't want him to do it, that would be tricky, because he most definitely was going to do it, no matter what.

He ate his soup and started to make notes about how much he could remember of those few days in Ibiza. He thought he might have a couple of snaps somewhere in an old album, probably not of the woman – Gina, Virginia, her name was, as he now had been reminded – but giving some dramatic illustration, good for a piece. It was more exciting than the latest fishing fly and much more lucrative on an hourly rate than writing about angling had ever been.

Nick knew that Roland had been a journalist, the editor of a fishing magazine, but had not expected Roland's instincts for story management to be so finely honed after twenty-odd years writing about the most boring popular sport – if you accepted a generous and flexible definition of sport – in the country. When Roland returned after lunch, Nick explained the payment Roland had been offered for his participation was not up for discussion; Rosalie wanted all the candidates to have the same terms and not to enter into individual negotiations. Roland just nodded when Nick said that.

'What if I can't remember anything?' he asked. 'How does that affect things?'

'It doesn't. It will be much more helpful to the story and – let's not overlook – to the medical research if you can.

But if you do not remember anything, truthfully do not remember anything, then we will ask you to comment on what the mother and any other contacts remember and that will be sufficient to discharge the obligations of this contract. The more detail we have, the more likely we will be to get a follow-up from the podcast. But you know, Roland, that if you don't know or can't remember something, no good will come of making things out to be otherwise.'

'I was absolutely not suggesting any such thing.' Roland's feathers were only slightly ruffled by the insinuation. By this point, both men were very clear on where things stood.

Neither had yet mentioned the potential reality of paternity. They had each preferred to leave that until more or less the end. Roland agreed to take the draft contract, find a lawyer of his own and get back to Nick within the stipulated seventy-two hours. Advice on that initial agreement had been given to Roland by another lawyer, not a member of Nick's practice, just after he'd arrived that morning. It was cloak and dagger, belt and braces, hush-hush top-secret all rolled in to one. While that lawyer had been sprung on Roland, was not of his personal choosing, the conversation had been recorded to minimise wiggle room if Roland was unreliable. Roland had taken his name and thought he might use him as the follow-up.

Finally, he broached the touchiest subject. 'How do the medics intend to establish paternity?'

'Very shortly after the birth it will be possible to rule in or out two candidates. For the others, including yourself, we will ask for DNA testing.' Nick paused. 'The dramatic aspect of this transaction – the podcast, print, scripting – is not dependent on your agreement to the DNA testing. My client and her client, the mother, think that the two should be separate. After the preliminary elimination, if there is still doubt about the paternity, then we will ask the other candidates to discuss the implications with the clinical lead and arrange counselling and family counselling as you wish.

'Roland, there are four reasons the mother agreed to this venture. First, the doctors feel it would be a major contribution to their medical understanding to know who the father is and how DESI happened in this case. It is very rare and could advance progress in infertility treatment. Second, she would like to be able to tell the child at some point. The third reason is that she feels – and has been advised by those well versed in these matters – that the story will get out and she prefers to retain as much control as possible. These are in no particular order. The final reason is that, given her age, she wants to be able to provide care for the child and ongoing financial security into the child's adult life. There is no question of the father being asked to contribute to the child's upbringing.'

That thought had not yet crossed Roland's mind and he said so. Not belligerently, but to make things clear. Then he said: 'I am not completely sure we ever technically consummated our relationship. Not completely. Not exactly. I don't want to participate under false pretences.'

Nick nodded to show he had taken the point. They agreed Roland would sign the agreement or not by Thursday afternoon, Valentine's Day and his birthday. Roland left with a sense of anticipation he hadn't felt in the thirty years since Eva was born.

*

The beach made it manageable. Eddie Grainger missed his psychiatric practice with an ache he could never imagine feeling for a person. Much as he loved Ines, when she hadn't been there the practice had filled that void, but she couldn't fill the void the practice left. They didn't talk about it and he wasn't sure if she suspected, let alone understood, the depth of his loss. They shared the caring – her father, his mother, their daughter – more or less equally, and managed with a haphazard and at times wafer-thin coalition of day centres, careworkers, respite homes, neighbours and charities, but it was still more or less a full-time occupation for both of them. Eddie took two hours off most days to drive the familiar miles from Inverness to one of the beaches on the Black Isle; once he'd crossed the bridge over the Moray Firth, dogs eager to get going, he temporarily closed the door on caring and was just a man walking his dogs on the beach, not a husband, son or father – roles he didn't feel he was especially good at.

Once a week or so, from the beach, he phoned one of the daughters from his first marriage, texting a picture of the sky or sea or, frequently, the dogs paddling with that in-the-moment *joie de vivre* dogs do so well. Mary lived in Ireland near her mother, and while Eddie and Mary weren't exactly estranged, there wouldn't be much doubt whose side Mary would take, had taking sides ever been required. He didn't blame Aoife for having the affair that broke up their marriage, although he maybe did blame her for giving him too much detail about why it happened. There had been a lot of truth in her tearful justifications: what did he expect, he was always working, they hadn't been out together except to an 'official' function like a family wedding or funeral since

Bernadette was born – and Aoife had just fallen into the arms of someone who noticed her. The classic 'it didn't mean anything' line was often repeated and more or less rang true. So he didn't blame her for the affair, thought perhaps, in general, people put too much store in sexual fidelity. As for the incontinent need to disclose: he had tried to lead a number of patients to the conclusion that they should keep a short fling to themselves. But he couldn't forgive Aoife for letting her lover into their house and their bed. He'd moved out that day, unable to look again at the bed without a weight of resentment and failure bringing him down, and then down some more. People, including his daughters, assumed he was the unfaithful one, and he had done nothing to correct it. Aoife would be a far better, more steadfast parent than he was, and if his contribution to the family's overall well-being – or the best that could come out of the mess – was to be the fall guy, he was fine with that.

Mary had decided to go to college in Cork, get in touch with her mother's roots to the extent of changing her last name to Ireland, Aoife's very apt maiden name, and, he suspected, away from people who knew. She joined the Garda, which took everyone by surprise, but it had been the right move. She was now the most senior female officer in County Cork. Aoife joined her a couple of years later, moving back home as soon as Bernadette finished her A levels. Bernadette went to Canada, married a man from Vancouver and had a child every year, give or take, or at least with such frequency that Eddie had to stop and think how many grandchildren he had. Ines put their names and birthdays in his diary, although that didn't always translate into cards or presents at the right time. He hadn't actually seen Bernadette for sixteen years. She phoned him very rarely, but she did take his calls if he got the time difference right and didn't clash with a yoga class or a school run. He had planned for he and Ines to visit when he retired, staying in a hotel near her for a few days before doing the Rockies. Then Ines's father had his fall, Eddie's mother's Parkinson's had an aggressive spurt, and their daughter Elke's sheltered placement was closed. Fucking austerity. He'd given up his studio flat with consulting room in Edinburgh's West End and moved back full-time to the family home in the Highlands.

Eddie's life had been filled by women. He sometimes thought he didn't really know any men at all except professionally, and then mostly patients, not colleagues. His father had died when he was eight and his mother never remarried. They tended to spend holidays with his aunts in various coastal locations in the east of Scotland, giving him an affinity with the beach in any weather. He only had girl cousins who felt sorry for him and let him into their games as often as he wanted. There was no family tradition of medicine, but he had wanted to be a doctor from childhood, probably a deep-rooted desire to somehow save his father. But he'd hated school so much he left at sixteen and started nursing training in Glasgow at seventeen, which was the norm in Scotland in those days. He'd been the only male, not only in his cohort but for several below and all above him. He did additional Highers at night school over five hard-graft years. The chance to make the change from nursing to medicine came through a pilot run by Glasgow University in the late 1970s. There was a shortage of psychiatrists – some things never change, he thought most days – and Eddie's transition was smoothed by those extra Highers, his mental health nurse qualification and his post as a community psychiatric nurse. He'd just about scraped through anything in his medical training not to do with the head. Then came the years in psychiatry that defined his self-worth; he was seen as no more than fair to middling by most of his peers, yet he was a saviour to many of his patients.

His romantic life prior to Ines rarely rose above the mediocre, tepid even when to all appearances he looked invested: an unremarkable set of short relationships, a few more mid-term relationships. The two serious long-term commitments ended in marriage: first Aoife, then Ines. He couldn't easily recall the names or faces of most of the girls he had dated, all but two had been nurses and one of those the sister of a nurse. He didn't for a moment, years later, suppose they could remember him either.

The mid-term relationships had not ended well. From time to time he brought to mind leaving Gina the morning after he'd been to Cambridge for her twenty-first without telling her why, or even that he was going and wouldn't be back. The day before, he'd received the letter offering him the place in medical school, and he just wanted to leave everything behind him. They'd had a patchy, very interrupted time together, Gina living in Paris several days a week or weeks a month, he couldn't be sure. The fairy dust of longing that distance had sprinkled on the relationship didn't provide the glue they needed. Still, he should have told her he was leaving. She was the non-nurse, they'd met through a friend, and he still kept a couple of photos of them on the Seine. The other mid-length girlfriend got pregnant and he'd wanted to emigrate – one person, one way – on finding out.

She miscarried around fourteen weeks and had never forgiven him for not caring more. Which made the break-up inevitable and messy.

As thirty-something crept its inexorable way up Eddie's timeline, there was Aoife the midwife, who he had liked a lot but probably never really loved. He'd thought they both wanted the same things and had a lot in common from their childhoods: windswept beaches, rainy picnics in the car and assorted relatives looking after them while a single parent worked, she in Cork, he in Glasgow and the Fife coast. Aoife wanted to get married, he wanted a wife: to pass that life milestone. And it had been fine – it had looked fine anyway – until she'd met that teacher at a PTA quiz that, predictably, Eddie had promised to attend but had missed. And she'd shared their bed with the prick.

Eddie's thoughts often ran like this on the beach. He picked over his childhood, women, patients, work, mistakes, the girls, his life as it had been, examining a short segment at a time and wondering if it would be too weird for him to get therapy now. He'd been friends with Ines a long time before they married. She'd had a one-night stand with her accountant – the accountant bit always made them both laugh – and got pregnant, much to her delight. She'd had enough of hoping for it. Eddie asked her to marry him: spur of the moment. Ines was forty-six and Elke had Down's syndrome. The subsequent twenty years had brought joy, crushing fatigue and, probably once a week, despair. They saved like misers, needing to amass enough money for Elke's care when they couldn't do it. A few months ago, Ines's father put money into a trust for Elke, which took the pressure off a bit, meaning the trip to Canada didn't seem so profligate. It may have been the last big thing Eddie's father-in-law did while of sound mind.

Eddie wasn't sure who knew that Elke wasn't his. He suspected his mother knew just from small things she'd said over the years, but he couldn't work out how. He referred to Elke as his daughter and he cared deeply for her, which was good enough for him and for Ines. Eddie couldn't imagine his mother keeping any speculative thoughts she might have had entirely to herself, so maybe his daughters had an inkling, and maybe some of the wider family. Like lots of personal things in his life, he didn't much care who thought what.

*

Walking back to the car that winter morning, darker in the Highlands than you'd like but more than compensated, Eddie thought, by the late, soft light of summer evenings, he knew he longed for a bit of excitement, for him and Ines, but not only couldn't work out what that would be – he definitely wouldn't be able to climb Kilimanjaro or even Ben Nevis – he had no idea how it could come about. Beds to change, meals to prepare, chairs to push seemed to be the limit of his world these days. Just as he opened his car door, a motorbike pulled up beside him in the shoreside car park.

'Mr Grainger, I have a legal letter for you. Please take it and read it.' Eddie was bemused for a few seconds, then wary, backed up against his car. He held out the keys and his wallet. 'No, sir. I just want to give you a letter. If you could nod to confirm you are Philip Edward Grainger, I'll just leave it here on the bonnet. Please make sure you read it.'

Eddie nodded with his thumb still on the emergency call button of his phone in his pocket. The motorcyclist turned a reassuringly lazy circle, placed the letter carefully on Eddie's car and left quietly, only turning the engine to a roar when he exited the car park.

*

Nick rarely left London these days. Why would he except for the weather, and that wasn't a big deal for him any more, though it used to be. Maldives, Club Med, South Africa. He left the meeting with Roland in time to get the 1800 Heathrow to Inverness, Eddie Grainger having been willing to meet but unable to travel. For an otherwise extremely well-travelled man nudging retirement it was somewhat hard to credit, but this would be Nick's first time in Scotland. He felt uncomfortable, some vague worry about the acceptability of his London accent, which he had smoothed down to the everyday side of posh – unlike his daughters, whose cut-glass intonations were sharper than the countess in Downton Abbey. He had a fear of being ridiculed and despised by nationalist Scots on the streets, in bars: anywhere public, in fact.

The taxi driver soothed his anxiety, asking if he had had a good flight and giving him tips – all of which were wasted – for a first time visitor to the Highlands. By the time he got to his hotel he had located his normal composure.

Eddie arrived at the meeting room not long after nine the next morning, explaining the short delay on caring responsibilities. Tuesday was always a difficult day for them because Ines had an early work start so Eddie did two drop-offs instead of one. He wasn't offering an apology, just an explanation. A local lawyer went through the confidentiality agreement while Nick had a coffee in the hotel lounge, staring out over the river Ness, which was wearing its black and broody getting-to-the-end-of-winter look. The meeting followed a similar trajectory to Nick's with Roland the day before, although the question of paternity came up much earlier. Nick went back to London on Tuesday evening with a decision from Eddie promised by video call on Friday. Eddie went home to talk to Ines.

*

'You know before I married Aoife,' he opened, 'I worked in Exeter? As a psychiatric nurse?' He'd wondered if he should save the conversation until the evening, when Elke was in bed and calls from either of their parents would be unlikely, reducing the risk of interruption. Eventually, Eddie decided it would be better to have the day to discuss it gradually, not consign it to a Highland night in winter when worries took hold easily in the dark, tendrils of doubt making sleep elusive. For him anyway. This way, he could get the shock out over coffee, pause for lunch with Elke, have a bit more discussion in the car on the care runs, then finish off over drinks at dinner. Psychiatry had taught Eddie the value of the rational, the practical, the pragmatic, as well as emotion, feelings and processing.

'Mmm. You don't talk about it much. Converting can't have been common those days. It isn't now. Are you ashamed – no, that's not the right word; reticent, that's better – about being a nurse first?'

'No.' Eddie was emphatic, firm without being angry, although there was an edge of irritation that 'ashamed' had been Ines's first thought. He was just certain. He was really proud of it, thought it was a sensible way in to medicine that should be widely available: a halfway house that he wished people would ask him about more often. Train to be a nurse, get an inside look at what you were letting yourself in for, then work for a year or two to fund medical studies once you were sure. Bring the caring and empathy and experience of nursing with you. Eddie estimated maybe half his colleagues over the years wished they weren't doctors, wished that they hadn't invested their lives in diagnoses, prognoses and patients with incurable ailments. But few had given up being a doctor. Proud families, job security about as good as it gets, status, occasional gratitude. Don't mention the downsides: the hours, the doubt, the dread of the wrong decision, being found out, covering for colleagues who diagnosed a slight tremor when it was obviously a fatal stroke waiting to happen, or dealing with the ridicule of blue-lighting a heart attack that turned out to be indigestion.

Ines was doing the crossword. 'Ines. I need to talk to you about Exeter. Well, Cambridge really.' Now he had her attention.

'Are you ill? Did you catch something there?'

'No. And no. But it's important.'

He told her. He told her about leaving Gina without saying anything and never contacting her to explain, knowing but not admitting – nor properly acknowledging until this week – what a devastation that probably was. Ines went to ask something but he said, in a jokey tone but clearly serious,

'No. Like a presentation. Save all questions until the end, then I promise I'll answer them.'

He didn't really understand why he'd just gone. The relationship was hard to sustain, exciting when they saw each other but Gina wasn't real for him. She had a sick parent, a job in France, endless travel, studying for exams while working full-time. She didn't have much left to give to a boyfriend trying to help contain mental health issues in south Devon. Except sex, which worked, and she wasn't needy, which suited him.

'Both good things,' said Ines, sitting hard on her questions and trying to let the story take its own pace, lost for why Eddie was telling her now. Something must have precipitated it. Elke came in, distressed because Teddy's eye had fallen out. As Eddie calmed and reassured her, Ines knew – short of being a master criminal – there was nothing Eddie could do to dent her love for him. She was as sure as anyone ever can be of another person's feelings that Eddie loved her. She didn't think this was a conversation leading up to 'It's not you, it's me, I'm leaving you', but then wasn't the partner always the last to know?

'I know we said no questions yet,' she said. Eddie held Elke close as he threaded a needle to repair Teddy's eye. 'But I need to know if there is someone else.'

'No. Never,' he said. A slight pause. 'At least, not in the way you mean.' He looked at Elke. 'We need a big hug with Mummy.' He kissed Ines over the top of Elke's head.

In the car, he talked about Gina, how he'd left and that he loved Ines like he had never loved another woman, and he had maybe only realised that recently. Like today. 'Better late than never,' she said, 'but why now?' Over dinner, he explained about Gina's pregnancy, about the project and the DNA and his meeting with Nick. Whether he should sign the contract.

'What do you think?' Eddie asked.

'I think,' said Ines, 'that the first thing you need to do is tell your daughters about Gina. About the possibility. We need to heal rifts, Ed. We've needed to do it for a while and we haven't. Don't wait until you have a terminal illness or I'm dead. Don't wait until you know, because that is shutting them out more. Share the uncertainty. Include them. Don't only tell them if you're the father. This is a gift. Let's use it.'

Eddie poked at the log fire for a bit. 'I wasn't the one who had an affair. It was Aoife. They slept in our bed. That's why I couldn't forgive her. She was always changing the sheets. Do you think I can tell the girls that? I'm not supposed to tell anyone anything about this except you. I signed a DNA. NDA. They paid me one thousand pounds for it.'

'Talk to their mother,' said Ines.

'The NDA? The project? Should I do it? I'd have to sanitise it a bit because of the confidentiality. Sanitise it quite a lot actually. Or just trust them.'

'God, yes. It's fabulous – so exciting! Blimey, I had an unexpected but much wanted pregnancy in my forties – hard as fuck. How in the name of hell does Gina feel at sixty-two? I mean, unexpected doesn't come close. Poor woman. Or maybe not, maybe she's pleased, how would we know? But no sixty-two-year-old woman would be pleased about an unexpected pregnancy, would she? Don't you dare *not* sign that stuff.' Eddie stared. It was unusual for Ines to be so openly animated. He began to plan how to tell the girls the truth and nothing but the truth. But maybe not the whole truth.

*

On Thursday morning, he checked the weather in Cork: dreich, as it was in Inverness. That made him feel better about ringing Aoife, though who knew why, as if sharing rainfall hundreds of miles apart somehow lessened the detachment between them. They talked very rarely these days, had no need since the girls were independent, and neither of them were much given to preamble.

'There's something I need to ask you. I want to tell the girls what happened when we split up. Not nastily. Bare facts. Something has come up for me and I want to start from basics.'

'Sure, I didn't think you were ringing to wish me a happy Valentine's. Are you ill?' asked Aoife.

'No.' he replied. 'I'm fine.'

'I can't stop you, obviously. And I won't deny it if they check with me. But I'm not happy about it. After all this time, I don't see the need.'

'I'm not exactly sure why, but it feels right. They're both adults, long-time adults now. It's not a revenge thing. I'm not getting at you, Aoife. And I'll also tell them that I would rather have you as their mother than anyone in the world. Including Ines. That I am equally responsible that we couldn't work it out, I put my patients before them and before you. But I want them to know it was not me who had the affair.'

'You've had another one.' Her accusation struck Eddie as being ironic, but he wasn't there to argue, just to… inform.

'No, I haven't, let alone another one. I didn't have an affair while I was married to you and I haven't since. Except,' he added, looking to soften the request, which appeared even less welcome than he'd anticipated. 'Except with my work. And that was just as much to blame. But you can tell them if you want,' he added magnanimously.

Chapter 15

People who told Jerome that he reminded them of Woody Allen – only vaguely, just a bit, it's not like he looked very like him or anything – were rarely given the chance to speak to him twice. It was a reasonable observation, he knew; but it irritated him out of all proportion to the offence, and he had long since decided one strike and they were out. He wasn't sure if his irritation was rooted in dislike of Allen's behaviour or of his genius, or because Allen was short and Jerome was… taller. He considered Allen to be vain, his public self-deprecation to be false, and recognition of these traits in himself probably added a grittiness to Jerome's antipathy. Before buying any new items of clothing, he searched for recent pictures of Allen just to make sure his look bore no resemblance. And in the end, as he reminded himself, Allen was American and he, Jerome, was French.

Most Saturdays he visited the market in the centre of town, walking from his stylish two-bed, two-bath apartment in a converted convent. He had breakfast, bought some groceries, had coffee, wandered around, had lunch and went home. He was lonely, although he hadn't yet named it as such. Divorced for more than twenty years, he had not been successful in a serious relationship since, let alone a second marriage. He came from a family of nine siblings, and his sadness at having no children of his own had eased only slightly as he grew older and more used to it. Although he had maybe twenty nieces and nephews, the downside of multiple siblings is that he had never been particularly close to any one of them, and it was too much to keep up with all of them and all of their offspring. He had drifted away. If he'd had one sister or brother, perhaps two, he'd have invested in that family unit, he thought. But he was fifth of nine and the only boy, his sisters above and below pairing off as they grew, leaving him isolated and sorry for himself. In recent years, mostly because she also lived in Lyon, had done all her adult life, he drew closer to one, Camille, and they met up a few times a year. Although, true to say, often at funerals.

He had married Nicole when she got pregnant, but she miscarried. More intense effort but little tenderness or romance did not result in another pregnancy, and she got fed up with his inability to make a life together for just the two of them. That said, her decision to ask for a divorce surprised her more than Jerome. After they separated, Jerome wanted another woman to be a mother to the children he craved, and attracting women had never been a problem. He was as ignorant of his strategy as he was of its inspiration: buying a new car, though that was appropriate enough given he owned several dealerships in central and suburban Paris. He slept around, test-driving various women, hoping to get one of them pregnant: a reversal of the usual intention of men indiscriminate in their sexual antics. It didn't happen. Or if it had, no one had cared enough for him to tell him.

Some time in his late fifties, he'd called it a day, sold the dealerships and retired back to Lyon where he had continued to be lonely for the last decade or so.

*

On a Saturday afternoon, back from the market, he'd open an expensive bottle of wine, a step up from the mid-range he drank during the week – although he certainly didn't always enjoy the Saturday bottles more. It was just a statement that this was the weekend. Jerome could afford to drink expensively every day, all day if he wished, but he felt around thirty-five euros was the right price to pay for a weekend wine; any more and the marginal, if any, increase in enjoyment was not worth the additional cost. Stopping himself drinking all day, every day was enough of a challenge in itself. He would have liked to write his memoirs, but if he couldn't remember the names of half his nieces and nephews, he couldn't see why they'd be interested. He thought a lot about contacting Nicole since she had been widowed a few years ago, to see if she might consider hearing his apology and reopening a relationship, but preliminary enquiries had led him to believe she had moved on very swiftly after that particular tragedy.

This cold, bright Saturday in mid-February, struggling to pull himself out of the tail end of winter, he'd fallen back on his idea of last resort and booked a sea-view cabin with a balcony on a round-the-world cruise. He would board the ship in Barcelona at the end of the week.

He was leaving his apartment to collect some US dollars for his trip when the young woman said his name and handed him the envelope, taking his picture with it in his hand, all without getting off her moped and in less than twenty seconds. He shouted down the street after her, but she'd whipped round the corner before he got to the end of the sentence and wouldn't have heard him over the noise of the engine anyway – it sounded like the moped was powered by a couple of Coke cans filled with laughing gas. The letter was in English with a copy in impeccable business French.

Jerome spoke excellent English but he appreciated the gesture of translation. He went back inside.

Like Roland, Jerome checked out Hewen Jones on the Law Society website, spent half an hour trawling LinkedIn and other social media for sightings of the partners, and concluded it was likely the letter came from a legitimate firm. One more check couldn't hurt. First thing on Monday, he rang the number on the letter, and apologised in his best American accent for bothering them, asking for Mr Hewen. Who was, of course, in a meeting. Jerome cut the call as the receptionist was asking if he wished to leave a message, feeling foolish. Why was he pretending to be American? Why not just say who he was?

He called back, this time speaking his fluent if very formal English, learned at Renault's business English school. He gave his name and Mr Hewen was available. Jerome agreed to get a flight to London the next day, stay overnight and then meet Nicholas at 11 a.m. Business class tickets, airport transfers and a reservation at a four-star hotel arrived on his phone within ten minutes. By the time he was on the return flight on Wednesday evening, he was Nick's first signatory, agreeing to be contacted further while on his cruise. He was thrilled.

Nick was also quietly pleased. One signatory, three to go. As a lawyer, he was always going to wait for the ink on the contract but he bet himself a new hot tub that Roland and Eddie's signatures would be with him that week.

*

Alan was not ready to retire, yet he couldn't be bothered to go on working. Sara talked of cruises and replanning the garden now that he'd have more time, although she herself wasn't planning to sell the shop this year, just take more holidays. Alan wasn't sure if he didn't want to go on a cruise or if he just didn't want to go with Sara. Bit of both – things often were. A year or so ago he'd dropped down to four days a week, and the other three days had been enough time to be at home with his wife. Now the big stop, as he thought of it to himself, had arrived and here he was at his retirement party. Surprise retirement party. Alan didn't believe Sara had honestly thought he would want a retirement party, let alone a surprise retirement party; no, she'd wanted a party and this was as good an excuse as any. She looked beautiful. In fact, he couldn't remember a day of their marriage when he hadn't admired her appearance, whether in gardening clothes or understated silk at their son's wedding. 'Moisturiser, mascara, lipstick, no smoking, stay out of the sun,' he'd once heard her answer when someone had asked what her secret was. And she was nice.

Alan was unlike nearly all his contemporaries, who saw retirement as the holy grail; those that had already retired spun the old line 'Don't know how I found time to work,' which grated on him, and those coming up to it made plans for golf and grandchildren. Baby boomers – many on final salary pension schemes after forty years in jobs in which they had thought themselves important but would be forgotten a moment after they left – sometimes had an aura of congratulation sharpened by the contrast of streaming services and central heating with the black and white TVs and freezing rooms of their childhoods. 'I've worked hard all my life' was their mantra, although lots of them hadn't; they had turned up to offices and pushed around papers, perpetuating useless bureaucracies or inequality-generating monoliths that failed in many very basic respects. Alan did not intend to join the ranks of their self-satisfied lunches and mini breaks. But he didn't know what he was going to do.

He didn't much like himself at the moment. Despising his class and contemporaries while living the life. It reminded him of visiting South Africa in the apartheid years for a university friend's wedding. He went into places that said 'Whites only' because he didn't know what else to do. It had never come close to being a justifiable way to behave and he had felt tarnished by his complicity. While not actually doing anything about it.

Tonight didn't seem the right time to lob a domestic hand grenade. A few more weeks of shuffling around his marriage, finalising his departure from the workplace and adjusting his everyday routine wouldn't make any difference. Picking up the mic now and saying 'I don't want to be here, I didn't ask any of you to come, I wish Sara had not organised this party, so please could you all leave' would probably just be unkind. True, but unkind. He briefly considered actually saying that but making it look like a joke – having your truth cake and eating it. Instead he said, 'Friends, family, colleagues, Sara: thank you all so much for coming.'

*

That morning of the party, Alan had rung his brother, whose sailing buddy and close friend was a lawyer somewhere in the City of London. 'Ade, can you ask Matt if this firm checks out? Some guy served a letter on me this morning, you know, like they do in US cop shows. "Mr Mackintosh, you've been served." They didn't actually say that, but he asked who I was— No, wait, asked me to confirm if I was me, and handed me a letter from this firm of solicitors asking me to contact them. I want to know I'm not being scammed or anything. Hewen Jones they're called.'

On Tuesday morning, while Jerome was travelling from Lyon to London, Alan was on the fast train from Leeds to Kings Cross. Enclosed with the letter had been a first-class ticket and he had taken up the option for a night in London and an open return. Sara had been no more than mildly surprised when he said he had to go to a meeting in London at short notice and that he'd be away for a night. She hadn't asked what for, although Alan knew her assumption was it was something to do with his final days at work, and he did nothing to remove that notion.

Nick took care setting out the purpose of the meeting. The jolt on Alan's face when he realised that the mother in question was the woman in Kirkcaldy in 1999 was stark as a firework going off. It was a lightning bolt of recognition.

'Does legal privilege apply to this conversation?' asked Alan.

'Not technically. You are not paying my bill and I am not giving you advice. You had advice from Serena when you signed the confidentiality agreement earlier. I am acting as a negotiator. That said, I will not divulge anything you say to me here to anyone in court.'

'In court? What would I be doing in court?'

'That is what legal privilege is.'

281

'I need you not to talk about it, full stop.'

'Unless it has criminal or safety implications, I won't talk about it.'

'I knew the mother because we worked together at—' Alan looked at Nick. 'Should I say the name of the firm?'

'Yes.'

'CPRL. It repaired mobile phones, cutting edge technology at the time. People broke them and we repaired them. General turnaround time was three weeks and it cost about a quarter of the cost of the phone. She was something in accounting. I'm not sure what and I didn't know her well.' He realised how unseemly that sounded, but it was the truth. 'That sounds a bit odd given why I'm here, but the finance department was next to sales, and six or so of us would meet most Mondays to go over the week's figures. I worked on channel relationships – not individuals sending us their phones but insurance companies for their customers, manufacturers, employers, that sort of thing. Corporate sales. B2B we'd say now.

'When I arrived, my boss was a guy called Will. He was a techie, not a sales manager, and he didn't understand the sales process so he moved back to manage the technical team. I then supposedly reported directly to the MD. Bit of a personality clash. I didn't rate him, I didn't like him and tried to avoid him. I was a good salesperson – really good – and as long as I made money I guessed he wouldn't bother me too much.

'The repair shop was in Kirkcaldy for legacy reasons, even though the head office was in Southall. I wanted to get to know the guys running the repair side – I was selling what they were doing, basically – so I booked a few meetings, flew up to Edinburgh the night before to see an old friend, then hired a car and drove to Kirkcaldy, getting there just after lunch. I was booked to stay one night so I checked into the hotel and dropped off my bag on the way. I remember it all very clearly. It was the defining two days of my career.' Nick nodded, said nothing but conveyed interest. It wasn't hard; he was indeed interested.

'Anyway, I got to the repair shop, which was an old RAF aircraft site with two hangars converted into workshops, maybe fifty or sixty staff in total. Most of it was a sterile environment, I remember that but I forget why, something to do with gold or chemicals or whatever, so I togged up like I was going to a crime scene and the site manager took me for a tour. I came out into the changing room to take off my stuff and the MD was there. You'd think I could remember his name but I'm not sure. Nothing exotic. John or Bob or Paul or something. Maybe Chris. He asked me what I was doing, I told him, and he said could I come to his management meeting that afternoon.

'So I did. There were about five people there: the MD, the site manager, the woman in question and a couple of others, maybe technical people based in Kirkcaldy.' Alan took a swig of coffee to catch his thoughts.

'I'm interested in your story,' said Nick. 'For itself. You seem to be building up to the denouement – how you came to sleep with the mother – and I can't see how you're going to get there. Please continue. You're doing very well.'

Alan was surprised that Nick seemed to think he'd begun to doubt himself. He hadn't. The potential for a story had been immediately obvious when Nick had first outlined it. He also knew – was certain with a conviction he had no right to – that the woman would still feel the same about that night in the hotel: they'd both known then that nothing would better it.

'When the meeting started, the MD asked me to what they owed the pleasure of my company in Kirkcaldy today. I said I was there to understand the repair process better, and build on my technical understanding to have better conversations with customers. I was just beginning to grasp an undercurrent. "And you think it helps sales – this racketing about the country interfering in departments that are nothing to do with you? Did you get permission to fly? Clear your travel with Will?"

'"Yes it does and no I didn't," I replied. The others round the table were looking either shocked or uncomfortable. I hadn't been there long enough, three or four months at that point, for any of them to know me. Then the MD said – and I'm pretty much sure this is a direct quote – "Andy, I know there's a lot of talk about sales being about relationships, but your most important sales relationship is with me. And you haven't got off to a very good start."

'If there hadn't been other people there, I might have handled it differently. Been a bit more conciliatory, known my place perhaps, the newcomer versus the MD. Or I might have hit him. I probably should have cleared the travel with someone, maybe even him. I'd not had a good week personally and wasn't up to this added humiliation. So I said: "It's Alan, not Andy. Sales isn't all about relationships, although that is a big part of it. When I started here, our corporate sales were under five per cent of revenue. Yesterday they were on a thirty-five per cent run rate for the year and, with me, they'll be seventy per cent by year end. All additional revenue. Not relabelling, not increase from existing customers – I mean, who breaks their mobile just so they can get it repaired? It's not like wanting a new dress. So, yes, I did get off to a really good start. But I'm not going to waste any more of my time working for a tosser like you who is more bothered about thirty quid on a plane ticket than an eighty-seven thousand increase in revenue in my first quarter." Or something along those lines. Very close to those lines, I've replayed them a few times in my head.

'And I left. Went back to the hotel, headed to the bar, ordered a Diet Coke. Sat down to think about stuff. About Sara, the children, my job. Stuff.'

'OK.'

'This all happened when I had decided, nearly decided, to leave Sara. I didn't but I think that is partly – mostly – because of Kirkcaldy. Because of the night in Kirkcaldy. So we're still married, me and Sara, but we might not be if I hadn't lived mostly in Rome and Sara mostly here. I'm in the process of retiring. So I'll be home more. Should be home more, anyway.' Alan let that sit in the air like a cloud that might just move over or might just release a deluge. 'Sara has booked a cruise for us. A surprise. She doesn't know I know. She also doesn't seem to understand I'm not the cruise type.'

'Maybe she wants to go and wants you to go with her, now you have the time,' offered Nick, noticing and understanding Alan's irritation as he said it. Nick would be repelled by someone booking a surprise cruise for him.

'Earlier that week, before Kirkcaldy, we'd – me and Sara – had an argument. Stupidest thing, about my brother and what we'd argued about years ago, just before our

285

wedding. Sara had said she hadn't wanted Ade, my brother to be my best man because he was shy, got befuddled after half a glass of fizz and wouldn't make a very good speech. So I said I hadn't wanted her father to do a speech either because he was a patronising bore, even more than usual after a glass of anything and would go on far too long. Both of these things were true and we both knew it at the time, and both speeches did indeed turn out to be dreadful. Well, Ade, my brother, was just dreadful. Patrick was excruciating. He said Sara's dress was the prettiest thing he'd seen since his mother made a lampshade out of old net curtains after the war. He said he'd always hoped for a successful, handsome, generous son-in-law and maybe he'd get one second time around. He thanked me for my magnificent offer to pay for my taxi to the church.

'I'm quite protective of Ade and Sara never got that. Instead of me and Sara working out a plan together before the wedding, it turned into a huge stramash and it kept coming up, years after, like shorthand for how much we disliked each other. We didn't. Dislike each other. But it felt like we did sometimes. We argued, picking holes in each other, unpleasant stuff. And it set the way we'd be together. For all these years. Niggling in private, perfect in company. A few days before Scotland, she told me she wanted to have another baby but I didn't. Wouldn't. Was too old. So I was thinking of getting the snip but not telling her. It was a mess. Instead of discussing a baby, we somehow, like always, got back to the wedding speech argument.' Alan paused. 'We still do sometimes though both of us try to make a joke of it now.

'I'd booked the trip to Kirkcaldy partly to have an excuse to get away. I had a friend in Edinburgh and we'd been out the night before the meeting. I told him I wanted to leave Sara.

'Anyway, in the bar with my Diet Coke, I was working the logistics. How to tell Sara. Money. Kids. Ride the storm. Move abroad. Probably had the fight with MD man to give myself an excuse.'

There was such a long silence, Nick eventually prompted Alan to continue.

'And I think that is what I would have done if this woman from work hadn't come in to the bar and sat down beside me.'

'Sliding Doors moment.'

Alan nodded slowly and deliberately, conveying years of regret with a few inches of movement. 'I don't live in the past,' he went on, 'but I do think about that often. If she hadn't come in, if we hadn't got in the lift together, I might have gone home that night, told Sara I was leaving, faced down the barbarians and— and what, who knows? But she did. She came in, walked over, ordered a large glass of wine. Told the barman, "I'm an accountant. It's not what I usually have at 5 p.m." The barman laughed and said, "Sounds like you need it and should do it more often." Then she turned to me.

'She said, "I can't believe I've put up with that for four years. I've got used to it. The belittling, the snideness, the management by making people squirm. God, I'm embarrassed I've sort of been part of it. I've resigned. Well, I haven't. I just left the room after you and I'm not going back. I was hoping you could give me a lift, but you'd gone by the time I'd got my bag. Well done. Will you be OK? Get another job?"

'We talked for a bit. She was easy to talk to and I needed to vent, but I wouldn't say there was much more to it than that. Not then. Not for another twenty minutes. She asked me what I was going to do. I said I'd been thinking of taking a job in Switzerland before this one came up, and it was still open so I might try that. If my wife didn't object. Or maybe even if she did. She said she'd be fine, always jobs in finance, and she had one in the pipeline and she was fed up with the commute to Southall anyway. I think we talked about trains and the Hayes bypass for a bit.'

'Let me know if it's too much' said Nick. 'We can take a break.'

Decades of what might have been were finding their way to Alan's face and, more so, his voice. Not regret for Gina; Nick didn't believe she was Alan's one who got away. But self-reproach: with sales, the futility, the wasted opportunities to live his best life rather than a life that was the acceptable face of a middle-class man with responsibilities.

'Nearly there.' said Alan. 'At around six she said she needed to go and phone her children and I assumed she had a husband. At this point, I was really grateful for her understanding, her offers of support – she had an internal network for things like personal possessions in the office, leaving formalities and so on that I hadn't – but nothing else. We got into the lift and there were four others. We got pushed to the back together. I felt like I'd been set on fire. In a good way. She did too. We spent the night together and agreed in the morning neither of us would ever tell anyone.

And I haven't until now. Except Ade. Nothing in my life, before or since, has come close to that night. And I knew that morning it never would again. So I might as well stay with Sara.'

Alan made it clear to Nick he did not want Sara to know that he had spent the night with another woman. It seemed likely the woman wouldn't be that keen on that either, although there was no one to be wounded by her behaviour. Not even her sons; it wasn't their father she had just started a relationship with at the time.

'I'm not sure I can take part without risking Sara being upset. But given it was years ago and hasn't happened again, I might be able to manage.'

Nick's instructions from Rosalie were that anonymity was not on the table at the moment. And also not to needlessly let a candidate get away.

'Do you want to have a think about it? And I will too. Maybe we can speak again tomorrow.'

Alan's bill at the Athenaeum was covered, including use of the spa and mini bar. He had afternoon tea with champagne, spent two hours in the spa, had dinner and in the late evening made a cup of decaf coffee in his room overlooking Green Park. He often found things settled in his mind if he left them alone for a short while. He decided he would simply tell Sara what happened and deal with any fallout. He didn't think she'd do anything extreme, like walk out, but he expected her to sulk for a good while. He could live with that. In fact, he might like to live with that. Might save him leaving.

Alan thought about Kirkcaldy often, at least once a week, but it wasn't about Gina herself. He knew that the reason he had never again been unfaithful to Sara, actually why he had not left her then or since, was that nothing would ever compare with that night outside Kirkcaldy. No dalliance, no sexual encounter could come close. Maybe only a deep abiding love could, and while he didn't have that with Sara he wasn't going to go on a likely fruitless quest to find it with all the messiness looking would bring. What he had with Sara was children, history, financial entwinement. And he wouldn't give that up for an affair that couldn't ever match up to Gina. He'd told Ade a few years back who believed him - this wasn't some adolescent mate's boast it was his fully adult brother - but simultaneously couldn't quite believe it. "Sort of sadly ecstatic", he'd said, and they'd moved on to talk about the Olympics.

*

Sara picked Alan up at the station, keeping her eyes on the late morning traffic as she leaned over to open the car door. 'Hi,' she said, pulling out as soon as she heard the door close. 'Good trip?'

'Interesting.'

'Was it the last handover documents?' Alan missed twenty seconds of Sara speaking as he wondered why she would ask that. Forty-five years of work had melted into irrelevance.

'No, it was more of a blast from the past.' The parallel tracks of their conversation were mutual. Alan still didn't have Sara's full attention. 'It was about a one-night stand I had when I worked in Southall for those few months in the late 90s.' Now he did.

290

'What?' The traffic was heavy and the car was in the middle lane, Sara intending to go straight over the roundabout and out to the west of the city centre before heading north. 'Why? Oh my god, is there a child?' When Alan didn't say anything she took her chances with the traffic and looked straight at him. 'Alan. Have you got another child?' The possibly accurate guess unnerved him slightly.

'It's complicated,' he said. And despite knowing how much Sara wanted him to tell her, he wouldn't. Not in the car. He needed terra firma.

At home, he took a cup of tea into the garden, the grass released from overnight frost, cold and wet as a result, and thought about that night, measuring it out in small pockets to savour it again, bit by bit, as he had so frequently all these years. He could massage the reality at this stage so Sara wouldn't know he had been planning to leave, but he wasn't going to. He could rationalise that: she deserved to know the truth; it would all come out anyway as the research went on; it was a long time ago. But he knew she would be deeply hurt. It wasn't that he didn't care at all about her feelings, but he didn't care enough to soften the story. Before they ate lunch, he told Sara what he knew.

'You were planning to leave me. We'd talked about having another baby. You slept with this woman who might now be pregnant with your child.'

'Yes, yes, yes. And yes but unlikely,' replied Alan, as gently as he could, but it all still sounded very matter-of-fact. 'We'd been in this disastrous meeting at CPRL. We both decided to resign and it sort of happened. It took us both by surprise. I never saw her again. Have never again been unfaithful.'

291

'While we were planning another baby and you were planning to leave? Why should I believe you?'

'Well, you were planning the baby. I wasn't. But I see why it is difficult to believe.'

'You haven't apologised.'

'No.' Confirmation was hardly necessary but Alan looked straight at her as he said it to emphasise the point. An apology was not in his thoughts, on his lips or in his heart. Sara could wait a lifetime for an apology but it would never come.

'Why did you tell me? Why not lie? Then it wouldn't have mattered.'

'I thought about it. But I think it would come out if the baby is mine and I thought it better to be straight from the beginning.'

'Well, it's hardly the beginning, is it? Was she better than me?'

'Sara, she was better than anyone or anything in my life. I was the same for her.' He saw Sara's face reflect an equal mix of pain and scepticism at his assurance. 'It was one of those things. I wasn't looking for it. It took me by surprise. Just that one night.'

Sara talked, dry-eyed, for another half hour or so. Flailing between what would they do if the baby was his, would they tell the children, the family, their friends, please don't tell them, why didn't he leave her then, did he really not want to stay married, was that it, why didn't he admit it at the time. Round in circles. Alan listened mostly, or looked as if he was listening. When she asked, 'And you've never been unfaithful since?' he was as sympathetic as concrete and it was brutal.

'No. And we have her to thank for that. Couldn't be matched. There would have been no point.' It seemed to them both that their life together was now, suddenly, a desert all around them. From playgroups to graduations, sick relatives, family holidays, meals, work and box sets: it was all at best second-best and at worst just a sham, the safety of a familiar life punctured not because of a one-night stand but because of that one-night stand. 'I'm going to sign the agreement.' Alan handed it to Sara. 'Do you want to read it?'

'Yes.'

'Let me know when you've finished. I'm going upstairs.'

When Sara came up later that evening, Alan was watching a chat show although his attention was clearly not on the well-worn host peddling his guest's wares under guise of an interview, fooling no one. She sat down on the end of the bed. Even the bed felt false, as if it had been bought in another life for someone else's home, because the home they had wasn't what they thought.

'Are you going to leave me?' asked Sara.

'If you want me to go, or to go for a bit so you can think, of course I will. Ade is away, I can use his flat.'

'Was she beautiful?'

'No, I don't think so. She was sexy that night, but I don't think I thought she was beautiful. I don't remember exactly. You are the most beautiful woman I know and I think that every day I look at you.' He couldn't tell if Sara's pain was eased slightly by this, but it was the truth and he hoped it helped.

'Are you going to see her?'

'I don't think so. Not unless the baby is mine. Then I guess I will, but not before, as far as I know. It's not in the agreement.'

'Would you see it?'

'I would hope so. I think it might depend on the mother, but I would try very hard if it is mine.'

'I've read it. Can you put in there that who you are, you and me, is kept confidential?'

Alan could see it was important to Sara, probably more so than any paternity issue, which he could understand. They'd neither of them ever been keen to wash dirty family linen in public. When their son had been cautioned for cannabis possession, they'd bought his silence with a skiing trip to Canada plus a lump sum if he kept quiet until he was thirty. Alan had gone along with it easily enough but now, on reflection, it looked ludicrous.

'They said the agreement is the same for everyone, all four candidates, so I don't think they'll change it. But I'll tell Nick Hewen your concerns and see what he suggests. And the lawyer who they got for me. I don't know if they can come up with something but I'll ask them to look into it.' He put his hand out to take back the agreement.

'If I ask you not to, would you refuse to sign?'

'Are you asking me not to?'

'I don't know. Maybe it's better to see it through or it will always be there. And there's the medical research aspect. I just want to know if you would.'

Alan thought about the decades they'd had together, the years he had been married to the almost stranger now sitting beside him. Someone else's crisis had opened a chasm of confidence in his marriage.

'Probably,' he said at last. 'It's a hundred thousand pounds and if I'm not the father, it's the closest I'll ever get to money for old rope. And wondering if I am the father might corrode my brain like battery acid. And if I am, the mother and, more importantly, the baby will never know for sure. But if you don't want me to, I probably won't do it.'

It was the unkindest of guilt trips. Alan registered the grief on his wife's face at his words. What was wrong with him that he didn't retract them? Was he blaming Sara for their marital mediocrity. It was horrible. He was horrible.

'I'll go to Ade's for a few days anyway and you can have some peace without me.' He stood up and left the room knowing she would try to talk about it more, and he didn't want to waste any energy on that discussion. Ten minutes later he was on his way to his brother's flat in Canary Wharf, three and a half hours at this time of night, if he was lucky. He detoured via Islington to put the unsigned agreement through the Hewen Jones letterbox. He stuck a post-it on the front: 'Need more time but probably not. Sara not keen on names and dates'.

*

Less than a week later, the four candidates had all had a call from Rosalie to reassure, flatter, thank, and confirm that Sophia and Brad would be in touch to 'finalise pre-birth information'. Alan had agreed to keep going until he made his final decision. Sophia met with each potential father methodically and sensitively checking the details gathered from Gina that might be relevant to the paternity questions, with gentle pushing to identifying variations. It was excruciating for all of them.

Brad's brief may have appeared less personal, but for the candidates it felt no less intrusive: mortgages, debts, career history, potential to breach Rosalie's agreement for a better offer, family weaknesses, arguments, previous addresses. All of them reached a point of push-back, asking if something was really necessary or insisting they absolutely weren't going to talk about that. Brad was unfailingly calm, polite and measured. He didn't remind them of the terms of the agreement, made no threats, gave no ultimatums. He didn't look menacing and he didn't sound menacing. They were all intimidated by him.

They had no reason to be. Brad was not going beat them up or disgrace them in the media, or drop a cruel word to friends or family. They knew he could although they were sure he wouldn't.

Rosalie read Sophia and Brad's combined report twice. She liked her job, always had. Never more than today. She phoned Brad to say thank you, spot-on results as usual, be in touch next time.

Chapter 16

Gerald rarely did scans himself, but everything was an exception for Gina Flowers. Rosalie said it was like the salon director washing a client's hair before it was cut. Like many of the male hospital staff, Gerald had his hair cut at the Turkish barbers near the access road to A&E. It had been there forever, long before Turkish barbers seemed to be everywhere, but had moved with the times. When Gerald first started going, a neat trim was all he expected and all he could have. He found neat hair a useful kick-start to his theatre prep, looking on as other members of the team tamed ponytails or curls beneath scrub hats, glad that he could use the extra ten minutes to think and centre himself. Now the place had a full menu from wet shave to head massage, and Gerald paid six times as much after his weekly visit than he had when he first became a customer.

The scan showed a foetus in the mid percentiles for every important indicator, with a strong heartbeat and moving around nicely. Gina confirmed Barney kicked and she could sometimes feel him 'rearranging the furniture' as she put it. To gauge the best time to operate, Gerald continued to discuss the case with the three colleagues he had invited to assist at the delivery. Viability was now over eighty per cent; another few days would get them over ninety. He suggested the twentieth of February – Wednesday less than a week away – for the working date of the Caesarean and asked Gina what she thought.

'I think what you think,' she said.

'A general anaesthetic would be best. I'll talk you through the reasons in the next few days, but that is the plan we are working to. After the birth, we will take the baby to the special care baby unit, so don't be alarmed when you come round and he isn't there. In these unusual circumstances, it is best we prearrange to take him up to the specialist paediatricians for a day or two so that if he does need some extra TLC, it's right there.' Gina nodded. She waited. It was obvious that Gerald had something else he wanted to broach.

'Gina, immediately after the birth, while you are still under the anaesthetic, we'd like to undertake an examination and a scrape of cells for tests. Arak Mudonak will be here from Cairo, and he is a world-leading – probably *the* world-leading – fertility expert. These tests are not directly for your benefit, although independent confirmation of what you have told us about your history will be useful for your project with Rosalie. But they will be enormously helpful to furthering our understanding of DESI and to pinpointing more accurately the timelines involved. It will help if we can take images of your womb and your other organs and a few small biopsies. You would be under anaesthetic for less than ten minutes additional.

'So, I am asking for your permission. But if you prefer not to give it, please let me assure you it will not affect your care in any way at all.'

Gina remembered nearly choking on a hard sweet when she was about nine, the feeling of panic when she couldn't catch her mother's attention despite being only a few feet behind her. And then the huge effort to finally cough it up, followed by washes of fear at what might have happened that came and went over several days. She hadn't told anyone at the time. It took her a few moments to identify what it was about the proposed tests that brought it so vividly to mind. Helplessness. Only herself to rely on, the terrible consequences of failure and swirling panic. Except for these immensely talented and dedicated men who wanted to scrape away at her innards.

'Of course. I would like to do whatever I can to assist. By way of appreciation for your care. Sorry, Gerald, that sounded sarcastic but it truly wasn't. I don't always get the balance right. Sarcasm sounds genuine and genuine sounds sarcastic. I've tried to stop being sarcastic as I've got older.'

Gina swerved back to matters gynaecological.

Why aren't there any women on your team? Do you think I could have a hysterectomy at the same time?'

Gerald paused for a moment. 'What makes you ask that? Unless we find something very unexpected during delivery, we would plan just a full internal examination, which would take maybe five minutes or so with us all working together, a scrape of the vagina and surrounding areas and a small sample from your womb. Is there a reason you'd like a hysterectomy?'

'So it can't happen again.'

It was a predicament to which Gerald had given no thought at all. The idea that DESI might happen twice was preposterous. But he saw immediately how Gina might be worried. DESI going to term once was unheard of. She was unique in evidenced medical history. Why wouldn't she think it could happen twice? He was surprised and irritated with himself that he hadn't anticipated the request.

299

'I need to be sure there isn't another embryo lurking. And maybe my womb might be of scientific interest.'

'A hysterectomy in a new mother is a significant trauma even for a much younger woman. It will more than double the recovery time. Let me think it through for a few days. Then I can give you a more considered opinion. I can't do your scan tomorrow, we've got triplets over the way, but ultrasound will keep me informed if there are any unexpected changes. I'll pop in on my way home.

'In a few years there will be,' he finished. 'Women on my senior team. The observing doctors, the ones who will be in the gallery, are 50:50.'

*

'Hello, Graham. We've met before. Well, not exactly been introduced but you were the first, the very first, person to know. I've wondered a few times if you got over the shock! Nice to see you again. How are you?' Gina Flowers smiled at Graham Neville.

'I'm, er, fine, thank you. Fine, yes.' Gray knew there was something else he should say, even as he controlled his terror. Amal had refused his request for a day off, made at the last minute when he saw the rota last night. 'Gray, there's only you and me on duty tomorrow and we've got to do the Flowers scan as well as the routines, so I'm half an hour down as it is. I'm sorry.'

'How are you?' Eventually he found the phrase he needed.

'Well, there's a question,' replied Gina. 'I should probably just say "fine" and leave it at that. I think I've been asked more times in the last three weeks how I am than the last decade.'

Gina remembered Graham's initial cheerfulness and polite chit-chat from that first scan, the way his steady hand had become suspended, still, above her body when he had seen the image. Today he was trembling, just slightly, his face had flushed the colour of a fading bruise when she spoke to him and he said nothing else except "all done", wiped away the gel and left.

She text Rosalie. 'Graham Neville, the scan man, seemed odd today'.

'Good to know. But don't worry, I'm fairly sure we're on it already and if not, we are now.'

*

Over the weekend, Evan came with the boys, who had developed a reserve with their grandmother that certainly hadn't been there before. They didn't get up on the bed with her or ask her to read with them. Their small faces were blank, their chatter absent. They didn't ask any questions and she didn't offer an explanation, Evan saying he'd tried and that would have to do. Sandra came. Gina's mother had been coming whenever she was allowed but this felt different. This time, all she could do was hold her daughter and hold back her tears. Stan and Alison came. By Sunday lunchtime Gina felt more like one hundred and two than sixty-two, exhausted, a freak show.

Greg stuck his head round the door just after 2 p.m. as Gina was resenting that of all her visitors not one of them had brought her lunch. 'Hey, Sis, can I come in?' Gina was pleased to see him with a force she hadn't expected. Although they got on well, they didn't interact in person all that much and hadn't for years: geography mainly, but lack of urgency too. There would always be another day or another Christmas to spend together, and so far there had been. He'd been a stalwart of admin efficiency for the funerals and aftermath for both the Georges. He started tackling a problem at the beginning and worked it through to the end. He focused on solutions, was calm and methodical.

'I've brought roast beef sandwiches and a bag of crisps – close as I could get to Sunday lunch. And do you think you'd like me to get you a doula?'

'God, yes. I need a doula. You do know it's a midwife and not a desert hideout or something, don't you?'

'Course. Live-in for three months, then live-out. Christine.'

'Who is Christine?'

'Been doing a bit of looking. Allegra's been on at me to get you a doula. She thinks you'll need someone when you leave hospital and a doula would be better than a nanny to start off with. But she didn't want to bother you or Rosalie.' Gina was momentarily floored that her brother was so au fait with things maternity and had found time for in-depth chat with Allegra. Rosalie was vetting nannies for discussion the next day, but a doula sounded spot on.

Greg was in his stride. 'Christine is a doula. Lives about fifteen minutes from you. Dan Rogers – started as an engineer with me, now works on the rigs – neither he nor Kasia, his wife, have got any family here so he got a doula for her. Christine. I remember him telling me when he put "doula" in an online Scrabble game one night. Everyone said it wasn't a word, but it was. I phoned him yesterday. He said Kasia said she was fantastic. Do you want to meet her?'

Trying to separate the details of Greg's work colleagues from the important bits, Gina absurdly felt Christine was a bit sudden, too much a fait accompli; which was unhelpful given it was what she needed. If she spent a couple of weeks post-natal in hospital, well – time was short for doula-finding. But a doula right here, off-the-shelf? Too perfect, all a bit much.

'Too much?' Greg asked. 'A bit "Here's one I prepared earlier?"' She nodded. 'How about I meet her, put a tentative feeler out there. At least if she's really irritating or doesn't know a steriliser from a soda maker, we can rule her out.' Gina nodded again but told Greg he'd have to run the whole thing by Rosalie, get confidentiality agreements, all of that. And it wasn't impossible Rosalie might already have someone for her to meet. Three days later, Christine was on board for three months, had a key to the house and was setting up a bed for herself in the baby's room. The shortlist of nanny candidates that Rosalie's assistant brought over on Monday was not needed.

'Mum seems to be doing OK,' said Greg when Gina asked. 'She says she's quite the talk of the wash house.'

Fear for the project swamped over Gina. 'No. She hasn't told anyone? She knew – surely she knew – she couldn't say anything. Even if it wasn't for the money, she shouldn't have.'

'She didn't,' said Greg, no hint of reproach in his tone but Gina filled that in for herself. 'Not about you anyway. No, she is buying a new car.'

'What? She hasn't driven her own car for five years. She's not really safe and she knows it. What is she thinking? Everything's going mad, Greg. I'm pregnant, so are both my daughters-in-law, Stan is married and his wife is a stranger who talks about flannies, whatever they are. Evan would be separating if Amelie wasn't up the duff. My grandsons think I'm an uncuddly freak and won't talk to me. You're organising doulas and Mum's buying a car she's scared to drive. I'll have to talk to her doctor. But they don't like taking someone's licence away, do they.' She put her fist in her mouth to shut herself up and closed her eyes to stop the tears.

'Well, I see what you mean about most of it, stuff, going on at the moment. It's a lot. My suspicion is that Mum is buying the car for you. She said the man told her it definitely has ISO fixings. She hasn't said so but she wouldn't, would she, in case you freaked out. Like that. At most she'll drive it home from the showroom. And I can go with her. But, as for the rest, yep, all a bit topsy-turvy.' As that sunk in, he added: 'Your niece is going to Seattle for a year. Some sort of reciprocal technical programme. She's really excited. It was quite competitive. There's a bit of normal.'

It was still hard to believe in the middle of her own crisis that the world went on around her. People caught trains, went out for lunch, did housework and the rest. And Laura had just clocked a triumph. 'She deserves it, Greg. She's always worked hard, but she's got a real flair. I'll take the baby to visit her.' Nothing like looking fantastically forward from the middle of the crisis.

He smiled. 'It's an SUV hybrid. Black with a cream roof.'

'I don't know if I'll need a car. What if I don't keep it?'

'The baby or the car? Sorry. Then we'll sell the car.'

'But it'll lose thousands.' What nonsense she was talking, but it felt good to get worked up about something banal like how new cars lose their value. 'If Rosalie's project goes through, and even if it doesn't, I'm guaranteed a good bit. I can afford a car.'

'She wants to do something, Gin. It's not because she thinks you can't afford it. She thinks you won't have time when you get out – excuse the prison analogy – to go shopping for a good car deal, and she wants you to have a car as soon as you need it. With a baby seat.'

'I won't be able to drive for at least six weeks, maybe longer.'

'No, but it will be able to be driven by Christine or someone like her maybe, and Stan can use it while he sorts himself out. He hasn't, they haven't, him and Alison, bought a car yet. I don't think.'

'Stan can afford to buy a car,' she said.

'Stop arguing about it. Unless you really badly want to upset Mum's efforts enough to veto a car that you will like and will need, then stop.

'It's got heated seats. You've always wanted heated seats.'

'What about you? Is she buying you a car. Keep us even?' She and Greg both felt the futility of the argument but he counteracted anyway.

'Do you remember when she gave me money for a house deposit when I had no money after Laura arrived? And you said you didn't need the same because you had some life insurance from George. And I accepted and never gave it another thought. Because you loved me, wanted me to have the house and wanted Mum to be able to help. Think on and change the subject. Anyway,' he smiled at her. 'I prefer to go by train.'

He left soon after and got Rosalie to set aside her shortlist of nannies and instead set up the whole Christine thing. Gina didn't drive the car until three months after the birth, but she was still driving it when she decided to relinquish her own licence. She loved that car.

*

Two days after he'd done that last scan on Gina Flowers, Gray lay sweating under his duvet, cradling a hot water bottle, nausea ebbing and flowing like a particularly unsavoury tide. He had to trust them. They said they wouldn't call the police or tell the hospital if he packed it in right away and gave them what he'd got. They took his phone, just took it – more or less robbed him although he'd said they could – and deleted all his back ups while he slithered around the leather bench in the upmarket hotel giving them his passwords. He'd resigned saying he wouldn't work his notice, citing a suddenly ill family member in Ireland; he couldn't face the chance of bumping into Gina Flowers at Valley. Amal had asked how close was the family member, so sorry to hear that, very sudden, he'd never mentioned Ireland, was it terminal, if he didn't work his notice it was really frowned on professionally, wouldn't do his chances any good, was he coming back, she could hold his job open if it was going to be short-term. Gray didn't know if she was being really kind or didn't believe him. He'd agreed to work a week, thinking Mr Howard would do all the final scans himself and by the time Gina came round after the birth, he'd be gone. But the coalition of lies and forced trust that was holding his life in one piece was fragile, so he lay under the duvet trying to sweat out his anxiety, thinking of ever more bizarre but legitimate ways he might not have to go to work on Monday which ranged from a fire in his block of flats (no one hurt) to a contagious disease outbreak at Valley (resulting in a world-leading vaccine).

*

After the weekly team brief on Monday, Amal caught up with him as he was sidling up a corridor.

'Gray, could you pop your head round Mrs Flowers' door please. She's asked to see you. Not sure why, didn't have time to chat to her. Let me know if anything comes up.'

Gray, listening fatalistically to Gina, was not surprised that it was a combination of money and who you know, two things he'd never had, that had found him out. Gina explained to him in an understanding tone that she had a PR agency looking for leaks and the 'incoming leads' section of every news desk knew to tip the agency off if anything like her story came their way, on the basis that if they published, they wouldn't just be damned they'd be in court and probably bankrupt soon after. And never get a lead from the PR agency again, which Gray inferred was a journalistic fate leading to oblivion. He wasn't even surprised the PR people knew he'd been to Oxford, into one internet café and come home; when only a very few people apart from doctors and family knew about Gina's story, it wasn't so hard to keep tabs on those few people. If you had money.

Gina said she knew how tempting it must have been, she was sure he wouldn't have gone through with it and she'd make sure there was a chance for him to get his story into the big one if he wanted, and even get paid a bit. He didn't know if she was really nice or taking the piss.

Chapter 17

Gina was frightened of the op, frightened of the aftermath, frightened of the responsibility. She had decided to give Barney his father's name – first name, surname, whichever flowed best – as a middle name, no matter what the father thought or wanted. Gerald came in to examine her, ask how she was and tell her the delivery team would be in place from 8 a.m. tomorrow. They talked through a few more logistics of paternity. If it was George Two's baby, which Gerald thought the least likely, it would be obvious at birth. The indicators available from scans and tests to date had not leant towards the baby being mixed race, and George Flowers's vasectomy meant the conception mechanics would have been the most obviously problematic. While not entirely excluding the possibility, Gerald did joke that Gina shouldn't book any flights to Miami. He had agreed to her having the hysterectomy. Dr Mudonak was very pleased at the now unlimited opportunity to test and study Gina's willingly donated reproductive organs.

Gina wanted to rule George One in or out before the tests on the others. She really wanted to be able to tell the boys if Barney was a full brother. Either way, she thought it might cause a lot of emotional fallout for them. Rosalie had suggested some talking therapy and as far as she knew they both had said they'd be willing. She should have arranged it years ago for them, growing up fatherless. She felt sad that something so obvious she could have done she failed to do.

Sometime after that point, the tests on the other three – possibly still four, Alan remaining undecided – candidates would go ahead. Gina insisted that the tests had to be done on all of them, and not just stop when one was positive, even if it was a George. She needed the negatives as well as the positive. Right now, she needed to talk to Rosalie about managing this and other stuff. Thankfully, Rosalie was coming in later.

'Gerald, what if none of them is the father?'

'One of them is definitely the father, unless you have forgotten a candidate. But if we don't get a positive test, we need to examine scientifically if the drift of time has weakened the DNA connection. I think that is highly unlikely. I am as confident as I can be that we will be able to identify the biological father after all the tests are complete.'

They went through the testing process once more. Results would be conclusive: '100% not the father' or '99.5% the father'. If it was the first test using the boys' DNA, the baby's chances of being a full sibling would be indicated as 99.5% either way. Gerald was arranging for a secure testing facility to be made available on site. She would be the first to know the father after the tester and Gerald.

During the last couple of weeks of bed rest, the issue of paternity had grown markedly for Gina. Despite the monitoring, the staff and visitors, and still being able to walk about, she felt very alone; decisions about Barney's future were hers and hers alone. The burden shrouded her every moment and it became gradually harder to let chips of light-heartedness find a way in. She wondered if her preoccupation was to displace her anxiety about the imminent prospect of caring for a baby; she couldn't understand why the paternity mattered so much. She didn't want a relationship with the men – she definitely didn't want to meet those who weren't the father. She hoped the one who was would want to meet and greet Barney, perhaps stay in touch with him, maybe introduce him to any other children or grandchildren. But she didn't intend to push for it. And what if they all tested negative; her confidence in Gerald was rock solid except for this, as she saw it, possibility. What if it was Alan? Would she meet him? Would he agree to meet her? And if he hadn't taken the test, would him being the father by default be good enough for her, for Barney, for the boys? Would people look at her then Alan and wonder how two old people were capable of such lust, think they'd made it up? Except of course they wouldn't know. Sometimes following her own thoughts was like tracking a snowflake in a blizzard.

Despite all of this, the paternity project was a boon she was grimly glad to have, for Barney's sake, yes, of course. But also for herself. She wasn't proud of it, but the media prospects were her saving grace in this gloom. She was quite excited about the podcasts. Maybe even a television drama with her played by—

Enough, she thought. But it had given her a small respite from the fear.

*

Dear Barney,

      If I never get the chance to meet you, I want to tell you that I love you. I was taken aback – you'll learn about British understatement,

311

no doubt – when I found I was expecting you, and it took me some of the very short time we've had together to get used to the idea. But now you are nearly here and I know we'll manage. Or, if you have to, you'll manage without me. You'll need the others, but you'll be OK.

I don't yet know who your father is. I hope I have done the right thing in trying to find out. Forgive me if I got that wrong.

Stan and Evan know all about difficult family times and their father would have been so happy to see the men they have grown into. I remember giving birth to them clearly, in a way I won't with you, and your childhoods will be very different. But I could not love any one of you more than I do, and I cherish the thought that if I am not there in person to tell you every day how much I love you, you will read this letter and know it to be true.

Gina's silent tears made small drops on the letter. She couldn't decide how to sign it. She wrote 'Mum' finally. But it wasn't right, only marginally better than 'Mummy', 'Your mother' or 'Gina Flowers'.

*

Dear Stan and Evan,
    Look after him for me in
whatever way you think best. Which
means you must first look after
yourselves – each other, your
children and their mothers. You have
been the joy of my life since the days
you were born. If I can't tell Barney
that, do it for me. And all the little-
ies. I love them so much, including
the ones that are yet to arrive.

    She had no trouble signing this one: the same way
she had signed emails, notes and scribbles to them for years.
'Lots of love, m xx'.

*

Dear George,
    Stan and Evan used to make
my heart break on a regular basis
because they couldn't know you. I
told them, often – too often – as they
were growing up how much I loved
them and how much you loved them
too. They were just small boys, then
teenage boys, and I was too much.
    I'm not sure we, you and me,
were ever really *in* love, but we did

313

love each other. I think we were both on the rebound and we didn't talk about it. Sally three doors up broke your heart, didn't she? And Eddie broke mine. We found each other and then we made the boys. So we owe Sally and Eddie big time. Sally's on the radio quite a lot these days. She's a bit niche in a good way. If you love a bridge, she's the woman and you really did love a good bridge. There's a new Forth Road Bridge now, the Queensferry Crossing. It's beautiful.

I am going to have Barney soon. I'm sixty-two. Don't ask. It's something of a story. I need S & E to look out for him. He'll be an uncle to their children (two here, two on the way) but we all think cousins will be easier for now. I know they will look after him, and you were always much nicer than me so I just wanted to say thank you because they get that from you.

Gina x

She wrote 'Stan and Evan – open in 2030' on the envelope.

*

Gina felt more in control of her outward composure than her emotions. Her insistence that paternity tests only be done when her six-week post-op period was over was written into a contract, together with instructions for what she wanted to happen if she died before then.

Gerald was talking. 'This is important pre-op stuff, Gina. Arak Mudonak and Hammy Maynard need to talk to you and do a final scan and examination. Around 7 a.m., if that's OK.'

Hammy Maynard was another eminent obs surgeon. He had five older sisters and the story was his mother had taken a bet that if he was a boy, she'd call him Hamlet after her favourite television ad with the hunk on a desert island smoking a cigar and being happy. The bet had been called off and his first name was Steven, but his family had always called him Hammy and it spilled into school and then his professional life. He'd grown into his nickname, looking somewhat hamster-like when he was concentrating hard. As he did when he operated. Gerald told Gina all this while moving his hand inch by inch over her abdomen.

Late in the day, Rosalie arrived. Kirkcaldy Alan, as Rosalie referred to him, had still not signed a contract for testing or further participation although he had been paid and the NDA was binding. Rosalie explained to Gina about timing, about his wife's understandable request for confidentiality.

'I wondered about that,' said Gina, 'once I knew a bit more. Well, once I knew he was still married, really.'

Rosalie looked at her. 'We have the five other potentials. If they are all negative, the father must be Kirkcaldy Alan. We will still know.'

'You say it "Kir-coddy,"' said Gina, 'not "Kirk-call-dee". Sort of like "Ark-en-saw", not "Ark-can-sas".' Both women smiled. 'I've written a letter for Sara.' Gina handed Rosalie several sealed envelopes. 'I seem to have letter-fever at the moment. This one, the one for Sara, is for now. The others are for if I die or suffer a life-changing injury having Barney. Can you get the letter to Sara? It's not to make her change her mind or get Kirk-call-dee Alan to change his. It's just to explain.'

'Of course.' Rosalie sent a text and the letter was delivered as fast as a motorbike could get to Yorkshire.

*

Dear Sara,

My need to tell Barney (I'm going to call the baby Barney) who his father is, and to get enough money for his future, has outweighed considerations I would otherwise have given to innocent parties in this – what am I going to call it – situation.

You have been caught up in it and I have thought about saying I'm sorry. But I knew what I was doing when I gave details of the men I'd slept with, so 'sorry' sounds like what I think of as 'politicians' regret'. I put Barney's needs, and my own, first. If I could have done that, made this

316

much money and satisfied the science without identifying Alan, I would have. But I couldn't, so I did. And I knew when I did it that there would be fallout.

Alan and I spent one night together. I knew he was married so, again, I knew what I was doing. He told me you were so beautiful, he felt privileged every time he looked at you. He also said you were 'commercial' (I kid you not and it was very definitely a compliment), you were kind and that you loved him.

My second husband proposed to me a few months after that night. I never told him about Alan and maybe – ethically, you know, full disclosure, no secrets – I should have. Perhaps George wouldn't have proposed if I had and that would have been the defining mistake of my life.

Sara, I don't know if I can say this without sounding patronising. I hate patronising. But sometimes things just happen. Kirkcaldy just happened. It was a moment. If Alan had wanted to contact me again, he could have. He didn't.

I might not be apologising
but I am sending solidarity. And
acknowledging the memory. It is only
a memory and it was never going to
be anything else.
Gina Flowers

*

Alan met Rosalie a few days later.

'Sara is still bothering me about confidentiality although she's gone a bit softer. I don't know if it's the money or what. She does not want her name, so my sleeping with Gina, to get out. She's OK with the rest of it. I know we've talked about it but just checking again: can you keep that confidential?'

Long having anticipated the rerun of this question, Rosalie explained that a key requirement of payment was truth as far as it was known, which Alan had provided to date. So had Gina, she said gently, and their truth was shared, matched, far more than was common after so long and in such unusual, delicate circumstances. It was not just Alan's story. But he could withdraw now without penalty if he wished.

'If you want to participate in any second phase, so a screen or full print version, that would be subject to what could be agreed. If it was a docudrama, then it's unlikely the producers would agree to either anonymity or massaging of dates. If it was a drama based on true events, which is my preference and at the moment Gina's preference, there would be more scope, but it is such a compelling detail the way forward there might lie in disguising identity. Maybe even making a feature of that. If you decide to proceed…' Rosalie paused, deciding how much further to emphasise that, essentially, it had taken two to tango, '…you'll also need to consider that Gina might want to be entirely accurate.'

'She might not if I ask her not to.'

'No,' said Rosalie. 'There is a good chance she might not reveal your identity. If you are not the father. But she will need to reveal the dates to fulfil her side of the contract, and if you are the father that would be complicated. Not insurmountable. And Gina is generous, open and reasonable. Whether that will hold sway in the face of producer opposition, we don't know.'

'So you're saying even if I don't take a test, the facts will come out but Gina and the producers might protect my identity?'

'I would need to undertake those negotiations, but it is certainly a realistic starting point. But it misses the main point. My advice, Alan, is for you and your wife to make your peace with it. Take up the counselling. Whether you hide it or not from the world, you can't hide it from each other now.' Rosalie realised he was not really looking for anonymity or to conceal the night but a sound basis to explain to Sara why he couldn't fulfil her entirely reasonable requests.

*

On Friday, a few days after Barney would be here, checked and safe in Gina's arms or at least an SCBU cot, the 'fathers' would be told of his arrival. Much consideration had been given by the production team as to whether to involve the fathers' families, but Rosalie had always said that was too much, especially for a podcast. Maybe if the story was expanded, that would be revisited later. For now it was Gina, Stan and Evan, Liv, Greg and Sandra. And three, maybe four, men who, like Gina, had found events from decades ago rip-roaring to the front of their lives. Well, not exactly like Gina. None of them were giving birth or preparing for twenty years of childcare.

Gina asked Rosalie if any of the fathers had wanted to meet her or know about her. What was that about? It sounded vain even in her own ears. Rosalie didn't have to answer directly because the contract expressly said no contact, no enquiries unless mutually agreed after the birth. Which Gina had forgotten. And then Rosalie told her she'd optioned the rights for a newspaper serialisation, a book and a television drama.

'I can't. I can't cope with that.' The sliver of excitement she'd felt earlier was gone.

'Which is why it's optioned,' said Rosalie. 'You have a two-year veto. We need to do the podcasts to get the financial security for you and Barney, but the rest is entirely – and I mean entirely – up to you. No pressure from me or anyone, and I won't let the media people anywhere near you unless and until you're ready. Which might be never.'

Gerald reappeared and told Gina to sleep, or rest if she couldn't sleep. Then he and Rosalie left. Gina and Barney were on their own.

Chapter 18

Everyone was in place. Evan was at home except when he was at Valley. The Rosalie-organised childcare was the thrill of his life. Alison was in Australia, Amelie in Berlin. Stan and Greg oscillated between the coffee shop and the waiting room, a ragged back-up band of anxious, fretful relatives. Four obstetricians and six midwives were in theatre. So were Gina and Sandra. Here he comes.

*

Gowned and masked, Sandra replayed the last few months. Gina had undoubtedly looked a bit fuller about the middle if you'd stared and cared, but it had not crossed Sandra's mind to ask if she'd reactivated her very dormant romantic life and might be pregnant. Even now, in a delivery room, the very thought seemed absurd. Sandra's maternity ward had been a leaking prefab, part of a repurposed wartime building that had been temporary in 1940 but somehow still in use in the 80s. In the mid 1990s it had deteriorated to the point where midwives only half-joked that expectant mothers should take an umbrella into labour to protect themselves from leaks in the roof. The site was sold for a few hundred thousand to end up, after lengthy appeals for change of use, making a few million for the developers.

This maternity unit, scraped bare by underfunding, was only a notch up from the prefab: at least the roof didn't leak. Ambitions to provide comfort, facilities for birth partners and a peaceful ambiance had been battered by budget cuts. Sandra was reassured by this being Gerald's home base: he hadn't parachuted in for Gina's pain and his glory. He delivered difficult babies here when presumably he could have settled for a comfy suite in a US facility for the well-heeled, where he could sprinkle a bit of obs and gynae fairy dust on celebrities and mommy CEOs. The downbeat waiting rooms with their peeling health and safety posters were his chosen patch and Sandra thought the more of him for it.

Sandra so badly wanted George Flowers to be the father of Gina's baby. She had known George since childhood when they'd stuck together at school, ridiculed and worse for their race, for being friends, for their clothes, accents and hair. Their families remained close even when the Flowers returned to America and after George went to college in Miami. Both families had believed, their assumptions shifting from certainty to wedding plans, that Sandra and George would make a match of it. But she met Wesley, fell tip-top in love and, whenever George had come to London for work, observed his broken heart from a distance she hadn't ever thought possible between them. George and Wesley were polite to each other for more than twenty years. Not long before Wesley left her, Sandra had introduced George, newly permanently returned to London, to Gina. She hadn't been matchmaking. To her private shame, when they properly got together she realised she didn't really want George to be loved up with another woman, let alone Gina, and her enthusiasm for their relationship was manufactured: bitch in the manger, she thought to herself. She felt a gravelly resentment even now, despite contentment enough with Leroy for a decade or more. Leroy was about to retire and Sandra sensed renewed pressure to get married coming down the track. That wasn't going to happen. She supposed she ought to tell him before he asked.

Even on the emergency service soaps, reality shows and hospital documentaries she was a keen fan of, Sandra had never seen so many people lined up for a delivery. Although Gina had unwittingly deprived her of George, she was still Sandra's closest friend, the one she would trust with her every secret (except George), and the executor of her will. Sandra looked straight at the medics with a hint of challenge, letting them know she was watching them, and took her place at Gina's side, by her face, at her heart. Sandra held Gina's hand as they put her under. As they started to count backwards, Gina said something no one could make out, but Sandra just managed to say, 'I will. Of course I will,' hoping, knowing it was the right thing, before Gina's face and body sagged into unconsciousness and she looked frighteningly old to be the mother of a newborn. God willing. It was, to be frank, shocking.

They cut into her as if it was nothing. Routine for them; less so this time but, nevertheless, something they'd all seen or done or both dozens of times before. Good. And they lifted Barney out, ten or so professionals immediately surrounding him, looking for defects or perfection, checking oxygen, counting toes, whisking him off to SCBU, almost as though his mother didn't matter. Baby first. Sandra caught a glimpse. George Flowers was not his father. This was an all-White baby. To her surprise, she fell in love with him. She was the first person on the planet who knew him, as it were, to see him – and she adored him.

The medics began removing things, taking pictures with tiny cameras, scraping and tying and prodding, talking through tiny mics to the watching students, several of them all around Gina at the same time. Gerald saw the fear on Sandra's face and went over to her.

'It was boring, Sandra, a routine C-section, a routine hysterectomy. We could not have asked for a more straightforward procedure. It is the next bit that is exciting for us. We are very thankful this bit was not exciting. Gina will take a while to recover, but the operations went well. And Barney is…' Gerald searched for a word. He didn't generally engage in congratulatory talk, was off to the next patient and left the new arrival's relatives to others. 'A cutie. Gina will come round soon. We have different surgeons doing different parts to minimise the time she is under and the stress on her body.'

Then Arak called out, 'Good to close. We've got everything we need. Thank you, everyone,' and Hammy started stitching, his needlework as neat as a Victorian schoolmaid's. Almost invisible.

*

Forty-five minutes or so later, Gina came round. Gerald Howard was there with other medics and midwives, but it was Sandra, at the back of her audience, that Gina looked for. Sandra smiled, nodded and welled up, moving to the front to take her friend's hand.

'He's fabulous, Gin. All White. And all right. Can I be his godmother? I know I've got Stan but I am good at God and you never know if he'll need Him.'

Gina smiled, cried and winced. 'As if there'd be anyone else. Just don't make him religious. Not hellfire and damnation, anyway. Love and peace, that will do.' Gina was drawn and weary, dark circles, red blotches and pallid undertones all battling it out on for pole position on her face. So she wouldn't be asking Amanda to be godmother. No American relatives for Barney. Or she might. Who says a boy couldn't have two godmothers? God, maybe. She was limp with exhaustion.

A voice cut through her postnatal fog. 'Gina, it's Gerald. Barney has been safely delivered. They have taken him to SCBU to check everything out, but to me he looks absolutely spot on. And I've seen a lot of babies. He's two point eight kilos. Ten fingers, ten toes. Breathing on his own. A cutie.' Gerald paused, please with his summing up. 'Well done.' He paused again. 'Would you like me to tell your family?' Gina nodded. 'I don't think visitors are a good idea for a few days so I'll tell them you're fine, Barney's fine but in SCBU, and you are both under observation. You can phone them tomorrow.' And then he slid out of the door and left just a crew to tidy up, Sandra and Gina.

Gina realised she had been safely delivered of a baby boy by Caesarean section, cared for by the world's best. 'Delivered of': they said that for the royal family – and the Virgin Mary, more to the point. She felt like she'd had no more part in conception than the Virgin Mary.

'He isn't a Flowers,' confirmed Sandra.

'I was so hoping he would be,' said Gina. Being on this side of the Caesarean let her acknowledge it. 'It would be best on a practical level if he was a Douglas, full siblings, that sort of thing. But I loved G2. He was my only true love, I

325

think. Men-wise. I love the children. And the grandchildren.' Gina was suddenly struck by how her grandchildren had dropped off her radar. Barney had outshone them like meteors in front of the sun. She tried and failed to remember their names. Everything has its price. Barney's safe delivery and— It began with A, no, there were two of them, they both began with A. The As had moved down the ladder. She was suddenly determined to move them back up again.

'Well, he isn't.' In her imagination Sandra had spent the proceeds of Rosalie's deals several times over, Now that Barney was here, she was hoping there might be more mileage in the story. She wouldn't have abandoned Gina had there been no money. Both women knew she would have been steadfast and sound whatever happened. But money makes most things easier. Who wouldn't want easier over not? Sandra had also hoped George Flowers was the father because a mixed-race baby added something to the story, but that fleeting wish was now replaced by a real desire to know who the father was. Not a Douglas, she hoped, because she suspected that would diminish Barney's media value. 'Gina, I need to leave you now. They're making faces at me like I'm the last person in the cinema when the lights went up ages ago. You need to sleep while Barney gets a meal, I guess. But I need you to know I love you. I love Barney. He's my new baby heartthrob. Thank you for today.' Sandra squeezed her friend's hand and Gina was asleep before she'd made it to the door.

Sandra went to the hospital coffee shop and turned on her phone. It seemed Gina's sons, brother and mother – Liv had not been able to get on the plane to Spain – were all in Valley, so she walked across the frozen lawn to join them. It wasn't yet 10 a.m.

*

Mr Howard came in and told everyone that mother and baby were well. Barney was in the SCBU, but initial indications were of a healthy baby, and while Gina was very tired she had stood up well, really well, to the operation and was now sleeping. He said that, subject to tests and overnight rest, they could perhaps see mother and baby in the next few days. Did anyone have any questions?

'Is the baby mixed race?' asked Stan.

'I don't believe so from the visual examination,' replied Gerald. He looked at the room. Stan, Evan, Gina's mother and brother, and her friend Sandra. 'We will be proceeding with the paternity tests for your father and step-father, just to confirm, this afternoon and expect the results within twenty-four hours.'

'So by tomorrow we should know if he is our brother or half-brother?' Even as he spoke Stan wondered why that was important. He hadn't even really known his biological father. He was going to be a good bruncle to Barney, no matter what. He saw that Evan had half an eye on his phone, trying not to look into his pocket for the next text.

'Yes,' said Gerald. 'Providing your material for DNA analysis in advance was really helpful.' He meant the strands of hair Evan and Stan had handed over in sealed plastic packets accompanied by signed consent forms, like a scene left on the cutting-room floor of CSI. Gina had given Gerald the packet of things she'd brought back from the hospital the day George Flowers had died. 'Rosalie is going to come over in about ten minutes and can talk to everyone individually or as a group, or both.' Gerald felt grubby talking about his wife's PR in the midst of a medical event. He moved on.

'Barney is in SCBU. He is there because of the unusual circumstances, as a precaution and because our view was that Gina's body, maybe her psyche as well, would be unlikely to adapt well to feeding. By early afternoon we will have observed all his reactions, measured every digit, checked his blood, his weight and anything else it is possible to check. We do not expect to find anything of concern.

'We – by whom I mean the medical team and the lead midwives – have a lot to do in terms of research and practice review in the coming weeks. Gina has enabled us, through her willing cooperation, to examine an area of medicine that will be entirely new. You have all contributed to this and so will the paternal candidates. We are very grateful. My professional excitement at the opportunities is fully informed by everyone's generosity. Thank you.'

A pause from Gerald, Stan thought, was there to let everyone prepare mentally to deal with what was coming.

'I am myself part of the project,' he continued. 'I am giving an interview. I will make sure Gina is happy with what I intend to say. I am not being paid, but I do expect an increase of interest, not all of it positive, in my professional persona.'

'Oh,' said Evan. 'I'm a bit surprised. Why?' Gerald understood immediately that Evan meant why give an interview, not why wasn't he being paid.

'Several reasons, including personal vanity. More important is that we need to ensure the rarity of DESI is communicated and properly reported wherever possible. We expect some wilful misreporting and sensationalism. I don't know if we can manage the expectations of prospective parents who might hope for progress as a result, or reassure women who may become anxious, but I need to try. One driver is that without me the story might lack credibility, and I am best placed to counter the rebuttals of the worst nonsense.'

Gina's backing band absorbed these thoughts, even as they processed the practical and emotional implications of the new arrival. Gerald was telling them nicely that without his participation, their fees might be in jeopardy, let alone Gina's. Like Sandra, Evan had mentally spent his already, he paying off a chunk of the mortgage, she on a family holiday from which she would derive as much pleasure in the planning as actually spending time away, and a new car, with a bit left over for whatever. Greg intended to bank it in trust for Laura. Liv had decided to split it between the other grandchildren, thinking that Gina's fee would be enough to see Barney right. She wondered if she should leave Stan's baby out of this legacy; she suspected Stan had plenty of money and Evan just about got by. She hadn't decided yet.

Gerald was hitting his stride. 'Having a baby is always, without exception in my experience, a life-changing event. For Gina, this life-changing event did not have time to take root before it happened. I have delivered babies of only a very few mothers, probably no more than five in thirty years, who did not know or – honestly – strongly suspect they were pregnant until their final weeks or, just once, when labour was underway. PTSD is not precisely the right term, but it is the best I can use to describe the shock.'

They waited for another pause, surfing with it when it came, enjoying the moment of peace.

'Gina is sixty-two, post-menopausal' – another pause – 'and has not been in a relationship since the death of her second husband. She is traumatised. So please can I ask that your actions and words over the next while have care for her at their centre. If you do this for Gina, and I know you can, you will also be doing it for Barney.

'My view is that we should see the project as a positive. For me, the science, the learning, the international cooperation, the excitement, the chance to know and care for Gina are gifts I had not expected. I am pleased – thrilled – to get a platform for obstetrics, for mothers and for babies. Barney was delivered in an NHS hospital. Gina did not need insurance to get the best possible medical care.

'My advice is don't agonise, wonder if you're doing the right thing. Don't think you're exploiting Gina or Barney. Celebrate. Share. Love. Give thanks. I have work to do. You have a baby's head to wet.' And he left.

Gina's family now needed to find their own ways through.

'Exploiting my own daughter?'

'No, Gran,' said Stan. 'That's what he said we weren't doing. I'm glad he gave it a name. Pimping out Mum is what I was worried about. Not any more. Let's all go and have lunch and talk Project Barney. I'm paying. There used to be a nice pub up the road that has a private back room.'

Stan got on his phone to book.

'It's only 11 a.m.,' said his brother.

'That's OK. They'll do coffee for those that can't face champagne.'

330

The day after Barney was born, Gerald updated all the men about his safe arrival. They knew already, of course, that there would be a wait for DNA tests, but he went over it again, explained why it was best to let Barney have his eight-week check and Gina a further period of recovery before they proceeded. Gerald now referred to Gina as 'Barney's mother', hoping to establish that Barney's paternity was the interest, not some sort of relationship, or rekindling of a relationship, with the past. The distant past. Gerald made provisional appointments for all of them, except cruising Jerome, with the senior profiling technician and himself for twelve weeks' time.

*

Barney's family called him Rubble from the get-go, and as he grew up people thought either that he just had an unusual name or he was nicknamed after one of the dogs in Paw Patrol, not the Flintstones character. It was of no consequence to Barney. He was a long, thin, serious baby and he would turn into a tall, slim, serious man. When he smiled, it had been earned, it was about something. He was not a baby who smiled just at the sight of his mother. He smiled when he had something specific to smile about, something more than the everyday minutiae of life. Like his milk being at exactly the right temperature, which was no more than once every couple of weeks; mostly it was slightly too hot, which made him cry, not because he burned his lip, but because it just wasn't right. Or slightly too cool, which was worse because it wouldn't get to the right temperature on that feed, which made him sigh longer and deeper than a babe in arms could be expected to.

*

Gina couldn't easily pick up Barney but she could cuddle him sitting down, which she did much of the time when one of them wasn't sleeping or eating. At first the nurses fed him, but as the days went on it was Stan or her mother or very occasionally Gina herself. She was much weaker than she'd expected. Cuddling him was one thing, but trying to hold a bottle and get the contents in to his mouth felt about as easy as the moon landing. Her milk never came in. She was grateful for that. She didn't have two unexploded hand grenades on her chest, which is how she remembered it from thirty-five years ago when a baby wouldn't feed on time. She lost track of time. February's short days and long nights made 5 p.m. feel like 11 p.m. and the outside world was flat, dispirited, waiting for spring. Gerald came in twice a day, Rosalie and Sandra every couple of days and it felt like Stan and her mother never went home. Nurses did the night feeds. Midwives and medics asked for short appointments to discuss discrete items of research. She cooperated, far too flattened to resist.

Allegra, by her side from the very first hour of the news, had been one of the first to see her after the birth. 'Congratulations,' she'd said and they had both laughed at the absurdity of it.

'I need you to be in my story, Allegra. I was so lucky to get you assigned to me that day. Can I talk to Rosalie about it? To work out something. You know, something?'

Allegra nodded and felt the welcome prick of recognition she'd thought would not come.

On Gerald's second visit after Barney's arrival, he told Gina there was no DNA match with Evan or Stan or George Flowers. Gina asked him to tell the boys that no Georges had been involved in the making of this baby.

Chapter 19

A few weeks after his meeting with Nick, on a grainy rainy sloshy Friday afternoon in April, Roland arrived at Valley to meet Gerald. He was half an hour early; Gerald was half an hour late after a difficult delivery. He apologised, although the explanation itself would have been sufficient. Roland sensed that when Gerald said 'difficult' it meant on the edge of catastrophe, and he ventured to ask if mother and baby were well. 'So far, so good,' was the reply, 'and in good hands.' Gerald moved straight on, like a train changing track, now with green signals all the way.

'As you know, my wife Rosalie McGrath is handling the PR aspects of this situation. My involvement with that is limited, but there is, of course, crossover. I am leading the research and led the clinical care.' Roland nodded. He appreciated that Gerald was upfront, and somewhat mousier than he'd expected from the headshot on Valley's website.

'Doctor,' he said, 'I think I remember from my initial contacts with the project, that you would request my DNA even if—' He hesitated, looking for a word, not wanting to mention Gina, to sound familiar when, in truth, he really hadn't been familiar with Gina at the time of their liaison, let alone forty years later. 'Whether or not the husband, one of her dead husbands, wasn't the father. Is that right?'

'Yes. Barney's mother wanted negatives as well as positives as reassurance. You'll no doubt appreciate the need for as much reassurance as possible. In a unique situation such as this.

'Gina Flowers was married and widowed twice. We now know, however, that neither of her husbands are – were – the baby's father.'

'Is the baby OK?'

'Yes, fine,' replied Gerald and carried on without further expansion. 'The provision, or not, of a DNA sample is your decision. If you decide to give a sample, then I can now talk you through the process.'

Roland just nodded and Gerald went on. 'I'll take you over to our senior profiler, who will ask a lot of questions, run some standard metrics such as blood pressure, weight, height and so on, take blood and hair samples – two lots – and then, in about another three to four weeks or thereabouts, she will run the comparison with the baby's samples to determine paternity. When we do this exactly will depend on the mother's and baby's progress, but we will give you at least forty-eight hours' notice of when we expect the results to be ready. We can upload these for you to access at a time of your choosing. But we will also make an appointment for you to receive the results in person from me, and you need only decide at the time what you'd like to do.

'I have tried to anticipate some questions. All the candidates will have the results available on the same day. The option for psychotherapeutic intervention will remain open for two years. The mother does not yet know if she would like to meet any of the candidates, or if she would agree to a request from one or more of them to meet her or Barney, the baby, although her preliminary inclination is that she will. The baby is now well over three kilos. If you do decide to give a sample, you can change your mind about it being used at any time until twenty-four hours before the testing date. If you are the biological father, there are implications for you and your family, some of which may be profound and far-reaching.'

Gerald was aware his delivery had been direct to the point of brusque. It improved in the next potential-paternal interviews, but covered the same material. He was glad he had left a decent interval between each one, not only because they all overran, but because he was personally exhausted. Elated and concentrating hard, a draining combination he long since had discovered.

*

Rosalie had made arrangements for a clinic in Lyon to take Jerome's DNA and send it with a secure chain of custody to the profiler before Jerome had left on the Reine de France. She would have much preferred that it hadn't been necessary to do so in advance, wanting his DNA to have been taken at the same time as the other candidates. But having made enquiries, she did not feel confident of the timing or the chain of custody if she entrusted it to the cruise ship's medical officer, who would have significant experience in dealing with emergency appendectomies and setting fragile elderly bones broken after a lurch on deck or some foreign pavement, but was less likely to be well versed in genome sequencing. Depending on the exact timings of the birth and results, Jerome would be somewhere between Bora Bora and San Diego. If he was not the father, his follow-up interviews could take place by video link from hotel rooms; if he was, Rosalie was working on the more intricate arrangements that would be needed. She had, in any case, tried to arrange for his sister to join his cruise at Sydney and to leave at Vancouver. Jerome wanted to tell Camille he had won the cruise in a competition, citing her absolute inability not to gossip about anything any time since childhood.

'Jerome,' explained Rosalie over a video call, 'this whole project is about truth. About who we are, the unforeseeable consequences of our actions, fate, science, and events we cannot control. I do not wish to introduce duplicity, however well meant, into our dealings. We need to tell her. Or accept it wasn't my best idea and leave her behind.'

'She will tell her oldest daughter, she won't be able to stop herself, and my other sisters and her friend Marie-Thérèse before you've left the building. She does not have a discreet cell in her body. She makes a fairground caller look like a nun from a silent order.'

'Then we need to ask someone else to join you.'

'No. She is the only one I can ask without the others being hurt.'

He added, more truthfully, 'I honestly don't know where they all are, so I'd have to ask Camille for that information anyway.'

He didn't elaborate on that but Rosalie guessed that his family, like many others, had their own dynamics and hierarchies that could be mysterious to non-members. They agreed eventually not to tell Camille yet and hopefully she would be free to travel at short notice. If required.

*

Colleagues warmed to Taono King, unusual in media which many thought had more than its share of wankers and talentless entitleds. 'To see ourselves as others see us', he sometimes thought, was not a gift distributed widely round the creative industry. His small team worked out of an office under the A40 flyover in a densely populated part of west London that nevertheless always managed to look desolate. When asked what he did, he generally replied 'radio producer', but he'd broadened out from that narrow field some years back. Now he concentrated on finding stories, collating people and cross-platform content. His was one of the few content-production outfits that was open to unsolicited ideas, and had taken on Rosalie's proposal, although no doubt helped by a call to Taono from one of her actor clients, who said she'd be a 'name' if anything came of it.

Now a couple of months or so distant from the meeting in February with Rosalie to agree the brief, Taono had got that settled feeling indicating he was comfortable with taking on the project, creatively and commercially. Gina had told Rosalie she preferred the idea of spoken or dramatic versions of her story over print, that in calm moments she almost quite fancied the idea and had passed some of the uncomfortable late pregnancy sleepless hours planning out her fantasy cast and watching famdram box sets for ideas.

Up-front work Taono still mostly did himself. He was going to draw out some of the backstory of each of the potential fathers, follow up with how they felt before anyone knew who the father was, and then track their reactions. The last section, following up with the father and family, was the piece that excited him most. They had to bring in the scriptwriter; Rosalie was satisfied that the combination of his highest fee ever, the threat of never working in the industry again and a hefty legal document would ensure the scriptwriter's discretion. Taono also said he was a decent guy to which Rosalie replied: 'We've got mind-bending science, human interest, a baby's paternity, a huge cast of real people, sex, maternal love, conflict, tragedy – and as close as we're going to get to a virgin birth in the twenty-first century. Decent will be stretched to its outer limits and might snap. But,' she added, 'decent is still good to have.'

*

Roland and Taono talked for an hour. Everything was recorded but so subtly that Roland didn't feel a thing. No 'testing, testing', no requests to repeat himself for the tape. It felt like a verbal hot tub, Taono wrapping him in empathy and interest and taking him seriously, as though his view mattered and he was important. It felt good. As they came to the end of recording his story so far, how he had met Gina, how he'd felt at the time, Taono asked if they could spend a little time on Ann and Eva and what it would mean if he was or wasn't the father.

'Well, if you've got time, I have,' said Roland. 'What do you want to know?'

'Why haven't you told them yet, and do you plan to tell them?'

'It's not because Ann would be upset,' said Roland. 'She's nothing if not rational and this was years before I met her. I had no idea a pregnancy was a possibility and I have not seen… Mrs Flowers… since then. I haven't told Eva because I should tell Ann first and as I haven't told Ann… I have told my brother. Chris. He's my brother.' This last admission came out abruptly, like deciding to get off at a bus stop just as the bus was pulling away. 'I got permission to change my one confidant from Ann to Chris so now I can't tell Ann anyway.'

Taono was surprised. Roland had not in the last hour mentioned having a brother, let alone one close enough to share secrets. 'My brother has a life-limiting illness. Maybe five years left. He once told me that since his diagnosis people don't share their lives with him any more, not even shopping or going to the movies in case it upsets him because he can't. So I decided I would, and now I tell him lots of stuff. This was pretty big, though, and he's really interested, so I am glad I told him. Not just interested in if I'm the father but in the science, the medicine, the techniques, how it happened. He was a chemistry teacher. The best. Kids who never thought getting pure salt from rock salt could be something they could do or understand. So I told Chris. I'm going to see him after this.

'He doesn't have any kids. His wife left him when he was diagnosed at fifty-one. He thought that was a sensible decision; not exactly true to the spirit of in sickness and in health, but he didn't want her to be stuck with him for up to fifteen – as it was then – deteriorating years.' Roland stopped for a few moments. 'I want to ask him if he got enough money out of the divorce, you know, the house, to look after himself for as long as. I haven't done that yet. But if I had enough, I wouldn't need to ask him.'

Taono nodded, said nothing, but was reassured, as he sometimes was in his work, that the world still had lots of quietly caring folk in it who did their best on a daily basis.

'Ann and I needed help to have Eva, and sometimes I wonder if Ann hedged her bets,' Roland continued. 'Two lots of sperm. I don't even know if it's possible. Eva has O-type blood. So do I, but I've not done a DNA. Not until now. I don't know if that means I don't trust Ann, or if I admire her more for giving us our best shot. And if I can't ask her about that, I don't see how I could tell her about this.' Roland's words seemed to roll on without his explicit permission, looking for a natural place to stop, a verbal breakwater.

'Might be an opportunity to do both together,' observed Taono.

They talked about how Roland would feel if he was the father, but he was so sure he wasn't – the time and method taken to conceive Eva were a factor in that feeling, but mostly he didn't think he'd had what he termed 'conception sex' with Gina all those years ago – he didn't seriously consider it. If he wasn't, he was very happy with a hundred thousand in the bank. He hoped they'd make a television series and he could double it.

With the sense of release he used to get after sending an edition of *International Angling* to press, he went home and asked Ann if Eva was definitely his. As soon as she said, 'What makes you ask?' he knew there was something there.

'Something and nothing,' he said.

She didn't push him to explain what had brought this on now. His question and her question sat between them like a stretch of quicksand. Thirty years of comfortable marriage and she'd been keeping this big secret. So he was quite justified in keeping one of his own. He went into Eva's room and took a hair from her brush, downloaded a home DNA kit from the internet, signed his consent and forged Eva's. He went back downstairs.

'Ann, I had a girlfriend a while ago. She's pregnant. It might be mine. It might not. The father might be one of her husbands or her other three lovers. Baby's due soon. I can only tell one person and I told Chris so you can't tell anyone or I'll lose all the money. And maybe the house, I think they'd sue for damages, I don't know.'

He wasn't sure what shape his life would be by the time of his next appointment with Taono.

*

Eddie was on track for his first proper project meeting, the water of explaining the end of his first marriage to the girls well under the bridge without any of the angst and backwash he'd expected. Bernadette, it seemed, had suspected at the time, having come home early from school more than once and known there was someone in the house besides her mother. But their father was never home long enough for them to gather the courage to talk to him, so she and Mary had made a pact, spoken of once and never again until now, to go along with things as presented. And, after all, it was Eddie who had left with a suitcase at seven o'clock on a Thursday evening. Aoife's lover had dissolved into a mist of irresponsibility and commitment phobia so effectively that she had given up on him in weeks not months, bought a new bed and new sheets, went back to work full-time and seemed hardly to notice her husband and lover were both gone, let alone miss either of them.

It had been different for Eddie and Aoife's daughters. They took their hurt, gathered up the betrayal and sealed it away, spending all their excess energy trying not to upset anyone in case Dad stopped paying for things or Mum left as well.

Eddie talked through the history of his first marriage and family, and then sat quietly for a bit. 'Tell me why you decided to marry Ines when she was pregnant,' Taono prompted. 'It seems unusual.'

'We were friends. After Aoife and I split, I had a few romantic relationships, six months or so at a time. I was always clear upfront that I had two teenagers and I didn't want any more children, but women – at least the women I dated – seemed to hope I'd change my mind. Each time I realised, I cut loose. None of them meant enough for me to agree to another child. And I don't think the road to a happy marriage is paved with denying your spouse children, so I never looked to change their minds. I'd known Ines for several years and it just seemed like a good idea. And, surprisingly maybe, it really was. I have never been bothered that I'm not Elke's biological father. In fact, I think it made things easier but I can't explain why. I didn't want any more children of my own, but Elke was different. And Ines didn't try to persuade me. It was all easy. I mean the decision was easy, because I didn't really feel like there was a decision. Caring for Elke often wasn't, isn't, easy.

'Ines did tell him, Elke's father, that she was pregnant. He was horrified – she was forty-six at the time and she's sure it genuinely hadn't crossed his mind as a possibility. Understandably. She knew she wasn't doing anything to prevent it, but she also didn't really think it would happen. Although she hoped it would.'

'How would you feel about meeting Gina?'

'Awkward. I behaved really badly when I left her. If I am the father, I'd like to meet her. But if I'm not, I wouldn't.'

'You don't want to apologise?'

'No. I will if I see her, but I suspect an explanation would be more use to her than an apology, and I don't have even that, except I was a selfish git.'

*

Jerome had not realised it was such a long way from Sydney to Hawaii. Even with an overnight stop in Auckland and three days in Bora Bora, there was an awful lot of ocean and it all looked the same. He loved his cabin, managed to be polite to fellow passengers and enjoyed some of the talks given by almost household names, who were all less impressive in the flesh than with the detachment afforded by screens or airwaves. Most of the speakers, he felt, were hiding boredom and a frosting of contempt, resenting the intrusion of amateurs asking about the forensic anthropology of Western Samoa or sharks and their prey or whatever their specialty was. Passengers acting as if they were somehow friends with the guest lecturer, paying for a cruise bringing with it an entitlement to interest in their humdrum anecdotes.

For ten days or so, Jerome took breakfast, coffee, tea and a sundowner on his balcony, looking at the endless sea until

344

finally they left Honolulu for the west coast of the US. Only four more days of ocean.

*

Arriving early for his meeting with Taono, Alan passed the time in an Italian café, chatting in Italian about the weather and Roman politics with the barista. Heading up the sales team of the Rome office of a tech company for twenty-odd years, English had been his working language and many of his British, Australian and American colleagues (and even a few of the Europeans) hadn't learned Italian, but he'd made it a priority. Now he wished he'd chosen Madrid when it was offered at the same time and had spoken Spanish instead.

Of the four candidates, Taono had been most interested in Alan. The idea of one night's life-changing, ever remembered never repeated sex was a bit of a stretch. Obviously you had to be there, thought Taono, with an internal, slightly smug smirk. He wondered if it was a smear of jealousy that made him sceptical. We prefer not to indulge what we don't understand or can't have. It was barely credible for a skylit Manhattan loft or an opulent room on the top floor of a luxury hotel, let alone a mid-market hotel in a business park in Kirkcaldy. He knew Alan was seventy and just retired so wasn't expecting a Bradley Cooper or Ryan Gosling type to turn up and fill the room in Soho with pheromones and complicated masculinity. Who then? He settled on Bill Nighy, never having been a fan of Michael Caine or Sean Connery, who, to be fair, would by now be pushing ninety. Or dead and he'd missed the news.

The women in Taono's family would have said that Alan made the best of himself, which was the highest compliment, albeit one Taono had never quite understood. The thing people noticed when they were the starting gun for it, as Taono was about to be, was Alan's smile. Taono could see how in a mid-90s lift after a bad day and feeling reckless having handed in your notice, the smile could tip someone off balance.

'Hello, Alan. Taono King. Good to meet you.' It was then that Alan smiled.

'You too. Strange circumstances.'

The men shook hands and sat opposite each other, Taono's slim-fitting shirt and jeans with turn-ups reminding Alan forcibly of what he might have worn at Taono's age. Turn-ups had gone the way of tank tops, and at about the same time, but both now seemed to be back. If you had the shape and style of Taono. Alan was dressed all in black except for a small multicoloured logo on his zip-up. He put Taono in mind of James Bond on a day off.

'Unsettling maybe.'

'Yes. Not so much for me. Very much so for my wife.' Alan paused. 'You know about the timing of my involvement? The short, very short, relationship with Gina?' Taono nodded. 'Initially, my wife didn't want me to do the project. Well, she still doesn't,' continued Alan. 'But, you know.' Taono nodded again; Rosalie had included this in the brief.

In the couple of months since Sara had asked him not to take part in the project, Alan's resentment had dissipated. He'd always known that appearances were important to Sara. Telling the world, her world, that Alan had

346

had sex - an unfathomable mix of science-fiction and bodice-ripping - in a chain hotel while he was preparing to leave her was a humiliation, as she saw it, he did not want to make her go through. She had been baffled that he didn't care what the world thought; appalled that 'people' would blame her for… something. They had eventually come to an agreement, negotiated an inch at a time by Nick Hewen and Rosalie, to provide full cooperation on the medical side, full story to the project and Rosalie would use 'all reasonable endeavours' to minimise intrusion. It was, like many compromises, equally unsatisfactory to all sides. The swing factor for Sara had been the thought that they would be uncovered and hounded anyway without Rosalie's protection and without the money.

The objective today was to get Alan's story in as much detail as he could remember. There would be a second interview after the DNA results. 'So,' said Taono, 'just tell me what you know. Don't worry about relevance. Don't edit yourself. Just start maybe with where you met and go from there.'

The meeting room was decorated in a somewhat grand, almost baroque style. Alan had been expecting minimalist London, hipster pared-back furniture and brick walls, but this room had opulent wallpaper and deep armchairs, chandelier lighting with the sense that there might be a door to a secret passage concealed within the decor. It gave him an unnerving sense of being cut off from the world, the view onto the underbelly of the A40 notwithstanding. He took a couple of mouthfuls of his third coffee in the last hour.

Taono sensed Alan was waiting for some reassurance. 'We will take care with the presentation of your relationship with Gina. It was short, fleeting, a single time, but there is a real sense from her that it was… transformative. As earth-moving as it's possible to get, exceeding any reading on an orgasmic Richter scale. Not that there is such a thing exactly. Dynamite sex. Let me quote – with Gina's permission – what she said to Rosalie: "Whenever someone asks what is the meaning of life, what are we here for, that was it." It is powerful testimony and won't be easy for a long-standing spouse to process.'

'No. But it is true,' Alan replied.

'It's really hard to believe,' said Taono.

Alan didn't shrug; he just leaned back a little in the wing-backed chair. 'Well,' he said, 'it doesn't matter to me if you or anyone else believes me or not. You would need to ask why Gina and I would independently say the same thing with no collusion or obvious benefit for either of us. But if you don't believe me, I understand why and maybe if I wasn't me, or Gina, I wouldn't believe me either.' It could have sounded impolite or defensive but Alan's tone was neither of those just straightforward, matter of fact.

'Noted.' said Taono, in recovery mode. 'I didn't mean I didn't believe you, just that— Back to the story. What we are doing, Alan,' Taono continued, 'is creating a whole story. A cast of people involved in Gina's story that listeners, viewers and readers will care about and invest in. Gina is the main one, but all of the others are important. So we will edit out or not use a lot of stuff that you tell me or that we record. But until I get it all, I don't know which bits will work best. So please tell me how it felt, what you remember of the evening. Don't censor it. That's our job.'

348

His tone was assertive, maybe a bit too firm, he worried. These were not professionals; they hadn't been bruised and numbed by the vicious actor-eat-actor of the casting world. This was Alan's story, one he was clearly protective of, and Alan was the only one who could tell it. Taono did not want to mar his series of interviews by making a damp squib of a potential golden goose. He shook his head, needing to get Alan back on side and tame the mixed metaphors.

The interview continued. By the end of the afternoon with the April daylight dimming, Taono had a good picture of Alan's marriage, family and professional life and the night in Kirkcaldy. As seen by Alan and now believed by Taono.

*

Arriving in Lyon the week after his meeting with Alan, Taono booked himself in for three nights at a hotel in the centre of the old town. It had a balcony and it was old, modernised and magnificent. On a weekday late-April evening there were a few smokers, inured to the cold after years of no indoor smoking rules, wrapped up in end-of-winter clothes, breathing deeply on their – he wrongly imagined – Gauloises outside the restaurants in the square. A light hum reached him, but it wasn't enough to disturb his thoughts as he gathered a composite picture of Gina Flowers and her lovers. Earlier that day, Jerome had spoken of his time with Gina without any clear recollection of who she was, and Taono had wondered if he really remembered her at all. When asked directly, Jerome answered that although he'd had a few promiscuous years in the 1990s, his lovers were

French apart from an Italian woman he'd met in Milan, three Americans – in America – and one English woman – Gina. So he could of course recall his short affair with Gina, he assured Taono, but perhaps some of the details merged with other relationships.

They talked about how Jerome had felt when he'd received Hewen's letter and first knew of the possibility of paternity. Taono was rarely surprised by a reaction, but Jerome's obvious enthusiasm to be the father was unexpected and somewhat moving. He didn't point out the implications of Jerome having so far not knowingly fathered a child save for the one he and Nicole lost. Jerome thought the miscarriage may not have been an accident.

'I have not said that aloud before,' Jerome told Taono. 'But I think it may be the case. I think Nicole did not really want children, and I wanted them so badly that after we got married I probably saw her as a baby-maker rather than a wife and a woman. She's very French,' he added, almost as if he himself were not. 'It is not enough to be *une maman*. You also have to be *une femme*. First, foremost, you have to be *une femme*. I did not give that sufficient attention.'

They met again the following day after breakfast in the lobby of the hotel. Impersonal international hotel space provided less chance of being seen or overheard, Jerome had explained. Taono thought the chances of that were very low to zero, and while Jerome didn't disagree, he preferred a neutral, business-like location. Otherwise, he said, people would speculate if they saw him having a conversation with a Black man.

'Do you not generally talk to Black people?' Taono enquired.

'I don't know any,' replied Jerome. 'So no. I have an Algerian friend and Syrian neighbours I am friendly with, but someone Black, no.' There was no undertone of apology or embarrassment in Jerome's voice, nor the unspoken shout of 'But I'm not racist' Taono would expect from an English person saying the same thing.

'What if we are seen here?'

'Well,' Jerome explained, 'this is now an American chain and they would likely think you were an American contact from my old car industry days. But this is not likely. In all my years living in Lyon I have never met a local who comes here unless it is for anonymity.'

There was a Starbucks concession in the lobby and Jerome ordered an iced latte. 'I know it's not quite summer, but it is the best thing they make.'

He did not want to dwell on how much he wanted to be the father. Que será. It was best to wait and see. And that was really all Taono could glean in ninety minutes of conversation that somehow had to be scripted. Which wouldn't be easy. But like all the interviews for the project, it did have what a lot of interviews – and therefore the subsequent scripts – lacked, which was truth. None of the candidates had to exaggerate or dissemble, the truth was quite enough. Jerome wanted the baby to be his but that was all he wanted to say for now, and the project would have to make the best of that.

Chapter 20

'I can't take time off at such short notice,' said Ann.

'Why not?' countered Roland. 'It's really important to me. It's not even short notice. It's two weeks from now. If you went off sick, they'd have to cope without two weeks' notice.'

'But I'm not sick and I don't want to go on holiday in April. It's cold.'

'It's a lot less cold in Morocco. Or Cyprus. Or wherever we want to go. You want to go. We can go wherever you want to go. Florida, California. I want to go to San Diego. And it is May next week.'

'We've been to Florida and California. We've been everywhere with dolphins.'

'We haven't been to San Diego. That's in California.' It sounded like an accusation rather than a suggestion.

'I didn't know you wanted to go to San Diego.'

'Well, you do now.'

They had acknowledged to themselves if not to each other that they weren't really arguing about holiday times, though they weren't sure what it was about. Were they tussling over whether Roland was more important than Sainsbury's, or that he'd never put Ann before his work so why should she take a holiday she wasn't keen on at a time that didn't suit her to please him? Perhaps it was about him maybe having another child, or agreeing to take part in the project without consulting her, or they didn't want to go on holiday together at all and this gave him an excuse to go alone. Or his doubts, still not explicitly shared with Ann, about Eva's paternity.

Roland had received the link with Eva's paternity test results. Received but not opened so far. He'd set up a new email account just for that with one of those strong, randomly generated passwords that he'd written backwards in his phone notes, changing caps to lowercase, lowercase to caps and adding one to all the numbers.

'Why can't you go fishing for a few days and we'll go on holiday in September like we planned?'

Roland, sounding like a petulant child who has just decided he doesn't eat beans, half-shouted his refusal. 'I don't like fishing any more.' Which, abruptly ringing true as it did, was as much news to him as to Ann.

'Seems like there's quite a lot I don't know.'

'So come on holiday with me and find out.' It felt suddenly and disturbingly like a seminal moment. If she did, they were OK. If she didn't, then what?

Without a top-up to his state pension, which in any case wouldn't come due for another couple of years, Roland had relied on inheriting a half share of his parents' house with the other half taking care of Chris. But they had both needed care costing a thousands a week each in their last years. Ann had asked him often enough to start a private pension but he just hadn't. So the hundred thousand from the baby – the project – was warmly welcomed by him, and if there was to be a follow-up he'd be first to sign; his big worry was that the non-consummation of his short relationship with Gina would make him a dispensable bit part in any development of the story. But now, even putting a good whack aside for his brother, he could afford to take them on holiday and not expect Ann to pay – but she didn't want to come.

'No, Roland. I'm not going. This is the first year I haven't had to organise my holiday around your publication dates or some who-can-catch-the-biggest-pike competition. The first year. So just because you've got a bee in your bonnet about a pregnant ex-girlfriend – and I can't even believe I'm saying that – when the chances of you being the father are at best one in six, I don't have to change my plans on a whim. And I need to keep my job for at least another five years if we're going to be able to go on holiday at all once I've retired, so I want to make it my priority. If you want to make a random baby yours, go ahead.'

'One in four,' said Roland. 'Neither of the two husbands is the father. Mr Howard told us after he was born.'

'Who is "us"? Why didn't you tell me?' asked Ann. 'What's that about?'

With a half-shrug, half-sneer, Roland indicated he didn't know. 'Rosalie says I can have therapy.' Realising how childish that sounded, he added, 'I mean that the project will pay for it.'

'What will you talk about? That you've held a torch for Gina all these years?'

'No,' said Roland. 'I'm not sure of much at the moment but I am sure of that. It was nothing more than a few days, a week at most. We didn't really connect then and I have not thought about her in forty years. But there are other things.'

He waited for Ann to mention Eva, but she didn't. She got on with the ironing, looking down at the sheets. She didn't much iron clothes, just sheets, because she liked how they felt – and so did he, although not enough to iron them himself. He wanted to ask her why she'd said 'Why do you ask?' but he just sat there listening to the faint hiss of steam.

'I'll do that as well. The therapy. As well as going to San Diego.' And he did.

*

Eddie's days didn't change during the waiting period, except for slowly picking up threads with his older daughters, enjoying the sluggish but certain creep to longer days and one less layer of clothing for the beach. He had often told patients not to drive themselves crazy with things they couldn't change, using exactly that terminology so they would recognise what they were doing. He followed his own advice, walked the dogs, visited his father-in-law, who he liked much better than his mother, looked after Elke and – once a week, no more – spoke to Bernadette and Mary.

*

Not minded to leave Ade's flat yet and grateful that his brother was safely scoping out road construction in some hot, remote location for a few more weeks, Alan worked to a routine. Alarm no later than 6.45 a.m. because if he didn't stick to that, he was frightened of falling into late up, early to bed with dinner at 5.30 p.m. like a nursing home. So he set the alarm, watched the news until about eight, did a few chores, a bit of admin and then went to the gym for 10 a.m. after the city workers had long left and what he thought of as the hardcore housewives were beginning to arrive. Three afternoons a week he 'did London', something like a gallery or a guided walk, and the other days he watched films, as many Italian ones as he could find on the multiple streaming services Ade subscribed to but was rarely home to watch. He spoke very little; a good morning to the brightly disinterested students handing out the towels at the gym was about it. He sent Sara a text a couple of times a week to say he was fine and to ask if she was, but she didn't reply.

As the weeks went on, it seemed sensible to stay at Ade's until the tests were over and the results out. He slept well, ate well and felt like he was on a retreat. If retreats had craft beer, takeout sushi and Netflix.

His son Jonas turned up at Ade's flat after he'd been there, Alan calculated, about eight weeks. Time had temporarily become something that mattered only to other people.

'Mum has told me about your affair,' was Jonas's opening line from the front door. 'You have to stop. We don't want another baby.'

'Who is we? What? And come in. Do you want something to eat?'

'Is there anyone else here?'

'No,' replied Alan. 'Just me.'

'Who is she?' Jonas had a flat face. Alan had joked to Sara he looked like an ironing board when he was born although the joke fell flat.

'Who is we?' Alan said again.

'Robyn and me. Not mum. She hasn't said anything except you had an affair and this woman might be pregnant and that you're living here.' Alan thought about correcting him to 'staying here' but he didn't. If he was going to talk

356

about that with anyone, it would be Sara. He gathered that Sara had told his son and daughter a version of the story but leaving out key details. He was grateful to her for protecting the terms of his payment.

'Well, I don't know what I'm going to do yet. And your mother will be the first to know. But I understand that the baby's mother wants to tell the baby who the father is.'

'So you know it's a boy? And the mother is a slag. Jesus, at your age.' Alan surmised from this that Sara was still angry – fair enough – but had not shared the full extent of her heartache with their children. He certainly wasn't about to do so.

'Yes.'

'I don't want a half-brother. I like our family as it is. Nuclear.'

Alan stared at his son. He genuinely had not realised that no longer being nuclear, which was in any case a remote prospect although on the basis of the information he had Jonas of course would not know that, would bother anyone.

'Jonas, think about that logically. It doesn't matter what you want or what I want. The mother is having the baby and I may or may not be the father. You will either have or not have a half-brother. It's not something I can control.'

He wondered, if this new baby was his, how like his children he'd be. Jonas was mostly, even at thirty-seven and the father of two children himself, what Alan had overheard Ade describe his nephew as 'an angry mix of bell-end, wimp and entitlement'. Robyn was still dancing in the corps de ballet of a world-leading company, understudy to the greats, just a couple of *pas de deux* away from being a principal

357

ballerina but with the chances diminishing every year in perfect inverse proportion to the increasing pain of training.

'Well, not now you can't.'

Alan was not going to facilitate his son's desire for an argument, nor further disturb his own tranquillity. 'I'll think about what you've said,' was all he replied.

*

The next day, at his second meeting with Taono, it was almost as if the words found their own truth without Alan having to do anything. Like they had sorted themselves out in his psyche overnight and knew what they were doing.

'I would like a baby to fill a gap in my life right now, so to that extent I'd like this baby to be mine. But I don't want a teenager when I'm eighty-five. I wasn't much good with them when I was forty-five and I doubt forty years would change that. I like babies. I like small children, then they go to primary school and you start a long slide downhill until you know for sure you've lost. You get to pick up pieces occasionally, when you are summoned or your better instincts prevail. Babies are cute for a reason. As dependency weakens, cuteness weakens. I would like a baby but not a child, so I hope this baby isn't mine.

'If it is, I will do my best. But if I were the mother, if I was Gina, I'd probably have it adopted. Though I suppose she'd need the father's consent once she knows who it is. I would give it. But that's too big a chance for her to take. So if she'd been going to do that, she'd not find out who the father is.'

*

'Hey, Roland,' said Taono and they had coffee, exchanged pleasantries and once again sorted out housekeeping practicalities like recordings, confirming permissions and what would happen next. The men sat down opposite each other. 'Just talk to me, Roland. Tell it as it is for you. Who you are, where you're at, how you feel right now, right here. We have all the time you need.'

'I don't want the baby to be mine. I agreed to the test partly for the money and partly because in some way I feel the baby, and maybe the mother, have a right to know. It's not her fault. The mother's. The shock and then some. Dear God, giving birth at her age. Even by Caesarean. Poor woman. I mean— Maybe she's not, maybe she wanted it. But I can't remember much about her or about Ibiza. I was in such shock about the pregnancy I'd left in England back then, Mary Batten, I mentioned her last time, and nothing else really registered. I have decided I will acknowledge the baby if it is mine, if he wants to know me. And if my daughter was his half-sister, then she might be keen. But I'm not. I told you I'd told my brother.

'I think if he was mine, I would see what the mother was thinking and fit in with that as far as possible. Money, seeing him, that sort of thing. Use the money from this to help if she needed it, I thought, though I know she has said the father doesn't have to. I'm guessing that she's getting a good chunk from this and maybe that is why she's doing it too. If she doesn't want money, honestly I'll be delighted. We've always had enough but never loads like this. Mostly I hope he isn't mine and I can just follow the story.'

Roland drew breath, finally. Taono smiled, delighted at this unexpected stream of consciousness.

359

'Glad to get that off your chest, Roland?'

'So glad. I feel like a deadbeat for thinking like that, but I have found a steady, comfortable place in my life. I am hoping to be a grandfather in the next few years, even if it's to a dolphin. My life has never been a rollercoaster exactly, but then I'm not the Big Dipper sort. And I don't want to start now. San Diego. A cruise round the Galapagos. A business class trip to South Africa. They might be nice. And if she doesn't want money, I can keep even more aside in case, Chris, my brother— You know. He and I, we couldn't imagine how…'

For the first time, Roland felt able to say Gina's name out loud, as if she were no longer the unnameable enemy.

'…how Gina is coping.'

'She has a lot of support,' said Taono. 'From her family, her doctors and other professionals. But I think it's still a very big deal for everyone involved and, of course, especially Gina. I haven't met her,' he continued, 'so I don't know first-hand.'

Roland stirred sugar in to his coffee. 'If I am the father, I'm going to blame her, resent her, resent the baby, resent Ann, who will encourage me to "do the right thing", whatever that is. And I will try because intellectually I know it isn't her, Gina's, fault, or the baby's or mine or Ann's or anyone's. Why couldn't she just have had a termination and not told anyone. Women have abortions all the time.' He stopped stirring, drank the whole cup and finished.

'I despise myself for thinking that. I know she was quite far gone before she knew. I feel like someone who has been against the death penalty all their life – which I am – and then wants it because they know a victim. I hate what it has shown me to be. And I don't know if it will go away because I'm not the father. If I'm not the father. I'm stuck with this horrible picture of my rotten heart. And if I am, I will be the father who wished his own baby dead. Baby. Not a shrimp on a scan. Baby.'

Taono left it a few minutes. Roland didn't fight the gathering tears but they didn't fall, staying on his lower lid like the old two-pence pieces on a fairground coin-pusher. He had the sorrowful, frustrated, needy air of a tired toddler who is refusing to go to bed but doesn't really know why. 'Bit melodramatic. Bit OTT. Sorry.'

'Roland, us looking at our darker thoughts doesn't mean it's what we'd do or who we really are. Voicing how you feel, it's cathartic. The contract includes therapeutic care, if you want to talk to someone. Short or long term.'

'I know. They've said. I think I will. I've thought about it. But I'm not keen on talking about my childhood. Not that it was anything dramatic, I just don't want to.'

'Well, you might just want some help to process how this has made you feel. Here and now stuff, not deep-dive.'

'Yes. Actually, I've made an appointment. Haven't started yet but I'm going for it,' replied Roland.

*

Taono was way out from where he wanted to be with Eddie. It was one thing suggesting therapy to a retired journalist, but to a psychiatrist? Also, he liked Eddie best and he needed that not to show to anyone. But he felt like Eddie might have some special insight and see right into Taono's biased psyche – literally read his mind. So he was very careful to manage himself. Short, firm handshake. Professional, not friendly. Exact same phrases he'd used for Roland about coffee and housekeeping. Sixty-degree angle to their chairs. And then he was stuck. 'Tell me how you feel today' was not going to come out of his mouth, not to a psychiatrist.

Eddie looked and waited. Psychiatrists were good with silences. Couldn't they sometimes charge someone for a whole hour, not say anything and call it a consultation?

Finally, Eddie helped him out. 'What would you like to know?'

'Do you want to be the father of the baby?'

'No,' Eddie replied, 'but if I am, I'll deal with it. Medically – though it's been a long time since anything obstetric has been on my radar – I find it very interesting and it's fascinating to be so close to something so rare. But no, I don't want any more children. And I'm guessing Gina didn't either. Until he arrived. Now maybe it's different. Not all mothers fall in love with their newborns. I've seen plenty of patients struggle with indifference to their baby or feel their own mother didn't love them. A few are a danger to the child, most rub along. Fathers too, but I didn't see many of those. It's still maternal love, a mother's attachment that is society's demon: the blessing and the curse. Fathers get more slack.' He stopped talking and Taono tried to stay with the quiet, which he had read somewhere was the phrase for it.

'How is Gina?' Eddie asked after a while, just as Taono was going to burst the wall of silence-induced panic in his chest.

'She has recovered well from the birth and is now able and keen to resolve the paternity question.'

362

'I would be surprised,' said Eddie, 'if after the way we finished – the way I finished us – she'd want me to be the father. I wouldn't want someone who walked out on me forty years ago to suddenly be a co-parent. But if the babe is mine, I need to know that I at least tried to make a relationship with him, so I'll have to get over my reluctance, and I guess Gina will too or she wouldn't have started down this route.'

'She did it for the money,' said Taono and instantly hated himself for it. 'And Barney, of course for Barney. So he'd know his father. Or at least know his identity if the father doesn't want to know him. She can tell him who it is and say she tried. And to advance infertility research.' It was a poor recovery but Eddie didn't seem squeamish about Gina's financial motives.

'All good reasons,' said Eddie. 'Nappies don't buy themselves.'

Chapter 21

Gina stood in her kitchen, holding her head and looking at her watch. Fifteen minutes to 5 o'clock, the earliest she was allowing herself alcohol. Thank God Gerald had advised against breast-feeding. Not only did the idea of her nosebag-like breasts being sucked dry by a self-centred infant revolt her, it would have meant wine was off the agenda for months. Alcohol was still her coping mechanism, though she was cutting back from immediately after the birth, when everything was just too much and had to be numbed or she'd implode. The sounds from the front room of sucking, snuffling and snoring meant Barney was feeding, cuddling with Christine or asleep. She had no idea which and for the next half hour she didn't care – after all, what else did nine-week-old babies do? Christine was marvellous. Gina had taken tea and cake to her, a personal best in hospitality since she'd got home.

Gina lay awake, or on a good night just woke up several times, with bad-mother thoughts. Barney was gorgeous, creamy, cute – but he was still a baby with all those baby habits that wear you down, like sleeping when you want him to be awake and being awake when you most need to sleep. Sicking up, needing to be changed, crying then suddenly stopping and, occasionally, beaming. He had a silky hair and his nose looked squashed. Cute, but squashed. She wondered if she should get him home-schooled so the other kids couldn't call him 'squash nose'. Gerald had said it would gradually not look squashed but she couldn't be certain. It wasn't these things that made her doubt herself; she just wasn't sure she loved him enough. Not as much as she had instantly loved Evan and Stan, she knew that. Was she just too tired, too old, too lonely? Might it grow on her, he grow on her, a maternal love develop? Or did the capacity for new maternal love just drain, drip by drip, through pores and orifices, running out as your hormones depleted over the menopausal years? She didn't know what to do. Barney was getting older every day. She had given herself Christine until he was six months to make space for decisions. And so there was another competent adult in the house.

Tomorrow, Rosalie was coming over with Gerald. Sunday. There would be time to discuss things. Gerald would only be called out if something unexpected happened, and Gerald's professional ethos was based on anticipating and preventing the unexpected. Anything out-of-the-ordinary in obstetrical terms was much safer dealt with Monday to Friday, eight to five if possible, and Gerald liked to make sure it was possible. Rosalie was going to bring her up to date on the project and find out what she wanted to do next. Gerald, clinical care of Gina now passed back to her GP, was going to explain about paternity. It seemed to Gina she would never be ready for either of these things so it might as well be now. She knew without the project money she wouldn't have Christine and that alone was enough to keep her in it. She felt Christine had saved her sanity once or twice already and probably Barney's life more than that. Gina acknowledged her own frailty, which was as brave as it was frightening.

*

Gerald had not moved house when they got married. He and Rosalie were rarely together in his compact flat for more than a day or two at a time, and he did not want the responsibility of keeping a larger house himself or getting a cleaner or a gardener or whatever else he'd have to do to manage somewhere, when really he just slept, read and made the occasional omelette. Similarly, while Rosalie had a stunning apartment with huge rooms, it had just one bedroom, although that had a balcony the same size as the room. It looked over the East River. Rosalie would have liked a two-bed, but despite earning what many people would view as obscene amounts for doing nothing very useful, she wasn't in that territory. Not if she wanted to keep looking over the East River, anyway.

So this weekend, needing to plan and prepare and perhaps be close to the hospital if they had to 'access records or whatever', as Rosalie put it, they were staying in the hotel across the road from Valley. Besides, as Rosalie had also said, Gerald's flat didn't do room service or have a pool.

They'd been out for the day. Gerald had researched train times but May bank holiday rail replacement services were not attractive, so he agreed that Rosalie's suggestion of a car with a driver was the better option. The day out reminded him that not only did he love her very much, but he really enjoyed her company. She was funny in that Southern US way that brought to mind Dolly Parton: a sharp, often self-deprecating, observational wit tempered with kindness – and a touch of New York street. Today she'd been wondering why grits had never caught on in England in the way that other American foods had. Gerald said, 'The clue is in the name' and was hugely amused by her genuine puzzlement.

The driver drove them to Gina's and they sorted out the agenda on the way.

'Project first or fathers first?' she asked.

Gerald thought about the question. 'Fathers, I think,' he replied. 'Start with the people, move on to the project.' Rosalie nodded. 'I want to check for myself the waivers of confidentiality,' he went on. 'I've never before discussed a patient, not that Gina is my patient now,' he reassured himself out loud, 'with a media person. Never anyone, except other healthcare professionals, the patient or family, friends… maybe a lawyer or two. I know you've got them, I know Nick Hewen drafted them, I know they've all had the independent advice, but I would like to read them anyway.'

'They all say that I am your wife.' Rosalie knew this was the area that made Gerald the most uncomfortable. He'd made his peace with involving a PR person because Gina would need both the money and media management, and he knew Rosalie was the best person for it. But they were married and he wasn't sure that the wider medical community would approve. 'Thing is, there's only four ways out. One, I withdraw and find Gina someone else for media. Two, you withdraw. Three, she pulls the project. Four, we go ahead with maximum bearable transparency.'

'I can see the headline. "Bus Pass Mother's Top Doc Wife Makes Pram Load of Cash from Selling Her Story".'

'That's goooood.' Rosalie smiled.

'Tomorrow, we'll ask Gina to pre-empt. I'm going to ask Gina to front it up. And the fathers. The ethics angle is much less problematic since she is no longer your patient, but we need to be in charge of the presentation. But,' Rosalie continued, 'if you want me to withdraw then tell me now. I want you and your career more than I want this story. And I have never wanted any story more than I want this one.'

'Not even the celebrity walkabout hero and the mother superior?' It was a serious question from Gerald, referring to Rosalie's most famous A-star-list client's desert liaison with a lifelong nun.

'Not even close. I think the way to do it is to ask Gina to open her episode with how she came to me. If her first line was "I wasn't the sort of grandmother who ever thought she'd need a media manager. Or ever need an obstetrician again", we could work with that.'

'Can we do our stuff tonight and review after we've seen what Gina has to say? And if she is OK, I need to update Arak, Evert and Hammy and maybe my ethics committee. Again, in case. Who might want to talk to Gina.'

'That would be good. Good back-up. And the right thing to do.'

*

The father candidates who weren't sailing the ocean eating midnight buffets and playing bridge with fanatical strangers were due to have their paternity tests, one every day, Monday to Wednesday, so they didn't bump into each other, three different patents of test for each man. Eddie, Alan and Roland would come to Valley, stay overnight in the hotel and have their tests the next morning. Gerald wanted time to talk to Gina and for Gina to think things through before the men were told the results, so it had been agreed they would all hear four weeks after the test – almost six months since Gina had first found out about the pregnancy. An appointment with a specialist counsellor was mandatory under the project's terms within seven days of the results being notified. The 'before' interviews already edited and scripted for production, the 'after' interviews with Taono would be a couple of weeks after the counselling appointment, and that would wrap up their contribution to the first stage of the project. Jerome, nearing the finish line of his seemingly endless voyage, would be in port with enough time for him to get the results on a video link. A counsellor would join his ship there and cruise until Jerome no longer needed her. He'd decided against inviting Camille. He felt she'd make it all about her.

*

Waiting while Gerald fetched his jacket, Roland could see the lab across two lawns behind him. The lawns marked the boundaries of the NHS and the private hospitals, a bed of rosebushes separating the two stretches of grass. The men walked over to the small outbuilding on the edge of the hospital grounds, which looked like an electricity substation. Security was tight; Roland wondered just who or what was tested here, apart from old lovers suddenly of medical significance, of course. Senior profiler Rasina was welcoming, her charm only slightly diluted by the clinical proceedings. She took Roland's hair and blood samples and a digital do-it-yourself platform provided readings of weight, height and BMI. How science could determine whether he was the father of the baby from a strand of his hair or a swab of saliva was not clear to him, but he had full confidence in the process.

The testing facility's roof had a leak in the corner near the centrifuge, drip-drip being caught in a plastic container. 'Don't worry. It won't contaminate anything. We don't let it overflow,' Rasina had joked. Roland had felt like going home to his shed, getting a bit of flashing and fixing the leak himself.

Fifteen minutes after arrival and Roland was directed down a one-way system to the exit where, like something from a political thriller, a car was waiting to drive him the less than half-mile to the hotel to meet the counsellor. He felt like a cross between an alien and a suspect in a crime drama.

Now, in a meeting room in the hotel, which he knew had been swept for bugs and was security patrolled – discretely, the minders looked like staff and guests – he wished he'd been bold enough to offer to fix the roof – to do something practical – though he was sure there were loads of reasons why that would not have been acceptable.

*

There were very few medical matters about his patients that Gerald did not understand with a high degree of certainty. His professional skills were tested most in unusual or distressing cases that required him to marry years of experience with the science. A teaching professor in his early postgraduate training had said that too many doctors didn't listen to patients in the way that too many detectives didn't listen to victims. So he layered blood tests and sats and scans and examinations with a mother's description of kicks or not, vague feelings of uterine heaviness and night terrors. So far, his diagnoses and treatment had kept him anchored in the world's top five. But he did not know who the father of Gina Flowers's baby was.

He had made lists and spreadsheets weighted by various factors resulting in improbable probabilities, studied the scans for clues to foetal position, carefully reviewed all the testimony for timings, factored in logical positives and negatives like frequency and contraception. Nothing empirical. Not a single decent clue.

Rosalie had wagered two weeks in the Maldives on it being Alan. He didn't want to go to the Maldives, but if she was right he would and he would also do his best to enjoy himself. She'd pressed him to write a name, seal it in an envelope and give it to her; if he was right, she'd stop her annual quest to get him on to a beach holiday. He hadn't, citing that it wouldn't be professional – although with no convincing rebuttal to her assertion that no one would ever find out – but he did not want to be wrong. If he didn't give a name, he might not be right but he wouldn't be wrong.

Apart from the frisson of betting against his wife, Gerald was troubled that he had no idea. On balance he thought Roland was the least likely because neither he nor Gina seemed sure they'd actually had sex, which probably meant they hadn't. On the other hand, if they had, Roland was youngest at the time of the relationship, which was a major point in his favour. There were doubts over the paternity of Roland's daughter, but having seen a picture of her, Gerald thought these were unfounded, although the need for assisted conception was another strong factor against him being the father.

On a straightforward reading, Eddie was the most likely. Frequency, length of relationship – but if these factors were key, George Douglas would be the father and that was not the case. George Flowers' vasectomy had been, for Gerald, a decisive no even before the scientific confirmation. Jerome and Gina were significantly older during their relationship, and while the timing cycle may not have been exactly right – for which they only had Jerome's hazy assurances – the lack of contraception or indeed any precaution at all made for something of an open goal. On the other hand, Jerome had a wife for several years but no children with her, although Rosalie's investigator had confirmed that Jerome's ex-wife had not subsequently had any children so that might be an indicator of why they'd failed to do so as a couple. Not failed. Wrong word.

Gerald really hoped it would be Alan. The idea of a lust so great but so short-lived having such a profound effect so many years later was an irresistible shiny bauble in the greyness of clinics and test tubes that comprised everyday obstetrics. It would make two weeks at the beach wondering how to fill the hours between breakfast and sundown almost pleasurable with something so momentous to mull over.

In a moment, he would know. The email with the results was in his inbox. He first phoned Rasina to check she was sure of the accuracy.

'Yes, Mr Howard, I am. Three of the men have a ninety-nine per cent no match on all three tests. Mr Pertus has ninety-nine per cent match on two tests and ninety-eight per cent on the Fismon test. Which is high for Fismon.'

No need for Gerald to open the email. He was annoyed he had not taken Rosalie's bet because he would have bet on Jerome, but he thought he'd book for the Maldives anyway.

*

'Jerome Pertus.'

Gerald leant back against the door of the Hazell room.

'You're sure?'

'Yes. Absolutely sure. Jerome is Barney's father.' Gina and Gerald both looked at Barney, who was wearing a dinosaur beanie and a T-shirt.

'I know it's June but I can't take his hat off. He won't nap without it and he wakes up if I take it off.'

Gerald smiled. Barney *was* cute. It occurred to Gerald that he rarely saw babies except newborns, when they were much less cute than a few months on. He hadn't realised exactly how much they improved, cute-wise.

'Remember that song?' said Gina. '10CC. One Night in Paris.'

'I'm sure you said it was three or four nights,' replied Gerald, and they both chuckled. 'Do you want to talk about it?'

'Just— It was the right thing. To find out. For me, and now I know, I know it's the right thing for Barney too, some day. Gerald, thank you. For your expertise, for your kindness, for helping me not feel like a— I don't know… like a mutant mother. For being married to Rosalie. What if I'd had my indigestion at another hospital. What then?'

What then indeed, thought Gerald.

373

Chapter 22

Sara's relief reminded Alan of when her mother got the five-year all-clear from cancer. This had been a six-month wait, not five years, but exposed the same strength mixed with fragility, her hands shaking, her voice wobbling in her repeated requests for assurances she hadn't misheard. They sat on Ade's couch, both now aware of the detachment between them and acknowledging it had been there for a long, long time.

'So who is the father?'

'I don't know yet. We will find out in a few weeks when they talk to us again about the screenplay, syndicate rights and so on.'

'Us?'

'Me and the other two not-fathers. There were six possibles. Gina's two husbands, me and three others.'

'And it's not one of her husbands?'

'No. We knew that a while ago. But they're both dead anyway.' A silence fell while Alan made them a sandwich. 'Sara, if you want me to leave properly, something formal, then I will. Otherwise I'll come home in a week or so. But things have changed, haven't they?'

'Are you sure she was the only one? No one else while we were married?'

'No one else. But I don't know if I can say that going forward. We've lost something. Or more like we've admitted there's something missing.'

'So you'll never get over it, that night? You'll always be trying to get it again?'

'I don't want to get over it,' said Alan quietly. 'It just is. And no, I am not trying to get it again. If I had ever thought it was possible, it would have got in the way long before this. I think maybe it's protected us.' It wasn't very flattering, to say the least, and Sara had no idea what to do.

*

Eddie contacted the girls first. They needed to know they hadn't got a new half-sibling. He had trusted them both with the story in contravention of his agreement and everything he always believed about patient confidentiality. He knew they were good at secrets.

He texted Bernadette because it was 4 a.m. in Canada. In Red Deer, Alberta at least – time zones were always a reminder of just how big Canada was. Mary was on patrol but answered anyway.

'The baby isn't mine, Mary. I'm pleased. Ines is pleased. Elke – well, we didn't really explain it to Elke. We'd have only done that if we needed to but we don't. But I am going to do some stuff. Media stuff. If everyone is OK with that.' He heard Mary munching a sandwich at the other end of the phone. 'Bacon or sausage?'

'Bacon, Dad. I needed it. Been up all night on a raid.'

Eddie felt put in his place, as he often did by Mary and her mother. He gave a small prayer of thanks for Ines. 'Did you get the bad guys?'

'Well, we arrested them,' replied Mary. 'Not the same thing as getting them, not yet, but we're working on it.'

Eddie wasn't asking for Mary's permission but he did want to protect his family from surprises. 'There's an agreement around the media stuff. It says I've got three daughters and two marriages but no more than that. It's

375

possible that fallout will come your way, but not being a Grainger should help. The angle they want from me is my relationship with the mother. I didn't behave very well when we ended it. When I ended it. So some dick of a journalist might ask you how it feels to be the daughter of a love rat. But the PR agency can help you with that. If you want, I can let them contact you. I expect to make a bit of money. I'm going to divide it four ways: you, Bernadette, Elke, and Ines and me. I'm also expecting to enjoy myself with my bit of the screenplay.'

Despite the pauses he'd left in giving this information, Mary hadn't filled any of them with a question or a reassuring word.

'Mary, I don't know what you think if you don't tell me.'

'Well, Dad, I don't know what I think either or – you know me – I would tell you.'

Eddie acknowledged this to be true. Since she'd become financially independent of him, his eldest daughter had decided direct was the best approach, and direct often felt to Eddie like a pitchfork battle except Mary had a pitchfork and he didn't.

'The money will be useful, thank you. I don't know if Bernadette feels like that but she's got eight kids so, blimey, what's not to like. Elke will need it. And it is your money so you and Ines deserve it. So maybe I do know what I think after all.' Mary finished chewing her breakfast.

Hot ice could not have surprised Eddie more. He had never expected that Mary would actively be glad about the money and less still that she'd say so. 'When it comes out that I'm involved, what if the press get to you? And eight? I thought it was seven.'

'Dad, I spent last night hiding in my car wearing a bulletproof vest. I was responsible for the safety of eighteen officers and four civilians. I was armed and ready to fire. Two young women depended on my team to get them out of hell in a basement. I can cope with gossip magazines. They might even do a feature: Cork's most senior Garda officer is the first openly gay woman in the force and her father is not the father of a sixty-two-year-old woman's baby. Although I'd hope they could find a snappier headline.'

'First time you've said you are gay,' said Eddie.

'Call yourself a psychiatrist? And it might be seven.' Mary laughed and cut the call.

*

Ann didn't see Roland immediately as he came through arrivals at Terminal 5. She hadn't seen him when he'd left immediately after his DNA samples, a taxi coming early in the morning. He had written her a note saying she shouldn't read too much in to it, just that he wanted to go away without much fuss. So she would have expected him to have luggage and have to wait for it to come through, but he had just a rucksack and a laptop and was one of the first passengers off. Benefits of business-class travel.

She had thought she was early and was standing in a queue for coffee with the private-hire drivers and other meeters and greeters. He hung back, waited to see if she got a sit-in or a takeaway, noting that she'd remembered to bring her reusable cup even to the airport, even to meet her not officially estranged husband for the first time in weeks. She paid, took up a place at the railing with a good view of the constantly opening automatic door. He was surprised she couldn't feel the half-nervous, half-resentful vibes pulsing out of him against her mid-afternoon skin as he came up unseen beside her. She must have taken the day off, he realised. Half-day anyway.

He had wanted to get a cab home but she had almost pleaded to be able to fetch him, and in the end it would have felt cruel to insist. He wasn't tired, wasn't jet-lagged, not yet, but absolutely he hadn't wanted to talk about anything to anyone who knew him even slightly, let alone talk about important things with Ann. Taxi drivers and anodyne enquiries about the flight were all he wanted, or a barista asking if he wanted his coffee to go and not caring about the answer.

'Hello,' he said. Ann turned, startled. The pulsing vibes announcing his arrival were in his imagination only.

'Hello,' she said. 'I'm on level three.'

She paid for the car park, drove them home and made not one enquiry about his trip or his flight or how he was. 'What time is your appointment tomorrow?' she said as they went into the house.

'Ten. Then eleven with the mandatory counsellor, and then one on Thursday to see if I want to follow up.'

'Do you?'

'Probably,' replied Roland. He didn't make a pretence of consulting her. 'But the Flowers baby is not mine. I am sure of that.'

'How can you be so sure?'

'Because I was there, Ann. I know what didn't happen at the only times it could have been me. And I need to tell you I've had a DNA test on me and Eva.' He saw the shock on her face as surely as if it had suddenly changed colour. He knew, whatever the DNA results said, whatever Ann said, that she had kept from him all these years that he might not be Eva's father. Presumably she'd kept it from Eva too.

'Why?'

'Because it occurred to me lately, as a result of this baby thing, that I might not be her father. What other reason would there be?'

Roland knew Ann was not, in general, manipulative or deceitful, not secretive or self-serving. He thought it likely, however, that Eva's conception was the one time in her life when Ann had been all those things together. He waited for her to say something to reassure him he was wrong to have got the test. He could see her carefully weighing what to say and wondered, from a position of great detachment, if she was looking for words that would not be incriminating, that could be taken in more than one way. *If* he was the father – which he didn't know yet. The results email had been sirening out to him from his inbox for several weeks. But it remained unopened.

'Did Eva consent? Does she know?'

'No,' said Roland. 'So the results, these results, wouldn't stand up in court.'

'You are Eva's father,' replied Ann.

'I mean biological, not the man who brought her up.'

'You are Eva's biological father.'

'So why didn't you just say that when I asked you before I went away? If you're so sure?' Roland was suddenly exhausted. It was as if the restful weeks of mornings at a pool, evenings in a bar watching sports with long bats and impossibly high nets had not happened. He was back in the place of unknown babies as surely as he had been at the start of last month.

At forty-two, with hopes of pregnancy fading by the month, Ann had persuaded Roland they should go to a private clinic in London for IVF. This much, of course, Roland knew. Four weeks earlier, while in Cape Town for an aunt's funeral, Ann had – spontaneously, rashly even - visited another clinic also for IVF. This he had not known. Just as neither clinic knew about the other. When Eva was born three weeks before her due date by the London appointment, Ann couldn't be sure which treatment had been successful. And she didn't much care. Over Eva's childhood, DNA techniques had improved and, just like Roland was to do years later, Ann had undertaken a DNA test. Roland was indeed Eva's father.

'I didn't see the need to tell anyone. It's not like I was proud of myself. And yes, I would have told you if it wasn't you. Otherwise why would I bother?'

*

All his life, he'd waited to feel like this, fall in love like this. As the years towards death ticked by, he had thought maybe it wasn't real, wasn't possible. No one ever did feel that way. And those that said they did were mistaken, lying, or at best simply exaggerating. And then he joined their club. He held his phone as if he was cradling the baby, slightly giddy with joy and holding on to his balcony rail, the last leg of the cruise almost over. Barney was staggeringly beautiful. He looked just like him, Jerome thought.

Chapter 23

Stan thought the washing machine was empty, possibly, for the first time in a week. Wherever he was living, he'd usually take his laundry to a service – or, better, they'd collect from his home or office – and it came back forty-eight hours later, clean, dry, ironed, on hangers or folded. Wear and repeat. But then, his washing didn't include kangaroo-patterned babygros or romper suits gifted by people who had forgotten that the only things that mattered for baby clothes was that they washed well and didn't have fiddly bits. Whoever thought putting pinging braces and tiny buttons on the front of a three-to-six months outfit was a good idea clearly hadn't done their fair share of this particular household chore.

The kangaroo pattern on the couple of babygros Stan was holding was less jaunty than the week before, when he'd put them in with a red towel. A few roos looked like they'd been half-hacked with a machete, small tears of blood dripping from their pouches and haunches, Stan thought, the drama of the last few months manifesting now even in the laundry. When the baby clothes from her sister had arrived, Alison sobbed into the bag of mini cheese biscuits she was eating for lunch. 'Sending all our love to you and Arlo and wishing you were here with us. These little mates will remind him of home. Miss you loads.' There was no mention of Stan, which bothered him very little, but Alison swung with a terrifying volatility between being furious with her family for so obviously ignoring her husband, and patiently explaining to him why they felt excluded and in return were excluding him.

'And anyway,' she deflected, 'how can they remind him of home when he's never even been there?'

His repeated assurances not to worry about it held things at bay until the next text, parcel or call, and then the draining round of justifications began again. Because they weren't exhausted enough.

He heard the front door click softly behind his grandmother as she tried to come in without waking mother, baby or even father. Like sleeping during the day, or night for that matter, had been a possibility for him since Arlo hauled himself into the world, he thought resentfully. The rented flat had suited them well: five minutes' walk from Gina's, minimally furnished so easy to clean and with loads of space for stuff, stuff and more stuff. Stan had now realised two things: babies have a lot of stuff and you have to keep them alive 24/7. The downside of the flat was that it wasn't particularly comfortable. But all the appliances were new, it was warm, had a small south-facing garden and Alison felt safe. What it didn't help with was decision-making. The agent wanted to know if they were going to extend for a further six months, otherwise the owners wanted to install new long-term tenants. Stan still needed to mention this to Alison. In the meantime, he put it off for a short while longer by taking coffee for him and Liv out to the garden where Arlo was dozing in his buggy. He was still holding the stained roo suits.

'It'll come out in the wash,' she said. 'Most things eventually come out in the wash.'

'It went in, in the wash, Gran.'

'I noticed the bleed last time so I've brought some stuff. Whitener. It'll get the red out but it'll also fade the colours a bit. So, injured kangaroos or anaemic ones?'

'Anaemic.' They sat for a few minutes, breath half bated in anticipation of Arlo waking up. He didn't mewl lightly for a few seconds as he emerged from sleep; he went straight from light snoring to an ear-splitting, angry lament that whirled out into the moment with the shortest possible interval between deep sleep and decibel levels that would put any self-respecting piledriver to shame.

Liv had determined to get on with Alison, right from her granddaughter-in-law's arrival if she possibly could. She put to the very back of her mind the word 'trapped', which had been her first thought. She refused to speculate, even with herself, let alone anyone else, on the rights and wrongs of Alison getting pregnant. She did not dwell on how Stan felt. If he was subconsciously angry, it didn't show; he was as even-tempered as it was possible to be with a shouty infant wailing twenty-three hours out of twenty-four. She had considered at length if she should be on his side, not Alison's. Liv had finally decided to be on Arlo's side, and that meant being on Alison's. Not that anyone had to take sides, of course, but if there were sides to be taken, Liv would be lining up with Alison who had got dressed in outdoor clothes for the first time since the birth and gone to the hairdresser, hoping she'd make it there and back before her breasts started their version of Victoria Falls.

All of this Liv had decided before she met Alison, before Arlo was born, the only discussion being with herself. It was a pleasant surprise, then, to find how much she liked her great-grandson's mother. And while Alison was

384

manipulative – there was no way of denying her getting pregnant had been manipulative – she did seem to be in love with Stan. Which might not be enough, but it would have to do for the time being.

Liv was also of the view that whatever Alison had told Stan about pills or precautions, he knew as well as anyone that there was always a risk of technical or human failure, or for that matter planning, so he was not entitled to feel totally blindsided. She also thought, having now met Arlo, that Stan should actually be grateful to Alison. He was, after all, just a few weeks off thirty-six. If he dallied about much longer he'd either end up with no children or becoming a father when he was too old to enjoy it properly, Liv thought. So Liv and Alison got on well. And Stan loved Arlo. So much for not speculating on the rights and wrongs, she acknowledged.

'How is Alison?' asked Liv.

'She's OK,' Stan replied. 'We've got an interview with the immigration people this afternoon. That's why she's got dressed and is having her haircut. You know, to prove we didn't get married just so she could come and live here. Which is tricky, because we did.' He finished his coffee and turned his chair to get the sun on his face. 'I don't know if I should just tell them we had a family emergency, we had to leave Australia, we discovered she was pregnant and so we got married and if that turns out not to be the right thing, it is at least true. Or if I should say we were the perfect couple in Australia, wedding plans thwarted by said emergency and so we got married on the way over here because we wanted to be married so much we couldn't wait.'

'They might ask you what the emergency is. Was. Well, they will won't they?'

'I'll say it's confidential. And so they won't believe in the emergency.'

Liv nodded. 'Get a lawyer. A specialist immigration lawyer and get advice. Tell the lawyer everything as it is and see what they say.'

'Do you think?'

'Yes. Phone Rosalie, she'll know someone. What time is your appointment?'

'4 p.m. Last one of the day. But it's in Croydon so we need to leave at lunchtime.'

'You'd better get straight on to that lawyer then.'

Stan put his hands over his eyes so he could think. To his grandmother, he looked as vulnerable as he had as a child when the other kids would tease him – bully him, but it wasn't called that then – about not having a dad. Even doing a heap of dirty washing, on tenterhooks in case the baby woke, he looked good. Attractive. Approachable. Alison was a lucky woman. Liv reminded herself she was on Team Alison. Stan was lucky too.

Stan tried to line up his thoughts. Did he want Alison to get her visa for leave to remain or whatever it was she needed to live here? Or would he prefer she was refused and had to go back to Australia? She would take Arlo. But there are planes and he could go three or four times a year, maybe live there again eventually. If he could get back into Australia when he was ready. But then she'd meet someone else who was there all the time and Arlo would think of this tall, blonde dude from Gold Coast who made a fortune working in mining derivatives and took Arlo surfing as his dad.

386

Then again, he liked Alison, liked her a lot, she made him laugh. But she had never, ever made his heart sing like Carran had. Never made him think he'd sell his soul for the sound of her voice, or made his heart stop when she got out of the shower.

And then, suddenly, like being handed a map in the wilderness, he was sure. Alison would never do these things. She would be what he could best sum up in the distinctly uncomfortable overtones of Victoriana as a good wife. But she would also not shroud his quiet moments in lovesick grief, compounded by reliving the naïve foolishness of his love, as Carran used to. And he would welcome the peace that Alison brought, the joy that Arlo brought just by screaming or laughing or sleeping, especially sleeping. And no surfer dude from Gold Coast was going to have first crack.

'Right, Gran, a lawyer it is. See about a visa. That's a good idea. Thank you. I'll text Rosalie. And Alison.' As he was typing, Liv ploughed on.

'Something else. I want to ask you something else.' The air felt suddenly still. Stan pressed send and looked up. He saw his grandmother wasn't about to ask him about the price of nappies or his view on the stock market. 'Before I talk to your mother.'

They sat there for a few moments listening to the distant domestic soundtrack of washing going round and round, the intermittent swoosh of the water an everyday buffer against the background of something momentous to come. Stan wondered if this was how kids felt when their parents told them they were going to get divorced. Although he had no idea what Liv was about to say, he saw all at once that she might be ill. Really ill. Terminally ill. She was eighty-five. Or maybe she was getting married again? She and Raj next door? Raj didn't look more than sixty but nothing was as it seemed any more.

'OK, Gran, go for it. What is it? I can cope.' He was half jocular in the face of imminent bad news. Lightening the load of mortality.

'You could adopt Barney.'

Stan felt like he'd been shot. Not a fatal wound but enough to make the world fade to grey around him and his life run through his head in multicoloured images. And enough to keep him stock still, because if he moved, he might collapse.

'It's an idea,' he said eventually. If Liv had been hoping for immediate acceptance and enthusiasm, this was not what it looked like.

'Jerome could be like a grandfather. You'd tell Barney the truth, of course you would, when he was big enough. Maybe four or five – or ten. But he'd have the certainty. You'll be doing school runs anyway. Kids' parties.' There was a long pause. 'Your mother isn't getting any younger.'

'No. Yes. I see. I do, I see the logic.'

Having half-expected to be hearing the news of his grandmother's imminent demise, Stan was horrified to find this request seemed almost as bad. Not quite but almost. It was like he'd been handed a very heavy box and steadied the load before a dozen bricks were placed on top.

'It's an idea,' said Liv. 'No more than that. I haven't said anything to anyone. I wondered if you'd thought about it, anyway.'

'No, Gran. I hadn't thought about it.' They were both aware of the gulf. It seemed so obvious to Liv, so remote to Stan. 'But I will.'

'And Alison?'

'Yes. No. I mean, I don't know. I need to think.'

Liv was embarrassed, flushing slightly across her neck and ears. Too late, she knew she shouldn't have mentioned it. If it was that obvious, Stan would have thought of it; the fact he hadn't was her answer in itself.

'Don't,' she said. 'I got it wrong. I wish I hadn't said it. Don't tell anyone, not Alison or your mother – especially not them. Or Evan. Don't tell anyone. Can we forget it?' The words tumbled out like she was a teenager hiding that she fancied a boy in her class, not a great-grandmother confiding in her family. The embarrassed flush of mortification spread upwards. Arlo's dozing stopped and his signature wail, half baby, half seagull, burst out. Stan picked him up, both adults glad of the cover.

'It's not a mad idea, Gran. I won't tell anyone and I will think about it. But I won't tell anyone. It's not like I don't owe you a few secrets. Can you take Arlo for a minute? Rosalie's just sent me a name.'

*

It was too much, all these babies at once. When Anton and Andre had arrived, Evan's mother had helped a lot with childcare, taking one or other of them for a few hours a couple of times a week, both together as Andre got bigger. She had cooked meals, dropping off what she called a 'just put it in the oven' most weekends: potatoes peeled,

389

vegetables chopped and ready to roast, something in a sauce. She'd put laundry on, take it out, dry and fold it, put toys back in toyboxes and leave. They'd wave and say thanks, grateful for the time it freed up for them to work. But not this time. This time Gina hadn't so much as folded a sock. Evan stared at the wreck that was the living room and wanted to cry the way Luc was crying in his cot, safely unhappy. He was getting to hate weekends when the childcare and the cleaner didn't come and he was getting to hate himself for that.

Amelie had returned to work three months after Luc slithered as gently as any baby could into the world, as if he knew that his mother would be pleased with him the less pushing she had to do. Evan had gone back after three days, but Amelie had to leave the house to work. Or so she said; he wasn't sure she had to, most of the time, more that she preferred to. He didn't, so somehow he became responsible for organising childcare, chores and all the other crap. It would be another three months before Andre went to nursery. Evan wanted someone over five years old to make him feel valuable. He made up a bottle, took Luc out of his cot and fed him with one hand, the other finishing the draft of a data architecture plan for a new customer, deftly typing single letters at a time into a table of figures hoping he wouldn't mistakenly add or miss a nought while balancing the bottle on his elbow. For all his technical creativity, Evan was also profoundly practical. But something had to change or he'd implode.

He quite liked Amelie and she, he thought, quite liked him. He supposed many couples reached their golden wedding on less, harnessed together by money or lack of it, children, habit and the creeping realisation that this was maybe as good as it got. For most people. He supposed that some couples did wake up every morning, years into a relationship, delighted to see their spouse, although he hadn't met any. He had realised he had no desire to get divorced, God no, although he wasn't sure Amelie felt the same. He didn't want to cope with a separation: all the mess, the explanations, the paperwork, the decisions. Unless Amelie pushed it and took on all the work – which would not be in her nature any more than sprinting round the block would be in the nature of a tortoise – separation wouldn't happen. And she couldn't afford it without generous financial support from him. Which, if he kept the kids, he would not give. Or it might actually happen but not be acknowledged in any practical sense.

So he thought he'd sell up, get a smallholding somewhere close to where Stan wanted to be in Scotland, with loads of room and a housekeeper. He hadn't dared voice the thought that if he was close enough and Alison couldn't work yet because of the visa thing, she might do some childcare – paid, of course – for a few months while he got organised. Amelie might not be thrilled; she'd either have to admit she did not need to be in the centre of town all the time or make some away-from-home arrangement. When work took her on location, it didn't matter much where she lived as long as it was no more than an hour from an airport and train station. Evan didn't think she had any friends to miss. As far as he knew, which he acknowledged probably wasn't that far, all her friends were work-related. He and Amelie might only spend weekends together, while looking like they were properly married. Not perfect, but the best he could suggest for now.

His bottle-steadying elbow was numb and he moved Luc to the other arm, reread the proposal, sent it and started looking for properties online. Best to have a few ducks in a row or at least a few places to look at and an idea of area.

Ten minutes later, frustrated and feeling Luc stirring, he texted Stan: 'Confidential but what if we move to Scotland, somewhere near you? Where are you thinking of? Need to be near an airport, station'. He got a list of six locations from Stan and a smiley face in under a minute.

*

Amelie was mildly surprised most days to rediscover she was the mother of three children. While she would not actively have chosen not to have children, neither had she felt the daily ache for them she knew some of her colleagues felt. Anton was the reason she and Evan had married – sort of. Her father had advised her that under French inheritance laws this was the best thing to do, and Evan was fine with it. Amelie could still bring a small smile to her face when she thought about her wedding photos. She looked simply stunning, so chic with the tiniest hint of a bump and a maternal glow. Evan wore a navy suit, made to measure in some trendy place off Brick Lane. No bridesmaids to detract attention. One hundred and twenty guests in a chateau. Truly the best day of her life and at that stage, everyone thought they were very well matched, including Evan. Amelie knew she wasn't really invested in being a wife or mother, but oh the wedding.

Her lack of attention to everyday details, and a tendency to alter the truth about whatever suited her, which the pill did not, had led to Anton and then, very soon after, to Andre. Followed by Luc. She'd been four months pregnant when she told Evan about Luc. Once Evan had overcome his shock, he'd made a decision. He, at least, would not be having any more children. For Amelie to think too hard about their domestic arrangements would be an acknowledgement of her own abdication, but she was aware vaguely that Evan was on the brink of not being able to cope with working full-time – and then some – from home, being the major breadwinner and looking after, even with additional childcare made possible by his – *mon Dieu* – mother's predicament, three small children. Gina used to help two or three days a week until Barney had arrived. Amelie gave a genteel shudder of disbelief and distaste. A baby at sixty-two. Amelie's sympathy for her mother-in-law was deep, real and tinged with disapproval.

But Gina couldn't help her son and his wife any more. Not much anyway, a couple of hours twice a week with Barney in tow, and she didn't do anything useful as far as Amelie could tell. Just passed the time while her nanny-person went to mass.

Amelie knew that she should give up more of her own time, as she saw it, to care for her children, but she rationalised it by saying she was just doing what men had done forever by leaving childcare to their spouses. She didn't factor in that those spouses, those mothers, typically hadn't worked full-time across three time zones and paid all the important bills.

She could see that if Evan cracked, everything would fall apart. It would be much more difficult to spend Monday to Thursday in town, on location or looking for locations, with Fridays half in the office and the bigger half at a spa. So she needed to talk to Evan and he needed to come up with a solution. Which he would, Amelie was sure of that. She hoped it wouldn't involve divorce because that would be messy, and she really liked having a husband to fall back on as an excuse not to overdo work contact opportunities; she liked being the stylish mother-of-three, recipient of envious enquiries of how she did it. Divorce would be a clumsy interruption. She didn't want anyone else. She liked Evan, still found him attractive if she put her mind to it. As husbands go, he was better than she could ever have wished for. She had enough insight to acknowledge this to herself, on a Friday, in the spa.

He came in to the kitchen. All three children were silent: two asleep, one watching a film. Evan didn't like them looking at screens alone but he'd got used to it.

'Mi, we have to do something,' he said. 'I'm cracking.'

'Yes,' she replied. 'I know. Thing is, I don't want to help you more with the children and I don't want to work less. I can't see how I can earn more so that you could work less. I can't do childcare – seriously I can't. Your mother is not much help right now, so what do you think?'

Evan laughed, despite being so tired, worried about a database crisis at a major bank in Florida and feeling guilty about Anton watching the film all alone. No, he really didn't want to divorce her.

He said, 'I thought if we sold the house, I took my money from the project and we bought a big house, I could get a proper nanny-stroke-housekeeper to help with the kids – even live-in, maybe, hands-on – but I'd be there a lot. But we'd have to move way out. I was thinking Scotland. Near Stan and Alison. Thought my mother might like to move too. And that might mean asking Gran, though she has got a whole ecosystem here, so she might just visit. Somewhere near Ullapool or Oban or Fortrose.'

'Where?'

'West coast of Scotland. Except Fortrose. That's east coast.'

'I think it's a really good idea, in principle. But location is my speciality. What about France? Near my parents. Warmer.'

'I don't speak French, and your parents don't do childcare,' said Evan.

'Yes, you do.'

'OK, I do, but not well enough to live there. Organise broadband. Arrange schools. Meet parents. Pay tax. I can't do that stuff in French.'

'I can do those things,' she replied. And they both laughed.

*

They were in Coal Drops Yard, the revamped space behind King's Cross. An hour ago Jerome had arrived on the Eurostar. Evan and Stan and their babies were waiting for him with Barney, by a stone wall opposite the Granary Square fountains. The end of August was behaving like it was still high summer and on this mid-morning the air was lazy, even here in the heart of London. It was an after-work and weekend venue really, Coal Drops Yard, except for invasions of teenagers going to the Nike store during school holidays, but it was too early yet for them so it was empty apart from a few tourists.

Jerome had walked straight over to them as they came into view: two buggies, one sling and a variety of bulging bags that so obviously weren't Eurostar luggage. They might as well have been wearing name badges.

'Jerome Pertus.' He held out his hand to the half-brothers of his son, who both shook it. Initial greetings over, they found him a spot on the wall. With Luc in the sling, Evan went to get coffee. And Jerome fell in love again with Barney, who was sleeping on his back with his arms above his head like a misshapen W.

'They say you should not wake a sleeping baby,' said Jerome.

'They do,' replied Stan, who had been taken aback by the look of adoration on Jerome's well-maintained, very lightly tanned face. 'But they probably didn't have this kind of meeting in mind, so if you'd like to hold him…'

'I would very much. But for now I am happy to look.'

Nothing more was said until Evan returned with the coffee.

'Do you know what your mother's plans are?'

'Not really,' said Stan. 'Or not so much we don't know, as she doesn't really know. It's a lot. The shock, the birth, the project and a baby. She's doing well, but at the moment she's still doing things day by day.'

'Can I do anything to help?' Jerome was surprised to find these words being said by himself. They hung, written in

396

the air in front of him, like an exam question he hadn't been expecting, on biology instead of literature. The brothers waited for a few moments, also to see if there was to be a retraction or a qualification.

'Well.' Stan began. 'She's OK for money thanks to the project. Phase two is going well. Mum has extended her professional help with babycare for the next couple of months. She has family, friends, Rosalie and her team.'

'Are you asking about doing the helping yourself?' Evan said. 'In person?'

'I wasn't, no, although of course I would like to when the time is right. I was wondering if I could do anything to help… your mother. Barney's mother.' He'd thought about saying Mrs Flowers and decided against it. 'We didn't talk about it when I saw her.' Jerome unexpectedly came into control of his side of the situation. 'When I met Barney, there was just me and Barney except for a few moments when I met her. Your mother. Gina. I am very glad to have this opportunity to talk with you.

'Does she call me Jerome or "the baby's father" or something else?'

Evan replied. 'Until now, "the baby's father". But I'll tell her you called her Gina and I think that will help.'

Stan took over. 'I think it would help to know what you'd like to do, Jerome. How you'd like things to be. Then we can find out how Mum feels about that. So we can see if it's along the same lines.' Stan and Evan had discussed at length what to say to Jerome, anticipating it would be awkward, maybe even a bit combative. They'd decided the best thing was to find out what he had in mind and take that back to their mother, who was today meeting with Rosalie and scriptwriters for a screenplay – much to her delight.

Jerome finished his coffee and walked slowly over to a bin at the other side of the public square with the cup, ignoring the one a few metres away from where they were sitting. As he got back, Stan was getting a bottle out for Barney who was mewling and puking like a tiny Shakespeare tribute act. Stan held the bottle out to Jerome. 'These two won't be far behind.' He waved his hand to indicate Luc and Arlo. 'My wife will be here in about ten minutes to feed Arlo.'

'I have never fed a baby before,' said Jerome.

'Me neither, until Barney arrived,' replied Stan. 'Haven't fed Arlo either, for obvious reasons. Whereas Evan has done pretty much nothing else for the last four years.' He lifted Barney out of the buggy, indicated that Jerome should sit down again on the wall and said, 'If you want to. If not, I'll do it.'

Jerome hesitated. If they didn't let him see Barney again, it would be better never to have held him. But they couldn't stop him, could they. He was the baby's father, he must have rights. He would have rights in France. Although they were obviously not in France. And the timeless fear of adults handed someone else's baby – but it isn't someone else's, it's his – might he drop him?

Barney was ramping up his call for lunch, untroubled by questions of paternal responsibility or competence with small babies. 'I'll start,' offered Stan. 'Let me know if you want to take over.' They sat quietly until Alison arrived.

'Hello,' she said to Jerome. 'I'm Alison. Arlo's mother. Stan's wife. Great to get some decent British weather, isn't it? Did you have a good trip over?'

The banal normality of her greeting was a shock to the three men. None of them said anything; there was no loosening of the stilted tension which had crept up on them. Jerome was calculating whether a relationship with his son meant getting to know Barney's half-aunt by marriage. It seemed likely these three babies would spend time together, being so close in age, so he supposed on some level he would need to engage with the wider family.

None of the men responded to her pleasantries. 'Stan?' she said. He turned Arlo's buggy round so she could take the handles. 'I'll go find someplace to feed him.' Alison's fragility, her lack of confidence in her marriage came boiling to the surface. For the first time, walking across the square past the bin Jerome had been to a few minutes earlier, she began to think about being with Arlo in Sydney, nearer her family. Without Stan.

Barney finished his bottle and smiled. Stan held him out to Jerome who continued to be as still as the stone wall he was using as a seat. 'Oui, ou non?' Stan tried to lighten the press of strangeness. Finally, Jerome made up his mind.

'I think I shouldn't until I know what your mother thinks.'

'Well, I need to blow my nose and Evan's already got his hands full, so can you just do me a favour and take him for a minute?' said Stan. He pressed Barney into Jerome's embrace while fiddling for a tissue in his pocket. A sneeze and two blows later, he went to take Barney back. 'If I could just have a moment longer,' said Jerome, holding the baby close, feeling helpless, looking relaxed, joy and nervousness battling it out.

'I think,' said Stan, 'Evan, listen up, see if you agree – that the easiest way to go on would be for you to say exactly, in very clear terms, what you'd like in an ideal arrangement. That probably won't happen, ideal rarely does, but it is the best place to start. Then mum can compare it with how she feels and go from there. No sanitising it, no holding back and slipping something in later. Tell it like you'd like it to be.'

'I'd like to go on the birth certificate. I presume it's father unknown right now?'

'You don't have to put a father on when you register,' said Evan, 'so it is blank. Actually,' he revised, 'as Mum a) didn't know when she registered his birth, and b) if she had known, didn't want to publish it, it was always going to be blank. Now, she'll have to fill in an affidavit or some form or something to get it changed. I don't want to pre-empt anything, but I can't see Mum objecting to that. It's the truth and my expectation is she'd agree. Although there might be a thing about timing and the press, but in principle.'

'I'd like to settle some money on him. Probably also my apartment when I'm dead. A lump sum, not regular maintenance. I'd like to see him regularly, say every month or two, and I'll come to him wherever he is. I'd like him to be bilingual. I don't think I can care for him at all while he is young. I have no idea how to do that and my sister, Camille, who wants to help is too old, though she doesn't admit it. She knows about the baby but not the circumstances. I haven't said anything I shouldn't. At least I don't think so. She presumably thinks I have had a late bout of *joie de vivre*. We didn't talk about that exactly.

'I'd like him to come on holiday to France sometimes. I would like to have a cordial, business-like relationship with his mother and his English family. I will not, I think, seek to go against anything your mother wants, even if it is not what I want. I, of course, do not understand what she has been through but I think it must not have been easy. I do not want courts, fighting, lawyers – except to confirm things if necessary – and I will not inflict this on her.'

It was a long speech but Jerome had not taken his gaze from Barney while he spoke. He didn't now. 'I think I may have said enough. Too much. If I can't have these things, I will take whatever your mother decides. This is probably the most reasonable and accommodating I have been in my adult life. I have not had a good reason before. If none of this works out, please tell Barney one day that I love him.'

Jerome stood up, passed Barney back and shook hands again through the trappings of babydom that his son's half-brothers had brought with them, then picked up his bag. Evan jiggled an unhappy Luc up and down in his sling. He said, 'That's really helpful. Can we go through Rosalie to sort things out?'

Jerome nodded. What he really wanted to ask was whether Gina planned to continue to care for Barney – how, how on earth could she do that? – but it seemed a step too far. He settled for a short closing speech, one that until that very moment he would not have thought himself capable of making. 'I love Barney. I didn't want to hold him at first because I was frightened. I don't have children. I don't know what to do. And I don't know your mother. But I remember

401

from our liaison that she was kind and funny. Please tell her that. And that I love Barney.'

Three hours later he was back in France, Googling 'how to make sure your baby is bilingual' at a café in the Gare du Nord waiting for his connection.

*

They didn't get many White babies coming to be blessed at Sandra's church, and it wasn't Gina's thing to go to a church of any kind. That said, she'd had no objection to Barney going or being blessed; he was unlikely to notice and it pleased her mother. Today, there were seven – four large, three small – in their subcongregation and the mid-autumn sunshine was welcome as they stood outside, raising their voices slightly to overcome the challenge of traffic which even on a Sunday was plentiful and fierce.

Evan had brought Luc, Alison was there with Arlo, and Sandra was holding Barney. Liv had come for the singing. She and Sandra had used to do that every couple of months; then Sandra stopped going when she fell out with the preacher. There was a new preacher now so Sandra was giving him a try. Gina was at a petting zoo, trying to repair the damage to her relationship with Anton and Andre though the media of cute lambs and too much sugar.

Gina and Sandra had been friends for about thirty years but they did not talk about racism. They talked about Black culture and history in the abstract but not the personal. So Gina had never asked Sandra about her experience of growing up, and Sandra had never asked Gina about being married to a Black man in Britain. Sandra was fairly sure it was because they were both frightened of saying things wrong or saying the wrong thing, Gina of revealing subliminal prejudice and then having to confront it. It would be easy to think it was just irrelevant to their friendship, that their love for each other transcended race, but that wasn't it. What Sandra hadn't expected was for Liv to come right out with it apropos of nothing.

'Sandra, did you get a lot of prejudice growing up? Remarks, people not wanting to be your friend? I've often wondered if it was hard for you.'

They were standing on the steps of a large, cement-fronted, unlovely church which made up in enthusiasm inside what it lacked in aesthetic appeal externally. Evangelical congregations often still wore Sunday best; those who didn't were no less welcome but nonetheless felt a frisson of failure. Sandra was wearing a fitted lilac dress, just the right side of too glamorous to wear at church. Evan was fiddling around with two bags of baby paraphernalia, shushing Luc and rocking Barney in the buggy.

'Don't worry,' said Sandra. 'The noise will soon drown them out if they get shouty. Shoutier.' She turned to address Liv's question. 'I did, yes. And it was hard sometimes. I was bookish and that saved me. But I don't worry about that, Liv. What I worry about is now. All these years on. We sort of expected it then. People feared what they didn't know. Now, things have changed, but I often think it's only on the surface. Or only at an individual level. Structures have deep foundations.'

'George – George Flowers – told me once that he loved Gina so much in spite of her being White,' said Liv. 'I thought it was an interesting thing to say. I've never asked

403

her if she thought the same. Or if he told her or if they talked about it, but I'm going to ask her now while I still can. I am not going to have much longer to raise these things and something about Barney's arrival has made it urgent.'

Sandra looked at Liv. 'I want to ask Greg how he feels about me. If he thinks we could form a relationship.'

'Ladies, we need to get these boys inside,' said Evan, no longer managing with the number of people stopping to talk babies with him. 'No, not twins. Cousins,' he said to the latest enquirer.

'They're not cousins,' said Liv. Evan looked at her.

'Not technically,' he replied, 'but I think practically it's best if we say they are. For now anyway.'

The singing was uplifting, though the pressure to 'Give generously, very very generously for the Lord's work' was alien to Liv, having been brought up in a church tradition where the offering was a bag on a pole passed silently along the pews often with an undertow of slight embarrassment – different indeed to the wholehearted entreaties, bordering on instructions, of today. She got out ten pounds, changed it to twenty and said to Evan, 'I've put yours in for you.' She made sure the man with the collecting plate got an eye on what she thought was generous donation. Then she saw others. Barney and Luc were held up to the roof and blessed, which made them chuckle in unison, one of the happiest sounds of Liv's life. Alison was more hesitant with Arlo who ended up in an ungainly shoulder hold instead.

'What about Wesley? And you know Greg's like a real Yorkshireman these days?' Liv resumed the earlier conversation with Sandra on their way out.

'Wesley is a lovely man but he is no George Flowers and no Greg Redcar. I've let him down gently. I was too much for him.' Sandra replied. 'And on Sundays, we can stay home and I'll make Yorkshire pudding.'

Chapter 24

Mrs Samson's triplets had been delivered, two of them alive, and they would be kicking after a couple of weeks in SCBU. She had known for a few days that the tiny third foetus was not thriving and he died thirty minutes before delivery. Gerald had spent three days monitoring all the babies to maximise the chances of the remaining two. He was comfortable with his judgment. Although it was not a popular opinion to express, he had found that having other children was a balm for parents who suffered a neonatal death. The Samsons would mourn baby Donald, but in Gerald's experience, they would find peace earlier than other bereaved parents because of the needs of their living children.

Pulling off his gloves and apron, he formally handed care to the duty paediatrician and walked over to Valley to write up the next instalment, as he'd come to think of it, in the Gina Flowers case.

Rosalie had been confident that neither his presentation to the International Society of Obstetricians and Gynaecologists, nor the forthcoming television drama would in themselves have endangered Gina's anonymity, but there was little chance of hiding her identity from every third party she met – acquaintances, Barney's friends as he grew up, random people the family came into contact with – without an elaborate set of new identities. Which were an option legally, if expensively. Gina had decided it was easier to manage the news now, get all the attention on her and not on Barney, and in that way protect him until he was at least eighteen and most likely had been superseded by new miracles. Rosalie's advice was that if Gina and the family could tough it out for the immediate aftermath, they'd get ninety per cent of the interest out of the way and making the drama would not incite more.

The conference fell inconveniently close after the birth of Barney but Gerald did not want to delay until the next one; they were held every two years and a lot could happen in two years. So he'd asked for a slot, something he had never done before, and now found himself as a keynote speaker with his session full. He hoped most of the audience were obs and gynae people, or at least healthcare professionals, but he was prepared to find a good number of lifestyle journalists in the room who were not used to dry graphs comparing egg viability in specified uterine settings.

He had another ten days to prepare, most of which would be taken up with what he thought of as the peripheries. Should Valley Healthcare Facility's logo be the same size as the NHS logo? Should there be no logos? Who should get a speaking credit and in what order should they speak? And get credit-listed? Sponsors. Such things he found fascinating in a detached way and he had begun to understand a bit more about the nuts and bolts of Rosalie's work as he answered questions from the client manager she had assigned to him. The conference was in Boston and his session had already been moved to a larger venue than first planned.

Gina and Jerome had, independently, been very helpful with conference data and agreed to share their personal medical histories. Those were, with the exception of Barney, unremarkable. Which was a little like Shakespeare being unremarkable apart from all that writing. There had been a sticking point for Gina; she had, quite understandably, been reluctant to include the highly relevant information about the number of potential candidate fathers, not least because she feared this would cause a frenzy as journalists tried to locate her past lovers. Rosalie had gently pointed out over a few days that they would do this anyway. So Gerald and Gina had settled their misgivings and Rosalie was meeting Gina later that week to map out the best way through the different players' assorted and sometimes conflicting desires.

Professionally, Gerald was thrilled with his research. Initial studies – very initial, preliminary of preliminaries – suggested new ways of looking at securing planned implantation in hostile uteruses. And, far more exciting, planned actual storage in 'non-exceptional' uteruses. Perhaps there was a better description than 'hostile uterus' that he could use in Boston. And one better than 'non-exceptional'. These were the phrases currently used by most of his profession. He was sad that he had not thought over the last twenty-five years how the phrase 'hostile uterus' might sound to a woman desperately hoping to conceive; and pleased that there was some campaigning underway to change it, although the suggestions doing the rounds – 'uterine lining implantation struggles' or 'uterine lining challenges' – were hardly poetic. But with news and features journalists at the conference, he thought he would use the new terms despite their imperfection. The fascinating thing for him, infertility not being his core area, was the egg. How had it stayed in such good condition all these years and what caused it to release? They were in the theory stage of testing hypotheses.

Gina had joked that she'd tried some new yoga moves last summer; Gerald was not entirely sure this idea was such a joke.

*

Rosalie had started the day on Australian time, slid seamlessly into GMT and was now gearing up for a conversation with the US West Coast. Gina was keen on a small, independent company to make the screen version of her story and so far had been unmoved by Rosalie's explanations of the millions more in upfront fees from one of the major US content producers. 'Hit the Decks' in Sydney was full-on about syndication rights. The podcast had been shelved as an independent distribution channel because it risked being too much of a spoiler for the drama, forming instead the backbone of the television script: twelve episodes, the pre-birth stages now being finalised. Which was not so difficult because all the agreements were in place for pre-birth.

Rosalie had read the final offer from the media giant in California, which was on the table for forty-eight hours only. She spent thirty minutes or so doing calculations, some financial and others about who she thought would agree to what. She texted Gina to ask to put their decision meeting back to 2 p.m. the next day because she had just finished collecting all the information and had the stay-at-home equivalent of jet lag familiar to global workers. Then she went to bed, knocked out by half a bottle of Merlot and a deep swig of cough medicine, careful both to pop the cough medicine into a drawer and not to wake Gerald as she lay down beside him.

ALL CHANNELS PRESS
RELEASE
Embargoed until 00:01 6 September
2019

A 62-year-old woman has become
the first mother confirmed to give
birth following a delayed embryonic
settled implantation (DESI). Baby
Barney was safely delivered by
Caesarean section in February in an
NHS hospital in London, England.
Mother and baby are well.

Virginia Flowers was more than ten
years post-menopause and had not
been in a sexual relationship since
she was widowed in 2009, when she
found out she was 32 to 33 weeks
pregnant in January this year. A
fertilised embryo had been settled in
her womb for a long period of time
before dislodging and growing to
term. The baby's father has been
identified using DNA profiling.

Mr Gerald Howard led the team,
which included experts from other

countries and disciplines, who cared for and delivered Barney, and he continues to lead on the science. He will be presenting the case at an international conference of obstetricians next month.

Mrs Flowers' story is under option with rights for a screenplay and novel expected to attract strong bidding.

Mrs Flowers' agent said: "Gina wants first and foremost to thank the medical and wider healthcare teams that looked after her and Barney, and her family and friends. She had not expected to become a mother again at 62. Her story of love, loss and a medical miracle will be released in 2021."

Press enquiries: info@32to33.com

*

Rosalie was surprised to find Gina alone, all her family elsewhere. She had rarely seen Gina on her own since they'd first met.

'Where is everyone?' she asked. 'You're on your own?'

'I'd forgotten how good it feels to have my house to myself,' replied Gina. 'Of course, of course, of course, I would never have managed without them but oh the relief of a few hours off. They've started asking me what I am going to do. It's exhausting.'

'And?'

'Not you too.' Gina put her feet up on the sofa. 'The thing is, Rosalie, I don't know. I can't bear the thought of having to have kids' sleepovers, mind whether Barney eats his broccoli, go to parents' evening, constantly have to think about where he is and what he's doing and is he using an iPad too young. Then teenage. I can't. But I have to. So, logically, I think we – me and Barney – should be close to Stan and Evan and their families. But I don't know where that is exactly. They are still looking and I don't know if I want to go there and wherever it is it will not be here. It won't be my life. And what if I up and move and then Alison goes back to Australia and Stan follows and Amelie insists on France and Evan follows and I am alone with Barney in the middle of nowhere? And what about my mother? She's not dependent on me but she relies on me and, honestly, I'd really miss seeing her a few times a week.

'But I do think I will go with them and you know what makes it bearable, Rosalie? Money. I will be able to afford help, travel and I am so, so happy about that. Thank you, thank you, thank you.'

'We're going to make it fun, not just lucrative.'

Gina felt a release that had been so long coming, she thought it would never happen. That she'd be forever stuck in a non-moving jam of worry, the burden of ultra-late parenthood impossible to reconcile with a life she wanted to live. She started to see how it could be doable, different from what she'd thought, but doable. Mostly doable, at any rate.

They had agreed the press release by email and discussed its implications over the course of the last few weeks. Barney's birth certificate would be changed to have his father's name after the story was out there. Arrangements were in hand for privacy and security, with everyone having extensive briefings and, in most cases, a minder. Or two.

Rosalie picked up the thread. 'Money, then. Let's discuss the screenplay.'

'This has to be my decision, Rosalie, and only mine,' said Gina. 'I don't really want to know what my family think and I definitely don't want to know if they don't agree with one another. No picking a side. No "I told you so" unless it's directed at me. The only way to do that is not to ask them. And I'm going to make the decision today. I think I know what I want to do but honestly the only opinion I'm really interested in now is yours, so if you could start with that, I'd appreciate it.'

Rosalie was startled. So far, Gina, apart from the production request, had been quite passive in the media negotiations, led by Rosalie, with occasional input from her sons and just once or twice seeking advice from Gerald. It was a bit like thinking you were dealing with Sleeping Beauty only to find she was awake all the time.

'I had a baby six months ago. At sixty-two. It knocked the stuffing out of me. I am beginning to think again but only just.'

Rosalie nodded at the explanation, embarrassed that her thoughts had been so evident to Gina. 'Right,' she said. 'I did a bit of squaring up last night, and thank you for moving our meeting. I didn't want to turn up tired. By not going with the big boys, you are giving up about six million dollars of confirmed funding. I think you will definitely recoup at least four million of that using your preferred route. So I'd say there was two million at some risk. To be clear, that is your personal share as the option holder on the story, over and above the base fee.' Gina nodded. She knew she had to think of Barney but the base fee alone would mean he never had to work and she didn't want him not to have to work.

'Possibly trickier for you, Gina, is how to structure our fee offer to the others. My view is we should go for maximum control, but that costs more and it comes out of your share of the cast pot.'

'I don't really have to think about it much. I want to keep production here and I will take the hit. If we can't find one of the big channels to distribute, so be it. I want to find a production company that will let me do some stuff on the side like have shadow interns, open workshops, guaranteed reads for new writers, include explainers on the science stuff, something about how the delivery had to be by the NHS because private maternity services can't cope, I don't know exactly what yet. And I want it to be up the road. Or at least up the motorway and not across a continent. And I'm just going to take your advice on control.'

'What if they don't want to do it?' asked Rosalie.

''That's fine. We'll do it with who we've got. We can sub something in or leave a bit out. Let's just ask them, see what they want to do.'

'Seriously?'

'Seriously,' confirmed Gina. 'I think they'll want to come, even on my terms, but if it is just you, me and Barney, we'll have to write in some random others. You know what I've wondered recently: it's all been about me and the fathers and privacy and controlling the story, but won't your agency come under the spotlight? Do you want that?'

Rosalie smiled. 'It's all under control but thank you for asking. I'll fill you in…..can you keep a secret?'

Gina laughed. 'I've got a bottle of champagne, Rosalie, that I have not felt like opening until today. I know you're working but will you join me? Not least to stop me drinking it all myself.'

'I'd love to. Where's Barney?'

'Out for a walk with his father. And their minder.'

Postscript

Dear Amanda,

I was so, so sorry to hear that Manuel had died. On especially bad days, hold on to how much Manuel loved you, how much better your love for each other made this world. Hold on to the goodness and the joy. Sometimes I'm not sure if I knew how much I loved George at the time. I surely do know now. I think he learned how to be a wonderful husband by being a wonderful brother with wonderful sisters. He taught my boys so much about being a good brother.

I have a long, long story I need to tell you and I hope next year I'll be able to come and tell you in person. What do you think about Buenos Aires next spring? But for now, this is just to say the woman in the papers that sounds like me, is me.

Grief is the price we pay for love, they say, so while yours will drag you under for a time, it will also lift you up.

Love as always
Gina

Printed in Great Britain
by Amazon

24202890R00236